2025
A STORY OF SURVIVAL

Carl Berryman

Author's Tranquility Press
Atlanta, Georgia

Copyright © 2023 by Carl Berryman

All rights reserved. No part of this publication may be reproduced, distributed, or transmitted in any form or by any means, including photocopying, recording, or other electronic or mechanical methods, without the prior written permission of the publisher, except in the case of brief quotations embodied in critical reviews and certain other noncommercial uses permitted by copyright law. For permission requests, write to the publisher, addressed "Attention: Permissions Coordinator," at the address below.

Carl Berryman/Author's Tranquility Press
3800 Camp Creek Pkwy SW Bldg. 1400-116 #1255
Atlanta, GA 30331
www.authorstranquilitypress.com

Ordering Information:
Quantity sales. Special discounts are available on quantity purchases by corporations, associations, and others. For details, contact the "Special Sales Department" at the address above.

2025: A Story of Survival/ Carl Berryman
Hardback: 978-1-959197-05-8
Paperback: 978-1-959197-06-5
eBook: 978-1-959197-07-2

CONTENTS

CHAPTER I	3
CHAPTER II	22
CHAPTER III	66
CHAPTER IV	88
CHAPTER V	155
CHAPTER VI	163
CHAPTER VII	183
CHAPTER VIII	185
CHAPTER IX	198
CHAPTER X	216
CHAPTER XI	233
CHAPTER XII	243
CHAPTER XIII	247
CHAPTER XIV	259
CHAPTER XV	263
CHAPTER XVI	266
CHAPTER XVII	273
CHAPTER XVIII	279
CHAPTER XIX	288
CHAPTER XX	292
CHAPTER XXI	295
CHAPTER XXII	300
CHAPTER XXIII	304

CHARACTER

Archer, Arlene, Ethan Bradley's secretary at the Pentagon.
Auburn, Robert, Captain, USN, Commanding USS San Antonio, SSBN
Billings, Captain, USN, Commanding, USS Minneapolis, SSBN
Bowen, Frank, Executive Officer, USS Minneapolis
Boyington, Kenneth, Captain, Commanding USS Andie L. Murphy, SSBN
Bradley, Robert, GEN Ethan Bradley's deceased father
Bradley, Joshua, Ethan Bradley's second son with first wife Martha.
Bradley, Samuel, Ethan Bradley's first son with first wife Martha
Cantor, Norma former Vice President Campbell, Naomi
Chandler, Mike Captain, USN, Commanding USS Kansas City, SSBN
Chinkov, Georgi, Deputy Premier, Russia, after Medvedev
Cruz, Felipe, *criminal*
Diaz, Hernando, *criminal*
Fitzgerald, Hugh, Chief of Naval Operations (CNO) SSBN
Frandson, General: four-star USAF, Commander, SPACECOM
Gordo, *waiter*
Johnson, Edward, Deputy Sheriff, Washakie, Co, WY
Ling, Wang Ni, Chief of Staff, PLAN
Lorenzo, Jesus, *criminal*
Marsden, Donna, a 17-year-old girl rescued by Bradley, Josh's girl
McCartney, General, four-star USAF, Deputy Chief of Staff, USAF
Medvedev, Alexi, Russian Deputy Prime Minister **Osborne, Robert,** General Commandant, USMC who replaces General Schenken
Perroud, Gypsy, Lee Gen Bradley's second wife, physicist
Proboff, Vladimir, *Russian Premier*
Reagan, George, *Chief of Naval Operations* **Santiago, Manual,** *criminal*
Saunders, Captain, USN, Commanding USS Fort Worth, SSBM

Schenken, General Commandant USMC, while Bradley is at the Pentagon
Sherman, Jason, Captain, USN, Commanding the USS Robert Howard, SSBM
Sikowsky, Fred, GS-20, NSA liaison officer in the Pentagon, CFR member
Stewart, Ronald, Secretary of State under Naomi **Thornton, John**, Physician, Washakie Co, WY
Waddell, Clayton Major General, USAF, SPACECOM, Satellite Program Manager
Wu, Ling, 33, Chinese President
Youngston, Carol, a 17-year-old girl, ultimately Sam's wife

CHAPTER I

PENTAGON BRIEFING ROOM, 1 March 2024, 08:00 Hours, for all General Officers at the rank of Major General and above. Briefing Officer: MG Clayton Waddell, USAF. Space Command (SPACECOM)

"We have one of our satellites in the same orbit as a Russian satellite we believe to be carrying MIRV, or multiple individual re-entry warheads. Its primary power source is solar panels, the same as ours. Our satellite, however, is registering traces of radioactivity consistent with plutonium. In other words, one of their MIRVs is leaking radiation. We have not informed the Russians that we are aware of the leak, which confirms the nature of the satellite. The Russians claim it as a meteorological satellite with a large onboard computer. We do not doubt the presence of the computer, but it has to be for programming warhead entry. We are uncertain as to the nature of the warheads, whether they are tailored primarily for heat, blast, or electromagnetic pulse, or EMP or other forms of radiation. If the warheads are EMP and are properly spread, they will destroy all digital instrumentation within the continental United States. This satellite circles the globe every 90 minutes in orbit opposite the rotational direction of the Earth. It can, therefore, be brought into position for launch within a 90-minute time frame. Should the circling the globe cease and its position be maintained over North America, we must presume it is being positioned for the launch of the warheads. If an EMP attack is planned, the best time to launch would be in early winter, say in early November, not later than early December, depending on meteorological factors. Crops would be harvested, and in storage, cold weather would be approaching or already onset depending on the location in the country. In short, such an attack at this time would shut down all distribution of food and fuel supplies and everything else. Those in the northern tier of states would soon run out of fuel oil for homes and factories, while the southern tier of states would manage temperature-wise. All electrical grids and transformers would be fried. All vehicles with electronics will be immediately shut down. Many will have magnetized engines and will come to abrupt stops with a large number of vehicle wrecks. Unfortunately, only the food supplies on hand in the kitchen pantry will be available. Those will last only a few days. Those within walking distance of grocery stores will pick the shelves clean in a matter of days if not hours. Make no mistake, ladies and gentlemen, we will be plunged back to the 1850s time frame. Only the farmers and only some of them will survive. Our cities will be rampant with looting, crime, and ultimately death by starvation and freezing in the northern states. Few, if any, city dwellers will survive. To do so, they would have to be able to walk to the surrounding country where they might or might not be taken in by local farmers. Small towns won't be much better off. Most likely, those who make it out to the countryside won't last long either, as they will most likely be shot for trying to loot from the rural population.

This will be an open door for any country with sufficient resources to walk right in. There won't be many of us left to resist. Expect starvation and cold to kill about 280 million Americans over the next 90 to one hundred and eighty days. That means Russia and China. No one else would have the resources to cross an ocean. A couple of dozen large ships say large oil tankers fitted to carry people instead of oil, could quickly place hundreds of thousands of foreigners on our shores. They could make the voyage circular, bringing in thousands each trip, continuing indefinitely, even for a couple of years. Our harvested food stores would feed them until they could plant crops the following spring. Of course, they would have to bring their own vehicles and farm equipment or the equipment and parts to repair ours to use them. Wouldn't you say this would be an excellent way for China to bleed off her excess population? All they would have to do is remove our decomposing bodies. They might even have plans to recycle the dead."

Ethan Bradley raised his hand. The speaker responded, "Yes, General Bradley? You have a question?"

"What does the intelligence community place on the probability of either an EMP attack or other forms of strategic attack, as in biological. I mean, what is the risk assessment?"

"We place the probability of an EMP attack at less than 5% General. The potential is greater for a biological attack that would leave the infrastructure intact. The only hitch here is that an EMP attack would destroy or greatly diminish our ability to retaliate. As a nation, we could handle a biological attack far better than an EMP assault. An EMP strike could cover the entire country in one fell swoop, literally in a matter of minutes. A biological attack would have to be initiated at multiple points with a very rapid acting agent to cripple us as a whole. That could take weeks but with no damage to the infrastructure."

General Officers Mess, the Pentagon, "Do you mind if we join you, General Bradley?"

"Not at all, Generals. Please sit down. It is always a pleasure to dine and chat with the United States Air Force."

"What did you think of this morning's seminar, General Bradley?"

"It's pretty obvious, though if it was not explicitly stated, we are now militarily in third place behind China and Russia. All three of these economies are in sad shape. So far, it hasn't resulted in a hot war, but that could happen at any time, although unlikely in the immediate future. China's military bases on those artificial islands they built in the South China Seas has given them control over the Spratleys and Paracel Islands. Their land-based fighter aircraft flying off these islands are superior to our carrier-based aircraft, and their land-based cruise missiles can threaten our Carrier Battle Groups before they can close to truly effective range. What concerns me more though is the possibility and potential of space-based laser satellites and nuclear missiles launched from their mini space stations the Russians have placed up there."

"What do you think we should do about that General Bradley?"

"Well, you are the Commander of SPACECOM General, I'd like to think that you have positioned our killer satellites in close proximity to their launch platforms and their laser-based satellites.

"You're in line for your third star, aren't you General Bradley?", asked General McCartney.

"I'm in the zone, but the timeline puts me at the bottom of the list. I have irritated enough politicians by being forthright, that I seriously doubt my selection will be approved. Besides, the United States Marine Corps has little use for three-star generals that aren't paper pushers. I'll probably be put out to pasture like an old war horse."

"What's your age, General, 50?" "46, General McCartney. Who knows, maybe it is time for me to retire back to Wyoming and chase the deer and elk instead of bad guys who are determined by the State Department."

"With the economy in shambles, inflation still running over 20% a year, do you think that's wise? What's the economy like in Wyoming, anyway?"

"Being agriculturally based General, it is pretty poor. The sugar beet industry crashed under the Trans-Pacific Partnership deal. Refined sugar can be imported at less cost than simply growing the sugar beets let alone refining it. People can't afford to eat much beef, and beef prices for lower-quality beef from South America and Mexico mean we Americans eat a lot more ground beef and far less steak than we used to. Also, the ten-year drought has reduced the alfalfa and corn grown in Wyoming, so beef prices are pretty high over the last decade. No, things are pretty depressing. Even the Mexican field hands are pulling out for greener pastures." Bemused, "Are you thinking of retiring to Wyoming, General Frandson? Can your satellites locate the elk for you in the timber?"

"Wouldn't that be cheating, General," asked General McCartney? "Indeed, it would take all the fun out of it, as well as being illegal General. Of course, Game and Fish could never prove it!"

"Aren't you a city boy General Frandson," asked Bradley. "New York City as I recall." "Indeed, I am General. I would have to rely on you, Daniel Boone types to do any serious hunting." In that case, the door will always be open for you to join me in Wyoming, Generals. And now if you will excuse me, I have to go see a man about some finances."

As Bradley rose with his tray, General Frandson remarked: "General Bradley, please join us in the General Officers' bar at 17:30 for further discussion." Bradley looked at the two generals and smiled, "If you are buying, I am drinking. See you there."

Bradley left, wondering why two Air Force four stars would want to meet with a USMC Major General. Is it because I commanded a marine division or any other possible reason?

Bradley ordered a Jack Daniels and Coca Cola from the bar while he waited and glanced around the room. Curious, he paid for his drink and with it in hand, he leisurely strolled around the room, noting who was present and with whom, and who was absent. He had already observed he was one of the very few two stars at the conference. Almost all attendees were three and four-star flag officers of all services. The only Coast Guard officer present was the commandant. The U.S. Coast Guard will fall under the auspices of the Navy in wartime. The all force conference was a presentation of future technological advances which would influence the coming decades of warfighting. How innovative research could be applied has yet to be determined for military purposes. The papers presented were mostly by scientists from the Defense Advanced Research Agency, acronym DARPA, and the Test and Evaluation Command, acronym TECOM. One or two were from medical scientists sponsored by Medical Research and Development Command, the acronym MRDC. MRDC presented two papers on radiation poisoning and advances in protection against it. A third paper was on the possibility of advanced biological weapons systems by foreign powers.

"Good afternoon, General Bradley," the two Generals joined Bradley at his table. "Are you ready for another?" "Only if you are buying, General Frandson." "But I shall" and he indicated to the waiter to approach and ordered three bourbon and colas.

"What do you think of the CNO's demands for more nonnuclear anti-sub submarines, General Bradley? He pretty much demanded ten and wound up with only four as the President reduced our DOD budget four years ago. Now three of those four are deployed and the fourth in sea trials, he still yells for more. His replacement will probably sing the same song. Since you marines come under the Department of the Navy, aren't you marines short of equipment that could be funded by the reduction?"

"Yes, Sir, we are. I have to agree with the CNO though. The size of the Chinese and Russian submarine fleets scares the dickens out of me. We need to be able to kill them all far from our shores, both their missile and attack subs. I believe our carrier battle groups are very vulnerable to their submarine fleets. We could all use massive budget increases. These new air-independent subs though are much smaller, more maneuverable, and quieter than anything else in the ocean, faster, deadlier and cost about a fourth or less than the cost of a nuclear attack sub. Our marine and navy air requirements are quite a bit shy of the ideal as well. We don't have enough carrier versions of the F-35 or non-carrier-based ground support aircraft for the Marine Corps. The yokel civilians who think we can do everything with drones and unmanned aircraft are a bit shy of practical experience. I'm not convinced that any killer types of satellite we might have up there in low orbit that I don't know about might be unable to eliminate tactical enemy aircraft."

"Don't you think General, those Chinese subs especially, are there to protect the massive trading fleet they have? After all, they essentially dominate international ocean shipping?"

"Protect their merchant fleet from whom, General McCartney? Certainly not us! Right now, they are in bed with the Russians and see no threat from them. European and Japanese and Korean shipping have fallen to their competition and are pretty insignificant. Russian subs, especially their Sea Launched Ballistic Missile Submarines (SLBMs) have prowled off our coasts for decades. I doubt we could get more than half of them at any one time before they launched."

The next day Ethan decided he would have lunch in the General Officer's mess rather than the brown bag lunch he hid in his briefcase. A tall, rather thin man in a suit and tie stepped up to his table as he was eating. "May I join you, General? It seems the place is rather crowded today."

Ethan looked the man over. His tie was loose and his suit slightly ill-fitting. Ethan looked at the identity badge hanging on a chain around his neck. It identified him as a GS-19, Senior Service Executive, one Ethan never heard of. "Certainly, Sir, please have a seat." Ethan figured his presence was no accident as he glanced around the mess and noted quite a number of half-empty tables. Ethan waited for the man to initiate the conversation.

"What did you think was the purpose of the briefing yesterday? Why would anyone want to launch an EMP attack on us?" Ethan hesitated for a minute, not wanting to insult the SES, if he was too stupid to figure it out, if he was simply testing Ethan's thinking, or tangentially trying to ferret out his position on something related, or something more sinister. Ethan did not notice him at yesterday's briefing. That means he was aware of its contents before the briefing occurred. Trying to phrase an answer that was not an insult, he replied. "The basis of it was geopolitics. We're still one of the big boys on the block. One way to consider it is Russia and China dividing the world along certain fault lines. Russia is a Eurasian power. Stress the Euro- part of that.

On the other hand, China is an East Asian and South Asian power that wishes to expand its influence over Southeast Asia and the Western Pacific. Russia wants to bring all of Europe into its fold. China has established a considerable footprint in Africa. I don't know how, or if at all, they will contend over Africa. The fault line in Asia will run through the Central Asian Republics, Kazakhstan, Tajikistan, and Kyrgyzstan. I don't know precisely where that line will be. I'm not sure Russia wants to contend with their Muslim population.

On the other hand, China has shown no restraint in annihilating them when they get too rambunctious, such as by establishing Sharia law. Russia gets Europe; China gets Southeast Asia, the Western Pacific. Where we enter the picture is from China's perspective, the garden spot of the planet. China wants our agricultural productivity, oil, and coal. They don't want our population. We are in the way, sort of a hindrance. They don't want us to eat. They want our food production for their own people. They have learned quite enough of our agricultural methods to step right in and take over. In short, they want our land. They have polluted their own to the point of serious degradation."

14 April 2024, 10:00 Hours

Flag Officers at the rank of O-8 and above.

Pentagon Briefing Room, MG Clayton Waddell, SPACECOM, USAF, Presenting.

"Over the past two weeks, our satellites have observed movements at night of Iranian forces moving towards the border with Iraq. The movements are from Ahvaz to Khorramashahr on the eastern bank of the Tigris River in the south, and from Sanandaj to Marivan in the north. The Iranians built a cantonment in Marivan last year, now we know why. So far, they appear to be company-sized units of mounted infantry. One, two or three companies are moving to these locations each night. They are driving using night vision goggles and no headlights. So far, no tank or heavy artillery units have been observed. Their objectives are uncertain, but their location around Marivan suggests a possible drive toward the oilfields around Kirkuk in the north. If so, they can expect fierce resistance from Kurdish forces. Such an operation would invoke considerable angst in Turkey. You can bet Turkey will go on full alert if the Iranians come within 100 kilometers of their border. In the south, the Marsh Arabs of Iraq are mostly Shiites, and would most likely welcome the Shiite Iranians. If the Iranians cross the Shat al Arab, they could take Basra and turn south against Kuwait, or turn north towards A Nasiriyah. From there they would have two roads to drive north to Baghdad if that is the final objective. One senior analyst thinks the northern force is a feint. The southern force could bypass Baghdad rather than get bogged down in urban warfare and drive towards Ramadi. Ramadi also has a substantial Shiite population. One single analyst, the newest on the Defense Intelligence Agency staff, believes their ultimate objective is Israel and Jerusalem. It is a long way to Jerusalem, close to 1000 kilometers in a straight line. By road, it is closer to 1500 kilometers. Refueling stations using fuel storage bladders protected by revetments have been established close to the border in each location. It would be difficult but not impossible for the Iranians to make such a thrust. If we observe artillery and armor units moving west, it could be consistent with a spring offensive. If chemical units are identified, count on it. A seaborne offensive by Iran as part of their operation is essentially impossible. The Egyptians would not allow their transit through the Suez Canal, and they lack sufficient blue water naval capability to sail around Africa and into the Mediterranean. It will be a classic land warfare operation."

MG Bradley's Office, Monday Morning, 10:30 Hours. "Good Morning Arlene, I don't have an appointment with the General, but I wonder if he is available for coffee."

"I'm sure he is always available for coffee with the Commandant of the United States Marine Corps.

Buzzing Bradley on the intercom, "General Bradley, GEN Schenken is here to see you. Shall I bring in two coffees GEN Schenken?"

"No thanks Arlene, I'm going to treat the General to coffee in the General Officer's Mess."

Bradley steps out of his office, hand extended, "Good Morning Sir, what's this about coffee?"

"Let's go to the Mess and chitchat."

Whatever you say, General, as long as you are buying." They strolled casually into the club and found a table in the open.

"What's on your mind, General? I'm sure you didn't want it recorded."

"You're right, Ethan. This whole damned place is bugged, and NSA fears everybody and everything. Who knows what or where the mikes are in here? Worse, who knows what the power structure backing NSA is? I suspect even the President is afraid of them, although I don't know why. Listen, I'm Hesitant, Bradley asked, "Just what is it that makes you so circumspect that makes you want to retire General? You still have a full year to go on this tour as Commandant. You could easily stay on after that if you choose."

"Things are going on that I don't like. I don't want any part of them. Ethan, there is a great undertow in effect to which the American public is totally oblivious. Mainstream media, if it is even aware of it, won't even think about it, let alone report on it. It is all behind the scenes, carefully guarded, part of it is a great debate on foreign policy. Even the Council on Foreign Relations is divided over it. Europe is falling to Islam. Some want us to invade Europe to help expel the Muslims. Another faction says to expel them here first. Our trade with Europe is declining to the point of going out of existence. The President wants to withdraw from NATO and Europe to make a Fortress America. Article 5 of the NATO agreement does not absolutely commit us to defend any NATO member if attacked. Rather, the NATO agreement states 'in consultation with other NATO members.' That's something the European heads of state and our military don't want the public to know. They want Congress and the American public to believe it is a total commitment. The President wants us to withdraw from NATO, but the military-industrial complex is resisting like hell. She won't give an inch and neither will the Joint Chiefs. You can bet your bottom dollar almost all of the four-star generals in all of the services are getting stock options at prices you wouldn't believe. Many of the CFR realize that Islamic Europe is the greatest threat to the New World Order. That's why they are pushing for us to 'assist' European governments before they fall to Islam and Sharia.

You have been here a little over a year. How would you like to get out of here, out of the DC area? Command of the Third Marine Division is coming open soon, and I'll offer it to you if you want out of here. I know you have had enough of this staff crap, and are really a field commander. You proved that in the past as a division commander. You're one of our top contenders for three and four stars, destined for Corps command if you stay in, that you are a warrior at every level is beyond dispute. Conceivably, you could become Commandant of the Corps if things don't go as far south as I think they will. You have proven that at every level of combat, from personal hand to hand combat to being one of the most successful division commanders in the USMC. You are needed for your military operational and demonstrated potential strategic skills. You are at that operational to a strategic level interface where you will be forced to make a decision for the edification of the inner circle hierarchy. You are either for them or against them, for or against the Constitution. Those who support the Constitution will be swiftly eliminated. That time is coming for you very soon. Sometimes I wonder though about your political philosophy. A military officer is an instrument of the perceptions of the geopolitics by the ruling elites, or ignorant politicians, be they tyrannical or republican, or anything in between. As Clauswitz routinely summarized, 'war is politics by other means.' You have played that very carefully, very close to your chest. Nobody really knows where you stand in the political arena. That's why you have been retained on active duty as a staff officer here for evaluation. Now to answer your question, let's just say I am sick of politics and let it go at that. I don't like the international situation that was covered in the recent briefing on EMP satellites. I don't like our national political situation. The country has forgotten its roots. We're rotting from the inside. I don't like the FEMA camps being staffed and stockpiled again. We had enough of them earlier. I just don't know how things are going to play out. There isn't a politician in either house of

Congress that isn't corrupt or power hungry or both. I don't like the smell of this place, Ethan. The capitol of our country is an overflowing cesspool. You better get the hell out of here, Ethan. If you accept a Division Command again, at least for the time being, I'll have the orders cut. Maybe I'll move to Wyoming too."

"I'll be delighted to get the hell out of Dodge, General. Just give me the written orders, and I'll get started processing. Gypsy will be glad to hear it. I'll still have the family move to Wyoming. I hear rumblings as well, but nothing definite. I have never cared for the rumor mill in this place, or the grinding politics or the ass-kissing or Congressional deities either, for that matter."

"I'll see that the orders are cut by the end of the month. I think you are wise to get the family out of the area. The change of command ceremony will, of course, take place in about 45 days at Camp Lejune, North Carolina. I know you will do what's right, no matter what happens, Ethan."

Bradley smiled. "Let's get some more coffee, General!"

Back in his office, Ethan thoughtfully didn't press the General after that last comment, just sipped his coffee and smiled. General Schenken submitted his resignation thirty days later with a retirement date of 31 October. General Osborne was named his successor to assume the office at the beginning of November.

Bradley was enjoying a late lunch alone in the general officers' mess when a tall, rather skinny man, dressed in a sport coat, striped tie, and white shirt approached his table. His identity card was hanging loosely by its chain around his neck. Ethan glanced up at the man, noting his identity card. "Do you mind if I join you, General?" he asked.

"Not at all, please sit." as Ethan motioned to a chair, fork in hand.

"I'm Fred Sikowsky, General," offering Ethan his hand. Ethan shook his hand and casually glanced around the room, noting a number of empty tables. Ethan immediately realized that this was a chance encounter. Ethan noted the security pass on Sikowsky's neck that identified him as a GS-20, a high-ranking NSA officer. Ethan continued to eat as Sikowsky settled in, salted his food, and placed a napkin on his lap. During the next few minutes, neither spoke. Finally, Sikowsky said, "I understand you are General Frandson's fair-haired boy."

"I don't know about that, Mr. Sikowsky. I am only a two star, not three or four."

"Well, that speaks volumes anyway General. I'm sure you'll soon gather one or two more." Ethan contemplated asking him why he said that. "Do you have the magic crystal ball, Mr. Sikowsky?"

"No, nothing of the sort, General. You are better known than you realize." Ethan nodded, saying nothing, just continuing to eat. After devouring half his lunch, Sikowsky asked: "What do you think of the situation in Europe, General?"

"You NSA folks are the ones with all the intel Mr. Sikowsky, what do you think? Us peasants only know what we see on the nightly news or what's left after you redact the news releases."

"It's pretty grim General. The Muslims are well armed, fighting house to house, killing anyone who admits or whom they suspect, of being a non-Muslim. Soon they will control some of Europe's major cities."

"What of the defense of these civilians, Mr. Sikowsky? The European civilians aren't allowed to own firearms for self defense, most likely the police have been targeted and slaughtered in their homes, and the Muslim militias outnumber the European armies, where the armies can't use heavy weapons in urban warfare. Seems pretty grim to me, Mr.

"Yes, it does, General, so it does."

Ethan continued to eat in silence.

"Do you think it could happen here, General? I mean open warfare between Muslim militias and civilian Christians?"

"It could if you continue to disarm American citizens in good standing and jail those who refuse to surrender their privately-owned firearms."

"So General, you are a member of the National Rifle Association?"

Ethan rose to return his tray to a dishwashing area and said, "You know I am, Mr. Sikowsky." Ethan walked away, wondering why NSA was trying to feel him out. He didn't think the Muslim uprising in Europe was Sikowsky's real agenda. He had the feeling he would meet Sikowsky again someday, and soon.

Ethan rang General Frandson's office at noon the next day. The General's secretary put him through to the General.

"Let's get some chow General if you can break away."

"Right, you are, Ethan. I'll meet you outside the General Officers' mess in five minutes." General Frandson knew that something was troubling Bradley.

After passing through the soup and sandwich line, the two generals found an empty table where they could speak in muted voices.

"I was joined by an uninvited guest at lunch yesterday, General. Some guy I never saw before. Said his name was Sikowsky. The name tag said he was a GS-20."

"What did you talk about Ethan?"

"He asked me what I thought about our world position. I voiced my opinion on Russia and China dividing the world but refused to answer his question on what our response should be. Told him strategic decisions are above my pay grade. Those decisions are for the shakers and movers at State and the Administration. I didn't mention what is referred to as the Deep State, the establishment elite, the New World Order people, the real controllers behind the talking head politicians".

"I'm glad you didn't, Ethan. He is a big wig over at State Department, one of the shadow government Deep State guys. Stays behind the scenes and pulls strings to make things happen. Council on Foreign Relations, New World Order advocate, might also have his finger in the International Monetary fund. He is potentially a very dangerous man. Glad you didn't touch on politics in here. You would have been out of a job in thirty days. I don't want to see you retire just yet."

"General, I know something is really bothering you. Is there something you can talk about? Any members of the Joint Chiefs feel the same way? I suspect something is going on way down deep in the bowels of the Deep State."

General Schenken was quiet, didn't say anything, but frowned as he looked at Bradley's face.

"Well, if your hunch is correct, the Joint Chiefs are probably in on it, with perhaps the exception of the Chief of Naval Operations. All I can say is that I share your perceptions. Let's let it go at that.

On another subject, Ethan, that greatly troubles me is this seemingly coziness between China and Russia. I think it is only superficial. The Chinese have long memories, actually stretching for generations. They remember well what they suffered at first the hands of the Japanese, then at the hands of the Russians after they entered the war on 8 August 1945. The Russkies were well prepared for their invasion of China. The Chinese peasants suffered just about as badly at the hands of the Russians as they did from the Japanese. Remember when the Japanese took Manchuria in 1931 and renamed it Manchukwo? How about Unit 731? That Japanese biological research that tested various biological pathogens on Chinese and American and Allied prisoners, then did live vivisection on them without the benefit of anesthesia? General McArthur gave them amnesty in exchange for their data, which turned out to be absolutely worthless. The commanding general of that Unit 731 became the head of the International Green Cross and died a multimillionaire. The Russians stripped everything they could from the Chinese territory they seized. They raped Chinese women just as much as the Japanese did. There is no love between Russia and China. The Russians have seemed to have forgotten all of that and would let bygones be bygones, but most certainly not the Chinese. I think as Russia orients towards Western Europe, the Chinese might just take advantage of it. Us idiot Americans, however, don't seem to read or understand the history and learn from it. We should be gearing up for the Pacific as well as Western Europe."

The Kremlin, 1 May 2024

Comrades, this plan is insane! It is total insanity! Economic competition is one thing. It is healthy and drives innovation. Political competition, however, leads to military competition that leads to war. This is now what you propose. The gains will only be temporary. More than anywhere at any time, the best minds of innovation and genius have concentrated in Western Europe and North America. Now you wish to destroy those minds, those abilities? For what reason? To destroy the competition? To allow a few thousand select elitists to rule the world. To form a bureaucracy that controls natural resources on a global scale in a top-down driven system. Do you think the mass of the world's humanity will allow this to continue forever? Yes, as long as you control the military and it remains obedient you can exercise control. At some point, however, the common soldier will realize the inequity of it. When that inequity overwhelms him, he will turn his gun on his superiors and the system. Yes, the old Soviet lasted from the end of the Russian Revolution in 1920 to 1989. Will your new installment last as long? I don't think so, not in this age of communication and commerce. Silicon Valley in California is the greatest concentration of brain power and innovation in the world. There is no place in the world where technology development rules as in Silicon Valley. There is nothing like competition that drives innovation and original thought. The results of what you propose will be impossible to predict or comprehend."

What of the Chinese masses? Hundreds of millions of unemployed, starving men and women and children moving in all directions. As they migrate out of the cities into what a few decades ago were rural areas that cannot absorb them, what will they do? I'll tell you. They will turn, violently against all forms of authority. They will not respect any international borders. Yes, I know the Chinese government has promised them all of North America if they will just be patient. For how long? Millions of Chinese crossing the Pacific Ocean even within a few years is not realistic; it is not the same as the massive land migrations of the eleventh through the thirteen centuries. The Chinese can't move enough people fast enough to alleviate their population pressure. What will it be today? This plan must not be put into operation.

Do we trust our Chinese allies in the global land war? Remember we have no friends, only temporary allies. When will the Chinese turn on us for our oil, uranium, forest, and food-producing lands? This temporary alliance is not a marriage made in heaven but an alliance forged in hell. When, if ever, after the Chinese conquer North America, why would they not look west and north on the Eurasian continent? That's where the oil is. That's where warm water ports are. That is where the proposed captive populations are. How far, comrades, how far?"

Already there are massive riots all over rural China. Chinese armies are marching through their rural areas to ostensibly restore order. The massive riots are spreading to their cities where millions upon millions of "unregistered" Chinese are living on the streets without housing, potable water, sanitary facilities, enough to eat, and jobs."

"Thank you Comrade Gorskin. Your views and concerns are well known to us. We have given them very serious and very long consideration that is their due. We have decided to proceed as planned. Our Chinese allies concur our first strike will determine the overall outcome of our operations. Unfortunately, we have found it necessary to order you and your family confined to your dacha in the Urals. Any attempts at outside communication will be dealt with most harshly. Your family is already in route to your dacha under guard. You will be escorted there to join them forthwith. We thank you, Comrade, for your views and your service.

CHAPTER II

1 MAY 2024

"GOOD MORNING, HASP REALTY, MARGARITA SPEAKING. How may I help you?

'Good morning, this fine Saturday morning, Margarita. This is Ethan Bradley, in Washington, DC. Is Roberto in?"

"Oh, Hello General Bradley, it is nice to hear from you. I'll put you right through. Roberto just got a cup of coffee."

'Good morning, General. How are things in that snake pit?"

"You got that right Roberto. It is really worse than that, which is why I am calling. Evict the renters in Dad's old place. Make sure all is well with it. Hold their feet to the fire on maintenance and damages. I want it to be ready to move into in 30 days from now?"

"Are you going to retire and join us, General?"

No, but I don't like the way things are shaping up around here. There are ominous rumbles beneath the surface that you never hear about on national news. The international situation isn't good either, and both are deteriorating. I want the place ready for Gypsy and the boys to move into on a minute's notice."

"That's both interesting and disturbing. Anything you can tell me?"

"No, nothing specific, just a lot of very bad intuitive feelings. Give me an interim update report in two weeks if you need to get a court order eviction notice or support from the local sheriff, don't hesitate to do so. Their lease expires this month, and I really don't trust them. I perceive them to be closer to squatters than civic-minded responsible citizens."

"Will do, General. Want me to call you at the office or at home?"

"Either will do. No classified information for the recorders but they will tape it if you call the office. It doesn't matter really, as National Security Agency, NSA has probably bugged every room in my house."

Ten Days Later.

"General Bradley's Office, Arlene speaking."

"Hello, this is Roberto, General Bradley's realtor in Wyoming. Is the General in?"

"One moment, Sir. Can you hold?"

"Sure, I have a couple of minutes."

Arlene buzzed Bradley. "A gentleman who says he is your realtor in Wyoming, named Roberto, is on line one for you, General."

"Hi, Roberto, Ethan here. How are things?"

"The renters skipped out several days ago. I checked on the place this morning. I ordered Bill's Lock and Key to replace all of the locks. They didn't bother to clean the place. It could use a thorough, top to bottom cleaning job before you put the family in it. I suggest the local company. They are reasonably priced and do a good job. Unfortunately, I think it will be a couple of thousand. Several windows in the garage need replacing, and they took a ceiling fan/light with them. The deposit will cover the repairs for the fan and windows, but not much more. Do you want the ceiling fan light combo replaced, and if so, immediately?"

"Roger that Roberto, I want it livable, ready by the end of the month. Pay the bills out of the account, send me the statements, and I'll cover the difference with a check to Hasp Realty. Gypsy won't like giving up her job though. She might be a little feisty when she gets there. Keep your eyes open for a job for her if you will. I know jobs for physicists working on a Ph.D. are hard to find."

"Will do, General. Don't get snake bit in that den of vipers over there."

Over the dinner table, Bradley said, "Boys, I have a surprise for you. This Saturday we are going to Six Flags for the day. Mom can use a day out of the house and job, you need to let off some steam from school, and I just need a day away from the office."

Gypsy looked at him with a wondering stare. "It's Ok Hon, we all need a day off."

After an hour's drive to the theme park, and paying an exorbitant entry fee, Bradley gave each boy $50 for snacks and drinks. He and Gypsy wandered around the park until they were relatively alone, no one within twenty yards of them. He spoke quietly. "You realize don't you, Dear, that every room of our quarter is bugged; even our bedroom and bathroom have microphones that record our sex life. The politicians and NSA officers responsible for it should be tried for treason in violation of the First Amendment and hung on the National Mall at the foot of the Washington Monument.

I don't know what or when or how, at least not yet, but I have a very strong premonition that something bad is going to happen soon. The vibes are pretty strong; an undercurrent is running through the Pentagon. I want you and the boys out of here, rather quickly. I told the realtor to evict the renters in Dad's place in Wyoming. He is having the house cleaned and ready for your occupancy. Keep the boys busy. They can clear the land down the hill, all the way to the river. They can cut the timber for firewood, cut the brush, maybe even level it some and turn the soil over for putting in a garden next spring. I'm tired, and I have had enough of this bovine scatology, politicking, and backstabbing at the Pentagon. I don't particularly want a third star. I am not sure when I'll join you there. Certainly, I hope by Christmas, but no guarantees. With the presidential election this fall, anything can happen, and probably will. I know this will play hell with your doctoral research, but I would much prefer a live wife than a dead one with a Ph.D.".

"You think it could be violent enough to spill over and threaten us?"

"Yes, whatever it is, it could be very deadly. I realize that things have seemed to calm down on the surface, but that is strictly manipulated by the White House in conjunction with the press. Things are not right and going downhill. Not just the economy, but something big, but I haven't discovered it. I don't want to take any chances with the loves of my life. So, you and the boys are going to get the hell out of here and back to Wyoming."

"Do you think the civil war still start all over again? Do you think we'll go into Europe to fight Muslims? Do you think the clashes with Russia over Arctic resources will bring World War III? So, what's the bottom line, Love? Who stands to gain from our destruction?"

"Frankly, everybody outside the western hemisphere. Based on the shortwave reports, probably China, Russia, and maybe Iran. China gets pretty much all of Africa with its oil and mineral wealth, Russia gets Europe, and Iran is expanding into the Middle East. Now, how long will that last? I don't know. I see that eventually China or maybe a Chinese-Russian coalition will turn on Iran. Those Iranian Shiite bastards devoutly believe they are destined to rule the world as a Shiite caliphate from Jerusalem. I wouldn't rule out a combined attack on Iran from China and Russia. I don't know if this Russian-Chinese-Iranian Alliance will hold together or for how long. The Shiite Iranian brand of Islam is antithetical to what is supposed to be Christian Russia. The Chinese don't like either Russia or Iran. It is a temporary marriage of convenience. When Turkey shifted to a theocracy of Sunni Islam, they pulled out or really were, kicked out of NATO.

Our illustrious Secretary of State Stewart is ridiculed as the "new Neville Chamberlain," for more or less failure to defend the Baltic states, Lithuania, Latvia and Estonia from Russia, after the asshole in British history who gave parts of western Europe, to Adolph Hitler. I suspect we are about to withdraw from NATO and Western Europe. They aren't willing to defend themselves, so why should we shed American blood and trillions of dollars in their defense.

Europe will be Islamic in a few years anyway. With the Muslims circling the Vatican and demanding the Pope withdraw, it is only a question of time. The Italian army could easily be overwhelmed in attempting to protect the Vatican. The situation is so bad the Pope is thinking of moving all of the Vatican's treasures to a special warehouse in Dallas, Texas. East coast cities, especially New York City, aren't considered safe enough from armed Muslim mobs to protect the art, the recordings of history, all the gold, and precious religious icons from confiscation and destruction. Oops, Sorry Love, that is classified above Top Secret. I never said that. The Muslim uprisings in Europe are far worse than the national media are admitting. There are serious riots in Denmark, France, Spain, Italy, Sweden, and Germany. Their demands for the institution of Sharia law and exemption from all other laws are becoming unbearable. There is a lot of unrest beneath the surface in Europe. I expect that it will turn hot, sooner or later, more likely within a year or two. It is a question of arms for the civilian population. Their national armies can't suppress it as they are so grossly outnumbered by the Muslims. Indeed, Muslims in their armed forces are expected to turn their weapons on their fellow non-Muslim soldiers. Unfortunately, Love, all those are possible, even probable. I don't know which will come first, or if we will continue to muddle along here in the good old USA. I want you to start stocking long term, as in years, food. Dehydrated, freeze-dried, whole, unground wheat, not flour, in 50 and 100 pound bags, bulk five-gallon buckets of honey, a couple of 50-pound bags of iodized salt, baking soda, spices, dried beans, and rice, in galvanized garbage cans or five-gallon polyethylene pails with watertight screw on lids. Buy galvanized garbage cans in several different places so as not to attract attention. A dozen might be sufficient. If you have to stack them in the basement, full or empty, so be it.

I'll see what I can do about acquiring some guns and ammunition. Being active duty military, I think I can get some exemptions to prove necessity as current law requires. I know Dad buried some, but I don't know what or where. I'll have to find the notes he left as to where he buried them. You know every room in our house is bugged, and everything we say is recorded. That is why we are here today to escape NSA.

I'll tell the boys that I am thinking of retiring, which is true. That you're going early to get the house fixed however you want it, and so that they can be ready to start in a new school. I know to change high schools is tough, but they are flexible and will survive. Pick out winter clothes for everybody. Lined blue jeans and down coats for each of you. Wool sweaters and socks and insulated hunting boots, heavy and medium weight polypropylene long johns for everybody. Get them ordered or buy them from Sierra Trading Post in Cody or Cabela's in Billings or wherever you find whatever you like. Don't worry about the money. You might even apply to teach physics in high school.

One big item is fuel. Try and decide where we can put an underground 500-gallon fuel tank in the backyard without cutting into the irrigation system. It will have to have a good hand pump, maybe installed at a slight angle for drainage to one end where the pump will be. After it is in, order it filled with stabilized premium gas for long term storage.

The next big items will be two chain saws one large, and one smaller, both commercial and professional quality. Make the smaller one a size you can handle. Make the larger one with at least a twenty-inch bar. Buy extra bars and three or four extra chains for each of them. Also buy the extras, such as sharpening files, oil, and extra filters. Roberto, our realtor, says they never did anything down by the river, so it is a mess down there, with lots of brush and small trees. It will keep the boys quite busy. They will want to get in on football when tryouts and practice start. That will be a relief for them from cutting brush and trees. All the wood should be cut short enough to fit in the wood-burning stove. Eleven inches is ideal, so it won't have to be cut twice. They can build muscles by splitting the sections of a log with an eight-pound sledge, wedges, and malls. Make them wear safety gear at all times. Get the boys and yourself steel-toed boots as well as insulated ones for winter, and chain saw chaps, hard hats with hearing protection and face shields. Make them practice liberal use of mosquito repellent down there. Being a physicist, I am sure you can direct the boys to build chainsaw boxes that you can make into Faraday cages. Order a 55-gallon drum of gasoline and add sufficient long-term fuel stabilizer. Don't touch it. Save it for emergency use only, as in save it exclusively for chain saw use. Keep it under lock at all times, preferably in the big garage out of sight of the neighbors. Get a fuel pump that fits it so we won't have to tilt it.

Dad left me a notebook. On the inside cover was a note, to be sure to read all the way through it. Mostly it was mundane, websites, addresses for e-mail companies, and even a few X-rated DVDs. There was one note though, very intriguing, but wasn't highlighted or circled or anything that would draw untoward attention to it. It goes something like three blazes on a big cottonwood tree, 10 yards from the center blaze, then a compass reading. I have no idea of the significance of it. It said your future and safety depend on it. Maybe on the weekends you and the boys can look for that cottonwood tree. If there are three blazes on it, on the east, west and north sides, it's probably pretty good sized. You might have to dig a little; I don't know if a metal detector would help or not. I can only hazard a guess no. Dad wouldn't want to make it too easy for just anybody. I suspect it is a cache of some kind to be recovered after The Shit Hits the Fan. It is up to you if you want to buy a metal detector if you think it will help. Dad buried some guns when they passed the idiot gun control laws, but I don't know anything about that. That might be what is in the cache. You can legally only own one bolt action rifle and one shotgun per person. No handguns are allowed for civilians. I know he buried more than that, along with several Government Model .45 ACPs and lots of ammunition for everything he buried. I'll just have to research my notes to see if I can find anything else as to where he buried them. You can bet he made them as hard as he could on the federal gestapo Bureau of Alcohol, Tobacco and Firearms boys. Lots of people tried to hide them in their septic tanks, but that is the first place the BATF assholes looked. Lots of people got their septic tanks pumped out for free if the BATF thought they had hidden guns.

The boys will want a dog. So, do I. Get a Chesapeake Bay retriever or a Labrador retriever puppy. Get two of them if the boys each want one. If so, get a male and female and let them breed after the bitch's first estrous cycle. Then get the female spayed, an ovario-hysterectomy. That is a lower priority, as you will probably wind up doing most of the day to day care for the dogs. You might have to search for a while to find a reputable breeder. Don't buy any dog whose parents are not certified to be free of hip dysplasia by the Orthopedic Foundation for Animals.

I don't know, but I hope the boys can continue studying languages. Both are getting pretty good in Spanish. Josh now has a year of Russian and Sam a year of Mandarin. I don't know if the public schools in Wyoming are that sophisticated enough to offer courses in those languages... I hope so. It will stand them in good stead. If not, get each one of the appropriate Rosetta Stone home study sets and make sure they continue to learn the languages.

The last thing I can think of is getting electronic parts for the little Toyota truck. Check with the Toyota dealership in Powell. Ask them what you will need. Put them in the Faraday cage along with the shortwave radio. Get or make Faraday cages for the chain saws you can use on a daily basis as well. Keep them in the cages when not in use. Make that at the bottom of the financial list.

Pay for everything in cash. Use credit and debit cards and checks as little as possible. I know you are limited in the amount you can withdraw as cash on each transaction as the government tries to eliminate cash so they can track everyone's expenses. Draw out just a little more than the maximum amount each week to reduce it being traced. We will make a wire transfer to a local bank in Worland from our account here. This will probably be close to cleaning out the bank account, which might not be a bad thing. I'll decide on selling some stocks for extra cash. I'll move into the Bachelors Officers Quarters on a nearby post. That will cost us our housing allowance for a few months, but we will just have to bite the bullet on that one. One last item: a good garden tiller. I'll make a list of all of this something this week. I know the boys will miss their current schools. They will have to accept it. They are flexible enough to adapt and make new friends. They might have a little trouble of getting rid of any possible elitist attitude they might have developed. Somebody once said there are three steps to war. First comes currency wars, then trade wars, then hot wars. We're heavily into the trade wars. With China controlling the Straits of Malacca, it could come at any time. A hot war with China could come at any time."

Gypsy and Ethan had sent his sons to a private school. Very expensive, but there they objectively taught history, mathematics and the so-called hard sciences and politics. Coat and ties are the daily dress. No flip-flops or Bermuda shorts allowed in the classroom. The young women were required to wear skirts or slacks and hose. Walking shoes are permitted, but many wore flats and squashed heels. Saddle oxfords were becoming popular again. Worth every damned penny, Gypsy and Bradley agreed. They insisted the boys participated in at least two sports, one of which had to be karate. Ethan encouraged wrestling to go along with that, but football and basketball and lacrosse were acceptable. Hillside College is the opposite of the Old Boys Club of Harvard and Yale for elitist liberal families. The Skull and Bones should be excised as the fraternity controlling access to the prestigious positions of industry, finance, and government.

Gypsy was quiet for a moment. "Do you think it is as bad as all of that? To separate us in the name of safety? Are you thinking of civil war again or a nuclear attack?"

"Both are possible, simultaneously or separately. If we have another civil war, it will be along racial lines. It will be a three-ring circus, blacks versus white versus Hispanics. Some of our cities, such as Houston, will really suffer. I'll learn more in the coming weeks to months about what exactly is going on. In the meantime, I want you and the boys safe, above all. In the opening days of the first two decades of the twenty-first century, China's military-industrial complex underwent enormous expansion. Funded primarily by selling rare earth minerals, uranium and oil from their business interests in Africa, and their engineer modified stolen plans of America's latest combat aircraft based on artificial islands in the South China Sea, they could choke the Straits of Malacca at any time they chose. The strategic threat was not lost on South Korea or Japan. Without the continued inflow of Middle Eastern oil, their economies would collapse within weeks, if not days. Their aircraft instituted flights day and night from South China into the Indian Ocean. India's response was to dispatch their fighter aircraft to accompany the Chinese overflights. The aviators always exchanged friendly waves, knowing someday they would fight."

"Darling, you know I love the boys as if I were their birth mother. I would die to protect them. I know there are many things you can't tell me. It doesn't take a nuclear physicist or even a first-year college student in political science or history to see what's going on. We, as a nation, are in critical trouble. The bastards in Washington, DC have kicked the economic can so far down the road we'll never recover. I've known that for several years. The bloat in the stock market is overwhelming. The FED keeps pumping more and more paper money into the economy. The only question is when will complete collapse come? That you want us out of here, up to Wyoming, very strongly suggests to you that total collapse is imminent. Am I right, so far"?

Ethan thought for a moment, just how much can he reveal? He sighed, "You're pretty close, Love. I can't give you the exact date, and a few more puzzle pieces have to fall in place. Unfortunately, they could do so at any hour. The economic situation is beyond repair. It will collapse, probably violently.

"Let me guess Ethan. Inflation has increased, now it is officially running 5% a month. I don't think it is so little. Hyperinflation is now defined as 10% per month. I believe we are much closer to that. Your two-star salary doesn't go near as far as it did just a few years ago. In fact, we had more purchasing power when you were an 0-6 when we married. I see an imminent collapse. The Middle East is an absolute disaster. Saudi Arabia is not just on the brink of collapsing; it is collapsing. Egypt has increasing riots. Jordan and Lebanon don't exist anymore. Turkey is reverting to Islamic fundamentalism and being kicked out of NATO.

That's a useless ally anyway. Our withdrawal from Europe has resulted in Russian expansionism. Riots in the Baltic states to rejoin a reconstituted former USSR cannot be suppressed.

Muslim refugees are demanding Sharia replace the constitutional law in France, Spain, Italy, and Germany. The Vatican is surrounded 24/7 by Muslims demanding it to be vacated so that they can claim it as the center of a new caliphate.

Russian Bombers flying off our coasts 24/7 out of Venezuela and Columbia threaten us daily. So how will the EMP attack be launched? Intercontinental Ballistic Missiles (ICBMs), from a submarine, launched ballistic missiles (SLBMs), or from space-based satellites or intermediate range missiles (IRBMs) out of Venezuela, or Columbia, space-based lasers to take out any potential responders? I'm sure you're aware of China's massive buildup of ocean-going cargo ships. I just read that article in your latest copy of the Naval Institute Proceedings. They are far in excess of what's needed for world trade. They already control most of the shipping industries through China Ocean Shipping Company (COSCO) and its subsidiaries. Why? The USMC doesn't even have the personnel, including women, to fill three divisions. The Army is down to eight divisions; the USAF is flying antiquated aircraft that are no match for MIG-5 Is. We're doomed, I know that. Just don't want to lose you. Soup kitchens are becoming all too common in our cities. Blacks are having demonstrations or riots on a weekly basis, complaining about everything, especially the Supplemental Nutritional Program (SNAP) being slightly curtailed. No more prime rib steaks on food stamps. Unemployment is above 25%. City folks can't even defend themselves as black rioters and looters terrorize whole white neighborhoods and the suburbs. Frankly, I am surprised they haven't hit our neighborhood. We have to be primed for looting.

Israel is fighting skirmishes all around its borders every day. China's People's Liberation Army Navy (PLAN) has developed a superclass of small nuclear fast attack submarines to counter our carrier battle groups that can't even be fully manned. Our front-line combat ships are sailing with only two-thirds of their full complement of crews. The Russians and Chinese know this. The Southeast /Asian nations are already negotiating with China for suzerainty. Only Japan is going nuclear out of deathly fear of Chinese retaliation for World War II. The collective Chinese memory lasts for centuries. In short Love, the world is a cesspool that is about to have barrels of gasoline added to it and ignited. It isn't going just to burn, but explode."

Ethan stopped and turned, taking Gypsy's hands in his.

"No matter what happens, you and the boys are the centers of my life. I'll be passing on tidbits for preparedness for you as circumstances permit. Let's get a hot dog and soda before the boys get off their ride.

One other thing. The Chinese hacked into the FBI database on firearms ownership in Clarksburg, W. They planted a virus in it that updates the FBI's files on a daily basis. They know where every registered gun in the country is located. If you get the opportunity to buy a gun you like on the black market, by all means, buy it regardless of the price. The FBI doesn't need to know who owns what guns."

The following Monday morning, Dr. Sikowsky again approached Ethan in the General Officers Mess.

"Good morning, General. May I join you?'

"Certainly Dr. Sikowsky, pull up a chair." Ethan continued to eat, waiting for Sikowsky to open the conversation.

"It seems that you are an up and coming General Officer, General Bradley. From the rumors, I hear you are on track to be a four-star general, possibly the Commandant of the Marine Corps."

"I don't know where you hear such rumors, Dr. I just do my job as I am ordered. I'm nothing special." "To the contrary, General. You performed brilliantly in the latest unpleasantness. Some people would very much like to make your acquaintance. Will you be available to meet with several people later this afternoon? I understand you keep a change of civilian clothes in your office. It would be better if you were not in uniform."

"If it is for official purposes, yes I can make myself available in civilian clothes."

"Very good General, please meet me with our friends in the Capital building at 17:00 hours. A friend who knows who you are will greet you at the top of the stairs on the south side and lead to our little meeting. She knows you on sight."

"May I ask with whom we will be meeting?"

"Well, General, in all honesty, it would be better if it is a surprise. Yes, it is official business. I think you will find it quite interesting. Enjoy your lunch, General." Sikowsky picked up his tray and moved off to another table across the room to join several people that Ethan did not recognize. All had to be GS-18 or higher to be in the cafeteria.

At 16:15 hours, Ethan changed into a dress shirt, tie, and sport coat. He caught a civilian taxi outside the Pentagon. He paid the driver in cash and casually strolled up to the steps on the south side of the Capitol building. An extremely beautiful woman in a summer dress that was nearly sheer greeted him at the top of the steps. "Good afternoon, General. You are even more handsome than your photograph." "Thank you, young lady, but I don't know where you get that information." She smiled.

"If you will follow me, General, some people are waiting to meet you. She led Ethan to a table in the cafeteria on the ground floor.

"Gentlemen, May I present General Bradly." The two gentlemen stood up and offered their hands. Ethan vaguely recognized one of them as the Speaker of the House but not the second. They introduced themselves as Speaker Thompson and Senator Bardston.

"Please be seated General, what can we offer you for a libation?"

"Just a Coca-Cola, thank you. I am still on duty." Both men smiled, and Bardston raised a hand signaling a waiter. The Senator and Speaker each ordered a scotch.

"I am sure you are wondering what this is all about, General."

"Well Senator, I am mildly curious as to why I am summoned to the presence of two of our most distinguished political leaders." Both men smiled at the flattery, but Ethan kept a straight face.

"Quite frankly, General, we will get straight to the point. I don't like keeping people in suspense. You have an amazing record and show great promise. What we are offering you is an invitation. An invitation to join an elite club, if you will, that can offer you a rapid promotion, choice assignments, and the opportunity to measurably increase personal wealth."

"I'm sorry gentlemen, but I am not in the contracting business. I have no input into that aspect of the Defense Department." Both men realized the remark as a ploy, and Ethan recognized that they knew it. *"These guys are sharp and not game players,"* thought Ethan. "Very well, gentlemen, what can I do for you?"

"We are extending an invitation to you to join the Council for Foreign Relations. I am sure you are quite familiar with our organization and what we can accomplish for our members."

Ethan glanced behind the two politicians. The young lady was standing off to the side. Bardston noticed Ethan's eye movement. Without turning around, Bardston remarked.

"Yes, she is quite striking, isn't she!"

"Indeed." Ethan knew she was bait. He returned his gaze to first Bardston, then Thompson, not letting his eyes return to the young woman.

"Your invitation is quite flattering, gentlemen. I really don't know quite what to say. Your club is amazing; it is really the power behind the political and economic structure of our country. Membership no doubt is a most distinguished form of recognition and accomplishment. I am not quite sure what I could contribute to such an organization. I really am nothing more than a soldier. I am aware of the power of your organization, but I seriously question what I could contribute to it."

"General, your military knowledge and analytical sense are what we need. We need someone who can look down the road long term for military assessment. You don't have to answer now. Think it over for a day or two and let us know by calling the office of one of us. Please let us know by the end of the week."

"I thank you, gentlemen, for your time, and I will most certainly get back to you. Thanks for the Coke." Ethan rose and walked away without looking back. The girl followed. She caught up to him at the stairs.

"You really should consider their offer, General." Her closeness was just a little too close. She pressed up against him.

"*I don't need this shit,*" thought Ethan. "I sure as hell don't need a honey trap." "Thank you, young lady, for the guidance."

"My name is Linda, Linda Martin." She put a calling card in his jacket pocket. "Call me General, any time for anything, anything at all." Ethan marched out as fast as he could without running. He returned to his office via taxi. He read the card she slipped into his pocket. Ms. Linda Martin, Staff Secretary to Congressman Thompson. It gave two telephone numbers, an e-mail address, and a Capital office address. Ethan trashed it, changed into his duty uniform, and headed for home on the subway.

15 May 2024

"Boys, this is a warning order. School is out after the week after next. That means you are going to have to do a lot of work on Grandad's place in Wyoming.

Unfortunately, that means you two more than me since I won't be there, at least initially. I have already made the arrangements with the Transportation Office to move household goods. The packers will be here the day after your graduation parties end. I told them that this is my twilight tour and we won't move again. Say goodbye to your friends and get your minds right. You will make new friends very quickly, I am sure. I know you will fall in love with Wyoming "

The Pentagon

"Good morning, Irene. Is the good General Bradley in and busy?"

"Right on both counts, General Schenken. He's terribly busy, but I'll buzz him. General B, General Schenken, is here to see you."

"I'll be right out, Irene." Bradley steps out, wearing a smile. "Good morning, General coffee? Club? It's my turn to buy."

"You can, Ethan, let's go."

"That's interesting. The Commandant comes calling for coffee twice in a month outside this office. Wonder if I should report it? Better be safe than sorry, besides, I can use the money" thought Irene, as she picked up the phone.

After filling their cups with hot coffee at the coffee bar, Bradley stuffed two $5 bills in the "feed me" coffee can for donations. After finding an isolated vacant table, Ethan could read the worry in General Schenken's face. He waited for Schenken to open the conversation while he sipped his coffee. Schenken looked at his best field commander and sighed.

"Ethan, I don't know how this will play out. President Naomi Campbell has made many enemies in the shadow government, or the deep state, or whatever you want to call it. I have massive, grave reservations." Bradley sipped his coffee and waited for General Schenken to continue. "She's trying to pull us out of

NATO; Proboff is massing troops on the borders of the Baltic states, she's damned near closed the Mexican border with troops out of Fort Bliss and Fort Hood patrolling it, she's fighting to repeal the Trans-Pacific Partnership treaty, she's fighting the Council on Foreign Relations behind the scenes to repeal the Federal Reserve Bank, which is owned by a cartel of privately owned entities, such as the Rockefeller Foundation, the Ford Foundation and a bunch of European banks. She wants to return to the gold standard and eliminate the worthless paper dollar backed by nothing except as Bernanke once said, 'confidence.' She wants to return to the gold standard, but the shadow government won't allow it. They have co-opted almost every federal politician, house and senate; some with cash, some with blackmail, some with promises of future wealth and position. I and a couple of Navy four stars are the only full generals who refuse to go along. In the USAF, all of the three and four stars have been sucked in. At least half by blackmail of their sexual exploits with young female service members. The "deep state" has used the National Security Agency, NSA, recordings of all e-mails and telephone calls as blackmail. A hell of a lot of the public doesn't understand or care, so long as the welfare checks keep coming and they can purchase with them. We're screwed, Ethan. I know it, and I think you know it.

The Muslims in Detroit and Dearborn demanding suspension of the US Constitution and replacing it with Sharia is only the beginning. You missed the briefing last month on the rise of Islam on Russia's southern borders. While Sunni and Shiite still fight each other, the Iranian mullahs felt strong enough to start agitating in southern Russia. Proboff is beginning to realize the error of his ways. His temporary alliance with Iran and Shiites is now biting him in the ass. The assassinations, bombings, and general agitation by Shiites for Sharia are growing in all the —stan nations to add to the fire. So, what the hell, a three-four-five ring circus? Is Shiite versus Sunni versus Russia versus Western Europe versus the economic and military collapse of the USA? I hope to God millions of hidden guns in the closets and basements of America are there. I predict our Christian, Constitution-supporting citizens will desperately need them in the coming times if only they can garner the ammunition. I pray there are millions of hand loaders ou there who hid the stuff, the reloading components. Ever since Barak Obama's martial law decree, we have been in a world of hurt. Your Dad was one hell of a fine soldier who resisted such crap. I know he is up there in Heaven looking down on you, and if pride is allowed in Heaven, he has a full measure.

Ethan, there is a great undertow in effect about which the American public is totally oblivious. Mainstream media, if it is even aware of it, won't even think about it, let alone reporting on it. It is all behind the scenes, carefully guarded and orchestrated. It is a great debate on foreign policy. Even the Council on Foreign Relations is somewhat divided over it. Europe is falling to Islam. Some want to invade Europe to help expel the Muslims. Another faction says expel them here first. Our trade with Europe is essentially nonexistent now thanks to European Islam. The North American-Northern European New World Order is very seriously threatened. The President wants to withdraw from NATO and Europe to make us Fortress America. Article 5 of the NATO agreement does not absolutely commit us to defend any NATO member, if attacked, rather it states "in consultation with the other twenty- seven NATO members." That is something the heads of Europe and our military don't want the public to know. They want Congress and the American public to believe it is a total commitment. While the President wants us to withdraw from NATO, the military-industrial complex is resisting like hell. She won't give an inch and neither will the Joint Chiefs. The intense lobbying behind the scenes is incredible. You can bet your bottom dollar almost all of the four stars in all the services are getting stock options at prices you wouldn't believe in defense industry companies. Many of the CFR now realize that an Islamic Europe is the greatest threat to the New World Order that ever existed. That's why they are pushing for us to 'assist' European government before they fall to Islam and Sharia. Some CFR uppity-ups are also pushing to try and split many Asian nations away from China. They think that is an even greater threat. Indonesia, Philippines, Vietnam, Myanmar, Japan, South Korea, or at least widen the gap between them and China. Taiwan and Hong Kong are moving closer together. Many coastal Chinese cities are secretly talking with Hong Kong and Taiwan about semi-autonomy from the rest of the mainland, from Peking. They have had a great taste of capitalism and love it. Japan and South Korea are about to bury the hatchet. South Korea will support nuclear weapons development in Japan if Japan swears to defend South Korea with them against Chinese aggression. Japan knows if South Korea goes, so will they.

Another thing that is closely guarded. We have been laying radio-controlled mines in the Straits of Malacca and the Strait of Formosa. The Chief of Naval Operations argued for them. The President concurred, ordered them laid by submarine. They are activated by a limited-very narrow-ultra high sonar frequency. Their specific locations are known only to the submarines that laid them. Submarine crews were informed they are sonar buoys to monitor submarine traffic as well as surface vessels. Even the sub skippers don't know their true nature. High ranking CFR members in the cabinet argued against any covert actions. That's one reason she was killed. They thought that might be the trigger to World War III. Some high-ranking Russians agree with the CFR on one world government. That is, as long as they are included in it. Given the Russian history of deceit, who knows what they are up to, but you can bet they are up to something behind the scenes, probably in accordance with China."

1 June 2024

Pentagon Briefing Room

Present: All Combatant Command Commanders worldwide, all 4 Star Flag Officers, All Services. Briefing Officer: Chairman, Joint Chiefs of Staff. Introduction by Secretary of Defense.

"Attention: The Meeting will Come to Order, Ladies and Gentlemen, the Secretary of Defense" called by the Adjutant.

"Thank you. I'll be as succinct as I can as will all of the presenters, so you can all get back to your respective commands and duties. I don't like having all of our major command commanders absent from their duties and gathered in one location at one time. Our first brief is from Admiral Fitzgerald, The Chief of Naval Operations. Admiral."

"Thank you, Mr. Secretary. The President has been engaged in highly classified briefings with our friends and neighbors in the Pacific. She has determined that it is in our best interest to withdraw from the western Pacific. We will draw a defensive line from Alaska to Hawaii.

Samoa is still in contention. The Samoans want us out. They see no threat from China or an increasingly militaristic Japan. The Philippines Islands want us completely out as well. Hawaii will be our central anchor, and we will pivot westward to New Zealand and Australia. That means we will be withdrawing our forces from South Korea; Okinawa goes back to Japan. You are all aware that we pulled the great majority of our forces pulled out after the explosion of Mount Pinatubo decades ago. The only forces left there are very small contingents of Army Rangers and Navy Seals that are continuing to help train Filipinos in anti-guerilla warfare against Islamists who want to establish an all Muslim state there. The large island of Mindanao is particularly troublesome. Indonesia has turned hostile as well. It is a nation with a population that is more than ninety percent Muslim. They are also agitating for an Islamic state. Christians there are quietly being killed off, particularly in the villages and small towns. The Muslims there have not openly attacked Christian churches or missions in the cities order to avoid adverse publicity. South Korea is going nuclear. They will be developing their very own tactical nuclear artillery deliverable warheads within the next few years, most likely in less than three with our help. Until then, we will continue to provide them with tactical nuclear warheads from our own arsenal.

Madam President has decided not to contest China for the South China Sea or the Straits of Malacca. If East Asia, notably Japan and South Korea, want Middle East oil they will have to pay for the protection of shipping it.

There will be no more carrier-based battle groups. In short, there will be no more aircraft carriers at all. She believes the Chinese Assassin's Mace, a hypervelocity Mach 7 plus missile that is nuclear capability has rendered our carrier battle groups totally obsolete. The most recent ones will be mothballed over the next few years and the oldest ones decommissioned. Her concept is that we will not be bogged down in a war in or around Asia and the far Pacific again. What it amounts to is that South Korea, Japan, the Philippine Islands Viet Nam, Indonesia, and Myanmar will have to face a militarized China without our air cover, or for that matter, without us, period. Having said that, it remains to be seen how the Muslim uprising on Mindanao and some other Philippine islands will play out. It is Islam versus everybody else. Muslims are killing non-Muslims all over the Island, burning churches, Hindu temples and possibly depopulating the island. They are raping Christian girls and women and beheading Christian boys and men. The Philippine government has decided to provide arms to the villages that are mostly Christian to defend themselves against the Muslim hit and run raids. On the other hand, the Republic of the Philippines is having a great internal debate on whether or not to resist Chinese hegemony. A tremendous amount of turmoil there. How all this will play out for the Republic of the Philippines is anybody's guess.

Indonesia is frustrated by the Chinese buildup. It is 90% Muslim and fears Hindu China to some extent. The Association of Southeast Asian Nations, ASEAN, has decided on a buildup of coastal patrol boats and aircraft. They are trying to build quick response teams to Chinese aggression masquerading as pirates.

They have captured a few of these so-called pirates who have revealed their Chinese duplicity under torture.

The President has decided that a fleet of smaller, faster, less expensive ships composed of frigates, destroyers, and a class of small, fast nuclear cruisers will be the Navy of the future. A new class of air-independent propulsion non-nuclear fast attack submarines will be built by several defense shipyards and contracts with private shipyards. She wants it done in a hurry. She bought into the concept that a killer submarine hunting other submarines is the best solution to the massive buildup of the Chinese submarine force. Our Pacific Surface Fleet is to be reduced until the new classes of smaller ships come online. Government shipbuilding contracts for capital ships not yet initiated are to be reviewed for relevancy in light of her pullback strategy and a smaller, faster navy. She has decided to push for space-based laser systems capable of targeting ships and land-based facilities. She is convinced that Russia and China are several years ahead of us in their research and deployment.

Our personnel will be drawn down accordingly throughout all fleets. The Bureau of Personnel is already working on staffing requirements and reductions. The President has indicated that contracts are to be let as soon as the elections are over. She feels she can corner enough votes to push this program through Congress.

Our budget is severely constrained as all of you know. The socialists are all screaming about proposed reductions in the social welfare state, demanding that the defense budget pays for all reductions. This is one way she seeks to reduce our national debt. That's all for the moment, Mr. Secretary.

"Thank you, Admiral Fitzgerald. Our next presenter is Army Chief of Staff, General Michelson."

"Thank you, Mr. Secretary. The President has bought into the concept that armor forces will disappear from the battlefield. She regards the tank as obsolete, an expensive piece of machinery too vulnerable to modern anti-tank weapons, both surface and air, useless in the mountains and swamps. She does believe in precision artillery and is advancing research and development in that area. Drone warfare with tank-busting capability and highly mobile anti-tank weapons are the wave of the future, in her opinion. Individual soldier capability, enhancement, and survivability is the order of the day.

The 5.56-millimeter rifle round as used in the M-16A3 rifle is now considered too small. You will recall that using the full metal jacketed bullet as required by the Geneva Convention is considered inadequate. It took an average of six hits from the 5.56 NATO round to put Somalis high on khat down for good in Mogadishu. That experience was repeated ad infinitum in Afghanistan. Our soldiers were screaming for M-l 4s to be taken out of storage and issued for their longer range and lethality. Larger caliber weapons are being explored. Old research data is being reviewed.

As we are all aware, the President's husband was a Non-Commissioned Officer who served tours in Iraq and Afghanistan as an infantryman. Since he returned to college and earned a degree in mechanical engineering, he has her ear. He is also an avid hunter of deer and elk, so he does have some personal experience. He has convinced her we need a rifle and cartridge combination of greater range and lethality. Test and Evaluation Command is attempting to determine if we can convert our current M-16A3 rifles to those cartridges of higher power and caliber. Early indications from TECOM are that we will probably have to purchase an entirely new inventory of rifles if this concept flies. It is also quite possible that the 7.62X51 mm NATO cartridge will return. Civilian variations of the M-l6 in .308 Winchester, a slightly different cartridge but one that is almost ubiquitous and will fire in 7.62x51 mm rifles that are no lighter than the M-l4 are more complicated with more parts and more expensive to produce than the M- 14. If that flies, we can expect the arms manufacturers to be jumping through hoops for contracts. We did it at the beginning of World War II, and we can do it again, according to my industrial analysts."

Right now, it looks like a 6.5 mm round, also known in the civilian world as the .260 Remington, firing a 120-grain bullet, is being developed for field testing in a semi-automatic rifle. Also, the old German 7mmx57 Mauser round of World War I launching either a 129 grain or a 140-grain bullet and the German 8x57 mm round of World Wars I and II with heavier bullets are being scrutinized for comparison. The 'pray and spray' concept of rifle fire on the battlefield is to be discarded as a total waste of ammunition. She has given the direction for recommendation to be firm and presented before the next election cycle so that she or her successor and make a decision early next year. She said 'heads will roll' if the drags out. All facts and figures to include retooling in government arsenals are to be presented before Christmas. Research teams are working around the clock to meet that deadline. Field testing will begin with a deadline of one year with a submitted rifle and cartridge combinations, as set by the President. 'No long-term fooling around here. Make a decision,' she said.

"Thank you, General Michelson. Start planning at corps and fleet levels and work down. PACOM (Pacific Command), EUCOM (European Command), AFRICOM (African Command), and CENTCOM (Central Command, Middle East) in particular with this general guidance. I believe the President will dramatically reduce CENTCOM, EUCOM, and PACOM. If you have further comments or questions, please pass them through the Joint Chiefs to your service secretaries to me. I'm all ears as to your thoughts and opinions. That concludes this briefing."

"That son-if-a-bitch sure left us, the Air Force, out, didn't he, McCartney?"

"Easy, General. Somebody might overhear you. Our time, or should I say, her time will come soon enough. I'm sure he was acting on her orders."

05 June 2024

"Coffee time, General Bradley. I have some personnel problems we need to discuss over a caffeine fix."

"I am your man, General Schenken. Is it my turn to buy?"

"It is my boy. Would you believe my wife raided my wallet last night and didn't tell me she was planning on going shopping today? How is that for putting a four-star general in a fix?" Ethan laughed. "I'll even throw in a doughnut this morning, General."

Once they had their coffee and sat out of earshot of everyone, General Schenken quietly whispered, "Your office is monitored; two bugs and your secretary are an informant. She really works for the deep state; in case you haven't figured that out."

"I figured as much. I don't like her on any level. So, what's new in the deep bowels of the five-sided waste basket?"

"Madam President informally submitted a reduced military budget proposal, pushed for a less expensive overseas commitment in favor of fortress America, minding our own business with much gnashing of teeth from Congress and the Joint Chiefs. The Chief of Naval Operations and I have been pushing for a new fleet of far less expensive non-nuclear air-independent-propulsion anti-submarine submarines to counter the Chinese submarine fleet, without success. The military-industrial complex wants more two to three billion-dollar boats. Even if the decision is made to reinforce Europe against their homegrown Muslims, we lack the sealift and airlift capability to get it there. Not only that, but as you are aware, our ground forces are inadequate in numbers of manpower, artillery, small arms, and ammunition. Too many big, expensive, wasteful big-ticket items and not enough boots on the ground basics are in the offing. The USAF is still clinging to the post World War II conviction that wars can be won almost exclusively through the application of air power, and that ground forces are not necessary or minimally needed at best. Those bastards refuse to learn or admit anything could be wrong with their grand strategy. The only really big-ticket items we need are missile defense systems, anti-satellite satellites, cyber security, and hardened communications against electromagnetic pulse attacks. I don't know how this will play out. Ethan, as a General Officer, you are authorized to carry your sidearm at all times. I strongly suggest you start doing so.

Ethan didn't say much, just staring into his coffee cup. When he finally looked up, he said, "Thank you for the kind words about Dad the other day. I have been thinking about him lately. As for the others, I have suspected for two decades, there is a force behind the facade of our government. I know some refer to them or it, as 'The Deep State.' They are not answerable to the electorate, or to the superficial fraudulent government, it controls but only to itself. I cannot imagine it polices itself except by threats, intimidation and ultimately, murder. First comes threats then the murder of close family members and relatives of members who stray from the central committee's decrees and finally by murder-assassinations of those members whose consciences get to them or who get too greedy for power within the organization. I have never known how to break in or gain insight into their organization, the CFR, the Bilderburgers, the IMF, the Bank of International Settlements, and the controlling elites' membership in overlapping organizations. I can only guess the outer circle is the CFR, the then next inner circle is the Bilderburgers, and finally, some very rare, highly secured central committee of no more than a dozen or two. I have no doubt they have and will continue to murder political opponents they can't control by one means or another. Accidents happen all too often and include what appear as medical emergencies. They are the kings and princes of the Western world. I suspect that somewhere there might even be a fourth ring, between the Bilderburgers and the elite council, one that includes a few of the world's heads of state, most likely the dictatorial types who cling to power. But hell, who knows? You should know that Speaker Thompson and Senator Bardston offered me membership in the CFR in the Capital Bar last night. They used some beautiful red-headed chicky-pooh named Linda Martin as some kind of come-on bait."

GEN Schenken grinned. "She is allegedly a staffer for that son-of-a-bitch Thompson. I hear that she is one of the most expensive and sought-after girls in the after-hours circuit. You didn't bite, did you?"

"Oh, hell no, General. I recognize a honey trap when I see it. That kind of trouble I don't want or need."

"What did you tell them?"

"Basically, that I was unworthy of membership in such a distinguished group. They gave me until the end of the week to accept or reject."

"And what will you do?" *Given the opportunity, I would murder every one of those bastards for surrendering our nation to the New World Order. Since that is illegal, I will politely tell them no thanks.*"

"Ethan, I always figured you for a bright boy. Now I see that I have underrated you. You still have the fight of your life ahead of you. I can't say any more than that. If you have any religious convictions, I suggest you adhere to them. At least that way you'll get to heaven because it is going to be hell on earth."

"Is there anything I can do, General?"

"No Ethan, there is nothing at this time. The forces have to expose themselves before you can act. All I can say is prepare your family and yourself in every possible way. I've said too much already. Let's get coffee refills and get back to work."

10 June, Washakie County, WY

"Boys, we are going to put in a massive garden down below on the river and a smaller one up here. That means cutting or pulling the weeds, leveling the ground as much as possible, fertilizing, and planting. Watering, and weeding it is necessary every week. Then there are the deer to contend with. We can't shoot the danged things out of season without a lot of potential legal headaches over poaching. Maybe we could set off some booby traps with fireworks and scare the hell out of them. I have no idea if that will work. We certainly don't want to start a fire down there, so we will have to be quite careful. We will fence the gardens in if it is necessary to keep the critters out... Perhaps a solar-powered electric fence, one wire high and one low will do. That will cover the rabbits and raccoons on the lower wire and deer on the upper one.

Nevertheless, it is off to work we go. I'll rent or buy a rototiller that will make things a lot easier. We'll plant a lot of potatoes, carrots, onions, beets, squash, maybe some cabbage down below, whatever the nursery lady recommends for this area. Up here we will plant corn, green beans, and squash, just like the old Native Americans did; what they called the sacred trio of corn, beans and squash. The beans climb up the corn stalks. We will probably use stakes. So, plan on putting several hours a day into gardening. We are going to grow and can lots of tomatoes for vitamin A. We will plant lots and lots of potatoes. They store well. We can make sauerkraut from cabbage for vitamin C through the winter. We will buy and plant half a dozen apple trees, ones that can best withstand cold winters.

I would like to see you practice with bows and arrows as well. I'll buy each of you your own bow and quiver full of arrows. One thing is for sure, an arrow is a lot quieter than a rifle bullet. Sam, take some of that plastic ribbon-type marking tape and go through our land and tie some around every dead tree you find. We'll cut it for firewood in the fall during cool weather. It will keep you in shape for college, Sam, and you for football next fall Josh. Happy graduation, Sam!"

"Ugh, Mom! Why can't we just buy what we need?"

"Don't argue, Josh; you need to learn to be a gardener. It will stand you in good stead all through your life. Besides, we don't know what will happen. Things do not look well on the global scale, and your Dad and I are both rather fearful. So, be farmers. We will use so-called Heritage seeds, not hybrids. That will give us seeds for many years. Gardening will help keep you in shape! One other thing; we are going to the shooting range once a week, maybe more often. Your Dad says he has trained you in the basics of rifle and pistol shooting. That's great. You can teach me quite a bit, I am sure. That means we will reload whatever centerfire cartridge cases we shoot. We'll stock whatever reloading supplies we can find so we can shoot on the cheap and develop skills. We'll stop at every little country store to shop for ammunition and reloading supplies. We'll stock cases of .22 Long rifles as the most versatile according to your Dad. That is also the least expensive way to practice. We have to keep rabbits and raccoons out of the garden. I understand rabbits are quite yummy. I don't know about raccoons. That means each of us will have his own dedicated rifles and handguns and accouterments. That means holsters, gun belts, speed loaders, speed loader cases, eye, and hearing protection. We have to have some fun too!"

25 June 2024

Gypsy was looking through the local rag that was supposed to pass for a newspaper. She was looking for an old bicycle from which she could salvage the frame when she came upon an advertisement for Chesapeake Bay Retriever puppies. She called the phone number to find that the breeder had three left, two males and one female. The breeder told her that both the sire and dam were certified free of hip dysplasia by the Orthopedic Foundation for Animals, that puppies should also be free of hip dysplasia. He guaranteed they would be, which is why he was asking the enormous sum of six hundred dollars. If they developed hip dysplasia before one year of age, he provides a written guarantee of a full refund. Yes, both parents were field dogs, not bench types. They were waterfowlers, pure and simple, not field champions, but great dogs nonetheless. If they were field champions, he said he would be asking $2500 for each puppy. He would hold them for one day to give them a chance to come and select one.

Gypsy got his address and said they would be there sometime in the evening. She gathered up Sam and Josh and told them that "we are going to look at some dogs." They drove to Greybull and found the breeder on the north edge of town, overlooking the Big Horn River. They strolled out to the kennel where the dam was penned. He had separated the puppies a week ago for weaning, and they were in the adjacent pen. "How does one select a puppy," asked Gypsy.

"Well, Ma'am, it depends. If you want them as a hunting dog, you put the emphasis on the confirmation. If you want them as a pet, you sit down in the middle of them and see which one or ones, is the most attentive to you."

"OK boys, you heard the man. Park your butts and play with the puppies. We can select only one. I don't want two males that are brothers nor a brother and sister." Sam and Josh sat down and played with the puppies. One, a little larger than the other two, couldn't stop trying to lick their faces. They chose that one. "Now boys, select a name for it." Josh spoke up, "Since it is a Chesapeake, how about Chess?" Sam nodded in agreement. Gypsy wrote the breeder a check.

24 July 2024

"Dear Gypsy, Sam, and Josh,

Sure, hope you are getting things squared away in the old homestead. I am looking forward to getting there. Can't wait to greet the new puppy either! Do you want a second one?

I was walking down the hall yesterday when I bumped into the Brigadier General of the Veterinary Corps. He recognized me by my name tag. He knew Dad and knew Dad had a son by the name of Ethan. He asked if I was the right man. He knew Dad when he was a junior officer under Dad. He was an 0-3, a Captain when Dad was an 0-6, a Colonel. I took him to lunch in the General Officers Mess (where brigadiers are not allowed as it is too crowded, but I can take him in as my guest) and we talked for quite some time. He is very pessimistic. We discussed a lot of things I did not know. Frankly, he scared me big time. This guy is quite brilliant. He is cross-trained; started out in public health and epidemiology, then went into pathology (passed the veterinary pathology boards), was a supporting researcher, then a primary investigator. He did some research in exotic tropical diseases that cross from animals to man, known as zoonoses. He thinks we are primed for a strategic attack, probably with biological agents. He really fears smallpox. There is a good chance Russia, China, and North Korea have weaponized it. He stated that back in 1975 after the Biological Warfare Treaty was signed by Leonid Brezhnev, the Russkies saw it as a golden opportunity. So, they genetically engineered a virus to get around our smallpox vaccine. Our vaccine isn't even really a strain of smallpox, but a closely related virus that provides some immunity. Back then, the Russians saw it as a great way to kill us all. Their ballistic missile submarines were loaded not with nukes, but with smallpox virus that would be sprayed over our cities. Our vaccine was worthless. Their vaccinated troops could walk right in and take over. All this was in violation of the 1975 Biological Warfare Treaty. Some kind of relationship exists between variola and vaccinia viruses or something like that, that provides cross-immunity. We haven't kept up with what genetic manipulation might do with the virus. Apparently, it is a very large virus amenable to genetic manipulation. It is possible that even genes for unrelated pathogens could be inserted into its genome, so it has a double whammy of two virulent diseases. That would really confound the issue. He argues that a biological attack is a much more likely scenario than an EMP because it will kill off the people but leave all the infrastructure intact.

On the other hand, if an EMP weapon is used, invaders would have to deal with hundreds of millions of dead as well as all digital and electronic and electrical infrastructure destroyed. The real key is if the bad guys have an excellent vaccine against the strain used in the attack. Then the invaders cold use the electrical/electronic infrastructure in place. They would have to deal with massive sanitation for the cleanup of all the deceased in either case. Scary crap, right? He figures if we suffer a biological attack, the attackers will all be immunized against it. Also, it might possibly be with some exotic agent for which we have no vaccine. We talked about nuclear weapons too. He doesn't think the standard strategic burst weapons of heat, blast, and radiation will be used, as there is too much collateral damage which the attacker would like to avoid.

Rather, he thinks if it is nuclear, it will be a tailored electromagnetic pulse weapon detonated high in the atmosphere. He says a couple of those would wipe out our country. I have had several briefings on this, all classified, and I must agree with him. He is more up to date on the threat of bioweapons than I am, but not on EMP effects. He recommended stocking lots of antibiotics, surgical instruments, and supplies. By the time he was finished talking, he was visibly shaken. Obviously, he is scared to death. He revealed things he probably should not have. He said The Secretary of Defense had ordered all the DOD Medical Departments to keep all of this quiet. I am not sure the Joint Chiefs know all that he told me. He felt obligated to inform me because of Dad. I have to agree with him. He said if a blast weapon is used, and there are blast effects regardless of the tailored nature of the weapon, the enormity of lacerations from flying objects is unbelievable. Therefore, lots of bandages, disinfectants, and suture materials are in order. An EMP weapon will also have some of these heat and blast effects as secondary to the magnetic radiation.

He advised his kids to move, take his grandkids and get to an isolated rural area, maybe north Missouri or somewhere out west regardless of the cost. They won't bother with the rural areas but will take down the population centers. The rural areas will be dragged down as the cities collapse.

There is no difference, really between human and veterinary antibiotics. He said to go to the feed store to stock up on them. He said penicillin's, both the kind that maintains blood levels for five days and the regular, which requires a dose every 24 hours, the various tetracyclines, and if you can find them, dihydrostreptomycin, leucomycin, neomycin, and others. Of course, an EMP attack does have some other radiation effects and antibiotics will be lifesavers as the white blood cell/immune systems of victims are wiped out. Secondary infections of otherwise ordinary bacteria can be overwhelming and highly lethal. In that regard, he said to also better buy some iodine tablets to protect our thyroid glands from 1-131, the radioactive isotope of iodine. Buy vitamins, especially vitamin C, but also Vitamins A, D and E, and selenium, as well as general vitamins with micronutrients. It is critical to guard against colds. Buy the boys each a razor and dozens of blades. He also stressed being able to grow your own food, raise chickens for meat and eggs, maybe ducks, rabbits, turkeys, and sheep. I don't think such critters will fly there due to the subdivision's covenants, but it is a good thought. You might explore that. If the neighbors are doing it, so can you. That's all for now; sure, do miss all of you. "

Love, Ethan.

Later that night, unable to sleep, Ethan poured his second whiskey and soda. Thinking about what was said that day, he decided he would start making subtle preparatory changes. The next day he called in his Division Surgeon and grilled him on what antibiotics were stocked and at what level. How prepared was the division, medically speaking, for either a nuclear attack or a biological attack? Is there any problem with overstocking? What discretionary powers can he exercise to exceed his basic load?

How well trained are his people in handling radioactive patients? Since preventive medicine is part of his command, how well-trained are his sanitarians and sanitary engineers? Can they decontaminate water supplies from fallout particles? What disinfectants are stocked to disinfect water contaminated with biological agents over and above their basic load? "Will you need my authority, Colonel? If so, you have it."

Bradley called his Chief of Staff into his office. "Neil, I want you to do whatever you have to do to ensure that there are no digital locks on any of our arms rooms. Revert to old-fashioned key locks in everyone if they are digital. I don't give a crap about regulations. Just see to it that it is done. Fund it out of our maintenance funds. If we can't get some blockhead in the system to make the changes because of regulations, go outside the system and have a private business locksmith do it. We'll just put the digital locks in the company storerooms. Get it done as quietly and as quickly as you can."

Gypsy first went to the landfill looking for an old discarded bicycle frame, preferably for adult women. Finding none, she went to the bicycle shop in town. Not finding the wreck she was looking for and not willing to spend hundreds of dollars for a new bicycle, she started going to the garage sales listed in Fridays' papers for the weekend sales. On the third Saturday, she found what she sought. It must have been 50 years old, one of the old heavy frame bicycles popular in the 1950s before the thin, lightweight multi-geared type bicycles became popular. With two flat tires, rusted spokes, and a seat split at the seams; she bought it for ten dollars.

The boys came up the hill soaked in sweat and ready for lunch and a break. When Gypsy unloaded it from the truck, the boys asked, "Mom, what's with the wrecked bike?" Gypsy smiled and replied, "This is, or soon will be our electrical generator. It will be you two that supply the leg power." With a laugh, she parked it in the garage and started lunch for the three of them.

Her next stop was to the salvage used car lot. After asking the attendant where the oldest vehicles were located, he directed her to the back of the lot where a hydraulic crusher was going to flatten them for recycling the metal. After twenty minutes of searching, she found what she wanted. It was an old Ford pickup from the 1950s. Gathering her toolbox, she removed the generator from the old truck. Over the next week, she sanded the bicycle frame and fenders and applied two coats of Rust-Oleum. She resewed the seat and treated it with several coats of silicone leather preservative. She degreased the chain and then dropped the chain into an oil pan of used motor oil to soak. Then she hung it over the pan to let the excess oil drip off. She reassembled it and in two weeks had a pedal-powered generator to which she attached two new but very expensive heavy-duty truck batteries. The generator kept the batteries charged. An inverter converted the direct current from the battery into an alternating current. It would provide sufficient electricity from thirty minutes of pedaling to power the refrigerator, a small deep freeze, and two electric lights for 24 hours.

Gypsy went down the hill to help the boys with the tilling for the garden. She took two, two-quart water thermos jugs with ice and water for the three of them. Sam ran the tiller while Josh and Gypsy hoed and laid out rows. Gypsy decided she needed to empty her bladder and so marched off into the woods. As she dropped her slacks at the base of a large cottonwood tree facing away from the garden, she noticed a blaze on it, a very crude arrow carved into it pointing down. Curious, she retrieved a shovel and started digging. She was about to give up when she hit something solid close to three feet down, below the frost line. She dug around it to reveal a piece of ten-inch diameter PVC pipe, more than four feet long. She called the boys over to help pull it out of the ground. Below it was another, shorter piece of PVC pipe of the same diameter.

The longer piece was heavy enough that it was a strain for the boys to carry it up to the hill. They were exhausted and soaked in sweat when they reached the top. "This thing must weigh a hundred and fifty or more pounds. Whatever is in it shifted around," noted Sam.

"I got the heavy end complained Josh."

"Break time. Let's get a soda and recover boys. Then we will retrieve the shorter pipe and see what's in them."

The three of them chilled out for thirty minutes in the shade on the back porch. Down the hill, they went. The second pipe was even heavier even though it was shorter, so still a bit of a struggle for the boys to get it up to the hill. The caps to the pipes were glued on to make them watertight. Sam got a hacksaw and started sawing on one end of the larger pipe. Josh got a crosscut saw and started sawing off the end of the shorter pipe. Sam tipped the sealed end of a larger pipe in the air and dragged the open end along the ground. A Dillon 550B progressive reloading press, followed by an RCBS Rock Chucker single-stage reloading press, spilled out, followed by complete sets of four tool heads for different cartridges for the Dillon press. Sam dragged the pipe until all its contents were on the ground. The presses were wrapped and taped in plastic, obviously heavily sprayed with some oil or water-repellant agent. Next came a case trimmer with pilots that fit into the case mouth to steady the case while being trimmed, taped to it, and also heavily wrapped. Then came sets of reloading dies for several cartridges taped shut. Then followed several small plastic boxes tightly wrapped in duct tape to keep them from breaking and spilling their contents.

Josh dumped the contents of the shorter pipe out. Tumbling out were four one-gallon polypropylene milk jugs full of cast pistol bullets and a box of 1000.30 caliber 150-grain rifle bullets Sam guessed each jug weighed at least thirty pounds. The box of rifle bullets weighed at least twenty-five pounds."

"No wonder we're pooped. I'll bet this thing weighed around two hundred pounds."

"Some necessary things are missing. Let's get this stuff into the garage and out of sight. After another break, we will go looking for some more trees with a blaze. We need powder scales, powder, primers, powder measures, and I don't know what else. I can't imagine your grandfather not having them buried somewhere nearby."

After lunch, the boys each took a shovel and proceeded down the hill. Gypsy went down to use the shovel left down the hill. On the next tree over was another crude blaze. Digging at the foot of it revealed another four-foot piece of PVC pipe. Josh and Sam carried it up to the hill and sawed it open. Inside the PVC pipe were four eight-pound jugs of reloading powders and a reloading manual.

"Everything is here for reloading except primers. Your grandfather would not forget those. They must be hidden somewhere else for safety. If anything were to blow, it would be the primers. He would not put them near the gunpowder or the other tools. We'll have to look for them later. Let's get this stuff into the garage and out of sight of the neighbors for now. Tomorrow we'll look for another tree with a blaze or whatever as a marker. Maybe there is a note somewhere in all this stuff about primers."

Josh was excited and not satisfied, so he decided to have another look around the tree. He went back down the hill with a shovel. Enlarging the hole by digging off to one side, he struck a much smaller piece of PVC pipe. It contained eight boxes of 1000 each of magnum primers, large rifle, small rifle, large pistol, and small pistol.

Elated, he carried it up to the hill, proud of himself.

"Alright boys, I have another project for you. You need to build a table large enough to hold all of these tools. We'll set it up in the basement so we can use it year-round in comfort and keep it protected. For right now, get the powders and primers inside in the basement. Your Grandad sure had a lot of foresight."

Gypsy wondered about the primers and powders, whether being subjected to the heat buildup in the ground over the last eight summers would cause them to be degraded. Only one way to find out, she guessed, reload several and test the loads out in the desert, away from prying eyes and ears.

In the evenings she wrote lesson plans for the high school physics courses she would teach in the fall. The Board of Education agreed to let her teach a calculus-based physics course as a college-level course provided that the majority of the students of the first such class tested out of the first semester of a college equivalent physics course. She would also teach a non-calculus-based physics course for those not interested in engineering or higher physical sciences.

Her next project was a Faraday cage for the large chainsaw. She built a wooden box to hold it with a top to it that would fit over it with a six-inch overlap. She took it to a local heating and plumbing establishment and for $100 had them wrap the two pieces separately with thin sheet metal. The curious worker asked what it was for as he bent the sheet metal on the bending machine used for ductwork. Not wanting to reveal its true nature, she explained she was the new high school physics teacher and wanted it for physics laboratory demonstrations on electricity. He shrugged and completed the wrapping process in an hour, making sure that the attaching screws did not penetrate entirely through the wood as Gypsy insisted. At home, she put handles on the ends of the top to prevent cutting her hands on the sharp metal edges of the overlapping steel.

Writing her lesson plans in the evening caused her a small amount of remorse. She wondered if she would ever have the opportunity to return to a major university where she could complete her research for her Ph.D. in physics. "It's a fair trade," she said to herself. "I have a loving, wonderful husband and two adopted sons. If only Ethan were here with us." She poured a jigger of scotch over three ice cubes and thought next month "I'll buy a case of good scotch for myself and a case of Canadian Club for Ethan. Perhaps a case of pints of cheap vodka for future trading materials wouldn't hurt. Hope Ethan gets here soon to enjoy it!"

The next day after breakfast, she and the boys piled into the truck for a grocery run to Walmart in Cody. They filled ten shopping carts, top, and bottom. Gypsy picked out 600 pounds of brown rice, whole wheat in 50-pound sacks, half a dozen 25-pound bags of sugar, two cases of oatmeal, all the honey that was on the shelf, orange juice powder, dried yeast, all the peanut butter in all varieties on the shelves, five gallons of olive oil, five gallons of canola oil, half a dozen cans of a different vegetable shortening, a dozen pound boxes of iodized salt, pepper and other spices, and all the bullion cubes of all varieties. She sent the clerk back for all the canned ham and Vienna sausages in the storage area and cleaned off the shelf of sardines and canned salmon. Then she went to the dehydrated and frozen dried sections. There she purchased all the cans of scrambled egg mix, whole egg powder, orange drink powder, and dried banana slices, and then she began to wonder if she brought enough cash. After that, she went to the drug and beauty products area. She took four dozen tubes of toothpaste, all the best toothbrushes, all of the dental floss, all of the aspirin, ibuprofen, and acetaminophen tables on the shelf. Antidiarrheals, rubbing alcohol, athlete's foot powder, antifungals, everything she could think of went into a cart. She threw all of the bars of bath soap into one basket. Then she went to the band-aids, gauze pads, adhesive tape and repeated the process. By the time she finished, she had a basket full of health and beauty products. The boys didn't know what to think. After filling a dozen shopping carts, Gypsy led the way to the garden center. There she bought every garbage can they had that had a tight-fitting lid? They started piling the groceries into the cans before they headed for the checkout line. The manager opened a checkout counter just for them. The total came to over eight thousand dollars. She decided to put it on the credit card and get the money out of the bank.

When they left, Gypsy laughed. She sent Josh for the truck while she and Sam guarded the groceries on the walk. After loading the truck, which filled the entire bed, Gypsy went to the liquor store and bought the two cases of liquor, one of Famous Grouse scotch whiskey for herself, one of Canadian Club for Ethan. As an afterthought, she picked out two cases of merlot wine. *"Now Eve done it,"* she whimsically thought. "I have sure put a dent in the bank account. No matter, I'll write the check in full and get the rest of the money out of the bank when I get the credit card bill."

Out of curiosity, Gypsy purchased a Billings Gazette at the local grocery store when purchasing some milk and yogurt. Casually perusing it, she noticed an advertisement for Chesapeake Bay puppies from a breeder in Billings. A phone number was listed. When she arrived home, she called the breeder. He had two females left. Both are certified by the Orthopedic Foundation for Animals to be free from hip dysplasia. No, they are not field champions, although he has used both parents for hunting both pheasants and ducks. He said they were pretty good swimmers. He was asking $1,800 for a dog. Gypsy explained it was a 170-mile drive each way, a whole day's worth of travel if they come. Would he consider a lower price, given the cost of gasoline to drive there? The man hesitated and said he would take $600 for either of them if they made the drive. Gypsy agreed to come the next day.

"OK boys, pile in the truck. Put two coolers, one with soda and ice, a half-gallon juice jar full of water, for Chess and a water pan in the bed. Put Chess in the back seat between you. We're going to Billings. We will look at another dog and do some shopping. Maybe eat BBQ for lunch at Famous Dave's."

The breeder brought out the two bitches while Sam and Josh held Chess on a leash. All three dogs played well together. The boys picked the one that did not have a white spot on her breast. Gypsy liked the other one. She wrote a check for $1200, and they all piled back in the truck, with the new dogs in the back seat. Each boy held one of the new dogs. Chess rode in the front seat with Gypsy. Josh mostly held one new puppy which he dubbed Suzy. During the drive home, each new dog and boy formed a special affinity for one another.

1 September 2024

"Dear Gypsy, Sam and Josh,

I have been here in North Carolina for just eight weeks and getting my feet on the ground. I am somewhat surprised at how much I miss all of you in spite of being extremely busy. I guess you could say I am homesick. My two deputy commanders have impressed me so far. My biggest challenge is to get this division trained. Finances have been so poor that the previous Commanding General cut back on training to satisfy nonsense political requirements such as Equal Opportunity for women in combat, race relations, and all that other socialist bullshit. I'm finding that less than five percent of the women in the combat arms can keep up with the men marines. A lot of them that can't are requesting combat service support in whatever slots can be found for them. Yet we are supposed to not lower standards or give them special treatment. God help us if I have to take a whole lot of women in this division into combat.

I really miss not being there for the boys' games. I guess that is part of being a parent, to support the kids. Seriously, I am beginning to think of retirement. Perhaps a year from now I'll cash it in unless I can't stand being separated from you guys anymore. I believe we could do well on my retirement pay and what you bring in as a teacher. My concern in that respect is I know you would like to finish your thesis and get your Ph.D.

Would you like to teach in the physics department at Northwest College up in Powell instead of the local high school? Would you want to commute on a daily basis? It's a pretty good trek, and winter roads might be a problem. Perhaps I could get on the high school faculty as a history teacher there, teaching military history. I am putting in twelve-hour days, but I still, have time to think in the evenings over a cocktail. I stay out of the Officers Club as much as duties will allow. I really have ominous feelings. I am not sure what it is or why, but I think we should spend the money while I am on active duty so we can get whatever we might need to cover any disaster.

I have been making another list of things for you and the boys to buy and do. I certainly did not want to put such information over the internet or phone to be monitored. Please buy all the one-gallon cans of fuel you can for the Coleman lanterns and stove. When you travel to distant towns for the boys' ball games, stop in at all the local hardware stores you can and buy all the Coleman fuel you can. Two dozen is not too many. Buy all the two-cycle engine oil you can find to add to the gas for chain saws. If you have two gallons of the stuff, it is not too much. I don't worry so much about gasoline as I used to, because in thinking about it, every vehicle has a gas tank, hopefully with a lot of gas in it. We can always tap vehicles that are abandoned or stalled if we have to. I can plunge an ice pick into the gas tank and drain it into five-gallon polyethylene gas cans. I'm thinking of gas and oil for chain saws. Make sure we have at least half a dozen five-gallon gas cans. Be sure to get a case of Sea Foam gasoline stabilizer. Gas turns to varnish over several months. We can't have that.

Make sure you and the boys have plenty of winter clothing, down coats, insulated boots, hats, socks and so on. You might even get some spares of larger sizes because the boys are going to grow some more, I am sure. Don't want them to have clothes that are too small! You too! Get yourself plenty of warm clothes, and long underwear; silk is great. Get yourself several sets of mail orders if you have to. How about a couple of down comforters?

Pure wool blankets from Pendleton Mills wouldn't hurt. How about cold weather sleeping bags? I think Dad had some two-man crosscut saws, wood-splitting wedges, and mauls. Make sure of that and buy whatever you think we might need. No use trying to save any money in this economy. If we have any leftover money, buy precious metals! Since you couldn't get much of a garden in, buy long term storage foods, dehydrated and freeze-dried foods that have a twenty-five-year shelf life if you haven't already. If the boys have time, take a roto-duller down the hill and turn over a large garden plot, get it ready for next spring. Yes, I know the weeds will be a problem. If we can get the soil turned once, it will be a lot easier in the future. I know Dad had some reloading equipment, so please go through that and buy whatever reloading components are necessary to supplement it. That is if you can find any brass, bullets, powder, and primers. That's all I can think of for the moment. You take good care of each other and hug those two Chesapeake puppies you bought.

I recall helping some farm friends of Dad's butcher hogs when I was a little kid. They used a great big iron kettle to make what they called scrapple. That was a mix of all the other organs and tissues, lungs liver, and so on, all tissues but red meat, chopped small and mixed with flour and boiled until it was a paste. They poured it into aluminum pans and then froze it. They would eat it as a breakfast food, slicing it and pouring syrup on it like pancakes. I don't envision us slaughtering hogs, but the kettle is a good idea. If necessary, we can boil dirty clothes in it with soap to get them clean. See if you can find one and a stand for it. They used a wood fire under the stand to boil the water.

I love you all,

Dad

CHAPTER III

NOVEMBER 2024

"WELCOME TO MOSCOW, MR. SECRETARY. I trust your flight was a pleasant one."

"Thank you, Mr. Premier. It is always a pleasure to visit Russia. I do enjoy the Kremlin and the museums in Moscow. There is so much history here. My colleagues in the state department find it fascinating that an American of Mexican descent can enjoy European history so much."

"Why would they find it unusual? Surely your surname of Santiago goes back centuries on the Iberian Peninsula. I would suspect as far back as the Roman invasion. Indeed, I am sure your ancestors fought against the Muslim Moors that occupied your ancestral homeland for over 200 years. Would you care for a cup of tea before we begin our discussions? I recall that you have developed a taste for tea the way we like it, with a bit of lemon."

"Yes, thank you so much, Vasili. That would be quite nice." Premier Medvedev rings for tea.

"Now, Juaquin, what can we do for you? It is not often that we have such a distinguished visitor as the Secretary of State of the United States."

"Frankly, Vasili, we are very much concerned with the troubles in Europe. As you are well aware, Muslims are slaughtering people in the streets in many cities. The Islamic State has morphed from the Islamic State in the Levant, ISIL, a Wahhabi based extreme Islamic fundamentalist sect, into a world force. It has grown beyond all projected proportions and power. When European nations allowed so many to flow in starting in 2016, they gave no thought to the long-term consequences. Cities are burning, women and girls are being pressed into sexual slavery, young boys being castrated, and adult men are murdered on sight. It is terrible. We cannot put an end to it from where we are. Obviously, your forces poised in the Baltic States have prevented the Muslims from advancing to the north and invading your former republics of the USSR. To be perfectly blunt, our intelligence community has concurred that you are the only force to restore peace to Europe and stop the slaughter and the Islamization of Western Europe. Undoubtedly you are aware that NATO dedicated forces of Belgium, Denmark, France, Italy, and the United Kingdom have pulled all of their troops out of NATO to fight Muslims in their respective countries. Only the U.S. has forces left facing your Russian forces in the Baltics. Non-Russian citizens would flee if they had someplace to go. Your heritage of Western Europe is as old as ours in the United States through migration of Europeans in the seventeenth through the twentieth centuries Our satellite reconnaissance shows your forces poised along the borders and that Muslim probes as reconnaissance in force have been turned back or annihilated. So much, the better.

We have our own problems with Islam. Muslims are coming out of the ground like gophers. The Obama administration has now been confirmed as essentially a Muslim administration, with so many appointees of Islam into high places, especially the intelligence and federal law enforcement communities, by former President Obama, it has led to a great deal of confrontation within our own borders. As you are no doubt aware, many of those appointees to high government office have disappeared, have fled the country or have been found murdered.

Certainly, their demise has not been ordered by the current administration but is believed to be the work of right-wing terrorist groups, the so-called patriots, really a bunch of assassins who liken themselves to the Minutemen of our Revolutionary War those centuries ago. In fact, I am sure that is what they call themselves, the Minute Men.

What I am saying Vasili, is that if your country decides to invade Western Europe to end the slaughter and prevent the establishment of a European caliphate, we will not object. We initiated small scale withdrawing our forces out of NATO some months ago as you undoubtedly know and will increase the tempo of withdrawal. We will have withdrawn several brigades of our armored forces from Eastern and Northern Europe within a few months and will have nothing left but a shoestring force that will be brought home very shortly after that. It seems that all of our NATO allies have withdrawn their forces home to fight the Muslims. Our budgetary woes have played a major role in our withdrawal. We no longer regard Russia as a threat to the United States. Indeed, we now consider China a greater threat to us since the days of the cold war when we previously considered the United Soviet Socialist Republics as our greatest threat."

"Obviously we cannot, or should not do anything militarily until spring, Juaquin. That is the time for an offensive. I am sure you realize that. Here's to a peaceful world, Mr. Secretary," as Vasili poured a shot of vodka into Juaquin Santiago's tea and his own.

GEN Schenken was found dead of a myocardial infarction in his home before the month of November was out. Bradley read the newspaper article and pondered over the General's death. Myocardial infarction can be easily induced with the right form and strength of digitalis or one of its derivatives in almost any drink. Ethan had a very strong suspicion that General Schenken was murdered by the Deep State.

"Here's a return receipt requested package for you General. Came through the mailroom this morning. It has your official position address on it."

"Thank you, Command Sergeant Major. Let me sign the card, and you can return the card to the mailroom by a runner."

Ethan signed the card, handed it to the CSM, and waited until he left. The address was from somebody in Roanoke, VA, somebody named Peterson he did not know. It was quite light. Ethan unwrapped one end very carefully to note that it was a cigar box. Peeling off the rest of the wrapping paper, he cautiously lifted the lid with the blade of his pocket knife. Inside was bubble wrapping around a compact disk. Ethan put it into the compact disk player and turned on the television. He was quite surprised when the image of deceased General Schenken appeared on the screen.

"Hello, Ethan. If you are viewing this, then you know that I am already dead. I had prepared this last year in the event of my untimely death and gave it to my sister to mail to you a couple of months after I am dead. I know they will send the FBI to scrounge through and confiscate everything in my home as well as my office. They are looking for anything that might incriminate them in their nefarious ways. Going through my sister was to preclude arousing any suspicion. It is possible that I have, or will die, a natural death. It is, however, quite unlikely. Much more probable is my murder by the powers that be. To my knowledge, I and the Chief of Naval Operations are the only ones in uniform who have stood up to the elitists of the "Deep State," the "Shadow Government", the ruling elitists, or whatever you want to call them. These are the people who control whoever is elected, so elections don't really matter anymore. They couldn't care less which party candidate is elected President or to Congress as they can control whomever it is, through bribery, or blackmail if necessary, or even murder of them and their families.

They are in partnership with their colleagues across the pond in Europe, to control the western economies. They have a much more difficult time than they ever imagined because of the Muslim immigrants. Nevertheless, if they can figure out a way to control the Muslims, they will. I guess they didn't count on the Muslims being near as violent as they are in their desire to establish a European caliphate. Even their so-called moderate Muslims who appeared to be in conspiracy with them have turned on the global elitists. What I am trying to convey is the possibility of civil war here. These elitists are out of touch with much of America. I fear that they have also made a gross miscalculation in our relationships with China and Russia. They don't see the potential of a coalition between our two most powerful adversaries on the international scene. I fear the national scene with the elitists in control as much as I do confrontation with Russia and China. I fear there is an unwritten contract or agreement with those two and the Deep State.

I overheard remarks from some in the intelligence community on several occasions that indicate a coalition of Russia and China is a done deal, with Iran on the periphery. The Russian-Chinese coalition promised us peace if the current administration can be overcome. Russia is to get Europe, and China gets Southeast Asia and the Middle East for its oil and Africa. I don't know how Iran fits into the picture. There was the promise of the continued inflow of raw materials, tin, rubber, chromium, Uranium, and so on into China. It is to be enough to sustain internal markets and trade with North and South America. I can give you several scenarios, but the worst is one in which our military is under their thumb and turns on the American people. The Department of Homeland Security will be their primary force but will be backed up by the Army. The Chief of Staff, Army is a son-of-a-bitch. He is an ass kissing traitor who sold out to the Deep State for his fourth star and Chief of Staff position. Be aware of him. He is your enemy. Guard your family well, Ethan. I have no doubt they would threaten them as a bargaining chip if you refuse to go along with them. As I see it, you have two choices. You can retire and let someone else battle them, or you can take them head-on and run the risk of paying the price. Hell, if civil war does come, perhaps you could lead a guerilla army. The choice is yours. I know whichever choice you make will be the best one for you and what is left of our Republic. God Bless you and yours, Ethan.

Your friend, Robert Schenken."

1 December 2024, Office of the Chief of Naval Operations.

"Commander Jeremiah Billings reported as ordered, Admiral," standing ramrod straight and rendering a salute before the Admiral's desk.

"Relax, Commander, grab a chair," said the CNO as he returned a loose imitation of a salute. Never one to stand on formality, the Admiral pushed away from his desk and sat in a chair adjacent to the Commander.

"Commander, you have the newest boomer in the fleet. I have sealed orders for you in this briefcase which will be handcuffed to you before you leave this office. These sealed orders are not to be opened until you are 200 miles out to sea, and 200 meters deep. Only you and your Executive Officer (XO) are to be aware of them. You have 12 SLBMs. As soon as you step out of this room, you will be provided with an escort of four Marines armed with shotguns and M-14 rifles as well as side arms. Each of them is at least a second dan black belt. They are to protect the contents of the attache' case at all costs. They will accompany you aboard your ship. They are part of a twelve-man detail, two of which will be with you at all times. When you are in your cabin, two will be on guard outside your door. They will work in eight-hour shifts of two men each. One will guard your cabin at all times. The remainder of this detail is reporting to your ship as we speak. Ask me no questions, and I'll tell you no lies. You are to proceed directly to your ship, communicating with no one in any way. A special detail will visit your wife this afternoon, informing her that you are on a special assignment and cannot be contacted by anyone. Two days ago, without your knowledge, I ordered your crew on board and your XO to make all preparations for getting underway without informing you while you were on leave. Your escort will accompany you on board to protect you and your XO at all costs, just in case there is a mole in your crew. Once aboard, you will immediately cast off. Your XO will take the ship out of the harbor before you assume command. Your route is already planned in your orders. The Marine NCO in charge of the detail will accompany you to your quarter and provide you with the special handcuff kay and observe you deposit this attache' case in the safe. He will have a rotary detail outside your quarter, shotgun and pistol armed until you reach your assigned location and depth provided to the XO. At this time, he will relinquish the command key to open the attache' case to you. You are to open, read, and share these orders only with your XO. Your crew is to know nothing. There are not five people in the world who know about this. I will not entertain any questions or comments. It is regrettable you will miss Christmas with your family. You have your orders, Commander. Good luck and smooth sailing." The Admiral stood and extended his hand to Captain Billings who firmly grasped it, looked the Admiral in the eye, and said, "Thank you for the honor and trust Admiral." Billings intuitively guessed what the orders contained. The Admiral handed Billings the attache' case and snapped the handcuffs on Billing's left wrist. Without another word, the Admiral escorted Billing to the office door where four Marines stood waiting, two with 12-gauge Remington 870 pump shotguns sporting slug barrels but loaded with double ought buckshot and two with M-l4 rifles.

The Admiral slumped back in his chair. "One down, five to go," he thought to himself. "Why oh why didn't those bastards in Congress fund us a fleet of nonnuclear attack air-independent propulsion subs? We could have had 10 or 15 for the price of one SSBN. Those New World Order sons of bitches behind the scenes control everything. They think they are going to reign over North

America and Europe. Those dumb bastards think they are going to control Muslims."

Commander Billings was putting away the contents of the attache' case when he noticed one sealed envelope that said open me upon clearing the harbor. It assigned the routine patrol mission and route to Commander Billings of a fast attack submarine. After thirty or more days of patrol, if no "significant events" happen, open the second sealed envelope. If a "significant event" occurs prior to that time, you are to open and carry out the enclosed orders immediately.

Commander Billings immediately hoped that the Russians and Chinese could not distinguish our submarine fleet by its acoustic signature, the way we can identify each of their ships, surface and submarines alike.

Reduced by budget constraints, both attack submarines and SSBNs had been greatly reduced in numbers. Only seven SSBNs remained in service. They are named after cities. Several are more than 30 years old. It takes almost five years to build an SSBN and costs over one and a half billion dollars. The plan to convert several Virginia fast attack submarines to a dual role was limited to two submarines, the first the USS Audie L. Murphy because of fiscal restraints. The U.S. Navy could have had twenty fast attack submarines that could launch forty SLBMs. They could have put two SLBMs on each Virginia class submarine so it could be armed with Tomahawk land-attack missiles in forwarding weapons tubes. If only they could have had a 50/50 mix, thought the Admiral. They could put six 475 kilotons W-88 warheads in each missile. One such missile carrying fast attack submarine could be a very potent force multiplier, let alone a fleet of twenty. That would be forty missiles for a total of 240 strategic warheads.

"Hey Chief, what's up with all these Marines around here? I can't get a word out of them. We got six in the forward torpedo room and six in the back-tube room. We have put up with them for ten days now. They never speak to us swabbies other than to say 'Semper Fi Sailor,' or Have a good day, sailor, or some such shit. There's always two of them outside the Captain's door."

"Sailor, you know as much as I do. You can bet though; this boat isn't headed for a picnic. Our own security detail wasn't considered good enough to guard the Skipper and XO, so you know some shit is going down somewhere. We carry the big nukes boy, not the usual tactical stuff. We transited the Panama Canal, so you know we're headed for the far Pacific, maybe with a stopover in Honolulu, but don't get your hopes up, kid. Like as not, we'll not set foot on dry land. We took on two weeks' worth of food just before we sailed. That is to present the appearance of a training mission so that we will have replenishment at sea somewhere. We aren't going to be home for Christmas, so don't get your hopes up."

The Chief of the Boat was right. The USS Minneapolis rendezvoused with a supply ship from which it took on five months' worth of provisions. The orders of the supply ship had no name of the submarine it was to meet. It was the first set of six sealed orders provided to the six resupply ship Commanders by the Chief of Naval Operations. It only provided the location and time of the rendezvous of each of the submarines. Two submarines were headed for the North Atlantic and one for the Indian Ocean.

Gypsy and the boys set up the artificial Christmas tree they found in the big garage two weeks earlier. They strung lights around the outside of the house under the eaves. Sam wrapped lights around the smaller spruce tree in the front yard and ran an extension cord to it. A great big Christmas wreath hung from the mailbox and another on the front of the garage. Ethan came home on the 23rd of December, flying into Billings and renting a car for the final leg of the journey. He couldn't help but smile at the decorations. On Christmas Day morning, they opened their gifts. Ethan had purchased a quality 6/8 straight razor made in Germany, a strop, a quality boar's hair shaving brush and a cup with shaving soap in it for each of the boys. Gypsy couldn't help giggling at the boys when they opened their razors. They didn't quite know what to think of them. Sam was ready for shaving, but Josh, well, maybe in a year or two. For Gypsy, Ethan had a gold chain necklace. Gypsy spent the day baking a twenty-pound tom turkey with all of the trimmings. They had a light lunch and were ready to sit down to a huge, early supper. Before serving, Ethan opened a bottle of Dram Bouie liquor. He poured the boys each about ten milliliters while he and Gypsy had double that in Waterford crystal glasses.

"Enjoy boys; I don't want you to have any alcohol outside this house until you are legal, that's twenty-one years of age, gentlemen! So, sip now and enjoy. If you are lucky, you might get one refill."

Ethan carved the turkey while Gypsy poured each of them, including the boys, a glass of pinot noir. Ethan said, Grace. "Let us not ever forget the real meaning of Christmas. It is to celebrate the birth of our Lord Jesus. We owe our eternal life to him. I regret that I have been remiss in your religious training, boys. It is far more important than you can probably imagine. The old adage, 'there are no atheists in foxholes' I assure you, is true. I hope that you will begin to attend a Protestant church. I suggest you visit several on consecutive Sundays to see which denomination appeals to you. You don't have to join any, but I hope you begin to understand and practice Christianity. Only the Good Lord knows what the future holds." So, holding his glass high, "Here is to Jesus Christ, secure life and happiness for all of us."

After supper, they sat down together to watch the evening's football game on television. It was one of the happiest moments in their lives for all of them. Three days later, Ethan flew back to Camp Lejune to report for duty.

Inauguration Day, January 2025, Camp Lejune, NC.

The Gunnery Sergeant burst into Bradley's office without knocking. He was out of breath, and the look on his face was a combination of fear and anxiety.

"General Bradley Sir, come quickly." Then realizing the General had a television in his office, strode over to it and turned it on without another word. He stepped back, and General Bradley directed his attention to the image on the screen. The presidential limousine was a ball of fire. Smoke billowed from all windows, and it was lying upside down. The bodies of the secret service agents who jogged alongside the limousine were on fire, most blown meters away from the limousine and mostly in pieces from the blast. Other Secret Service agents more distant from the presidential limousine went down from machine fire emanating from other MRAPs. Dozens of spectators were mowed down along with the agents. Mine Resistant Armored Personnel Carriers (MRAP) had burst through the side streets, crushing the barriers as they went. One broke through the motorcade in front of the presidential limousine and one behind it.

Pedestrians who could not move aside quickly enough were simply run down and crushed. The Tube Launched Wire-Guided (TOW) rack on the lead MRAP in front of the limousine was empty. The first woman President of the United States had just been assassinated by mutinous U.S. Army troops. Overhead, Apache helicopters circled the scene without firing on the MRAPs for several minutes, then assembled in formation and disappeared low in flight over Washington, DC.

Armored columns had moved by truck from Fort Bragg, NC overnight and by morning were in position around the city. At the last moment, they moved from staging grounds in the city parks to position themselves around the city. On cue, they moved to surround the Capitol, all of the attending crowd, and the Pentagon.

Bradley cursed to himself. Madam President-Elect Naomi Campbell was widely acknowledged as the most controversial president since Abraham Lincoln. Now the first black woman president just elected for a second term and one who granted general amnesty restored the gold standard, revoked the charter of the cabal of privately-owned banks known as the Federal Reserve Bank of the United States, was reduced to a cinder. Bradley immediately realized that high treason involving personnel of much higher rank than himself had to be participants if not the major perpetrators. Flag officers of the United States Army and most likely of other armed forces had to be culpable. Bradley pondered if it was a military operation unto itself. "No," he thought. Controlling forces higher up the ladder ordered it. Is it new, or old, are the Joint Chiefs of Staff in on it? Is it a rogue division commander? Not likely. How loyal would lower-ranking personnel, company grade officers, Non-Commissioned Officers (NCOs) and troopers be to a higher authority to commit to this? Was it a unit specifically assembled, permanently or temporarily, only to be disbursed to complicate identification? No, it was too broad, involving too many people to be restrained. As a battalion commander, Bradley knew his Marines had greater loyalty to the country, the Corps, the brigade and the battalion that could never develop in the army. "Crap," he thought. How soon will my marines be fighting U.S. Army dog faces? The military hit unit had to be an integrated unit not too distant from D.C. What outfit would have air, armor, and mounted infantry assets? No National Guard unit would do this. It has to be a Regular Army unit, at least of battalion size if not a brigade. Could they convoy from Ft. Bragg? Too far, and the Special Forces folks would probably not go along with it. It could be hard to maintain the necessary secrecy. Almost all flag officers today are members of the Council on Foreign Relations, the advocates for one world order, headed by the United Nations. There are no tactical units of this nature in Virginia, West Virginia; New York is home to the Tenth Mountain Division, light infantry, mountains and that is pretty far from D.C. Bradley could not recognize any division patches on the television. Due to requirements for logistical support, the farther away from D.C., the more tenuous the objective becomes-unless it was supported by the USAF to air ferry the strike force in. That suggests the duplicity and authority of the Joint Chiefs of Staff, at least of the USAF and the US Army. No, it would take at least two brigades. As he was working through his thought process, the television switched to scenes developing in other areas of the city. They portrayed army battalions surrounding selected federal buildings. It had to be an entire army division participating in the coup. The army had been reduced to less than 300,000 personnel. A fact greatly resented by many senior officers. Now, there was a division of at least 12,000 troops participating in a military coup."

Turning to reasons why the President was assassinated, Bradley recalled the theory of some historians, never discussed in public, why President John F. Kennedy was assassinated. Kennedy would have returned the U.S. Treasury to notes backed by gold and silver. The Federal Reserve Bank greatly resisted this move as it would destroy its power to print money and control the economy based on nothing more than confidence. "How in God's green earth did a cartel of privately-owned banks, mostly European at that, known as the Federal Reserve Bank, come to control the American, and then most of the world's economy?" thought Bradley.

"Maybe I should have read that book that Dad was always trying to get me to read, "The Creature From Jekyll Island," by Ed Griffith, on the history of central banking in the United States. Who coined the phrase 'Follow the Money'? In this case, who benefits, and follows the power? Who craves whatever results occur from this? Obviously, the Vice President assumes the throne, but who else benefits? The Secretary of Defense? The Speaker of the House moves up to the Vice President's office. Vice President always craved power and was terribly disappointed when he didn't get the democratic nomination for President. The backroom deal of the Democratic National Committee bought him off with the Vice President's slot. Okay, so he's suspect number one. Who has been his main man in the Department of Defense? I am too far from the political flagpole to know. Sure, hope the USMC commandant isn't in on it? Perhaps GEN Schenken was retired and murdered because he didn't want any part of it. Maybe it is just a matter of economics and politics. Maybe the re-election of a real conservative who cuts the welfare budget to pieces, tries to balance the budget and reduce the national debt, cuts the defense budget, demands we return to fiscal responsibility, has pulled us out of Europe, the big bankers and screaming, the Federal Reserve is threatened. I can't rule out the Russian Chinese coalition, but it would make no sense. Their new rail link is fantastic; trade between them has enormously increased. They sit on the two largest piles of gold in the world. Russia is China's main oil supplier, and China provides uranium and rare earth metals to Russia for power plants, nukes, catalysts, and other purposes. Iran eyes them both very cautiously, as Iranian oil is in direct competition with Russian oil. Then too, the mullahs are stirring the Muslim communities of both Russia and China into acts of terrorism. Still, Iran would be foolish to tweak their noses at this time. No, more likely this is an internally driven disaster."

It had been almost three years since the end of what was called the second civil war, real anarchy in the streets that lasted for months. As a division commander, Bradley had instinctively subjected his brigade and battalion commanders to intense scrutiny. Those he suspected of lack of dedication to restoring order, maintaining objectivity, allegiance to their oath of office to the Constitution (and not to the Office of the President, as Barak Obama demanded) and otherwise politically neutral he eliminated from his command by the forced retirement of those eligible and transferred to other commands of those he could not retire. The Chairman and all of the joint chiefs of the respective services were forced to retire under the blanket amnesty. Bradley would have much preferred to try them for treason, as all were members of the Council on Foreign Relations (CFR), dedicated to the New World Order, one world government, directed by the United Nations. As such, all had betrayed their oath of office to the Constitution. As a student of history, Bradley immediately suspects that the same forces that assassinated John F Kennedy in 1963 were involved. Many members of the CFR had escaped to Europe and South America where they had stored much of their wealth in gold, stashed in private banks and warehouses. Over the last two years, many had returned to the United States to reclaim their positions as captains of industry and especially finance. The majority of the Supreme Court judges survived the riots of the Washington DC area and countryside. Some conservative organizations wanted to bring some of the flag officers and politicians and federal judges to trial for treason. Unfortunately, President Campbell did not agree. Now she was dead. Bradley always thought she was too forgiving. Obviously, the "shadow government" of the "eastern establishment" is alive and well through Bradley. Bradley told the sergeant to schedule an officer's call for 16:00 hours, no exceptions down through company commanders and their company sergeants.

Would the Vice President continue the deceased president's policies? Rumors abounded that he was a 33rd degree in the Scottish Rights Mason. Previously he denied any affiliation with such a supposedly secret organization. What about the rumored Skull and Bones club that so many elites were supposed to be members?

Bradley surmised that the eastern establishment and its twin, the European establishment was delighted to see the assassination. Was the President-Elect murdered because she fulfilled her promise to revoke the charter of the Federal Reserve Bank? Is it a military coup? Did some rogue Army general conduct the assassination operation because he was not selected as the Joint Chief of Staff (JCS) or office in the civilian side of the house, as in Assistant Secretary of Defense or something? What is the fate of subordinate officers and troops who refused to participate in this operation? Perhaps that is why a large number of officers and Non-Commissioned Officers (NCO) and their troops were recently assigned to African Command (AFRICOM). How will this fit into what is happening in Europe? Is this a rogue operation by the Department of Homeland Security that has become a second military force, nearly the size, and capability of the Regular Army? How could that be, with the heavy weapons deployed?

Europe's social order is collapsing. Second and third generation immigrants, Shiite and Sunni, and native-born Muslims of Europeans of several generations' descent create a three-ringed circus for political control. The elitists are struggling mightily to maintain any semblance of order. Programmed famine had encouraged anarchy to be crushed by military force, tying the elitists and their military services closer together to control the masses. Islam in Europe was proving to be far more incalcitrant than the non-Islamic population. Muslims had long smuggled small arms and ammunition buried under minerals and food shipments originating in Africa and the Middle East in ocean-going shipping containers into European ports. Now many European cities are more or less under siege or civil war. How does all of this tie together?

"Is this their game plan?" thought Bradley. The ruling elite supported by a large military organization in turn supported by the elitists responsible for the control of the masses through the economy. Is it because President Campbell refused to send troops into Europe to help defeat the Muslim uprising? God, only a few tens of millions of Europeans died while we had our own internecine conflict. The Muslims have almost made it, especially in France, Spain, and Italy, when they burst out of their mosques armed with rocket-propelled grenades and automatic weapons, especially AK-47s.

They slaughtered everyone they thought not to be Muslim, both sexes, and all ages. Many young women were violently gang-raped before being killed. Some of the more attractive and young ones were retained as sex slaves in what were previous hotels. The local police forces were quickly eliminated, not just in their stations, but also in their homes, along with their families. The result was the national armies of the respective nations surrounded their enclaves, cutting their electricity and water supplies. Then the bombing of the enclaves was initiated. Finally, tanks and infantry have been committed in the desperate house to house fighting where the situation now rests. As the national armies slowly closed in throughout the enclaves, they returned the barbarity. Men, women, and children were slaughtered, no questions asked. The appearance of being of Middle Eastern origin was sufficient to be a death warrant. Many sections of many cities suffered as badly as they had during Allied bombings in World War IE Worse, the elitists were now back in control. The elitists, backed by the military, are making the masses pay for their own stupidity of relinquishing control to the elitists. Dumbing down the education system had been an enormous help. The "working class" was rather like Socrates's man in the cave. He had never seen the sun, so he did not know what it was like to breathe clean air and feel the rays of the sun. Come out of the mine; so, it is with individual liberty. "Old Ben Franklin was right," mused Bradley. "Those who would surrender their freedom for the promise of a little security will, in the end, lose both and deserve neither." The Muslim uprising certainly threatened the elitists of the International Monetary Fund, the World Bank, the Bank of International Settlements and their attempts to control the world's economy. Bradley couldn't sort it all out without time and more information.

Too many of our own law enforcement elements, from the Department of Homeland Security's notorious army that was Barak Obama's private domestic army, through the FBI, to the local county sheriffs and city police forces that bought into Agenda 21, engaged in domestic terrorism against all they considered as enemies of the state. Too many innocent citizens died, too many went into FEMA camps. Some of the local and state politicians who acquiesced paid with their lives. A few secretive militia units formed that were responsible for their local assassinations, as they knew who the traitors were that sat on county commissions and city councils in small towns. A few such militia groups were compromised by useful idiots who infiltrated them under the threat of blackmail. Locally operated law enforcement drones, flying high enough to be out of small arms range, played a major role in the police monitoring suspects. Only the most closely-knit militias survived, rather like the vigilantes of California during the gold rush days.

The Kremlin, January 2025

"Mr. President, the Chinese Premier is on the red telephone for you."

"Thank you, Natalia." Russian President Proboff answers the red telephone on his desk, speaking English. "Mr. Prime Minister, this is an unexpected pleasure. I am sure you have something profound in mind."

"President Proboff, I am sure you are aware of what just occurred in the United States. I suggest an immediate face to face summit, at the place of your choosing, within twenty-four hours to discuss our options on how to best address the situation that just developed in the United States."

"I quite agree, Mr. Prime Minister, what if we meet in your country at an isolated military base far away from prying eyes, where satellite reconnaissance can be negated as to our meeting? What about your secret base in Yuman?" Say tomorrow, about 12:00 hours your time in Yuman?" "An excellent suggestion, Mr. President. My staff and I will be there."

City of Dunhuang, Gansu Province, northwestern China, meeting of Prime Minister Wu and President Proboff.

"Mr. President, do you think this is the golden opportunity, handed to us on a plate? It is entirely unexpected to us here in China, more of an opportunity than we could have ever dreamed. True, it is not the ideal time as we had previously planned, differing in three months later than our planning, but still, with the weather still in our favor, the mass hysteria, disruption in the chain of command, and overall uncertainty of who is responsible and turmoil within their Congress could not but be in our favor. Their political structure is entirely in disarray. With the demise of their newly elected President and then the swearing in of the Vice President, we have the opportunity of the century. The new President is a coward, a wealthy woman afraid of hard decisions, especially commitment to war. She would rather talk and surrender than fight, especially if it comes to a strategic nuclear war. In our ongoing discussions with the US Department of Defense, we do not believe the Secretary of Defense, and his Number Two would believe us. Their traitorous murder of their own Chairman of the Joint Chiefs of Staff and assassination of the President showed how wrong we were. They truly believed they are preventing World War III, but have provided us an open door for the annihilation of the United States and the seizure of their lands. The Chinese and Russian peoples will not experience hunger for another hundred years. The lesson in diplomacy and geopolitics will be forever studied. Never negotiate from a position of weakness. As Sun Tzu said, 'When you are weak, appear strong. When you are strong, appear weak.' The Americans came to rely entirely on digitalization. As in the destruction of the Twin Towers on September 9, 2001, they refused to believe that anyone would launch such attacks as Pearl Harbor, 9-11, and now, January 24th."

"We must ensure complete isolation of the Americans' ability to communicate with their forces and weapons systems. They must not be able to communicate with their Submarine Launched Ballistic Missile submarine fleet or their strategic aircraft."

"Mr. Prime Minister, we can negate their ICBM force while their missiles are still in the air or perhaps still in their silos with our laser satellite weapons or our new precision-guided small nuclear-tipped missiles launched from the International Space Station or our satellites or through an electromagnetic pulse attack. The key is that they must not be able to communicate. Can your submarines carry out their mission of severing the communications cables on the floors of the Pacific Ocean? We can do so in the Atlantic. Our submarines have already laid mines adjacent to their undersea cables. All that is required is a radio signal, and they will all be simultaneously detonated, just a few minutes before our electromagnetic attacks. Say 12:00 hours January 31, in New York City? That would be a pleasant New Year's evening surprise. The traffic jams would be insurmountable. Our satellites are positioned such that we can achieve maximum kill on the American communications satellites. Many of our so-called weather satellites are actually anti-satellite killer satellites. We can disable the American satellites in a matter of minutes. One or two might escape complete destruction, but they will be rendered useless, floating hulks of space junk."

"Mr. President, we would like to move more of our submarine fleet in position around the Hawaiian Islands, Diego Garcia in the Indian Ocean, the Philippine Islands, and Japan in case they should exercise any folly. I do not believe South Korea is in any position to react. I would suggest that we plan a party for our friends."

"Comrade Proboff, on further consideration, we do not feel that an attack limited to EMP effects will be sufficient. Some ships are moderately shielded against an EMP attack, but many are not. Our concern is that not enough of their offensive capabilities will be downgraded by EMP. Therefore, we will also attack some of their west coast assets with more traditional nuclear weapons. Rest assured, our attacks will be strictly limited in nature. After all, we do not wish to destroy valuable assets we want to gain. The naval bases in San Diego and, Honolulu will definitely be destroyed. We are discussing their assets in San Francisco and Bremerton, Washington. Perhaps you wish to consider similar redundancy in Norfolk, Virginia, Washington, D.C., New Haven, Connecticut, and New York City.

Since the current US administration has reduced the DOD budget especially that of the US Navy, about two-thirds of ships are now in their home ports at any given time, their crews ashore. Even if there are ships are insufficiently degraded, they cannot sail without crews to man them. Perhaps the demise of their crews is even more important than the destruction of the ships themselves. With only one carrier battle group at sea at any one time in each ocean, their defeat should not be too difficult. With the loss of their satellite communications, they will be isolated. We are aware of which of their civilian satellites have built-in military capabilities as well. We will destroy those satellites in a timely manner. Complete isolation by the destruction of all means of communication is essential."

"What you propose Comrade Wu makes excellent sense. We will consider your recommendations, especially with regard to Norfolk. Perhaps Savannah, Mobile, and Pensacola should receive modest nuclear strikes as well. Weapons in the 50 to 100 kiloton range should suffice to melt their ships, burn out their electronics, and kill their crews. Unlike Europe, much of the American civilian population is armed, especially in rural America. Of course, idiotic American politicians, especially in the liberal coastal states, have disarmed their constituents, particularly in California. We should thank them. Starvation will eliminate most of the civilian population threat, and save the farmers, which will be easily overcome in isolation. Recall the submarine-launched rocket we fired just off the coast of California a few years ago. They had no idea our submarine was just a few miles off their coast.

Our submarine fleet will be quietly waiting outside their harbors for any warships that sail out of their other homeports. Rather like in World War II when Americans could read their newspaper at midnight by the light of their burning ships sunk by German U-boats off their east coast. They have made no preparations, no means of detection, of penetration by submarines off their coastlines. We will deploy the traditional nuclear weapons from submarines. Our ballistic boats will serve as bait to draw any of their anti-submarine assets out to where our killer submarines will destroy the-would be pursuers. Their anti-submarine air assets won't get off the ground. All fuel tanks will explode from the heat and blast. We'll use nuclear weapons tailored to heat and blast to minimize radiation contamination. We won't attack New York City because of the Federal Reserve Bank, the financial records, the art work, and museums. We have already hacked into the FBI Center in Martinsburg, West Virginia for the BATF 44473 records of gun owners. It is the end of the United States and the rise of China America. How soon can you be ready?"

"I quite agree, Mr. Prime Minister. We can be absolutely ready in less than twenty-four hours to initiate Operation Bright Flash for an attack. What is your time frame for attack?"

"12:00 hours on January 31 in New York City it is. It is agreed, Mr. President."

CHAPTER IV

JANUARY 23, 2025

"HEY, GORDO, WHO IS THAT HOT MAMA IN THE RED DRESS?"

Gordo, looking over the tray he carries, replies, "That is Sam and Josh Bradley's mom. Sam is on the football team and with my son, the basketball team. They just moved here in June. I think her man is some kind of Marine general in the Pentagon right now. Maybe Quantico, I don't know for sure. At least that is the rumor. She teaches physics in high school. She is some kind of smart woman."

"Smart or not she is a real MILF, Mother I Would Like to Fuck. She is really hot. What's the celebration, anyway?"

"It is for the basketball coach. I think he has some kind of birthday party. Yeah, she's hot, but you wouldn't want to mess with her hubby or even her kids. Her boys are on the basketball team with my older son. They say he was some kind of guerilla leader around here in the civil war, one tough dude with lots of followers. I don't think you want to mess with the Marines, Manuel."

"Do you know what she drives, Gordo?"

"Yeah, that little Toyota truck with the purple topper."

Manuel thinks about it for a moment as he studies Gypsy Lee. Outside the Hoot Owl Cafe Manuel uses his cell phone. "Jesus, you and Hernando up to a little fucking tonight? There is this hot MILF partying at the Hoot Owl Cafe, some kind of party. If you bring your van, we'll pick her up, take her to Manny's garage and have a little fun. If there are any others in the club who want to join in a little action, they can come too."

Manuel hides in the alley until Jesus appears with his van. He climbs into the passenger's front seat. Hernando and Felipe are in the back.

"We'll snatch her as she leaves the party, real quick like. They park next to her truck, that little Toyota and when she starts to open the door, we'll jump out, put a sack over her head, throw her in the van, then off for a little fun."

Most of the partygoers had left. It was 11:30, National Guard time, 23:30 for the military. Gypsy paid no attention to the black van with its engine running, parked on the driver's side of her truck. As she inserted the key in her car door, Felipe and Hernando jumped out of the sliding door while Manuel exits the passenger door of the cab. As Gypsy turns around, Manuel slides a grain sack over her head and down her arms. Felipe and Hernando grab her legs and waist and shove her into the truck. Hernando pulls handcuffs from his hip pocket and handcuffs her ankles was Manuel slides the side door shut. Felipe delivers a powerful punch to Gypsy's solar plexus. They shove her over on her stomach and handcuff her hands behind her back as Jesus drives off. Once inside the garage, they pull her from the van. Still cuffed hands and ankles; they stand her up so that Felipe hits her again in the solar plexus which makes her buckle to her knees. Hernando raises the grain sack, just enough to expose her mouth. Holding his hand under her chin to keep her mouth closed, Felipe duct tapes her mouth from behind to prevent her from screaming. They remove the grain sack so Felipe can blindfold her from behind. Once blindfolded, they remove the handcuffs from her wrists and remove her coat, then recuff her.

Standing her up, then remove every piece of clothing with switchblade knives. Felipe hits her hard in the rib cage, feeling the bones break under his blow. They lay Gypsy on a mattress, and each rotates holding her legs apart to rape her vaginally. After each had his turn, Felipe puts a cushion next to her and rolls her on it, so her pelvis is elevated. He sodomizes her. Gypsy is semiconscious when they load her in the van. They replace the handcuffs with rope, tying her hands behind her back and binding her ankles together. They drive by the emergency entrance of the hospital, slowing down but not stopping, pushing her out of the side door of the van. The temperature is five degrees Fahrenheit. The security camera at the emergency entrance records it all.

Sam wakes up slowly. He puts the two puppies out the back door into the fenced enclosure. He lets his brother Josh sleep while he showers and shaves. Sam dresses quietly, but Josh sits up and looks at the clock. It is 07:00. Sam slippes on clean jeans, wool shirt, and boots, pulls on a down coat and hat. He goes out the back door, opens the gate top to the enclosure and with the dogs following, walks to the end of the street for the puppies to run, play, and relieve themselves. When he comes in, he is surprised that Gypsy is not up making breakfast. He peaks into her bedroom to discover she is not there. Concerned, he checks into the garage to see her truck is gone. Sam fries bacon and eggs with toast for the two of them. It is now 09:00. Worried, Sam calls the sheriffs office to report Gypsy is not home, her truck is gone, has she been involved in an accident?

"An as yet unidentified woman was attacked last night and dumped off at the hospital. Can you describe your mother?"

"Mom is about five foot, eight inches tall, 125 pounds, shoulder length hair, a brunette, 38 year of age, and a very attractive woman."

"That description fits the woman. Can you go to the hospital for confirmation of identity?"

"My brother and I will be there in 30 minutes." Sam hung up the phone. "It sounds like Mom is at the hospital. We need to go now. She's been hurt bad."

The brothers jumped into the Toyota Tacoma and sped to the hospital. Gypsy was conscious but heavily sedated. The hospital staff had completed the whole-body radiograph. She has three broken ribs, a broken jaw, and a mild concussion. She recognized the boys and tried to hold up a hand. Each stepson, one on each side of the bed, took her hand. Both Boys had tears on their faces. They stayed until Gypsy drifted off to sleep. The Red Cross representative asked Sam and Josh for Ethan's phone number so she could call him. Sam pulled Ethan's office phone and quarter phone number off his cell phone for her, then called his father. Ethan was at church without his cell phone, so Sam left a message.

"Dad, Mom was brutally attacked last night. She is in serious condition in the hospital, where I am calling from. They tell me she will survive physically but has broken ribs and a broken jaw. Love you. Will call again later, Sam."

After church, Ethan started making his lunch when he noticed a call waiting. After hearing Sam's message, Ethan made airline reservations and packed a bag. He called the Corps Commander informing him he was taking emergency leave, uncertain when he would return, to hell with the confirmation and paperwork. He then called his Assistant Division Commander for maneuver and informed him he was in command of the Division until he returned, a date not yet known. Ethan ate his lunch, drove to the airport, and waited. From Denver, he called his sons and told them to pick him up at the Worland airport from the 18:30 flight. They did, and after hugs, Sam drove them to the hospital.

Gypsy was conscious but in pain. They had a nasal cannula for oxygen to ease the pain of respiration. The county sheriff and Worland police chief were there, gathering as much information as possible. Gypsy remembered the black van parked next to her little truck, but could describe no other details except how she was restrained and attacked. She did relate that they spoke mostly Spanish, occasionally relapsing into English. The hospital security compact disk revealed the van as it pulled through the ER driveway. Part of the license plate was legible. An investigation of the license plate revealed it was stolen last month in the Riverton Walmart parking lot. The perpetrators of the license plate theft drove away in an old pickup, but it was never further investigated.

The next day the city police investigator questioned the attending party members. One remembered Gordo speaking with someone, a Latino, but could not identify him. When questioned, Gordo denied speaking with anyone.

Two days later, Ethan took the boys to the Hoot Owl Cafe for supper. Their waiter was visibly nervous; it was Gordo. When asked by Ethan for his name, he admitted it was Gordo. Ethan took the boys home and watched football with them until 20:30. He drove alone back to the Hoot Owl Cafe and waited. When the restaurant closed, Gordo emerged from the back door. Ethan, wearing a ski mask, stepped behind him. Gordo never saw or heard the whirling of the chain-linked rosewood nunchaku that struck him from behind, just below the left ear. When he awoke, he found himself cold, naked and staked spread eagle on the rough desert ground. Sitting on a stool by the light of a camp lantern, was Ethan.

"Now, Gordo, we're going to play a little game. You lied to the police about discussing something with some Latino at Saturday night's party. You are going to tell me everything you know."

"I don't know nothing about nothing," replied Gordo."

"You're lying, Gordo. I know it. We're 30 miles from town, you're naked, alone in the desert. It is close to zero degrees. You can scream all you want, no one but me will hear you, and I don't care. I am not the police, and in your present condition, I can do anything I want to you. No one will hear your screams or come to help you. We'll start with who you were talking to that night, your Latino buddy."

"I know my rights, man. You can't do anything to me." "My wife had rights too, Gordo."

Ethan slipped on a pair of vinyl gloves and picked up a pair of slip joint pliers. "I know you are just shaking mostly from the cold right now, after all, it is near zero, and you're naked on the ground. But you are also shaking in fear, Gordo because I have total control over you. Now I am going to crush your testicles, slowly, one at a time. Then I am going to pull your fingernails and toenails out one at a time, then your testicles, until you tell me everything, I want to know about who attacked my wife."

With that, Ethan took one testicle in the jaws of the pliers and began to squeeze gently. Gordo screamed. Ethan backed off, then squeezed again, a little harder.

Gordo screamed again, the pain absolutely sickening. He started to wretch. Ethan didn't want him to die just yet, so he rolled his head to one side so he wouldn't drown in his own vomitus. Ethan watched his agony with detachment. When Gordo regained his breath, Ethan said, "This time I will not stop until your testicle is like a squashed grape. Gordo screamed again, "OK. I'll tell you. It was Manuel Santiago who was asking about your wife. That's all I know, man."

"Well, now we're making progress. That will do for starters. Obviously, you know this Manuel Santiago well enough to converse with him. I want to know where he lives and who his close friends are."

"I don't know the man; I honestly don't."

Ethan palpated the crushed testicle and decided it could be crushed some more. Ethan applied the pliers. Gordo screamed and vomited. Some he inhaled, choking on it. Ethan waited until Gordo quit trying to cough it up.

"Gordo, I just might let you drown in your own vomit. Do you want to tell me something?"

"Manuel's closest buddies are Felipe, Hernando, and Jesus. They all run together. They all live in those crummy little cubicle houses on Culpepper street, right next door to one another. They all do drugs and deal. Felipe, he is the meanest. He's the one you have to watch out for. Manuel left town yesterday, and headed for Mexico. Maybe to get more drugs? He took Jesus's van. That's all I know, man."

"Because you weren't involved directly in raping my wife, Gordo, I'll let you live. Now, you know who I am and what I am. You know I command 12,000 of the most bloodthirsty marines in history. Be aware that if you attempt to press any charges, such as kidnapping, torture or so forth against me, some of my people will pay you a visit. There is no place you can run and hide, not even in Mexico. Some of my best marines are Mexican Americans. Their personal loyalty to me is unquestioned. They will not only come after you but your parents and your brothers and sisters. What I did to you tonight is child's play compared to what they will do to your family. I'll leave you now. You have a 30-mile walk back into town. You could have avoided all this unpleasantness if you had told all of this to the sheriff."

"You can't do this to me, man, and get away with it. I'll see your boys killed."

Ethan looked at him for a moment, then slowly spoke. "I take all threats seriously and personally, Gordo. Threatening my sons was a very bad thing to do." Ethan walked over to Gordo and delivered a karate chop to his larynx that crushed it. Gordo began to immediately wheeze and choke. Ethan removed Gordo's bonds and pulled up the stakes to which Gordo had been tied. He put Gordo's clothes and shoes in a plastic bag in the back of his truck. Gordo was still wheezing when Ethan helped him to his feet. Gordo never saw the nunchaku in Ethan's hand as it came across the back of his neck. A second blow to the larynx with the rosewood nunchaku insured its fracture and that Gordo would choke to death on his own body fluids, from the edema of the multiple fractured bones of the larynx in a few minutes. Ethan left Gordo's body behind a big rock 100 meters off the desert road.

When he passed a trash dumpster in the alley behind an automotive garage, Ethan tossed the bag with Gordo's clothes and shoes into it. He collapsed in bed after a hot shower. He slept soundly until 07:30. The boys were very quiet so their father would sleep.

"Vladimir, do you think it wise to initiate our Operation Rub Out considering we are about to obliterate the entire country."

"Of course, Alexi. Why take the chance? Our predecessors' term for these traitors to their own country was 'useful idiots.' Why should we take any chance at all of any of them surviving to rally any stupid survivors? Besides, who is to know who killed them? With the anticipated riots, rapes and looting going on, all of them rich and famous, why shouldn't they be singled out as targets for local violent elements. It is quite possible that the locals will accomplish the job for us. It is important that none of them survive to establish any kind of government or control. They had their opportunity. They squandered billions of dollars, and threw away tens of thousands of lives of their youth to achieve their own ends of financial and physical control through both the Korean and Vietnam wars. They made billions of dollars on defense stocks, weapons, and munitions. They could have won both wars if the elitists and the neocons would have allowed the military to do so. No, instead they retire the war-fighting generals who oppose them. Can you give me one good reason why we should take a chance and let any of them, any at all, provided they survive, a chance to rise like the Phoenix from the ashes? On the second or third day of Operation Bright Flash, we will send a signal to all operatives in Operation Rub Out to proceed as planned."

January 26, 2025

Ethan went to the hospital after a breakfast of bacon and eggs. He questioned the attending physician and requested Gypsy be administered a shot of estradiol to prevent fertilized egg implantation and prevent an unwanted pregnancy. The physician wrote the order in Ethan's presence. Ethan walked into Gypsy's room. The intravenous fluids had been discontinued. Gypsy was sitting up and gave him a weak smile.

"That's my girl. You'll heal in no time. I see they have put a compression bandage on your rib cage to stabilize those fractured ribs. How about other injuries?"

Gypsy pointed to her jaw. "It's broken, green stick fracture" she mumbled. The attending physician and nurse entered, bearing a syringe and clipboard. The nurse administered the estradiol intramuscularly.

"How about other injuries, Doctor?" asked Ethan.

"Well, she has a green stick fracture of the left mandible. We're still evaluating how to best treat that. We sent the radiographs to an oral surgeon in Billings and to a local dentist, who, while not an oral surgeon has done of a lot of repair jobs on similar injuries. We also have a local orthopedic surgeon who might want the job. We'll let you know as soon as we get some responses. On other injuries, we'll let you know as soon as we get some answers as well. On other injuries, we did a camera proctology exam earlier this morning. There are several tears in the rectal mucosa, but the basement membrane seems to be intact. We stored a semen sample we recovered for future study. We also recovered some semen vaginally for DNA analysis for proof of guilt. I'm about to arrange for psychological counseling for full psychological recovery. It is pretty much standard practice. I'm sure as hell hope the law gets the guys that did this. We see more and more cases like this every year. Not nearly enough are brought to justice. We hope none of them have transmitted HIV. I have ordered prophylactic antibiotics for syphilis, gonorrhea, chlamydia, and other bacterial susceptible diseases. We don't have a vaccination history for papillomavirus, so I am considering ordering one of those. The vaccine does offer some protection against the most common strains."

"Thank you, Doctor. I was vaccinated some years ago when I was in my twenties."

"In that case, Mrs. Bradley, I'll order a booster for you. I'm sure your immunity has waned, and the vaccine hasn't been highly immunogenic. Nevertheless, it would be an excellent medical move. We'll do it this afternoon so you won't feel so much like a pin cushion."

"Thanks, Doctor, I know Gypsy is in good hands. I very much appreciate your professional skills."

"And I appreciate yours, General. I'm aware of what you did in the recent troubling times."

Ethan smiled and nodded a thank you.

"How long can you stay, Hon," mumbled Gypsy.

"As long as you want or is necessary. I want to see these bastards caught."

"How are the boys handling it?"

"They are mad as hell, as mad as I am. They love you very much. You are their real mother. If they find out who did this before the law or me, I doubt the law or me will be necessary."

"Don't let the boys wreck their lives or ours by doing something rash. Let the law handle it. Promise me."

"Now Gypsy, you know that I am a man of peace."

"Promise me!"

"Love of my life, I make no promises. I can only promise to do my best to control myself."

Two hours later, Dr. Thornton returns to Gypsy's room. "We have heard from all hands. Our orthopedic surgeon said 'it's a piece of cake.' He'll put a small titanium plate on your mandible. He'll approach it from the bottom of the mandible so you won't even have a noticeable scar. You're scheduled for surgery at 07:30 tomorrow. It will heal well, I'm sure."

27 January 2025, 15:00 hours

Ethan walked in with a bouquet of flowers and kissed his wife on the forehead. She smiled and glanced behind him as others entered the room.

"The surgery went without a hitch, General. Your wife is under sedation for pain, but she will heal without any expected problems. My colleague who did the surgery is around here somewhere and might drop in later. She has a few other visitors if she is up to speaking. Thanks, Dr."

The Sheriff and a deputy approached the foot of her bed.

"Well, good morning, Sheriff, Deputy Johnson," said Ethan.

"Good morning, Mrs. Bradley, General. If you are up to it Ma'am, we would like to ask a few more questions. We started at the Hoot Owl this morning, talking with the staff. We can't find one of the waiters, but that's not unusual. I'm sure he will show up sooner or later."

"Yeah, a whole lot later," thought Ethan to himself.

The security camera revealed a dark-colored van. Four men were involved. We have a tracer on the van. There are very few around here like that. One seems to have gone missing, and we have an All-Points Bulletin out on it. The owner is a single Latino male, not known for being a nice guy. He isn't at home either. We very much want to chat with him. Can you remember anything at all about the location where they took you, Mrs. Bradley?"

"I was blindfolded and gagged the whole time. They laid me on what felt like an old mattress. The place smelled of oil and gas like an old garage. I can't say for sure, but I think it had a concrete floor. They spoke mostly in English, but would occasionally lapse into Spanish."

The Sheriff and Deputy glanced at one another. The look was not lost on Ethan.

"You suspect something, Sheriff?" asked Bradley.

"In the past year, two high school girls were raped at knifepoint, with the same modus operandi. Neither girl nor their families would cooperate. They are terrified. We suspect the perpetrators threatened to kill them and their families. We have DNA samples from those two cases stored in the state forensic lab. I'll request a cross-match of the samples to see if they match. I hope a sample of semen was recovered from you,

"It was, Sheriff. It is frozen in storage here for shipment to the lab."

"Thanks, Dr. Thornton. I suspect the samples will match."

"Sheriff, if there are any suspects, is there any way we can legally get a DNA sample? Get a search warrant of their premises, cigarette butts with dried saliva, hair of a hairbrush, used condom or whatever? How about the owner of the missing van?"

"General, if we can find any shred of evidence that will allow the issuance of a search warrant, we will. We'll talk to the judge today. Can you think of anything else, Mrs. Bradley?"

"Not at the moment, but if I can recall something, I'll contact you."

"Thank you, Ma'am, we won't bother you for a few days. Get well real soon. General, Doctor Thornton."

The Sheriff turned to the Deputy, "Johnson, see if we can get any phone call records, even recordings, to and from Jesus Lorenzo. The truck, the garage description, being Mexican, might be enough to generate a search warrant. If NSA has cell phone records or recorded and digitalized calls, they can send us a copy. I'll see the Judge, you call the FBI and put the request to NSA through them. Tell the FBI Jesus is a suspect in drug running and child molester. If we get a search warrant, maybe we will get lucky enough to lift fingerprints at his pad. One other thing, General Bradley is one tough son-of-a-bitch. Even at his age, he could probably kick the crap out of three men in their twenties at the same time. He is a killer. Recon Marines who make general are as rare as 40-year-old virgins. He has killed a lot of men in a lot of ways, and some up close and personal, barehanded I'm sure. Don't give him any excuse to take you down. If you stand between him and a suspect, he thinks is guilty, he might kill you to get to him."

28 January 2025

"Sheriff, Deputy Johnson here. We hit pay dirt. Jesus and some guy named Manny, using code words of course so they would think they weren't being recorded, ordered a truckload of drugs from the Sinaloa cartel warehouse in El Paso. The NSA is making copies on disk, one for us and one for the FBI. I guess that means the feds will muscle in though."

"Good, let's welcome them with open arms. Marijuana we can tolerate, but no LSD, methamphetamines, oxycontin, or dangerous designer drugs. If we can get charges of drug dealing on top of gang rape, so much the better."

"Good morning Beautiful. How do you feel this morning? Dr. Thornton says you can go home as soon as you feel up to it."

"I feel much better Darling. When do you expect the crap in DC to be settled? "

"I don't know, Gypsy. I don't like the idea of a military coup seizing the government. The Vice President-elect refused to be sworn in. So, the next in line is, or was, the Speaker of the House. Still, the idiot now in the President's Office, the former Speaker of the House, is one of the Democratic loyalists. If they couldn't steal the election, they would possibly murder for it. It is anathema to the Constitution and me. I expect the entire election process was set up to be fraudulent but didn't pan out when the DNC lost. Of course, that is only my guess. My guess is also that it runs much deeper. There is a lot unknown that might never be known behind this seizure of government and power. I suspect Russia and China might have had a hand in it, but that is incongruous. The president elect was not a socialist; a half step away from restoring the Constitution, reversing the totalitarian type of government ruled by an elitist oligarchy with enormous wealth and power, the New World Order cabal. All military units were put on hold as I left, and I have not been contacted by my Executive Officer (XO) to report any developing situation. I just might resign and come home to you and the boys. I find the death of Commandant Schenken highly suspicious. The President wanted to reduce the DOD budget to the point where we could just defend the Continental United States. Maybe the military-industrial complex had something to do with the assassination. It is so big, though, and I don't know how they could keep any role in it quiet. The Council on Foreign Relations and the Bilderburgers are another story. Those bastards should be seen in the light of day. They should all be rounded up and coerced into spilling their guts on pain of death as traitors. I just wish to God we were better prepared here. Think I'll go grocery shopping for long term groceries, dried beans, rice, canned meats, vegetable oil, that sort of thing. I'll put it on the credit card and pay it off at the end of the month. My Assistant Division Commander for Maneuver is capable; he can handle the Division command if I resign. Today is the 28th of January. One week after the coup.

We'll take you home in the next day or two. DOD gets the hospital bill."

After the boys drove to school in the SR-5, Ethan drove into town and parked on Big Horn Avenue. Wearing a hoodie under a down jacket to reduce the probability of recognition, he casually strolled down Culpepper Street, noting names on mailboxes and neighborhood activities. At 10:00 hours and a temperature of 15+ degrees Fahrenheit, there is little of the latter. He noted which yards were well cared for, which had children's toys present and which were unkept. A row of four houses in need of paint with weeds in the yard garnered his attention. He feigned adding a note to one mailbox and noted the name of Felipe Deniz. Good enough, thought Ethan. He repositioned his car on an adjacent block where he would watch the houses.

At noon someone entered the third house. Ethan could not distinguish facial features due to a closely drawn sweatshirt hood, even with binoculars. After fifteen minutes, a sheriffs patrol car pulled in front of that house. Ethan recognized the deputy who emerged from the patrol car as the Hispanic one accompanying the sheriff into Gypsy's hospital room. After several minutes the deputy left. Ten minutes later, Felipe emerged and walked to a battered car down the street where he deposited a duffel bag in the back seat. It proceeded south on Highway 20. Ethan followed.

Felipe stopped at the McDonald's drive-in in Thermopolis and went inside. Ethan parked on the blind side of McDonald's parking lot. He slumped down in the seat as low as possible to reduce possible observation of himself. After twenty minutes, Felipe emerged, so Ethan nonchalantly emerged from his car and walked to the passenger side of Felipe's car. Ethan opened the passenger door and sat down.

"Hey Man, what are you doing in my car, asked Felipe? Ethan mumbled something half in Spanish and unintelligible but plainly held a $100 bill in his hand. Felipe climbed in behind the wheel and closed the door. Ethan held the $100 bill firmly in his left hand. Felipe pulled on it, took it for a moment, and glanced at it. Pretending to scratch his right leg, Ethan pulled up his right pants leg to remove a knife from its sheath, a cattle bleeding knife. It has a razor sharp doubleedged eight-inch blade. Its purpose is to be plunged into the thoracic inlet of cattle in a cattle chute on the kill floor of an abattoir, cutting the great veins immediately above the heart, so the meat bleeds clean as the heart continues to beat. As Felipe looked at the $100 bill, Ethan used his left arm to push Felipe's arms upward and plunged the knife into Felipe's chest just under the xiphoid cartilage, driving it through his coat upward, left and through the diaphragm into Felipe's heart. A wild look of surprise covered Felipe's face as Ethan moved the blade side to side, slicing deep into the myocardium. Felipe tried to scream but could not. The immediate loss of blood pressure caused circulatory collapse to the brain. Felipe lost consciousness and died in six seconds. Ethan wiped the blood off the knife on Felipe's pant legs and placed it back in is sheath lashed to his right calf. He exited the old car, reaching behind the seat to remove the duffel bag. He casually walked to his truck carrying the duffel bag. He threw it in the truck bed and drove south to the Wind River Canyon. At the second pullout, he turned around to observe traffic for five minutes to be certain he wasn't being followed and drove home. " One down and three to go, but why the deputy's visit to Felipe," Ethan wondered.

At home, Ethan examined the contents of the duffel bag. It was full of cash, drugs, and clothes. Ethan deposited $100,000 in cash in the gun safe and put the drugs he could not identify along with the clothes in a thirty-gallon trash bag; he drove into town and dropped them off in the dumpster behind the thrift shop. He arrived home thirty minutes before the boys arrived home from basketball practice. Sam, at six foot two inches and 180 pounds of pure muscle, had played tight end in football and was a starting forward on the basketball team. Josh, still growing at five feet, eleven inches and 175 pounds was as mean a linebacker as a rattlesnake. He was a feared guard on the basketball team, a starter as a sophomore.

"Okay, Dad, it's time. We want to know who did this to Mom?" What have the sheriff and the police told you?"

"They told me they would handle it, not to do anything stupid, not to go off on my own."

"What do you think, Dad?" "I don't know what to think. I don't know how capable the local cops are. Time will tell. Have you heard something? Anything at all at school?"

"No Dad, nothing at all." Both boys shook their heads.

Outside in the front yard, Sam asked, "Do you think Dad is holding out on us, Josh?"

"Nope, but I don't know how much he knows, what, if anything, he has done. It's not like Dad to take something like this without acting on it. He's trying to protect us, to keep us from doing something on our own. Sooner or later, something will come out. I wish I knew who to hit. We haven't wasted Mom and Dad's money on Kuk Ki Do lessons for nothing." (Kuk Ki Do is a Korean martial art that is not a sport. Rather, its philosophy is to maim and kill as quickly as possible. Very few karate studios in the USA teach it. It is considered the most lethal of all martial arts. All Korean soldiers guarding the Blue House, the Korean equivalent of the U.S. White House, must be Third Dan black belts in Kuk Ki Do as a minimum).

"You and me both, Sam. Together we can really kick some ass. Have you noticed how people in school have kind of stayed away from us since Mom's assault was published in the paper? Yeah, they know something we don't or else they are afraid of us. I don't know which."

Unknown to Ethan, several rural counties in Wyoming had formed informal militias over the last several years. Their rationale was to protect their homes and their local community. Those with prior military experience, both Noncommissioned Officers (NCO) and officers formed the core and leadership. Particularly interested were native sons who were former career soldiers who were eliminated from the USMC and US Army under earlier reductions in force. Many who had not reached retirement eligibility and were eliminated without any benefits for almost 20 years of service were particularly bitter about having to start over with new careers and their lives. The undercover FBI and other federal agents who were assigned to every county in the country made maximum effort to infiltrate such militia units. The natives who spent their lives in the county, who knew each other from grade school on and everyone else, were distrustful of all those who were not born and grew up there. Every effort was made to ferret out information on each individual who attempted to join such units. Most of the undercover agents were soon identified. Most were relative newcomers who had lived there for less than ten years. Their histories were examined and cross-examined in secret.

In some cases, their fingerprints were lifted by trusted deputy sheriffs and run through the National Criminal Investigation Center. Their wives and children were subtly questioned about family history in coffee acquaintances and church activities by other wives. Sometimes simple remarks made by spouses and children were sufficient to arouse suspicion. Those agents who had government jobs at all levels and met the criteria and whose history was suspect were identified in a year or two. Many had government jobs at local, county, state, and federal organizations. They were placed there by agreement between state and federal officials with the federal government paying for their employment. They posed as officers of the Bureau of Land Management, USDA, US Forest Service, state brand inspectors, highway and bridge engineers, state police highway patrol officers; a few even founded front companies, such as small construction, merchants, cattle and livestock traders, irrigation and state game and fish officers. No opportunity for deceit was left untouched. One of the most intractable problems was who in local and state law enforcement was legitimate, who was a real patriot, and who were turncoat officers and their snitches. Blackmail for past indiscretions was a common weapon used by the undercover agents to plant informants into these informal groups. Extreme suspicion with no trust involved was practiced by core leadership. The casual observation was practiced at every opportunity. Those trusted central members with computer and communication skills in information technology tapped phone lines and computers of all those who claimed true patriotism and desire to join the militias. Several of the more sophisticated technicians even figured out how to receive and record the cell phone communications of suspected agents. Some county militias attempted to recruit long-standing members of local law enforcement to gain insight on who might be providing information on members to federal authorities. On several occasions, when suspicions reached a critical point, a secret tribunal was held and how to address-or dispose of the suspected agent.

29 January 2025

"Alexi, put our evacuation plan into operation commencing tomorrow. Our embassy and consulate personnel have purchased a sufficient fleet of multiple personnel vans to load everyone in and drive directly to the port of embarkation for their respective city. In Washington, DC, that means Dudalk, MD. At Dundalk, they can drive the vans directly onto the freighter waiting there for them. Round trips from the consulates elsewhere might be indicated. All our embassy personnel and friends will leave at noon tomorrow. No stragglers allowed. No one will be left behind. Everyone must be out no later than 08:00 on the morning of 30 January regardless. Get all of our agents out. Send the coded message. The convoys are to take different routes to the ships according to the plan for each embassy and consulate. The helicopters are to be standing by for any disruptions that might occur."

The Russians have purchased an enormous fleet of vans through various useful idiots as well as embassy and consulate personnel across the country and parked them in a variety of garages in the neighborhoods of each consulate and the embassy.

Russian personnel had quietly shipped most of their personal belongings home through various shipments over the last three months. All they were abandoning was their furniture. Each Russian family and agent knew when and where to go. The vans departed the Russian consulates every five minutes to avoid arousing any kind of suspicion. Russian freighters especially equipped to negate the effects of EMP were in the appropriate harbors of the cities where their consulates stood.

08:00 hours 31 January 2025 aboard the International Space Station.

"Communication from Russian Central came in for you, Pyotr. I think you want to read this yourself."

"Thanks, Jack. Let's see. Hey, I am going to be a daddy again. It says my wife is about to deliver the twins."

"That's great Pyotr. I always figured you Russians liked big families."

"I'll check on Dimitri and tell him the good news." Pyotr climbed to the back of the ISS. He told Dimitri that his wife was about to deliver twins!

"That's great news! I'll get something of a surprise ready." Dimitri went to his so-called room and extracted a small syringe from his ditty bag. He put it in his breast pocket.

Hey Phil, I'm getting hungry. Are you ready for some breakfast? I'll think I'll plug us in some meals if you are. If not, I'll wait a few minutes," said Pyotr in perfect English.

"Sure, go ahead Pyotr, heat us up some phony food!" Pyotr took out two microwavable complete meals and plugged them into the microwave and set the timer for two minutes. When the timer dinged, Pyotr lifted the saran wrap off one and dropped it in the disposal. He lifted the wrapper off the second but glanced around to observe anyone else's presence. Noting no one, he poured a few drops of a colorless liquid on the second and resealed the saran wrap. He set both down on the table opposite one another. He began to eat the unwrapped one. Commander Phillip Kinnington, USN, senior American Officer on the space shuttle, joined him after a minute. He unwrapped his lunch and began to eat. Halfway through his meal, Kinnington began to choke. "What's the matter, Phil?" ask Pyotr. Kinnington was experiencing considerable difficulty in breathing. Pytor arose and went to the other side of the small table. He looked in Kinnington's eyes, felt his pulse, and called to the other two crew members, one Russian and one American. "Steve, Dimitri, come quick. Something is wrong with Phil."

The other two astronauts rushed in to examine Phil. Lieutenant Commander Johnston never felt the karate blow behind his ear that rendered him unconscious. Dimitri removed the small unbreakable plastic syringe from a zippered breast pocket of his suit. He felt Johnston's jugular pulse and injected two milliliters of saxitoxin into the vein. Their bodies were expelled through the emergency escape hatch into the coldness of space.

The Russian supply ship launched from Kazakhstan delivered two small missiles each containing a single twenty-five kiloton nuclear warhead capable of being launched from the ISS. They are there for back up, should one of the four submarine-launched ballistic missiles fail or be intercepted. Launched from the ISS, they would be impossible to stop. Pyotr guided the replenishment rocket to the docking module. As soon as he manipulated the operating boom to lock the retaining bolt levers in the slots on the rocket in place, Dimitri opened the hatch. He unloaded the fresh food and water, then the mailbag. It contained four printed microcircuit cards, one for each area of the United States which was targeted by the Submarine Launched Cruise Missiles. Then Pyotr donned a space suit and unloaded the assembly arms for attaching the missiles to the external surface of the ISS. After fixing the assemblies to the external surface, he re-entered the space station. Dimitri then donned his space suit and exited the

ISS. Next came the missiles which he carefully locked in place in their carriers. Dimitri would insert the printed microcircuit cards into the rockets to guide the missiles as required. They would watch the explosions from the portholes of the space station as the ISS passed over the continental US to determine if there were any failures. A message would confirm success or launch. Any such attack was bound to be successful because the National Command Authority would not have time to respond. The missiles would be over their targets at the preset altitude within two minutes. The nuclear warheads would detonate by altimeter triggers at the appropriate height of forty miles before the President could respond.

12:00 hours 31 January 2025, Boston, New York, Philadelphia, Baltimore and Washington, D.C.

The people on the streets looked up, looked around, and asked themselves and everyone around them, "What the hell was that"? It was as if a giant flash bulb went off over their heads. As they looked around in wonderment, some noticed all the electrical lights in stores and street fronts everywhere were out. All motor traffic came to a cruising halt. The vehicular collisions were innumerable as cars and trucks lost their power steering and power breaks. Many pedestrians were struck by uncontrollable vehicles. Ten seconds later a similar light flash occurred over Houston, Texas. Ten seconds after Houston, a third enormous flash occurred over Chicago. Another ten seconds, one occurred over Los Angeles. The first electromagnetic pulse blast, detonated from a missile fired fifty miles off New York City at an altitude of forty miles, blanketed the east coast from Maine to Virginia. The second blast fired from an SLBM in the Caribbean covered west to El Paso and east to overlap the panhandle of Florida. The third, over Chicago, launched from a Russian satellite 120 miles high and detonated at an altitude of forty miles, collapsed the electrical grids and all digital equipment of Minneapolis-St. Paul, St. Louis, Kansas City and east over Ohio. The fourth EMP, fired from a submarine off the coast of southern

California, destroyed all electronics in Los Angeles, Long Beach, and San Francisco north to Puget Sound. Every piece of equipment that was digitally controlled was fried. The bursts over Houston and Los Angeles extended deep into Mexico as well. Every piece of digital electronics not protected by a Faraday cage was fried. Simultaneously, both Russian and Chinese killer satellites in near positions targeted all American and European communications and observational satellites with laser beams or large shot, similar in principle to a shotgun that destroyed their communications capabilities, their solar panels, or their cameras focused on earth.

15:00 hours 31 January 2025, Kremlin Inner Circle of the Politburo

"What do our satellites show? They should not have been affected by the EMP, as they were not in a position to be exposed? Do we need to follow up with the space station or Strategic Rocket Forces Launch, General?"

"Comrade Premier, so far there has been no detectable response. Their Intercontinental Ballistic Missiles were fried in their silos. There have been no detectable signals for them to launch, at least nothing our satellites have detected. Their fleet of B-1B, B2 and B-52 bombers appears to be frozen on the ground. Their ballistic submarines at sea are being tracked and hunted as we speak. Those in their ports seem to have suffered from the EMP and to our knowledge, have received no orders to deploy. We are not aware of any communication to them by any means. Our attack satellites are maneuvered into position and have killed, so to speak, many of their satellites, particularly their communications and spy satellites. A few of their submarines are unaccounted for. Our naval assets, as well as air assets, are searching for them as we speak. So far, we have no reports of their locations. I will keep you informed Comrade Premier, of any further developments."

The loss of satellite communications destroyed the US Navy's capability to communicate with its fleets. The Pentagon was completely in the dark. Somehow, numerous naval ships were not protected against electromagnetic pulse attacks. Ship to ship communications was initiated by hand held high powered signal lights as used in World War II. Aircraft in the carriers lost all means of electronics, rendering them useless. Chinese submarines practicing Sun Yat Sin's philosophy of when you are strong, appear weak, suddenly went quiet, to become the quietest on earth. What little US Navy sonar that was shielded from an EMP could not detect or track them as they disappeared into the depths of the South China Sea and the Pacific Ocean? Releasing a signal buoy from the depths, they received the coded message to initiate attacks on the U.S. Pacific Fleet from their satellites.

16:00 hours 31 January 2025

India received word of the catastrophic attack on the USA through its embassies in Europe that were still operating. All Indian forces were immediately ordered to full alert, Condition Red, in anticipation of multiple nuclear strikes from China or possibly Pakistan. The Indian government did not know China's role in the attack on the United States but feared they would take advantage of the situation and launch a nuclear attack on India. The readiness posture lasted for two weeks until India grasped the full situation. Now, with China in control of the South China Sea and Indian Ocean, with Muslim Pakistan on its western border, and Shiite crazy Iran a few hundred miles across the Arabian Sea, India considered itself completely surrounded. A state of emergency existed, and all forces were mobilized. Whatever small arms could be found were distributed to Hindu young men in the civilian population, even those with no military training. Arms factories for small arms were ordered into massive production around the clock. Every kind of rifle that could be found and was operative was handed to those who requested one, no questions asked except to those who were known to be

Muslims. The armed Hindus now turned upon their Muslim neighbors out of fear of them serving as a fifth column, a cadre of religious fanatics destined to install Sharia as a state religion. Entire Muslim families were slaughtered throughout India except in Kashmir, where Muslims were a majority. In Kashmir, Hindus packed what they could carry and immediately began walking south and west. China ignored India for the time being. They had bigger fish to fry.

Upon reaching the position and depth skippered by the XO, Captain Jeremiah Billings, and the XO, Commander Frank Bower aboard the USS Minneapolis, opened the attache' case. Their orders were succinct. Every night at 24:00 hours they are to release a communications buoy from a depth of 200 meters in the middle of the thermocline. If no receipt of a meaningless scrambled signal by protected communications is received by 00:45 hours they are to reach a specific rendezvous point from which they are to launch all twelve preprogrammed ballistic missiles at precisely 24:00 hours. Their guidance systems of the missiles were developed for the exclusive use of the stars for positioning, rather than GPS modules using satellites. The target areas were not specified in the orders, only the launch codes. A CLEAR SKY WAS IMPERATIVE. No cloud cover over the submarine or target areas to confound targeting upon launch. Without clear skies over both, no launch should be committed regardless of any other circumstance.

Gypsy was leaning against the cranial portion of her hospital bed, raised to a forty-five-degree angle. Fortunately, the broken ribs were only greenstick fractures, not penetrating the lining of the pleural cavity. She was moderately sedated for pain, but still able to read the latest edition of Scientific American. A sudden bright flash of light came through her window. The lights of the hospital went out three seconds later. "What the hell was that?" she thought. The emergency power system did not come on. The interior rooms were in essentially total darkness. Only natural light that was shining through adjacent rooms provided any light. Surgeries in progress were disrupted. The hospital staff stumbled around into hallways only dimly lit by light beaming through the patients' rooms and exterior doors. Surgeons were all yelling for power restoration. Some elderly patients were screaming. The digital controls of the emergency power system were fried as were such controls across the country.

The Maintenance Director reached for the emergency flashlight he kept at his desk. His office was in total darkness. With his six-volt battery flashlight, he proceeded to the control room to check on the circuitry, wondering why the emergency power system failed to engage. The main power panel showed him only that all circuits were off. He repeatedly tried on different circuits to initiate power flow without success. Cursing, he proceeded to check the emergency diesel-powered unit immediately outside the hospital. Unsuccessful with the electrical starter, he tried to initiate power manually with no success. He paused, noting cars stalled in the middle of the street in front of the hospital. He returned to the interior of the hospital where the chief administrator caught him in the hallway, demanding to know what happened. All he could say was, "At this time, all I can say is that all power systems have failed. I don't know why." The public address system of the hospital was nonfunctional. He proceeded to the surgical suites to ascertain the status of the procedures in progress. Thankfully, he insisted on an emergency flashlight in each surgical suite over the objections of the hospital administrator who didn't want to spend a few hundred dollars for flashlights and batteries. Only by flashlights were the surgeons able to continue. In those cases where it was possible to close without proceeding, the astute surgeons did so. After five minutes without power, Gypsy had a sinking feeling of what occurred. An electromagnetic pulse attack had occurred, probably across the entire country. "Oh, Shit!" was all she could think of. Gypsy waited for an hour to see if power could be restored. When it did not come on, she very carefully rose from her bed and dressed as best she could then lay back down on the bed. She knew Ethan would do something.

The boys were home playing a video game when the power went out. Ethan was preparing lunch for the three of them. He recognized the disaster immediately, as the bright flash came through the windows. "What the hell was that Dad?" asked the boys.

"I'm afraid it was the result of an electromagnetic pulse attack high in the atmosphere. We have been plunged back about 200 years if it is multiple pronged and the entire country is affected. Right now, boys, get your holsters and magazine carriers on your belts. From now on, you are to be armed at all times. I'll open the safe. Thank God I had selected a dual-purpose safe lock, both an electronic opening that is now fried and manual dial that will allow opening via a standard dial combination lock. I'll get your Government Model 1911s out for you. Put them in condition one. Chamber a round and put the safe on as I have trained you. Carry two loaded magazines at all times as well. Finish making your lunches. I'm going to the hospital to go get Gypsy."

"Dad, aren't the trucks down as well? We never did get the spare electronic parts for the little truck"

"Yup Josh, Gypsy told me. I'll ride a bicycle. I'll take an AR-15 and go on the bicycle. Gypsy will have to ride behind me. It will take me a couple of hours, depending on how well Gypsy can travel on the back of a bicycle if she can ride at all. We'll probably wind up walking. I don't see how she can really sit on the back of a bicycle that has no seat. I'm not sure she can even walk. We might have to take a lot of rest breaks."

Ethan put on a down sweater, insulated gloves, and hat, put on his one-size-larger combat boots over an extra pair of wool socks, packed Gypsy's down coat, wool socks, insulated boots and a pair of insulated slacks in a backpack. He took a DPMS-15 out of the safe, pressed in a 20-round magazine and chambered a round, then put the safety on. He slipped on a shoulder holster and put a

Government model 1911 in it after chambering a round and putting the safety on. He put on a light down jacket because he figured he would be burning a lot of calories bicycling. Then he slung the AR-15 over his shoulder. He manually raised the garage door, took the bicycle off the wall hangers, and peddled off. Thirty minutes later, he had covered the eight miles to the hospital. He noted all the stranded vehicles on the road. Many people were standing around outside their vehicles in the cold, shivering, wondering what happened. Many had their vehicles' hoods up, wondering what to do. "Too bad they didn't carry emergency gear and clothing in their cars, they might have a long, cold walk home," Ethan thought. Ethan could never comprehend why the government refused to share vital information with the citizenry. He could only believe that the government didn't trust the people not to panic and require the politicians to address potential problems. That might cost money that would otherwise go to social welfare programs to buy votes keeping themselves in office.

While pedaling, Ethan had an interesting thought. "Why not a wagon? Maybe I could put Gypsy in a wagon and tie it behind the bicycle to pedal home?" He went to the largest hardware store in town where he found a large Radio Flyer wagon. He took a skein of rope as well. Ethan laid a $100 bill on the counter as the clerk jabbered away. He tied the tongue of the wagon to the frame of the bicycle and pedaled off. When he reached the hospital, Ethan put a lock and chain around the rear tire and frame. Inside he could appreciate the administration's panic. "Too bad," he thought. "They should have built a Faraday room around all their controls." He recalled that estimates of the number of Americans that would die, mostly from starvation in such an attack, would be between 250 and 280 million people. The cities are doomed. Only those in the countryside who could grow a vegetable garden and perhaps kill an occasional cow stand a chance for survival. He recalled that in medieval times, families usually only got meat once or twice a year, usually in celebrating some significant event. Meat was reserved for the barons, not the peasants. That's where the term "bring home the bacon" came from. The peasant family with the least domestic discord was awarded a pig each year on the estates of the nobles. How many Americans could defend themselves from roaming gangs on foot going through the cities and suburbs? Ethan found Gypsy in her room dressed in her clothes and lying on the bed, waiting for him. He gave her the garments he carried for her.

"Well, Ethan, it's happened. I don't know how it will all play out, but it isn't good."

"Yup, you are right there Love. We'll make it though, the four of us. We're prepared. Damned, few others are. I have no doubt we will have to kill some people real soon to protect ourselves and our food supply. I rode in on a bicycle and bought a wagon at Ace Hardware to pull behind it. You'll ride in the wagon." Ethan held on to Gypsy as he guided her out the manual door to the bicycle and wagon. Gypsy climbed into the wagon and felt like a little girl again, with a big smirk on her face. She sat face forward, hanging on the wagon tongue to keep the rope free and the wagon running straight. It was almost dark when they reached home.

The boys had already brought in the Coleman lanterns and stove. They filled them with fuel outside before bringing them into the house. They had one lit on the kitchen counter. Josh was fiddling with a small wind-up AM/FM shortwave radio he retrieved from the garbage can Faraday cage, trying to find a broadcast. Ethan and Gypsy were sure proud of the boys. They had already wheeled the wood-burning stove into the kitchen and connected it to the stovepipe previously installed by their grandfather. They had to take a board out of the ceiling to run the pipe up to connect to the pipe just on the other side of the ceiling. Sam had filled the firebox with kindling wood and was attempting to light it. Gypsy headed straight for the bed, and Ethan watched as Sam got the fire going. From now own, that wood-burning stove would be their only source of heat and means of cooking. "The Coleman stove will serve for supper tonight, but after tonight boys, we use the Coleman fuel only for the lanterns. You have done very, very well. I am proud of you. You're great kids. I expect we will be invaded. I am not sure by whom, possibly by millions of Mexicans in an unplanned mass migration looking for food and loot. China and Russia would have to cross oceans. I don't know if they are prepared to do that. That would require an enormous scale of resources. At any rate, things will never be the same, probably not in your lifetimes."

From the International Space, Station Colonel Pyotr Rubikoff watched with fascination, glee, and a touch of trepidation as the ISS sailed over a completely dark North America each night. Rubikoff wondered if they had done the right thing. *"Was killing our fellow astronauts and destroying a nation and people in the pursuit of world dominance for my own super tribe, right? What if someone, some nation, could do the same to Mother Russia? How long would it take before North America recovered? What would it look like? Is there any way the Americans could retaliate? He remembered his strategic military classes when Russia decided to violate the 1975 Biological Warfare Treaty by equipping their Submarine Launched Ballistic Missiles with smallpox virus to be sprayed over the United States from their nuclear submarines which prowled off America's coasts. Could/would the United States do the same? What if the Russian plan failed to cripple all communications with the United States' nuclear submarine fleet until their anti-submarine forces or Chinese forces in the Pacific could hunt them down and destroy them? What of the United States Carrier battle groups strike forces? Did the United States have a contingency plan for such a catastrophe? Thank God we did not have to use the missiles delivered to us here to be fired from the ISS. I am a soldier, but at what cost? Will we burn in hell's fires forever?"*

Even the backpack weighed fifty pounds, the man carrying it felt that it was quite light. Extremely physically fit, he smiled as he thought of the carnage just delivered upon the United States of America. *"Or should I say, what was, the good old USA."* He enjoyed his own thoughts so much that he laughed out loud. "Out here, who would hear me? Why should I not laugh? My country's main enemy has just been defeated."

Oleg had purchased a small farm in Greenbrier County, West Virginia when it came on the market several years ago. Or at least that was the name on the deed and the title insurance. Very few actually ever saw Oleg. He stayed in the house that the old couple had occupied for nearly sixty years as man and wife. When the elderly man finally died, their grandkids moved grandmother into an assisted living home so that the farm came on the market. The location was ideal. The heirs asked for a premium price for it and got it. As soon as it was discovered on the market, it was snatched up by Russian embassy personnel. Several hours drive from Washington, DC, the location in the mountains was perfect. It was within a mile and a half of Greenbrier.

The old house was renovated to some degree by hiring local contractors. A treadmill, weight bench with weights and several exercise machines were installed in the back bedroom. Oleg understood that he was required to maintain himself in top physical condition to complete his mission. It was used on rare occasions as a location for a love tryst for Russian embassy employees. The same vehicle with darkened windows was always used, no matter who was driving or who were the occupants. No contact with the natives of the area was allowed. Fuel was purchased before leaving Interstate 64, and the pantry was always maintained as well, stocked with food and liquor. An occasional embassy van brought propane tanks, plenty of canned goods, fresh fruits and vegetables and an enormous supply of Grey Goose vodka and American liquors. No one ever really saw Oleg. When neighbors came to call to introduce themselves, Oleg was never at home. Whenever the sensor and video camera positioned 500 meters down the road signaled an approaching vehicle, an alarm sounded, giving Oleg time to retreat into the woods behind the house if it was not an embassy staff car or supply truck. He would lock the front door and rush up the hill behind the house where he could observe the visitors. He maintained an AK-47, a quality bolt action rifle in a .308 Winchester cartridge, a 9mm Makarov pistol and a quality bolt action 22 long rifle. He indulged himself in occasionally hunting squirrels and rabbits in the season with the .22 long rifle. The others were kept strictly for nefarious purposes should armed violence become necessary. All of the property was posted, not that it initially meant much to the locals. After one or two ventured too close, a rifle round would buzz close to their heads. It didn't take long for the natives to realize Oleg did not like company. He was a caretaker really, but a very discrete one when the video revealed an embassy staff car approaching. He would make himself scarce, very scarce. He had a small log cabin, like a trapper's cabin, ten feet by fifteen feet 25 meters from the house. It was equipped with a propane four-burner stove, a propane driven refrigerator, propane space heater, and stocked with liquor and canned goods. He would simply "disappear" for the convenience of his seniors when they brought their mistresses. A television and stereo provided him with weekend entertainment. He loved American Western movies and had a library of several dozens of them to prevent boredom and possibly his stupid interference with the lovers. On the last weekend of every month, a trusted prostitute would drive herself to Oleg on a Saturday morning. She would leave late Sunday afternoon. With sexual service provided, Oleg would have no reason to seek feminine companionship among the natives.

Now, as he trudged along with his backpack, he relished the thought of unwrapping the motorcycle from its EMP protected cocoon in the small barn that had a room also shielded from the EMP and riding to the rendezvous point near Baltimore. Now, it was time for the completion of his mission. After eighteen months of essentially solitary life, he was glad to be done with it and return to Mother Russia. In his backpack, he carried a bomb, a very, very dirty radioactive bomb that was delivered by the prostitute on her last visit. He reviewed the explicit instructions that told him how to type in the key to give him forty-eight hours to escape. Detonated on the ground, an enormous quantity of dirt particles contaminated with radioactive alpha particles would be sucked into the low atmosphere, only to settle out, especially with the next precipitation. The alpha particles would rain down in a ten-mile radius. Beta particles included. Everything exposed would suffer massive radiation poisoning.

Oleg trudged with his backpack and canteen to just outside the Greenbrier Inn. It was a cover for the massive underground bunker that the administration and senior political leaders were to retreat to in case of nuclear war. Nuclear war occurred all right, just not the kind the government was prepared for. Now, the last application of nuclear war, of a more conventional type was deployed, the kind that was expected. The contaminated area would be uninhabitable for close to sixty years. If personnel were inside, they would be trapped forever. If they emerged, they would die within days of radiation poisoning. When Oleg typed in the last letter of the code, detonation occurred.

"OK Dad, how long will it be before we get power back?"

"Josh, in all seriousness, it might be decades. All of the transformers on the national power grid, the digital switching equipment, and only God knows what else, will have to be replaced. How long it will take to build the transformers and switches or buy them from who knows where and install them, I don't have a clue. Mom might; I don't. Without previous government preparation of replacement equipment stored in safe places where EMP can't fry them, we could be in the dark and cold for decades. About 350 transformers control our entire power grid. It takes two to three years to build them, one at a time. They are now all built overseas, I understand in Europe and South Korea. Siemans Company is, or was, the company that built them in Europe. They can't build any new ones while they are fighting Muslims. With our infrastructure, and our industry burned out, how would we pay for them anyway? Delivery? I see ten to twenty years or more before we can restore much at all; it might even take a generation to rebuild our country. If this is worldwide, it is conceivable that we have been plunged back to the Middle Ages.

I'm sure glad you boys cut plenty of wood this last summer, ditto for Mom building a Faraday cage for the chainsaws. We can tap any vehicle's gas tank for saw gas as long as we have two-cycle engine oil to mix with it and bar and chain oil. The gas supply might last a year before it turns to varnish. We'll have to protect most of all, each other and our wood and food supplies. I'm sure glad you boys are young, healthy, strong, and have pack frames suitable to carry wood up the hill. As soon as people run out of food in their homes, they will begin begging, looting, and killing for food. I expect it to start at any time. That is why I want you boys armed at all times. Keep your .45s in Condition One at all times. That means loaded round in the chamber, safety on. Sleep with your pistols under your pillows. People's refrigerators, deep freezers and electric ranges are useless now without electricity, nor natural gas for gas stoves and furnaces. The natural gas is pumped around by diesel-fueled pumps. They store only a twenty-three-hour supply of diesel fuel at the pumping stations. Without resupply, the pumps cannot run, and the gas distribution system will fail. From now on, it is wood heat. If your bedroom gets too cold, you can move your mattresses into the living area in front of the wood stove. I suspect; however, you will be warm as you were last night or perhaps with an extra blanket. We will start cutting wood in earnest as soon as the latrine is finished. We will start with the trees on our land and slowly work towards the neighbors' lands on both sides of ours. We want the trees down while the sap is stored in the roots. We can cut them into firewood lengths later. Right now, we just want them down so they can continue to dry out. As the weather warms, we can cut and split them into right-sized pieces for the wood stove. I really don't know how much will be necessary for a year's supply.

Without water, the toilets won't flush. That means we have to start building a latrine immediately. Sorry boys, but that means a lot of digging. We need to dig a pit about five feet deep, three or four feet long and two feet wide. As soon as the pit is dug, we'll start to build an outhouse over it. The upper foot or so of the ground is frozen, which means we will be swinging a pick and manning a shovel. You can take turns with the pick, alternating about 10 minutes each. The frozen ground should come out in chunks. In the meantime, anybody that has to have a bowel movement will have to take a shovel to bury their excreta and go down the hill. One of you will have to help Mom when she has to go. She will have a hard time going up and down the hill, let alone digging a cat hole to relieve herself.

On that note, I am not sure how we are going to do laundry for clean clothes. Sure, hope Mom stocked a lot of bath and laundry soap. I wish we had one of those huge cast iron kettles that hold twenty or more gallons. We could boil our clothes in soap water to get them clean then rinse them in hot water after that if only we had a large kettle or better still, two, one for soap and washing, one for rinse water. We better start saving wood ashes to make our soap. One of those books in the basement, in the Foxfire series of books, shows how to make a trough and drip lye from your wood ashes to make soap. I'm not sure how to preserve the wood ashes until we get a sufficient amount to drip the lye. We have to keep them out of the rain until we get a sufficient quantity to drip our lye. Perhaps we can store the wood ashes in a washtub until we accumulate enough.

Most people who haven't prepared will be dead in three months. A few might make it to six months if they become cannibals. None who haven't prepared will live beyond that. A big garden down below the hill is the reason I wanted all that land cleared and tilled in case we have to grow enough vegetables to hold the four of us over for a year or perhaps two if the first year is bad. We will, and we must kill human scavengers on sight to protect our woodpiles, garden, and orchard. Even from our neighbors. We will have to kill a rancher's cow sooner or later and hunt deer and make dried or canned meat for animal protein. Starving people will kill us for our food, even people we know. Remember reading about famine in the Bible? The two women who agreed to kill and eat their children? So, Josh and Sam, start mentally preparing yourselves. You might have to kill your friends and neighbors to survive. The only exception might be two young women of interest to you. I know that sounds really terrible and stupid, but if this lasts thirty or forty years, you will need mates. We will take them in as a family, as your wives.

With Europe in the throes of Muslims waging war on everybody else, we can't expect any help from Europe. China or Russia, independently or together in perhaps a temporary coalition, have brought us to this. I have no evidence, but I suspect North Korea has attacked South Korea in coordination with our destruction. There will be some ionizing radiation effects, although the majority of the energy expended will be as an EMP pulse. It will probably be enough to push the seriously immune compromised, the fragile diabetics, the HIV/AIDs infected, and others compromised into their graves. Expect to see bodies in the streets of the cities before too long. What would otherwise be harmless germs will become disease-causing pathogens very quickly in such people. In a few weeks, I expect infectious diseases to begin to take their toll, especially dysenteries of various kinds. People will die of dehydration in association with dysentery and consuming contaminated water before they die of starvation. There are Iodine 131 tablets we should be taking every day to protect our thyroid glands. Thyroid glands are the tissues most susceptible to radiation damage. After that comes intestinal epithelium, the lining of our guts. People will develop serious diarrhea, often sloughing the lining of the intestines, to the point of dehydration and overwhelming gut bacterial infections and death."

"Why, Mom? Whoever did this, why did they do it?"

Gypsy thought for a minute. "Well Josh, my guess is they wanted to kill us off without hurting the infrastructure. Maybe they want our farmland. We have the garden spot of the planet. We have such a variety of climates in the country, from semi-tropical to cold continental. They can wait for a little while for us to starve to death. The urban population will not last long at all. The surviving rural population won't stand a chance. Their timing is pretty good. The great majority of us will be dead by the springtime planting season. If they are prepared, they can move right in. That, however, entails quite a massive logistical effort. It will be the biggest the world has ever seen. I have no idea how prepared they are to do that. The sealift would have to be enormous. Perhaps they would conduct it incrementally. The coastal port cities on each coast hold millions of people I guess the invasion would wait for those tens of millions of people to starve to death so they could move in unhindered. God, what a cleanup mess that would be. How do you dispose of millions of dead? Make fertilizer out of them? Mobile rendering plants? Hardly. They would have to have detailed, intricate knowledge of our infrastructure and be ready to replace whatever is destroyed. To me, these problems seem insurmountable. They would require decades of planning and preparation; still, only God and the enemy know."

"Will there be any survivors? Will we survive?"

"Of course, we will. We are prepared. Others will survive as well, although in small, probably isolated numbers. For instance, the north Woods of Minnesota and Upper Peninsula Michigan will survive. There are lots of small farms there that have unlimited amounts of forest for firewood, thousands of lakes filled with fish, loads of deer, some moose, and even bears. Those farmers will survive, especially if they have draft horses and a plow and harrow the horses can pull. They can plow and plant and eat and live."

Both boys were silent and looked at each other. The precariousness of their predicament was sinking in. Noting their sudden fear, Ethan thought for a moment of a useful way to distract them. "Your Mom built that bicycle generator. In the basement, you will find several of Dad's old books on ham radio. I want both of you to start reading those books immediately. I expect both of you to learn Morse code and figure out how to communicate using the radio in the Faraday cage. There is a telegraph key attached to a nine-volt battery to learn the code. I want one of you on the radio every day for about thirty minutes. You can take turns, or one of you can assume it as a primary duty. It is between the two of you, but I want both of you to learn the technology. I have read that you can get around the world with ten watts of power on a single sideband with that bicycle driven generator. Learn it, boys. It is the only way to communicate with the outside world. Do not send, only receive for the time being. That will be our only contact with the outside world. Mom and I will discuss an antenna. She is most knowledgeable." Gypsy heard the comments from the bedroom and walked into the kitchen and sat down.

"Guys, when warm weather arrives, we will move the flagpole in the front yard to the rear of the house, immediately outside the sunroom. That will be the mast for the antenna. In the meantime, I will work on building an array so we can receive on multiple wavelengths. I don't know enough about radio hams to know what frequencies they broadcast on. It would be a great thing if we can pick up international broadcasts, both in code and voice. We will have to work on that. I'll start planning for the antenna so it will be ready when we can move the flagpole in warm weather and set it in a concrete base. It is a simple task to drill a hole through the wall to run the wire from the antenna to the transceiver. We'll prowl around when warm weather comes and see what materials we can use for an antenna array."

Ethan was right, at least partially right. The Mexican invasion was like an invasion of army ants. They just kept coming and coming by the thousands. Some crossed at the bridges but most simply waded across the Rio Grande. The Anglo population of El

Paso held out for a little more than a week. When the Anglo population ran out of ammunition, it was reduced to ball bats, shovels, knives, and hand to hand fighting. Ultimately almost all of the white population was murdered or driven into the desert. Many, if not most of the young women and teenage girls captured alive were gang-raped. Potable water soon became the limiting factor. After ten days El Paso was an empty shell of what was a city. A few individual homes held out because they filled all the bathtubs and containers they could with what water could be drained from the distribution system. The Mexican bodies scattered around a house identified those who held out. When their water was exhausted those close enough to the Rio Grande or other natural sources of water used household bleach to disinfect the water in double or three times the recommended amount to kill any pathogens. After the occupants of most homes were murdered or forced out of their homes, their houses were raided for food, bottled water, canned soft drinks, drugs, alcohol, and any precious metals and jewelry. Cash was deemed of no value; firearms were regarded as the ultimate prize. After the first few days, the invaders realized just how limited their options were. Many headed north towards Las Cruces, New Mexico. Some headed east toward the Guadalupe Mountains National Park in hope of finding wood, water, pinion nuts and cattle for food. Similar scenarios played out in smaller towns all along the Rio Grande. Presidio, Del Rio, Eagles Pass, Laredo, McAllen, and Brownsville soon became empty shells of towns and cities. Many tried to walk the 150 miles from Laredo to San Antonio. Not ten percent of those who started out survived. Fighting over water and food among themselves soon became a macabre spectacle of predator and prey. Houston was reduced to a raging battleground along racial and ethnic lines, blacks versus whites versus Mexicans versus any others. Some in the suburbs who were well armed and had swimming pools filled with water held out for about a month. When the water ran out, they too became desperate.

Those sections of the Midwest where wood and water were abundant, those backwoods areas of so-called rednecks fared much better. Some isolated areas of Appalachia and the northern tier of the midwestern states, similarly endowed with wood, water, gardens, farm animals and sufficient distance from towns, also survived. They had kerosene lanterns, Coleman type lanterns, wood burning cook stoves, garden tools, saws and axes, wood splitting mauls and sledgehammers, and home canned foods, so they survived to till and plant next spring. People In small rural towns fared a little better. Those who had relatives in outlying farms gathered what they could carry and trekked to their more rural relatives. A major problem arose when it came time to plant a garden. Almost all garden seeds were hybrids. The seed companies bred hybrids not only for better yields but also so that the seeds from the plants would not be fertile for future generations of gardens. Heritage seeds became a prized commodity for future gardens and survival. Many neighbors died at the hands of their neighbors when they attempted midnight raids for garden produce, especially for vegetables carrying heritage seeds.

The cities became utter jungles within twenty-four hours. With no energy from any power plants, and no natural gas for heat, electricity, or water, everything became untenable. With no water to flush toilets that soon overflowed with urine and feces, people started defecating in the streets, in open elevators and stairways. Those who needed daily injections of the type of insulin that required refrigeration were among the first to die. After three days, hunger and cold began to drive people mad. Neighbor turned on neighbor for whatever resources could be found. Furniture was burned in apartments which soon filled with smoke making them unlivable by ignorant people. Churches began to fill with people; some to pray and some to hope for food. Fires were built on street corners. Fights broke out for places near the fires. Hungry children unceasingly cried with hunger, but distraught parents could do nothing. After a week, the first signs of cannibalism appeared. That is when the devastation of urban populations really began. As people in cities died, there were few means of burial. Those homes which had yards and their owners had shovels buried their dead as their energy permitted, often in half-frozen ground. Without food, the gravediggers could barely manage to dig graves three feet deep. Apartment dwellers had no choice but to simply wrap their dead family members and friends in a sheet and lay them on the sidewalk or in alleys. As the weather warmed with the coming spring and more died, the stench became unbearable. In some single-family dwelling neighborhoods, a few of the more capable survivors piled the bodies at street corners where the probability of winds to remove the smoke and stench was greatest. Siphoning gasoline and diesel fuel from vehicles and mixing it in a 50/50 ratio where possible, they ignited funeral pyres.

One by one, the families on Bradley's street disappeared. Their Mormon neighbors joined the long trek; some of the non-Mormon families or family members walked into town seeking relief, never to return. A few simply succumbed to hunger in their homes. Some asked for food from Ethan and Gypsy but were refused. One or two threatened violence, but Ethan informed them that their entire family would be killed if they tried to carry out their threats. Ethan made the rule that the chainsaws would be used only to fell trees and cut the trunks into twelve-inch sections. Once down, crosscut saws and axes would be used to limb them for firewood to conserve two-cycle engine oil. Mauls and wedges would split the sections into sizes suitable for the wood burning stove. It was a tedious but necessary task, requiring several trips carrying firewood up to the hill each day. In early May Ethan decided to use gas to till along the river for a large garden. Gypsy and Ethan were concerned about the weather but said nothing to the boys. It was far more cloudy and cooler than normal. Both knew it was the result of far off nuclear explosions, the possible dreaded nuclear winter. They could only silently speculate that somehow; the United States had retaliated. The ground from the garden put in during the previous spring made it a lot easier. Ethan tilled, and the boys hoed, raked and leveled the ground. They staked out rows with stakes and string. They planted carrots, kale, broccoli, lettuce, cabbage, and more potatoes than anything else, with heritage seeds.

All prayed for a good garden to prevent starvation. The deer population was greatly reduced by hungry hunters. It reduced the potential for deer raiding the garden but also reduced the probability of venison. It would take four or five years for the deer to return to acceptable population levels. Cattle that were turned loose from feedlots and herds grazing on public lands soon became feral. Whenever a cow was sighted within a mile of the house, it was shot and slaughtered where it lay. It was boned out, and edible organs such as kidneys and livers were consumed fresh as quickly as possible. The meat was otherwise salted, made into jerky by drying or cut into small squares and canned with the heavy-duty propane two burner stove. The hide was scraped and the brains used to tan it as practiced by Native Americans. Ethan found a book on the method in his Dad's library. The climate was turning colder due to increased clouds as a result of the nuclear bombs detonated over Russia and China, but they didn't know that.

Right after a hearty breakfast, Ethan told the boys, "OK boys, after your brush your teeth, we are going on a treasure hunt. I'll tell you more in a little while. We will need shovels and perhaps mattocks down the hill. So, get out your leather gloves, warm jackets, and boots. Be ready to work. Once down the hill, Ethan said, "I don't know exactly what, but whatever it is, we'll find it. Look on every side of every tree more than a foot in diameter. Look for a blaze from knee height to ten feet high. When you find such a tree, tie a piece of this ribbon around its waist high." Ethan handed each boy a roll of blaze orange fluorescent marking tape.

"Don't yell and alert anybody who might be hanging around or still in their house, just come and get me and your brother. I'll take the north side of the clearing, and you take the south side. Josh found such a tree twenty meters from the end of the steps. Ethan carefully looked over the tree Josh found. It had a blaze cut on the north, east and west sides, nothing on the south side facing the small open field. Ethan checked his compass. He pulled a tape measure from his pocket and fighting the brush, measured off the distance specified in his Dad's notebook. "OK boys, get the shovels and start digging here. Don't go any deeper than two feet. If you don't find anything two feet down, go to one side. If nothing, move to the other side and dig again." Five minutes later, Josh hit something with his shovel. Digging carefully around it he uncovered a 36" long piece of PVC 40-gauge sewer pepe ten inches in diameter.

Sam came over to help him dig. They lifted it out of the ground. Josh went to get Ethan. Ethan came with a crosscut saw and let the boys take turns sawing off the end. Inside were two rifles, an M-l Garand and a bolt action Mauser 98 action rifle with a .30-36 barrel. Ethan looked inside the tube. He picked up the intact end of the pipe and dumped six bandoliers of ammunition in clips for the Garand. "Thanks, Dad," thought Ethan as he hung two bandoliers of ammunition on each boy and himself. He handed Sam the M-l and Josh the 98 Mauser that was customized into a sporting .30-06.

"Take the rifles upstairs and give them a thorough cleaning. I'll fill in the hole. Don't load the rifles just yet Guys.

"That's one cache," thought Ethan as he began filling in the hole. After filling the hole, Ethan continued to look until he found a similarly blazed tree. Stepping off what he believed to be approximately 10 meters, he began to dig. On his third try, he found another piece of PVC Schedule 40 plastic pipe. When he sawed the end off, he found a Springfield Armory M-1A, another 98 Mauser bolt action rifle that had been rebuilt into a .308 Winchester sporting rifle with a laminated stock, adjustable trigger, a 3-10X-40 mm variable scope and sling. As previously, he found several waxed paper wrapped boxes taped shut along with three magazine bandoliers for the Ml-A, with a 20-round magazine in each of the six pockets. When he looked into the PVC pipe, he noted the weight at one end that unbalanced it.

There was something stuffed at the end. He shook the tube so that two carefully wrapped packages fell out. He unwrapped one to find a Springfield Army stainless steel Government model 1911A1 in .45 ACP. He opened one of the taped packages to find it contained two plastic shell boxes, each holding 50 rounds of .45 ACP Ammunition. Ethan set it all aside and refilled the hole. He dropped the magazine bandoliers at the foot of the steps, picked up the two rifles and carried them up to the hill. He sent Sam down the back with a backpack to bring up the rest of the ammunition and Josh to bring up the shovels and mattock.

1 February 2025

President's Office in Beijing, China..

The Japanese ambassador has been summoned to the Office of the Chinese President.

"Thank you for coming, Mr. Ambassador. You will forgive me, but I will speak most bluntly. Without the United States nuclear umbrella and the United States Navy to protect you, your nation is extremely vulnerable. You are without nuclear weapons, and your Japanese Self Defense Force will not last a week in the event we, China, decide to conquer you. Most of your forces will be destroyed on the ground. You are a nation of over one hundred million citizens today, living on an archipelago that cannot grow enough food to sustain your population. How do you view your position in relation to the Peoples Republic of China?"

"I'm not at liberty to make any official statements, Mr. President. I must contact my superiors for guidance. I recognize the might of the Peoples Republic of China, and I hope we can continue in the most peaceful relationship."

"Mr. Ambassador, please inform your nation that we require complete suzerainty over Japan. If you fail to surrender to China, our Navy will completely surround your home islands within twenty-four hours, eliminating any inbound shipments of food, fuel of any nature or anything else, or any outgoing shipments of any nature. In short, Mr. Ambassador, your nation, will be under a complete naval and air blockade. Any attempts to alleviate your desperation by air will result in all aircraft taking off from your country will be shot down. We are monitoring every airfield in your country by satellite. You can do nothing but submit, attempt to hold out as long as your food supplies last or commit to war against China, a war that will completely destroy your nation. The choice is yours. Please inform your government. You have seventy-two hours to decide to submit, go to war, or wait and see."

3 February 2025

The Kremlin

"Are you having second thoughts about the 'insurance squads' Georgi"?

"Not at all, Vladimir. Those people will ensure the total destruction of political leadership. Why wait to see if any of the politicians and apparatchiks survive or make it to Greenbrier? Not that they won't have an unpleasant surprise when they arrive if they arrive at all at Greenbrier."

Proboff smiled. "Indeed, why take a chance on any loose ends. Let us be complete so that there is no rallying point or persons. The squads are well-trained and equipped. Local police forces will remain in their homes to protect their families. The military is totally immobilized. Let's be done with them."

A radio signal sent out from the Kremlin at 24:00 hours Eastern Standard Time, U.S.A. At 23:45 hours each night for two weeks, some apartments on second and third floors of apartment buildings in Washington, DC and New York City had a single wire trailing out of a window. It served as an antenna for short wave bursts radio signals from satellites. The recipients were Russian agents in scattered locations throughout the two cities. Those apartments held two or three-man teams of Russian sleeper agents. They had been planted in their environment, in ones and twos, over several years. Initially, there was only one occupant who would rent a satisfactorily large apartment. Over time, he would be joined by other agents, some entering the country legally, as refugees, others clandestinely over the Mexican or Canadian borders. All were fluent in English, and skilled in a trade or profession. Jobs were waiting for them in Russian front companies. Some had Russian girlfriends and some did not. Extreme caution had to be exercised in seeking American feminine companionship. In those instances, their brethren watched them like hawks. Some of the agents who lived on the second floor had bicycles that they routinely carried up and down the stairs. Other agents had rented private garages where they stored compact cars wrapped in appropriate materials to protect them from the electromagnetic pulse. These vehicles were to be used very sparingly, kept full of gas, and ready to move at an instant's notice.

They were the lucky ones. In each case, their apartment location or rental home was chosen with care, close to those individuals who would be their targets. Each apartment was quietly stocked with dehydrated and freeze- dried foods. Coleman camp stoves and lanterns with abundant fuel were stashed in closets. Short wave radios were kept wrapped in reflective aluminum blankets until brought out each night at 23:45 hours receive one-second radio bursts of code. Hidden in locked footlockers were AK-47s with hundreds of rounds of ammunition and hand grenades. They were brought in through diplomatic pouch, although some were smuggled in onboard ocean-going merchant ships.

These men lived close lives, constantly watching each other. They were the classic sleeper cells according to the definition. They were closed-mouthed, interacted as little as possible with neighbors or workplace personnel, and engaged in any activities that would draw attention to themselves. They read, studied, occasionally attended movies or theaters and played chess. They had no contact, indeed, no knowledge of other sleeper cells. Each was given a list of targets which were to be assassinated on receipt of the appropriate radio signal.

On February 3rd, they all received the appropriate signal. Their targets: political figures, but mostly members of the Council on Foreign Relations. Of the 2,450 or so members, most were located in New York City and Washington, DC. They included many so-called captains of industry, as well as politicians, bankers, bureaucrats of high order, and prominent businessmen/citizens, were espoused nationalism. Those on bicycles slung their AK-47s over their shoulders, took canteens, a liter of vodka, extra magazines, and hand grenades, and traveling together as teams, sought out their targets. Few citizens standing around who witnessed them dared not to stop or interfere with them after observing the Kalishnikov AK-47s. More than one mob had second thoughts when the Kalishnikov was swiveled around into their faces. These agents were never informed about the small amount of alpha or beta radiation that might pose a hazard. They were considered expendable. If they survived, they would be rescued later by specially equipped squads.

The Kremlin made the decision to evacuate their embassy personnel immediately prior to the EMP attack in spite of the potential warning. They did not want to repeat what Japan did on DEC 7, 1941. Consulates in other cities were not notified and left to their own devices. The Russian embassy discretely purchased a number of large passenger vans over the course of the year. All had been ordered with four-wheel drive and limited slip capability. They had their own carpentry staff line the garage compartments with appropriate materials to insure against their vans being incapacitated by the EMP. Each Russian staff member was allowed one suitcase as luggage, to be placed in the roof luggage rack. The problem would be negotiating around or through or somehow bypassing the dead traffic en route to Dundalk, Maryland where a Russian freighter protected against the EMP awaited them. Side streets, alleys, and even on the median of highways were utilized. Drivers had surveyed routes months before as part of contingency plans for evacuation. Looters were to be avoided whenever possible. Each van had a designated driver and a guard in the front passenger seat. He carried a Kalishnikov AK-47 with several hundred rounds of ammunition and three hand grenades in addition to his handgun. The vans were required to maintain visual contact with one another for mutual support.

Office of the President, Beijing, China.

Thank you for coming, Mr. Ambassador. Has the Japanese government formulated a response?

"Mr. President, my government recognizes the overwhelming military superiority of the Peoples Republic of China. My country, however, has decided to resist any and all attempts of subjugation by your country. We will fight with all of our might to resist you. To borrow from Mr. Winston Churchill's famous speech at the opening of World War II, 'We will fight you in the air, on the sea, and on the beaches.' You will ultimately overwhelm us, of course, but you will pay a heavy price."

The Chinese President smiled. He hoped that would be the reaction of Japan. He grew up on the stories of atrocities the Japanese had committed against the people of China from 1931 to 1945. He looked forward to the destruction of the Japanese people; not the land or the infrastructure, certainly not their technological centers and expertise, but the people. He remembered the atrocities of Unit 731, which waged a biological war against the Chinese peasants. No one knows the death toll from Unit 731; it could have been in the tens of thousands or millions. He read of Japanese officers having contests to see how many Chinese peasants they could decapitate with their samurai swords in one hour. In one documented contest, the winner decapitated 110 people. The runner-up decapitated 109.

"Thank you, Mr. Ambassador. Please consider yourself and your family under house arrest. You will be notified of any further action."

Within the fifteen minutes, massive radio beams penetrated the Japanese embassy in an effort to destroy or disrupt any communications equipment. Electrical power, water, and heat were immediately shut off. Sappers blew away the gates to the Embassy after a brief firefight with the guards. A main battle tank blew away the main door of the Japanese embassy. Chinese troops poured through the door, shooting anyone, both men and women, who did not have their hands raised. The people in the embassy who survived the assault were escorted into trucks. All files and paper and equipment within the embassy were loaded into trucks and moved to a secure location for study. The families of embassy personnel were taken into captivity. All were placed in an underground compound immediately outside Beijing. Chinese rockets rained down on Japanese airfields before the aviators could reach their planes. Chinese destroyers, frigates, and cutters steamed from both east and west to seal Japanese ports. Military posts, airfields, warehouses, fuel depots, storage depots of all kinds received intermediate range rocket strikes. Chinese surveillance planes kept a twenty-four-hour vigil over the four main islands. Any warships that attempted to run were attacked by aircraft or rockets from Chinese destroyers and frigates. Freighters flying foreign flags were not allowed to continue to unload or receive cargo. They were ordered to immediately leave the harbors.

7 February 2025 Chinese Central Committee

"Comrade Minister, are things proceeding according to schedule?

Yes, Comrade. We give the Americans six months to starve, freeze, and kill each other off. The tremendous looting, rape, murder, and pillage, especially for food, fuel and potable water that our satellites have revealed has been incalculable. It has made

America a jungle, survival of the fittest. With the draconian firearms confiscation policies of the previous Obama administration and subsequent Democratic governments at all levels, there will be very little active resistance. A few criminal gangs might still exist but will possess only sporting arms and military-style small arms, no heavy weapons or explosives. Resistance will essentially be nonexistent. The first ship will carry sanitation crews to dispose of the cadavers. Specially trained troops will provide whatever security is necessary for them.

Our Chinese firms have manufactured virtually all of the digital equipment for the models of the American brand vehicles for the last fifteen years. Each year we have set aside five to ten percent of those parts. We have them cataloged and prepared for shipment. Our first priority is to establish shelter, water, and food centers for our troops. We can utilize their structures for the farmers as soon as the bodies are removed. Our second priority is to replace the damaged controls in the American made trucks, which will allow us to utilize them. True, it is a logistical nightmare, but we believe we can manage it. We will immediately establish distribution centers whereby our mechanics can draw on these parts. Our mechanics will initially use their own motorcycles built by us as part of their original shipment to retrieve the necessary parts for each vehicle they are repairing as required. A special messenger service of motorcycle riders has been established as a backup as required, to retrieve the parts so as to keep the mechanics busy. Repaired vehicles will grow exponentially in numbers once the process is started. Priority will be given to trucks. Portable solar systems will be utilized initially to provide them with power where possible, and gasoline generators will be utilized where solar is impractical. The EMP attacks on 31 January will cause many to perish by starvation and freezing. By the first of June, our invasion force will begin to maximize warm weather and use of solar power.

By the first of June, we will have replacement power transformers shipped and on location. Unknown but to all of us on a select committee, we have ordered one of the huge transformers that control the America power grid from Siemens in Europe and one from South Korea every six months through middle companies for the past few years. We now have several dozens of them that we have purchased on hand. We also initiated building our own five years ago using those purchased as models so that we will be able to restore a considerable part of the American power grid in a matter of months. Installation at select sites should be complete no later than one August, but we hope by 15 July, thus restoring more important parts of the power grid. To completely restore the power grid will require about 340 such transformers. That will require several more years.

By that time our sanitation crews should have buried all the dead in mass graves. God knows the odor would be overwhelming in the cities if they fail to complete that mission by spring. Initially, we will use our own disposal trucks, but as more American vehicles are repaired, they will be put to this use. That is what I mean by exponential growth in the completion of the disposal process as more and more of our people make the voyage. We are training and enlarging our disposal cadre to ensure maximum haste in the cleanup. Mass graves will be created in city parks as a matter of convenience. Burial at sea has also been discussed. Of special use for this will be the garbage trucks, apropos, don't you think? These sanitation trucks will be utilized as well as all other dump trucks and others that can be pressed into service.

The first convoys will sail from several of our ports to arrive in Long Beach, San Diego, San Francisco, and Seattle to immediately establish bridgeheads. Each of our oil tankers converts to troop carriers that will carry thousands of troops and will steam in a continuous circle between our ports and the Americans. We can have one million or more people in what was the USA by fall. We intend to push into the Midwest as rapidly as possible so we can be ready to plow and plant by spring. Repairing their farm equipment is a high priority for the Midwest region. While their food stores will be empty, their grain elevators will still be full and free-ranging livestock will provide some protein for our troops. Converting our ships into modules so that they can carry troops or cargo in any combination was brilliant. They can be divided into sections and modules installed, making A, B, C, D units essentially independent of each other. Modular kitchen units, sleeping units, latrines on deck, storage, refrigeration units, dry goods storage, tailored to the needs of the moment allowed battalion commanders complete control.

We believe our air-independent submarine force is more than capable of sinking the U.S. Pacific Fleet. Recall the exercise in the North Atlantic in 2015 when a single French nuclear submarine sank 11 of the 13 ships of the U.S. Atlantic fleet. Our submarines are much more numerous, smaller, quieter and far more lethal than the so-called killer antisubmarine submarines of the U.S. Navy. Much of our fleet has been sitting quietly on the ocean floor, rising only on occasional nights to recharge batteries and air tanks through snorkeling. Thus, their locations are invisible to American satellites. The Americans will not be allowed to come close enough to our shores for the launch of their carrier-based aircraft. Their President Obama curtailed Their sea-launched ballistic missile program. What they have is outmoded and vulnerable to our anti-missiles systems at any rate. Their ships and aircraft simply cannot communicate one with another.

One curious thing has arisen. Somehow, Iran is aware of our plans to occupy the United States. The Iranians are now demanding that we include them in the occupation of North America. They have given us no good reason why we should do so. Our Russian friends have had about enough of the Iranian intransigence along their southern border. Iran's continued support of Shiite guerilla warfare along their southern border will probably come to an end in the immediate to intermediate future. Their Shiite fanaticism has invoked retaliatory concerns. I would not be surprised if our Russian friends used tactical nuclear weapons against Iranian nuclear facilities and some of their major cities. It is felt that the majority of the Iranian population has had enough of the Revolutionary Guards fanaticism. Perhaps the Guards units feel the same way. No doubt they will try and blame any attack on the Americans.

Our Russian friends are closing in on Eastern Europe as we speak. The Baltic states of Lithuania, Estonia, and Latvia are the first that will succumb as Spetnaz units have been in place for some time and up to 45 percent of some of their populations are of ethnic Russian origin.

No doubt they will welcome their Russian brethren with open arms and gladly return to the Russian, nay, Soviet Union, fold. NATO is useless and will not be able to defend itself against the Russian steamroller. We believe the western European countries of France, Italy, Spain, the United Kingdom, and the Scandinavian countries will welcome the Russians as a better alternative to the rioting, raping and burning the Muslims are conducting against Christians in their major cities. We are not so certain about Germany. Hopefully, the Russians will be more polite. Time will tell.

The American Strategic Air Command is laughable. They thought they could reach us with outdated heavy bombers, B-52s, albeit they claim they are upgraded with avionics, and a hand full of more sophisticated bombers, the BIB. Three fourths of their bomber fleet are unable to fly. Their digital electronics are also totally useless since their so-called upgraded avionics are also burned away. They did not protect their strategic aircraft from EMP attack with hardened hangers because of the cost. They would have to fly low and slow over our borders. Our anti-aircraft missile system will blow them out of the skies before they can penetrate our borders. What is your assessment of the situation in Europe, now that the Americans have been neutralized?"

"Europe is in utter turmoil over the Muslim invasion. The stupid Europeans failed to realize they were welcoming a religious fifth column into their midst. Even with the massive crime waves of rapes, robberies, and murders of the infidels on their streets throughout Western Europe prior to the coordinated attack on the USA, they failed to result in the sufficient expulsion of Muslims back to the Middle East and North Africa. Can you believe it? Those idiot Europeans actually prosecuted their own citizens for speaking out against the acceptance of millions of Muslim refugees. What a manner of self-destruction! Muslims in the countryside have no concept of farming in the European climate. They don't realize that they will not be able to generate sufficient food or livestock production to feed themselves after they have liquidated the farming communities. Certainly, they cannot expect food shipments from their home nations. The house-to-house fighting continues, growing ever stronger as Muslims with small arms outnumber the European national armies. The Muslims must have shipped millions of small arms and tons of ammunition into the European nations. No doubt that after his conversion to Islamic fundamentalism, the Tyrant of Turkey allowed the use of his country as a pipeline for the shipment of small arms along with the millions of migrating Muslims into the rest of Europe. The European national armies can't use heavy weapons to good effect in house-to-house fighting. They are killing many of their own ethnic citizens. London, Bonn, Rome, Munich, and all across Europe, Iran has supplied massive quantities of small arms to be hidden in their mosques, that over time, the European national armies will be annihilated. Ignorant third parties funneled the weapons to Sunni organizations so that their origin would be difficult to identify. Sunnis would get the blame. Barred from ownership of privately-owned firearms, the European citizenry cannot protect itself. The fundamentalists are dynamiting all the Christian churches and charities. They are castrating captured boys who have not reached puberty. They have established houses of prostitution for their fighters, using kidnapped young girls and women. Their holy war is most admirably succeeding. Their economies are those of failed states, that is, nonexistent. Their paper money is useless. Barter, especially for food, is what is occurring. Russia is letting the Muslims and the Europeans thin each other out, much to their benefit. They have halted their advances on all fronts to let the killing there continue. Rather like killing two birds with one shotgun blast, wouldn't you agree, Comrade?"

"Of the United States, Muslims there will die alongside Americans in Operation Bright Flash. We must thank our Iranian friends for sending so many Shiite fundamentalists across the Mexican- American border, along with cash and weapons being stashed from California to Texas for transit north into the cities. Apparently, they willingly go to Allah, killing as many infidels en route to paradise as they can. Operation Bright Flash has affected much of northern Mexico, as much as the southern United States. The leaders of the Mexican cartels that controlled the drug and sex slave trade and human trafficking across the border are being ruthlessly destroyed by our agents. Mexico will be left as nothing more than a narco-state and perhaps not even that. We can easily control the Mexican cities if we choose, but we will not even attempt to control the rural areas. Most likely, Mexico will also experience the emergence of warlords on a regional basis. They will be capable of resisting any effort by whatever is left of any central government, the army, regional or local police forces. We will leave that to local warlords. Mexican citizens have not been allowed to own firearms, so they are helpless against the armed drug lords. Politicians controlled by the drug cartels will also be eliminated."

"Our political bureau has the program of seeking volunteers ready to launch on the first of April. Our propaganda machine will publish the opportunities for free, rich land in North America. Free for the taking, along with all the necessary machinery and structures for successful farming. We will advertise it on the radio and television across the country. We will show videos of the rich land available for taking at no cost. I expect we will have millions of volunteers flooding into the regional offices. Those farmers who have served in the armed forces, especially if they are active militia, have been identified and have priority. We will offer free land targeted to specific elements of our own population. Those from our southern provinces will be selected for the southern and southeastern United States, the gulf areas with their rice, sugar, and citrus crops. Our more northerly-raised citizens will be targeted for the Great Plains. Our wheat growers will live from southern Canada to Oklahoma. We lack the expertise in feedlot raising of cattle, but that will not take long to learn. No doubt their cattle population will, as they say, 'roam' on the Great Plains since they cannot maintain them in the great feedlots. They will have to turn them loose or let them starve in place. I don't think they will do the latter. Perhaps we should train some cowboys in the American style. Our populations from the western desert areas will no doubt like the southwest, although they might not be initially aware of the hot temperatures. Of course, we will have to contend to some degree with Hispanics across the border, but I do not see that as a major problem. Our armed forces will eliminate them on sight as invaders to the New China Republic.

We will provide food, and information on the American farm machinery and implements that are on the farms and ranches so that our farmers can learn as they settle in over the winter and replacement parts arrive to make them functional. Our city, dwellers, will have to wait for some time. We must clear the cities of cadavers first and re-establish the entire power grid before they can be inhabited. Food production must have our highest priority."

25% of the population of many rural western counties in the USA consisted of Mexican migrant workers. Officially, the percentage of migrant workers was 15%, but many illegals were hired and paid in cash because they worked so cheaply in the agricultural sector. They worked in the feedlots, did the ditch irrigation by hand, drove the tractors towing implements and drank ice-cold Corona beer at the end of the day. What little money they could save over and above their salaries, was mailed to Mexico in the form of postal money orders that could be cashed in American cities along the border or wire transfers or cashier's checks to branches of American banks in Mexico. By the fifth day of the attack, the employers of the migrant workers could no longer pay them or feed them, which, along with providing rooms, was a primary part of their pay. The migrants figured they had no way to return to Mexico other than a two-thousand-mile walk, so they began to look for what they thought they needed to walk back, and occasionally rape when they could find a vulnerable victim. Some had acquired firearms through private sales. Some had legitimate green cards, but most were illegal workers who figured they had nothing to lose by pillaging. Outraged Anglo citizens who managed to retain hidden firearms resisted. In spite of the hazards of the journey, many started walking south along the highways, mostly at night, usually in small groups. When they thought they could escape retribution, they would poach a cow and butcher it for as much fresh meat as they could carry. Second and third generation Mexican-Americans who maintained their Latino heritage through marriage only to others of pure Mexican descent, legal and illegal, were not spared out of fear.

Meeting of the Peoples Liberation Army Navy (PLAN) With Select Committee Members of the Central Committee of China in Peking.

"Admiral Shu, you believe you have no difficulty in defeating the United States 7Th Fleet in the next few days?"

"Mr. Premier, I am absolutely convinced the battle will be over in a matter of hours, not days or weeks. The Obama administration for eight long years allowed the United States Navy to stagnate. It has not maintained currency in electronics, in weapons systems, in maintenance, training, and personnel. All this negligence was to provide money for social welfare programs at the expense of the Defense Department and its global stance. Not only has its hardware declined, but so has the quality of its personnel. The best officers and noncommissioned officers left the service for more lucrative jobs and better working conditions as soon as conditions were personally favorable. The training was vastly reduced as a cost-saving measure. It is not a stretch to say that less capable officers man their Navy with inferior training and weapons systems short of maintenance.

Our Assassins Mace missile will obliterate their carrier battle groups that are out to sea in the first few minutes. Our submarine force and air force will quickly defeat the remainder of the fleet. Our submarine force, which has been on picket duty for several weeks, is now forming a cordon around the approaching American fleet. A "U," if you will, a wide semicircle, with the ends moving around to enclose their fleet in a classic envelopment maneuver. With their carrier as their central capital ship and the loss of its aircraft, one of the significant sources of their antisubmarine capabilities will be lost. Their missile cruisers are the next priority targets, followed by their missile destroyers and frigates in turn."

"What makes you so confident of such a swift victory, Admiral Shu?"

"Our Assassins Mace missile, as you know, is a hypersonic missile that travels at a speed of Mach 7, and is capable of carrying a conventional warhead or a small nuclear warhead. The Americans have nothing like it and no way to defeat it. It will overwhelm them. It has a standoff capability similar to a modern anti-tank round. That means it will penetrate deep into a ship before it explodes. We have armed it with a small nuclear warhead tailored for maximum heat effect that will literally melt the aircraft carrier into a useless hunk of molten steel. There will be no survivors of the extreme heat. All will die in one or two seconds throughout the ship. Sinking within minutes removes the threat of radiation contamination. All ordnance aboard will immediately explode for secondary effects. It will be fired from a standoff distance as a surface skimmer that is undetectable until it reaches the target. That is within seconds. There is no way to respond to it. Without their air assets from the aircraft carrier, our submarines, and air force aircraft, long-range bombers initially, from our island bases, then follow-on fighter-bomber aircraft, will work in coordination to destroy the remainder of the fleet. We will overwhelm them. For ten years our submarine fleet has practiced what was referred to in World War II as the Battle of the Atlantic "wolf pack" tactics of the German submarines. Our submarines will attack in unison and coordination with our aircraft to overwhelm their antisubmarine defenses. Our submarines, being smaller, more maneuverable, and quieter than any of the American submarines that specialize in antisubmarine warfare will swiftly defeat the few submarines that are part of the American fleet. Between the coordinated air and undersea attacks, the remainder of the American fleet has no chance. As added insurance should something fail, our frigate fleet will be standing by just out of range of their aircraft from their carrier as a follow-on force.

One thing that concerns me is my mission to control the Straits of Malacca. To place the resources necessary to enforce a toll on all ships for passage through the Straits removes ships and men and planes that I could use to hunt the remaining Americans. I believe we should delay controlling the Straits until we have completely eliminated the United States Navy. After all, much of that traffic is destined for Japan, which we now have under blockade."

"That seems good, Admiral. Make it so."

February 8, 2025

Telephone Conversation between Russian Premier Proboff and Chinese Premier Wu

"Premier Wu, there is no doubt the Europeans are losing to the Muslims in the streets. Europeans are defending themselves with shovels, clubs of every kind, hammers, saws, cricket bats in

England, and anything they can find that will suffice as a club. Even kitchen knives are being brought into play, mostly by women fighting off attempts of rape. The European armies are faring much worse than we anticipated. They are simply too small and cannot be in many places at once. The Muslims will return Europe to the Dark Ages with their fundamentalism. Can we afford to allow that to happen? Of what value then would Europe be to us? With NATO now an organization in name only, can we allow that to happen with Chechnya and the Iranian Shiite Muslims conducting guerilla warfare on our southern border, how do you suggest we handle this, Mr. Premier?"

"As you are aware President Proboff, our own Muslim populations are causing a good deal of consternation. I do believe, however, that we will contain, not crush it. We are unleashing part of our two hundred-million-man militia on them with the purpose of eradicating the menace once and for all. There will no longer be any adherents to Islam left in the Peoples' Republic of China. We expect to have this menace eliminated in about six months. Our problem with this is our shared border with the previous member states of the United Soviet Socialist Republics, the Central Asian Republics of Kyrgyzstan, Kazakhstan, and Tajikistan. Our informants tell of us of restlessness within these Muslim nations. We are uncertain if they would come to the aid of their Muslim brethren. If they can be quieted or influenced not to interfere, it would be most helpful. That way, we can continue our efforts to secure North America as our pantry. We believe that NATO without the United States in Europe is so hollow that cancellation will allow us to continue to pursue our grand strategy together and separately. With the neutralization of the US, Europe will be in the palm of your hand. You have Ukraine with all the graineries and all of the Eurasian continent north of the Black Sea.

"President Wu, I just spoke with the Iranian ambassador. Iran is demanding we include them in occupying North America. They have more or less demanded a specific, well-demarcated region of North America, a particularly verdant one for food production. I have informed the ambassador we will consider their request. They have no resources sufficient to even contemplate invading North America independent of either of us. Their request is ludicrous. Ever since joining the nuclear club, they have become increasingly belligerent. It must go along with their belief that the entire world must be bathed in blood for the return of the Twelfth Imam who will rule the world as a caliphate from Jerusalem. The continuing unrest the Iranians are committing along our southern border is only going to increase. They are supplying arms to Chechnyans, encouraging them to agitate for an independent state by combining Dagestan, Chechnya, and South Ossetia. How long should we tolerate their intransigence? They are waging subtle unrest in the independent states that were formerly part of the USSR. Having the fourth largest known oil reserves in the world gives Iran considerable economic clout, or at least it did. With Japan and Korea, Malaysia, Australia as major customers, they are financing jihad on a grand scale. So, Mr. President, what suggestions might you offer to end their campaign of Shiite fundamentalism? I am open to any recommendations you have, Mr. President. My basic question is how much the Iranians civilian population supports this fundamentalism. I do not wish to invade Iran alone, nor do I wish to use nuclear weapons so close to both of our borders. Could a revolution that disrupts the power of the mullahs be initiated? I would not trust an EMP attack against Iran. A massive chemical strike with nerve agent gases might be a better alternative. Will it require an invasion by us from the north combined with an invasion by you from the east, thereby splitting their defenses? Right now, I would prefer to consolidate our gains in Europe, as I suspect you would prefer maximum effort in your North American excursions."

"Thank you, Comrade. I will drink a toast to our continued mutual success. I must admit; however, I will miss the occasional American bourbon and Canadian rye whiskies as alternatives to vodka. Here is to our continued success." He tipped a glass of vodka to his lips and drank.

"Thank you, Comrade, let us ponder it as a last resort and entertain less drastic responses for the time being."

After hanging up the speakerphone, Premier Wu laughed. "Russia fails to realize what our strength will be when we own North America. We will be able to feed our population here at home, enjoy the United States' manufacturing and technological capabilities, as in Silicon Valley, its agricultural productivity, and place our now North American Chinese people in their houses and apartments without having to add additional construction. Canada will shortly follow. They have no choice. They are afflicted for hundreds of miles inside their borders. Only their northernmost reaches have escaped. Sooner or later, we will occupy them as well. Their timber, oil, iron ore, uranium, gold, and coal resources will be ours in due time. It will be a bipolar world for some time in the future. We need not worry about South America. We already own Africa with its oil and mineral wealth. Our navy controls the Horn of Africa and the Indian Ocean. Japan and both Koreas are forced into surrendering to us. I look forward to eliminating that little bastard in North Korea along with all his minions. Our control of the South China Seas allows us total, utter dominance over the Philippines, Indonesia, and the Malayan Peninsula with Viet Nam. What will Australia do?

What can Australia do-nothing! In the meantime, Russia will have acquired a very damaged Western Europe. Eastern Europe? Not so much. The Russians will have to rebuild much of what the Muslims have destroyed in Western Europe. Of course, they will have to control the surviving European populations, much as they controlled the Eastern Europeans after World War. The sum total of Europeans will fall under the heel of Russian boots. As for the Middle East, let Russia become bogged down in sand dunes and the martyrdom of Allah. They already have their own oil supply. To whom will they sell Middle Eastern oil? It is merely more cheap energy for them. No, the threat from the Middle East is really Iran. Sooner or later Russia will have to face a nuclear Iran, albeit one of very limited nuclear capability. Still, how many megatons of nuclear fires to destroy a country? Russian cities are mostly in the west and southern parts of their country. Iranian Shiite fanaticism will be Iran's undoing. As for South America, the land of corruption, coups and police states, perhaps they will be next."

The Chinese have immigrated to Africa in massive numbers, starting in the late 1990s and accelerating in the last ten years. Bribery of local and national African officials contributed greatly to increased Chinese immigration. Money paid as bribes to regional and national black African leaders flowed into bank accounts in Switzerland, Britain and the United States. Small towns became the sites of small factories which were expanded over time. When Peking felt the time was right, these towns expanded in physical size. They started out as small operations in rural areas, sometimes as developing mines for gold, vanadium, uranium, tungsten, cobalt, palladium, platinum and oil exploration. Some were agricultural experiment stations for plant genetics as well as commercial crops. From a few dozen initial Chinese efforts, the enclaves grew into hamlets, then small towns. Solar energy power plants were developed where feasible in African villages where the Chinese wished to utilize local labor to exploit the mineral wealth. The thirty-foot by thirty-foot concrete block homes the Chinese built for the African workers had ten solar panels installed on the roof of each house as a supplemental source of home power to supplement the power to the village solar power plant. Solar energy provided television and hot water to many Africans for the first time in their lives. They were furnished with indoor plumbing with water from locally developed wells and a water distribution system that was carefully monitored. Each home had a septic system, or in some cases, a small local sewage treatment plant was built. Many had never experienced indoor plumbing before. The Chinese did not neglect the urban areas. Realizing the value of communications and propaganda, the Chinese purchased or developed local television stations. Satellite dishes were not allowed. The African workers were paid a modest wage. Company stores provided inexpensive Chinese merchandise. What developed was similar to the coal mining towns of Appalachia in the nineteenth and twentieth centuries in America. Health clinics and in some cases, a small hospital were built.

The native Africans had never experienced such services from their governments as the Chinese provided. Within years the native labor force transferred their allegiance from their national governments to the Chinese managers.

In regions dominated by Islam, the workforce was extremely monitored for any Muslim discontent. Basic education was provided for the workers' children. Education was stressed by Chinese managers. While not required, education to the eighth-grade level was strongly encouraged.

The most gifted students were selected to attend a regional high school. If they excelled there, they were offered university scholarships to universities in mainland China. Political education was always part of the curriculum initiative at the sixth-grade level when the children could grasp basic political concepts. When Muslim fundamentalists began to demand the Koran be taught and Islam practiced, and education for girls be limited, they and their families were removed from the community. They were never seen or heard from again. The official explanation was that they were "transferred" to an unnamed district or community where allegedly Islam ruled.

The professional class who came in the early days of colonization remained to become citizens of their host countries, experiencing more personal freedoms than they experienced in mainland China. Now children of the first waves have reached adulthood. Educated in Europe, China, and the United States, the children of the professional class became the second and even third generation managers, engineers and agronomists. The process was not limited to the educated class. Many middle and lower-class Chinese also immigrated as skilled workers and craftsmen. They helped develop solid entrepreneurial enclaves in their adopted new homelands. Carpenters, electricians, miners, merchants, industrialists, educators, and agronomists, all flowed into Africa. Over time, the enclaves developed their own law enforcement capabilities. Many of the law enforcement community were, in reality, active duty military police in the guise of civilians. At first, the military additions to the enclaves were infantry platoons or companies, depending on the size of the enclave for providing security against bandits and Muslim raiders. Some African young men wanted to join the Chinese army units but were denied because of the potential for questionable loyalty. The Chinese deployed only light infantry and air assault units to Africa. The appearance of armored units would appear to be an invasion force, and a perception Peking wanted to avoid at all costs. Rather, it is to be a "stealth jihad" takeover. First, it would be an economic and agricultural effort by providing jobs and a raised standard of living and health care for native Africans, to help ensure their loyalty. The manufacturing and mining followed, then with the assumption of political power at the village level. Once the second and third generation Chinese established themselves as local leaders, managers, bankers, agronomists, they are encouraged to seek local political office through "democratically held" elections. For the black Africans, their jobs and continued occupation of their company, provided houses which depended on how they voted. Chinese petroleum engineers leading exploration teams spread across central Africa. From Leopoldville, they marched westward. Sometimes they built rough roads; on occasion a small airfield for resupply, medical emergencies, and equipment needs. Chinese army platoons provided security for each team of engineers. By 2023, there were over twenty million ethnic Chinese scattered across Africa south of the Sahel.

The flow of Nigerian oil at first came to a dribble as the Chinese force invaded Nigeria. The airfield at Lagos was the first objective. Lagos itself and its civilian population were relatively unscathed. The requirement was simple. Stay away from the airfield and the seaport. Security arrangements between African national governments and the Chinese government allowed Chinese army units to provide security for oil fields and other infrastructure but no more. The Nigerian politicians were taken completely by surprise by the landing of Chinese troops. Brigade and battalion-sized units of the PLAN soon became permanently established bases in the oil fields and mining districts. These were soon supplemented by Chinese air force-built airfields where Chinese helicopter gunships and troop transport and support aircraft became home-based. The Chinese Politburo had long debated how to eliminate Boko Haram and perhaps any vestiges of militant Islam from Nigeria. Biological warfare using a modified agent, such as Ebola or Marburg received serious discussion since they were endemic to the country. Chinese satellite reconnaissance for three years revealed all that was necessary to know the geographic centers of Boko Haram. Two Chinese cruisers accompanied the troop ships that landed two divisions of infantry well trained in jungle warfare. Their orders were simple. Kill anyone suspected of being Muslim or Boko Haram. Take what you like from the civilian population in the interior when seeking out Boko Haram. Resupply of the individual battalions will be by air if land routes are contested or difficult. Effectiveness was monitored by satellite.

Quick reaction forces delivered by helicopters and supported by fixed and rotary wing aircraft struck swiftly and without quarter. Initial efforts to separate terrorists from subjected village populations proved unsuccessful. Whole villages which had served as bases for Muslim terrorists such as Boko Haram or ISIS or ISIL were then totally destroyed. Over the years Boko Haram had slaughtered tens of thousands of Nigerians and displaced over two million. Many Nigerians starved to death at the hands of Boko Haram. As a Chinese battalion approached a nidus of Boko Haram, air cover was provided from the Lagos airport or one on the interior, and no one was spared. On some villages, deeper in the interior short life binary anti-cholinergic nerve gas was deployed from four-engine aircraft equipped with agricultural sprayers. With major air bases outside the capitol use of tactical bombing that was initially discarded as too ineffective became tactically plausible. The use of hunter-killer battalions seemed the most likely tool to use deeper in the interior. Afterward, all surviving villagers were executed when sweeps passed through the gassed area. Rape was permitted as was looting as long as there were no survivors. Livestock was released or killed for fresh meat and desirable foodstuffs were confiscated. Further support for Islamic fundamentalism withered on the vine. Diehard local imams were pointed out in some villages. They became hunted men. Several Chinese enclave towns built small Hindu chapels. The raising of pigs was encouraged by local enclave managers. They provided good dietary protein, a means of edible garbage disposal, and identified any Muslims trying to remain incognito. Christianity was tolerated but not encouraged. Catholic and Protestant missionaries were allowed to continue, particularly where they operated schools, but further proselytization was prohibited. In less than six months oil pipelines were repaired and fully operational. Chinese engineers had petroleum filling Chinese oil tankers.

CHAPTER V

GLANCING OUT THE WINDOW in the rear of the house, Ethan noticed a man loading firewood that the boys had previously cut and stacked about 30 yards from the shore. He was using a boat he had tied to the shore. Ethan grabbed his boots, coat, hat, and an AR-15 rifle, and headed down the hill. The man did not see Ethan until he was at the bottom of the hill. He started to walk to his boat. Ethan called out, "Stop or I'll shoot." The man didn't stop, so Ethan fired one round into the air as he ran to the man who was just getting into the boat when Ethan reached the bank. Pointing the rifle at the man, he told him "Unload the wood back up on this bank, now. I will kill you if you do not." The man gave him the finger and said: "Fuck You!"

Ethan angled sideways to him so that his body would fall into the river. The man had a surprised look on his face as Ethan shot him in the middle of the forehead. The body tumbled backward out of the boat and into the river. It broke through the thin layer of ice along the shore but stayed there. Ethan climbed into the boat and pulled it against the shore and threw the wood up on the bank. Then he pulled the boat up on the shore and dragged it into the woods. Sooner or later, the current would move the body downstream. Ethan wasn't worried about it at all.

Ethan slept well, snuggled against Gypsy. He realized now just how much he had missed her and the boys. He did not touch her but just snuggled against her as she softly breathed. He thought, "Just how lucky I am." He awoke at 06:00. He softly dressed and closed the bedroom door behind him. The boys were still asleep, but he lit the Coleman lantern by flashlight. The firebox still had coals in it, so he threw in several pieces of firewood. He opened the damper wide. It didn't take long before a roaring fire was going, which soon heated the kitchen. He dug out a skillet, found a pound of bacon in the still cool refrigerator and put three pieces for each son and Gypsy and two for himself into the skillet. He lit the Coleman stove and began to slice four potatoes. While the bacon fried, he took the lantern and dug through the old camping box in the garage that contained the camp cookware. He found the old wire toaster that held four slices of bread that can be used on a camp stove. He put on a pot of coffee on the second burner. "This will probably be our last breakfast of fresh bacon and eggs," he thought. When the bacon was fried, he placed the bacon on their plates then he put the toaster with four slices of bread on that burner. He put the sliced potatoes in the bacon grease when the toast was finished. Then he started frying the eggs as the boys got out of bed. Gypsy came into the kitchen and smiled. She didn't say anything but poured herself a cup of coffee. Ethan just smiled and gently kissed her on the cheek. Now, as the boys came out dressed, he set a plate of bacon and eggs and a piece of toast before each of them. They all sat down, and Ethan said grace.

"I'm going to take a bicycle and look around the town. You boys keep your loaded guns on and protect your Mom. She isn't well, and she should go back to bed."

"I'm going," Gypsy said, "Right now." She closed the bedroom door and climbed into bed.

"You boys take turns carrying a load of wood up the hill. The other stays in the gazebo with a rifle to cover him. I don't want anyone trying to steal our wood. It is up to you if you shoot somebody. I certainly would not hold you accountable in any way. That is your work, our wood and we have to protect our very limited resources. I should be back before lunch. Maintain the fire to keep the kitchen and living room warm. I love you, boys. You're great sons!'

Ethan holstered his .45, chose a Mini-14 rather than the DPMS-15, slung it over his shoulder put two magazines in his pocket, took the same bicycle from the garage and peddled to the National Guard Armory on the edge of town. He unslung the rifle and held it at the ready position as he checked the main door, then walked around the building inspecting and trying each door. They all had combination/key locks on them. Every window had iron bar guards across it. Ethan thought about what the armory might contain and how to enter it. "I'll need a portable oxyacetylene torch to cut the window bars, punch out the glass rather than fight the maximum security doors. By regulation, secondary doors should be barred on the inside as well. Where do I get a portable torch outfit?" he thought as he pedaled home. Once there, he asked the boys if they knew anyone on the street who might have a portable oxyacetylene torch outfit.

"Well Dad, we don't know him very well, but the guy next door is an oilfield worker. He might have an outfit. His name is Matt. I know he has ogled Mom a few times, but I don't think he ever approached her. I think he was a little afraid of us and by reputation, you. Why do you need an oxyacetylene welding outfit?"

"Frankly, Sam, I'm thinking of committing what could be construed as a federal crime. That is breaking into the National Guard Armory to see about small arms and ammunition that might be stored there. Of course, these are extreme circumstances, and I do wear two stars. Legally, as senior officer around here, I can take command. I'll talk to Matt. I really don't know how to use one, though. I might have to enlist his help."

"No need Dad. I learned to use one in a shop. If we can get our hands on one, we're good." Ethan smiled, 1 think I'll go meet our neighbor." Ethan knocked on the door, and Matt invited him in. The sun was sufficient to provide interior lighting."

"No, General. I don't have a portable outfit. What I have is a big outfit on the truck. I have no idea how we would get two big tanks to wherever you have in mind. They are full, and they are heavy. The welding supply company might have a portable one if you can make some arrangement with them. I don't know if anyone will be there given no electricity." "Thanks, Matt. I'll see if I can rouse someone."

After lunch, Ethan shouldered his rifle and peddled back into town pulling the wagon. It took him fifteen minutes. At the supply company, someone had thrown concrete blocks through the front window to gain entrance. About a dozen people were standing around outside. He could see and hear people inside rifling through the building's contents. Ethan parked the bike and chained it. He unslung his rifle as people watched him. He eyed the crowd and then climbed through the broken window. People inside stopped for a minute and watched him as he held the rifle at the high port and surveyed the situation. He walked slowly over to the man nearest him and asked, "Do you know about any portable welding outfits in here?" The man had a pile of clothes in his arms. "Nope, I don't know nothin' about nothin'. I just wanted to get some work clothes." With that, the man climbed back out of the window, looking at Ethan over his shoulder. Ethan asked the next man who said, "They can't keep gases in this building. They are in the building behind this retail store." Ethan nodded and climbed back out the window.

One man was starting to try and walk away carrying Ethan's bicycle even though it was chained, pulling the wagon behind it. Ethan said, "Put the bicycle down, or I will shoot you," as he pointed the rifle at the man's head. The man let the bicycle with the wagon still attached to it fall and backed away. Ethan unlocked and removed the chain, picked it up and carried it with one arm to the building behind the store, pulling the wagon behind it. The building was locked and the windows barred. He leaned the bicycle against the side of the building and walked to the door. He removed the magazine loaded with 64-grain soft point bullets from the rifle, removed the round from the chamber, inserted it into the magazine and inserted a different magazine filled with full metal jacketed bullets in the magazine well.

Standing ten feet away, Ethan put ten rounds all around the lock and door handle. People gathered to watch. Ethan pulled on the door handle which only gave way with considerable effort, held by incompletely severed metal. It finally came out in his hand after much twisting. He inserted his gloved hand in the hole and pulled the door open and walked in.

Inside he found a new portable outfit in a carrying case. He set it on a table and looked around until he found the appropriate goggles, gauges, welding gloves, igniter and some welding rods in a case. Other people started to enter the building but gave him a wide berth as they began to loot. He found some binders twine and duct tape and put the smaller items in an empty cardboard box of suitable size. He taped the box shut and put it in the wagon along with the portable outfit. With the rifle dangling around his neck, resting on his chest, he pedaled home. He stayed warm with the effort, in spite of the single-digit temperature.

That night as he snuggled against Gypsy, she put her arms over his chest. "Ethan, I love you. It was not my fault I was attacked. Are you blaming me for what happened?"

"No, I'm not. I desire you very much. It has been extremely difficult to lie next to you night after night and not hold you and make love to you. I have wanted to give you plenty of time and space to recover. I don't want to hurt you in any way. I know your ribs must still be extremely sore. I have been waiting for you to say or do something to tell me we can have wonderful sex again. Sex with you is the most wonderful of all my emotions."

"Close the door, Ethan. I'm ready now."

After breakfast the next morning, Ethan loaded the wagon with the portable welding outfit. "Sam, you and I are going for a little heist. Dress lightly, sling a light rifle over your shoulder and put on your .45. Grab your bike and meet me in the driveway when you are ready. Josh, you guard the home front. Take care of Mom and warn off all beggars. Be armed when you do. Let them know you mean it and will kill if necessary."

Together Sam and Ethan pedaled to the armory. The building was still deserted. "Sam, fire up the portable oxyacetylene outfit and cut the bars off the window. We're going into the building." Sam did. Ethan broke the glass out of the window, reached in and unlocked it. He climbed through the window and told Sam to pass the welding outfit to him. Sam then followed him through the window. After searching the building, they identified the arms room. The jail cell type door yielded after Sam torched the bars and lock off. They gathered weapons after cutting the chain, locking the rifles in the rack. Ethan looked over several lockers and wondered about the danger of cutting into them in the search for ammunition. He figured he could do the cutting after watching Sam. "OK Sam, exit the arms room and stand way back. I'm going to torch these lockers and see what's in them. Hopefully, I won't set off any ammunition." Ethan very carefully cut away the locks, first the padlocks then the cabinet locks. He hit a bonanza. Inside were four Beretta 9x19 mm. pistols with magazines. Sam carried cases that contained GI cans full of 5.56 ammunition to the window and passed them outside where Ethan loaded them in the wagon. They found a case of hand grenades and a case of 9x19 handgun ammunition. They filled the bicycle saddlebags with the grenades and packed what they could loosely around the cases of rifle ammunition along with as many rifle magazines as they could. Ethan duct-taped four rifles on top of the cases in the wagon. They each put a Beretta pistol in their belt, slung an extra rifle across their chest and pedaled home. Ethan pulling the wagon had to stop and switch bikes with Sam halfway home.

After a week, it became obvious that power would not be restored any time soon. Mormon families, together or in neighborhood-based groups, gathered to trek to the Bridger Depot warehouse in Lovell. As an organization, the Mormon Church was far better prepared for a catastrophic event than the Federal Emergency Management Administration, known by the pseudonym as FEMA of the US government. FEMA's preparations consisted of a massive storage of plastic coffins and gulag facilities scattered in strategic classified locations across the country. Cattle cars were prepared with manacles to transport large numbers of prisoners who might resist federal tyrannical efforts. Not all went to the government's game plan. FEMA and DHS strategic plans required 100% cooperation with the National Guard units in each state.

Such units could not be mobilized. Neither could Regular Army units. Military vehicles experienced the same loss of function as civilian vehicles. Nothing could move.

The Mormons set out on organized marches. Each individual carried as much food and water as they could reasonably carry. All non-Mormons were excluded unless they had something of value to contribute to the welfare of the marchers. A few were included because they contributed extra firearms and were known to be skilled in their use. Others were included because of specialized skills or professional expertise, such as physicians, dentists, nurses, and veterinarians. These people often carried their professional instruments and pharmaceuticals. March marshals on horseback maintained order and discipline. Those marchers who carried firearms protected the march route perimeter and flanks to support the marchers in case of firefights and to protect the columns' weaker members. Selected rest stations had been pre-planned every ten miles. Those who could not maintain the progress of the march dropped out to rest at the rest stations. They would join the next marching group. The more vigorous covered twenty miles a day. Others barely made it from rest station to rest station.

Nevertheless, good order and high spirits were maintained most of the time. "It's all God's work, God's plan" was the belief of the Mormon Church. Those in the Midwest began to move to Jackson County, Missouri. On rare occasion, an isolated family or small group was ambushed for food and women. The men and older boys were murdered, and the women and girls gang-raped. Those who resisted were killed after being beaten and raped. A few of the more compliant women were kept as sex slaves in hidden locations not too far off the line of march. Food was more important than women.

CHAPTER VI

14 FEBRUARY 2025

"I'M AFRAID OUR IRANIAN NEIGHBORS ARE CAUSING CONSIDERABLE consternation in our Islamic Republics, Comrade. Do you have any ideas on how to curb their insolence?"

"No, Comrade Proboff, not short of either massive assassinations of the mullahs, or nuclear destruction of the mullahs at the next meeting of their Supreme Council."

"And of the two, which would you recommend Comrade?"

"Frankly, a well-placed tactical nuclear device on their meeting would get the great majority of them in one fell swoop. We would have to plan the strike when the meteorological data is most favorable to blow any resultant fallout over Afghanistan and Pakistan or out to sea. I should think a strong westerly wind would be sufficient. A check with our meteorologists should provide an answer on the time frame. A medium sized device, say twenty-five to fifty kilotons, should also serve as a warning to our rebellious Republics which are clamoring more for Sharia and more influence on us here in Moscow. I think it would certainly get their attention. My greatest concern would be what our Chinese friends think. Certainly, they have enough trouble with the Uighers in their western areas. If we include them in discussions; however, it would probably tip our hand. We have not resisted their aggrandizement of the African continent. We left that for their exclusive use. They have African oil, uranium, cobalt, nickel, and gold. Iran is much closer to our borders than theirs. I would like to think they would not begrudge us Iranian oil. Besides, any elimination of Muslims from Afghanistan, Pakistan, and possibly Tajikistan would be welcome. The Himalayas should prevent all, or almost all, of the fallout from crossing into China. It will wash down the southeasterly slopes, ultimately flowing into the Bay of Bengal. Now would be the time to attack, as winter winds blow from the cold north."

"We have done well, Georgi. Turkey's withdrawal from NATO since it has become a Sunni Muslim theocracy has left Europe's southern flank open. Not that it matters much. Muslim Albania is tearing into Greece. Once potent fighters, Greece is now economically hamstrung through years of living beyond its means. The civilian men are soft, and the army is weak and small. Muslims are tearing Italy apart. Sooner or later, they will destroy the Vatican. That would be a shame. Perhaps we should rescue the art and library of the Vatican? What do you think, Comrade Medvedev?"

"I think we could send some of our Black Sea Fleet through the Straits with a modestly sized flotilla consisting of transport ships carrying several logistical battalions of trucks and troops to rescue the art wealth and library. They could land at Anzio and drive to the Vatican before the Italians or the Muslims could figure out our objective. After all, we would be saving Christian art for Christianity. If the Muslims take the Vatican, they will destroy everything. Perhaps two dozen transport ships and 100 trucks along with several heavy cruisers and one aircraft carrier would provide sufficient covering force. Five thousand of our better troops, but not Spetnaz, a tank battalion and one of armored personnel carriers I think would be sufficient. We can work around the clock and accomplish such a mission within several days if properly planned. After all, who cares if we slaughter hundreds of interfering Muslims or any pathetic Italians who try to stop us? The US Fifth Fleet will be unable to stop us. They would not consider it anyhow if we give them our objective when we approach from over the horizon. Besides, most of the Fifth Fleet is now stateside. Very few of their ships are on the waters. Most of them are in their Mediterranean ports or hovering just offshore. If they have any observational or communications capability left, they will recognize the validity or our mission and not interfere. Their chain of command is disrupted, and they will not act without orders from a higher authority."

"Excellent thinking Comrade, but just how many Christians do you think will be left in the world? Now that spring is arriving; there are very few Americans left alive. After the unusually bitter cold of winter months of February, March and first weeks of April, without fuel, hypothermia has killed millions. Millions more have starved to death and murder over food, water, and sources of heat has killed millions more. The Muslims are killing all the Christians in Europe they can catch as infidels. Russia will be the last bastion of Christianity."

Deputy Premier Chinkov chuckled. "How right you are, Vladimir. I had not considered the enormous casualties of Christians around the world. What of the Pope, provided he still lives?"

Premier Proboff smiled. "We'll leave the Roman Catholic Pope to the Muslims. Our Greek Orthodox Church will survive. Whether our Church will be joyous or sad is of no matter. Let us call in our military elements to discuss a previous staff study and plan that included such a rescue. The Russian Orthodox Church and the Russian people, and indeed, any Christians left alive in any other parts of the world, will thank us. Of those who are left, how many will renounce their faith in God? After planning is completed for such a rescue of the Vatican art, let us turn to a discussion of what to do about Tehran."

Medvedev was grinning like a Cheshire cat. "Our Chinese friends do not have a clue, do they not?"

Proboff chuckled. "They really do not appreciate the lion's mouth; they are about to enter. True, they will control the urban areas, but the rural areas, what they really seek, never! At least not without great cost, especially in Appalachia. Those so-called armed rednecks will play absolute havoc practicing guerilla warfare, eighteenth-century style against them. As I understand it, those so-called rednecks hid their guns from the government. They didn't turn anything in except the old useless antiques. As the guerillas gain mobility and heavier weapons from their Chinese tormentors, the movement will grow. The Japanese recognized the folly of attempting to invade the United States in World War II for that very fact. They will discover how well-armed rural America is. Thankfully for the Chinese, military service has not been required of the young American male as it was prior to the Viet Nam war. Think what difficulties the Chinese would have if, 50 million men and women, some young, some old, and some women, had prior military training. Clever how many American politicians feared a trained and armed population might turn against them. The Americans best hope is to annihilate the Chinese before they can deliver enough men and material to dominate the interior. If the Americans are smart, they will attempt to stop the Chinese at the Sierra Madre Mountains, then at the Rocky Mountains if not at the sea coasts. Only the southwest is open to them, but then there are the deserts. Of course the Americans will have a most difficult time of massing more than a few men in any one place at any one time with the appropriate heavy weapons. Possibly, what they might need is an old fashioned horse cavalry. That, however, is laughable under all but the most extreme environments such as heavily forested mountains. In World War II, the Polish horse cavalry lasted about five minutes against German armor. Of course, how much armor does China have and how fast can they get it into action? It would be difficult for horse units to deploy heavy anti-tank weapons.

Can the Chinese friends deploy drones, such as the American back packable Switchblade drone, to detect any resistance by more than a few individuals armed with sporting rifles?? The American cities will be littered with corpses who died of starvation. What a stench! Only the rural areas will have any survivors. 80% of the urban population will be dead in 90 days. 90% will be dead in less than six months. Civilian urban survivors will eat the dead. It will take a decade, perhaps two, but our Chinese friends will have to learn the hard lesson that if you wish to control or assume a large nation, you must kill everyone. Everyone, every man, woman, and every child older than five years, must be dealt with. Ah, North America for them, Europe for us; an unarmed Europe where the Muslims have done much of the killing for us. We will be greeted as liberators."

Coal miners in southern Pennsylvania and West Virginia and eastern Kentucky took the liberty of helping themselves to the dynamite, blasting caps, and fuses from the mines. This was particularly true in all of the coal mining regions of Appalachia, but also to some degree in northeastern Wyoming. Some were uncertain as to why they should help themselves, answering only to an innate feeling bound with the desire to survive.

As the number of urban dead began to mount, burial became a significant problem. In the northern tier of states digging graves in the frozen ground was impossible. City dwellers, apartment dwellers, had no option but to place the dead on the street. Sometimes ravenous dogs fed on the corpses. Some turned their pets loose and roving gangs of dogs formed. Others bludgeoned their pets to death and ate them. Suicides became more common. Apartment dwellers took the stairs to rooftops and jumped off.

Suburban families went scrounging for wood to build fires, in fireplaces of those who had them, in backyards if they did not. Those with barbeque grills tried cooking every kind of food they had on them. A few people wheeled them into their houses and tried to use them as a source of heat. All law enforcement officers abandoned their duty after the first day, choosing to remain at home to protect their families. Anarchy only increased with time.

Over the weeks as the cattle freed from feedlots spread across the prairie onto adjacent lands, some took the liberty of shooting one of them for fresh meat. Those who had propane barbeque grills or and camp stoves and home canning equipment, canned as much meat as they could and dried the rest into jerky. The more knowledgeable ranch families soaked the long dried thin beef strips in salt solution for several days prior to drying. They used their wood burning cook stoves to dry the thin strips placed in pans. It saved many of them from starvation until their gardens would flourish. Home canning was the first or second priority for rural families across the country. Their first priority was physical security, of defending themselves and their food supplies from starving neighbors and looters. Many men deserted their families in search of food and whatever loot they thought they could carry from wherever they found any, by force or theft. It was a repeat of the Great Depression of 1929-1940, only much more severe and fatal.

Feedlot managers opened the cattle pens and drove the stock out to roam free. They could not feed or water them without vehicles and power to run the water pumps. Many cattle attacked the haystacks and ensilage pits on premises. Hired hands tried to drive them from the ensilage so they would not overload on it, resulting in bloating. Severe bloat could result in death; relief would require puncturing the rumen to relieve the gas pressure on the heart and diaphragm. Soon the freed cattle sought water. They smelled the river and headed for it. Those who overloaded on the ensilage and now filled their rumens with water died of bloat. Those in greater distress from lack of water headed for the river without raiding the ensilage pits; they survived.

Ethan thought of Gypsy's family. He wondered how they were surviving. "Did I make a mistake in moving the family to Dad's old place? Should I, could I, have gone somewhere else for a greater chance of survival? Northern Missouri comes to mind; milder climate, greater garden variety of vegetables possible, longer growing season, a lot more wood, more rainfall, more steams, and natural waters. The EMP grounded all the urban and suburban people. They can't move to the country. If they try to move on foot, they will surely succumb to weather, starvation, and banditry. Best to be in place and prepared, first and foremost. Debts are meaningless. Food, warmth, protection, meaning possession of firearms and ammunition, and the skills to use them, are the key to survival. Perhaps I should have purchased a place in northern Missouri where Dad originally came from. Too late to move now. At least we have water, and semi-wild cattle will be all over the Basin in a year or two. Sure, hope there is a lot of fish in the river".

The third week of February a blizzard struck the high plains and Great Lakes region of the upper Midwest. The temperature plunged to -35F for overnight lows in Minneapolis. Six inches of snow followed. Those in the cities and smaller towns, especially the very young and the old who were without heat, froze to death in their homes. The living wrapped the dead in a sheet and placed them outside. Blankets were too valuable to use as shrouds.

Sam and Josh moved their bunk bed mattresses into the living room in front of the stove each night. In the day they moved them back into their bedroom which otherwise remained closed to conserve heat. Ethan and Gypsy just added another blanket and snuggled closer together. Each day Sam, Josh, and then Ethan carried two pack frame loads of wood up the hill.

One day in early March a stray cow ventured along the river, and Sam made a one-shot kill with his .30-06 from the bluff. Ethan took the liver, spleen, and kidneys and diced them into a five-gallon stainless steel pot. When the contents of the pot were boiling, he added flour, a little canola cooking oil, salt, and pepper and boiled it down to a thick gruel while the boys boned out the meat for canning and jerky. When he thought it had boiled long enough, he poured it into pie pans and set it outside to cool. He had read about farmers doing this when home slaughtering pigs. They would freeze it after it hardened. They called it scrapple. The farmers' wives would slice the hardened scrapple into a frying pan and serve it with syrup for breakfast.

Sam and Josh switched places. It was Josh's turn to carry a load of wood up the hill. Sam sat in the gazebo with the scope sighted .30-06 resting on a pad on the gazebo rail. Sam noticed movement in the brush about 60 meters from the woodpile where Josh was loading his pack frame. Repositioning himself and the rifle, Sam scanned the area for movement. He saw it first with the naked eye. Keeping his eye on it, Sam pivoted the rifle and pad to scan the area. He observed the first one, then two, figures attempting to move stealthily towards Josh. Both had a long arm of some kind. As Josh was attaching the bungi cords to keep the loaded wood in place, the two figures crouched. Josh mounted the loaded pack frame on his back when the leading figure raised a gun. Sam didn't hesitate. The 150 grain Winchester Power Point bullet designed for deer sized game caught the figure in the middle of the rib cage. Since the figure was kneeling the bullet had sufficient energy to knock him off balance, laying him flat. Sam worked the bolt and shifted the reticle to the second figure. The second man below looked up, just as Sam squeezed the trigger. The bullet him hit high in the chest. He too fell over and lay still.

At the first shot, Josh dove to the side of the path, hoping the load of wood would protect him. He looked up to see Sam scanning the scene with binoculars, looking for a third possible intruder. Then he watched for movement from the two people he just shot. He motioned for Josh to be still. After several minutes,

Sam waved to Josh to get up and bring the wood. Exhausted, shaking, scared, Josh said: "What did you shoot?"

"Two men who were about to shoot you. I wasn't going to shoot until one of them pointed a rifle at you. Then I had no choice but to shoot both of them. We'll wait for Dad and watch."

Gypsy came out the back door. "I heard two shots. What's going on?"

"Two men were sneaking up on Josh at the woodpile. One of them pointed a rifle at Josh, so I shot both of them." Gypsy said nothing, turned and walked into the house. Gypsy poured a cup of hot tea, added sugar, and sat down. *"God,"* she thought, *"What have we come to when sons have to kill to protect each other over a woodpile?"*

Two hours later, Ethan arrived home. He put his bicycle in the garage, entered the house, and hung his hat and coat in the closet by the door. No one said anything. "What's wrong," asked Ethan, reading their faces.

Sam spoke. "Dad, I shot two men a couple of hours ago. They were sneaking up on Josh at the wood pile. One of them pointed a gun at Josh, so I shot both of them."

"Have you checked them out?" asked Ethan. Both boys shook their heads no. "Get your rifle, Sam, and let's go to the gazebo. Josh, get your pack frame and rifle and come with me. You can bring up a load of wood. Sam, you can point them out to me from the gazebo when we are down the hill."

Once Ethan had a general idea of where to look, he took a Mini-14 and proceeded to where they lay as Sam pointed from the gazebo. Both were dead.

Josh, load your pack frame with a load of wood and take one of their rifles and head on up the hill.

Dark was closing in, but Ethan didn't want to wait for the bodies to freeze or rigor mortis to set in. He stripped them of their boots and clothing and wristwatches as fast as he could down to their feces and blood-stained underwear. He dragged the bodies to the river's edge and pushed them in with a long stick. Now with only a few minutes of twilight, he gathered their ammunition, the remaining rifle, and some clothes, leaving their bloody and fecally stained clothing behind. *"I'll get the rest tomorrow,"* he thought as he climbed the stairs.

"Do you know them, Dad? No, I guess you wouldn't."

"You're right Sam; I would not know them. No, I didn't even look in their wallets or for some other means of identification. I'll do that tomorrow. Both were older men. You did what you had to do, Sam. You saved your brother's life. That first one had a .270 Winchester pointed at Josh. The other had a scoped rifle in .30-06. I am sure they were going to kill him. If they had their rifles mounted to their shoulders, they meant to kill Josh for sure. They were close enough that there was no need to point their rifles. They could have observed Josh easily with the naked eye. Let's brew a cup of hot tea from the kettle on the woodstove." Ethan lied.

Apparently, it was a father and son, both armed and dangerous. Ethan silently prayed that the river would wash the bodies away before the boys could view them.

The next morning Ethan took two plastic thirty-gallon trash bags and a Mini-14. "Sam and Josh, I'm going down the hill. Keep watch from the gazebo while I gather their remaining clothes."

Their clothes were stiff with blood and frozen, but he managed to stuff them into a separate garbage bag for each. He looked through their wallets then threw them in the river. *"I'll soak the clothes in cold water and then boil them clean in hot water and soap in a tub. Gypsy can sew the bullet holes. Some day we will need them,"* thought Ethan.

Iranian armored columns poured westward into southern Iraq. In each hamlet, village, and town, they distributed small arms and ammunition to the Shiites. Local Shiite mullahs knew the faithful, Shiites who were willing to murder their Sunni neighbors. Iranian forces lacked such local knowledge and therefore decided to allow their fellow Shiites the privilege of killing their Sunni neighbors.

"Mr. Premier, Iran is invading southern Iraq, reported the Colonel General. We believe their ultimate objective is the destruction of Wahhabi Saudi Arabia, where riots against the Wahhabi royal family are occurring in epic proportions. The Saudi air force fell to waves of Iranian fighter bombers striking their airfields in low-level dawn attacks overnight. To date, no nuclear weapons have been used.

"Pyotr, what happens if Iran seizes all of southern Iraq and moves ground forces into Saudi Arabia? If they control Iraq, Saudi Arabia, and with their own production, they will then control at least 50% of the world's oil supply. That leaves Africa, Venezuela, and the South China Sea oil. North American oil is out of the question for the immediate future. China will soon control the South China Sea oil, much of the African oil, the shipping lanes, and most of Southeast Asia. China exerts tremendous pressure and influence over the oil-producing Central Asian Republics. While we can still supply our own needs and those of Europe with our natural gas lines and refined oil products, our pipelines will have to cross much of untrustworthy Muslim states such as Kazakhstan. They are vulnerable to guerilla attacks at innumerable points along their lines and pumping stations. It is conceivable, if they choose, the Chinese could cross the Amur River and invade us in the east. Now, much of the remaining world fears China. I wonder what India and Japan think of that! It is too bad Japan did not develop its own nuclear weapons program. They had the reactors to produce the plutonium. Why were they so stupid to depend on the Americans? Did they think the UN could control, or would control China? The riots in western China are increasing. Kazakhstan is becoming increasingly wary of China's intentions. It quietly put its small armed forces on full alert. Western advance by Chinese forces would require crossing some of the most mountainous, inhospitable terrain in the world. The least formidable land route would be over Kazakhstan. The alternative is the sea route through the South China Sea. Do they have the resources for such an enormous sealift? They cannot move so much so swiftly in opposite directions across the Pacific and Indian Oceans." Proboff said nothing. He just poured two glasses of vodka and handed one to the Colonel General.

15 March 2025

The USS Kansas City surfaced from the depths of the Norwegian Basin in the Norwegian Sea where she had quietly laid for two weeks. Unknown to Captain Chandler their patrol route was usually assigned to a fast attack submarine so it would appear the ship was not a boomer. Then Captain James Chandler opened his second set of sealed orders on the specified date.

If you open these orders, it means that the United States has been strategically attacked. The attacker could be either Russia or China or most likely a combination of the two. What it means is that the United States, as we knew it is destroyed. Consequently, your orders are to inflict maximum damage upon Russia.

Your orders are to retaliate for nuclear strikes against American cities. I do not know their official targeting priorities for our cities; I can only hazard a guess. Certainly, some of our cities have a higher strategic priority than others. Yours is a mission of retribution. I hope you will unflinchingly and without remorse carry out these orders as an act of revenge.

The targeting codes are hereby included in the attachment of these orders. You are to reset the coordinates in your missiles upon reading this order and launch when the opportunity is presented. Other ships such as yours have received similar orders. Do not hesitate to do your duty. Good Luck and God's speed,

George Reagan
Admiral
Chief of Naval Operations

By word of mouth, Captain Chandler ordered maximum quiet. They are going to sail inside Russia's territorial waters. He proceeded into the Barents Sea. He ordered the ship to rise to periscope depth. He ordered the radio antenna to be released to receive a hoped for a signal that never came. After fifteen minutes he ordered the antenna reeled and a return to 500 meters depth. He sent a runner through the ship telling the Executive Officer, the Diving Officer, the Chief of the Boat and a Lieutenant, the Chief Engineer, to join him in the officers' state room.

He read the orders to them clearly and distinctly. All missiles and codes are to be prepared for launch. At 03:00 hours they were to surface to confirm their position by sextant, prepare to receive any message that might be sent, and if no signal to abort received, launch all missiles and retreat to the depths. The missiles were launched one by one. The Russian Naval base at Murmansk, St. Petersburg (Leningrad), the Kremlin in Moscow, Gorki, Kiev, Archangel, Novogorod, Tula, Vologda, Vorkuta, Severomorsk, and the last at the Duma in Moscow.

The USS Kansas City submerged on running quiet and headed under the ice for the North Pole.

"Come quickly!" shouted Ilya. "There are mushroom clouds all over Mother Russia! We have been attacked. The Americans have surprised us. They must have been submarine-launched missiles. No missiles came from the continental United States. Our navies must have allowed some of their nuclear SLBM submarines to escape. They must have waited until our defenses were down when we thought there was no chance of retaliation. A surprise attack! Our country is destroyed."

"What of our families? What have we done, Ilya? We have initiated World War III! How will this end? Have we opened the doors to others? What will China's reaction be? Will China now turn on us? What of the Central Asian Republics? What will they do? Will they break away? We launched this war to gain Europe and eliminate a meddling United States. We economically took it down when we crashed their economy by going to the gold standard. How well have we succeeded militarily? The United States is no more. Now it is us and China."

The Russian astronauts gazed in horror as the mushroom clouds billowed over Russia. The International Space Station circled the globe every eight hours. Shutters snapped as pictures were taken at each revolution.

"Try and contact Space Center in Yekaterinburg. Perhaps they were sufficiently shielded."

16 March 2025

Captain Jeremiah Billings aboard the USS Minneapolis, brought his ship to the surface at 00:01 hours. No one aboard said a single word except the Commanding Officer, the Exec, and the radar and sonar operators. The submarine surfaced as quietly as possible. It lay still for five minutes with active sonar and radar to detect any other ships or planes within striking any detectable range.

Captain Billings in the conning tower spoke into the microphone. "Open outer doors." He scanned the horizon out of nostalgia one last time. "All hands below. Initiate launch sequence." Two minutes later, the Executive Officer stated "Launch sequence completed, will launch on your order." Captain

Billings ordered "launch number one." The missile arose propelled by compressed air out of the submarine. Its engine ignited 200 feet in the air and sped off over the horizon. The orange flame steaked upward, arched over, and disappeared into the night sky. "Launch two." And so, it continued until twelve SLBMs, each carrying a 475 kilo ton W- 88 warhead, steaked toward mainland China in low earth orbits.

Without a missile defense system, China's defense ministry scrambled jet interceptors to meet the incoming missiles. Launched from less than 200 miles off China's coast, not enough time for a defensive response. One at a time, the missiles detonated over twelve different Chinese coastal cities. Each had a specific area of the targeted city as its detonation point. The most important area of each city was incinerated under a weapon designed for maximum heat and blast. Military installations and port facilities, followed by political assets, had the highest priorities. One hour later, the USS Pueblo followed a similar pattern. This time nuclear facilities and political and command centers suffered incineration.

The third strike force, Captain Auburn aboard the USS San Antonio, remained deep and silent for the moment. One week later, Captain Auburn surfaced at 24:00 hours on a moonless night. He took a sextant reading from the stars to ensure he was in the right position in the Yellow Sea. He launched his cruise missiles uncertain of their preprogrammed flight paths and targets. The first five long-range missiles hit the dams of the Five River Gorges on the Yellow River. The remainder landed on Harbin, Ningpo, Shenyang, Darien in China and one on Pyongyang, North Korea. The USS San Antonio slipped quietly below to cruise five meters off the ocean bottom at five knots headed for the open Pacific.

Unable to destroy the incoming SLBMs traveling at five hundred meters above the surface of the earth, the furious Chinese Navy ordered five of their air-independent submarines out of Shanghai to cordon off the Yellow Sea. They formed a picket line from Qingdao to Gwangju, South Korea. They lay at neutral buoyance in the thermocline and waited, listening.

"Sir, I am picking up noises. It sounds like a submarine opening its outer doors!"

"Which direction, depth, and range, sailor?" "It sounds like they are about 8000 meters just off our starboard bow, Sir."

"Anything more?"

"Sir, there is definitely another submarine out there. I'm picking up some very faint noises, but there is definitely another sub close. I am getting just a hint of engine noise now. It seems, no, it just stopped."

"You're sure about opening the outer doors to torpedo tubes?"

"Yes, sir, no question in my mind."

"All stop! All quiet throughout." The USS San Antonio sat quietly for an hour. No one breathed any harder than necessary.

"Sir, I'm picking up faint engine noises, but it is coming from another direction. The range is about 10,000 meters, running quiet, from the east."

Captain Auburn did a quick mental calculation on the speed of a torpedo, both Russian and Chinese models. He figured if they were Chinese and launched any closer than 2000 meters, he could not maneuver fast enough to avoid a wire-guided torpedo. The Russian navy developed an enormous torpedo that blows an air bubble ahead of itself so that it essentially is travelling in the air. It is impossible for an enemy ship within range to escape it by the maneuver.

"If it is a Russian sub, I don't stand a chance. If they are Chinese, maybe!" thought Auburn. He figured if he was being boxed in between two Chinese submarines he might escape by aggressive action. Now, he figured his only chance was to maneuver, so they sunk each other or run, or both.

"Engine room, give me all the power you have. Sonar, direction, and reading of the first sounding!"

"Sir, they are at 7500 meters range, 265 degrees."

"Steer 265 degrees. All hands man your battle stations, torpedo attack. Exec, maximum speed, close the range. Forward torpedo room, load all tubes, wire-guided torpedoes. So, depth won't matter. Sonar, keep the readings coming."

"Sir, both subs are now moving, about 15 knots, closing on us. Sir, I was wrong. There is a third sub out there. It's directly in line behind the first or was, and it is moving laterally to be alongside the first sub. The first sub screened the second. The one that opened its outer doors is still in its position. It hasn't moved."

"Exec, target the two subs to the east as a priority. Launch on my command. Aft torpedo room, load all tubes, wire-guided. First Mate Marshal, the plot for the sub to the west. When you think it appropriate, open rear doors?"

Unfortunately, SLBMs ability to conduct undersea tactical warfare is limited. With only four torpedo tubes forward and four aft, a minimum basic load of eight torpedoes, their primary mission being strategic, self-defense options were eight torpedoes.

"Sir, range is 1500 meters and closing fast. The second sub is opening outer doors."

"Exec, launch forward two torpedoes at each submarine."

"Fire One, Fire Two, Fire Three, Fire Four."

"To all hands, this is the Captain. We are engaging three enemy submarines. I wish to thank each of you and am proud to have served with you. God Bless you all and your families."

The two Chinese submarines could not maneuver quite fast enough. The stationary submarine had kept its engines quiet and could not build power fast enough for a rapid turn. It turned to starboard and took the first torpedo amidships. The second torpedo hit the back half just aft of the propeller. The oncoming submarine tried a zig-zag to confuse the torpedo but was struck forward of the conning tower. It immediately broke in half. The second torpedo hit two seconds later.

Ten seconds later, a torpedo struck the USS San Antonio from directly behind. It immediately arced forward and turned straight down to the depths.

"All hands abandon ship."

Very few of the crew made it to the escape hatch using a rebreathing apparatus, and the great depths precluded any survivors. There was no time for decompression, so those who made it to the surface died of what is known as the bends- bubbles of gas forming fatal emboli in the bloodstream.

One hundred and twenty miles to the southeast, Commander Layne Boyington of the USS Audie L. Murphy stood in the conning tower, binoculars in hand. Named after the most decorated soldier of World War II turned cowboy movie actor, the USS Audie L. Murphy was a Virginia class submarine recently remodeled for dual duty, strategic and tactical. Boyington had not received any communication in any form from COMSUBPAC in Honolulu or anywhere else. The Navy screamed bloody murder over having one of its own named after a dog face soldier of World War II, but the Secretary of Defense only laughed when confronted by the Secretary of the Navy and Chief of Naval Operations. He said, "Heroes from all branches of service should be recognized. The Army doesn't have any ships, only tanks, so suck it up."

The Audie Murphy had two modified launch tubes each holding a Tomahawk missile, but it is first a fast attack nuclear submarine carrying guided torpedoes as well. The Audie L. Murphy was one of the first Virginia class submarines to be armed with Tomahawk land attack missiles in its forward weapons tube. This class of submarine was modified to carry twenty-four warheads per submarine. Now the Audie Murphy lay very silent in the Pacific Ocean, noise discipline in force, only the conning tower above the water line. One hundred and fifty meters in the air above the conning tower a helium-filled balloon held a basket with a transistorized radar capable of over-the-horizon monitoring. The sonar/radar operator "listening" to the battle one hundred twenty miles away described it to Commander Boyington through their headsets. Having no word from COMSUBPAC or any other higher headquarters, Boyington had been extremely reluctant to take any kind of action.

"Commander, two ships just got sunk by a sub, and one sub just sank the one that sank the first two."

"Sonar, bridge. Check the recordings of the vessels just sunk. See if you can identify it as one of ours."

"Sir, I am convinced that three of those are Chinese subs. There is no mistaking the signature of Chinese subs. One of them just surfaced to look for survivors." The sonar operator placed a disk with the recordings of all American submarines into his computer. The sounds of the sunken vessel matched those of the USS San Antonio.

"Sir, it was the USS San Antonio that was just sunk by three Chinese submarines. The San Antonio got at least two of them. It sounded like the San Antonio launched its SLBMS about an hour before being engaged by the Chinese. Sir, I take it we are at war, Sir."

"Reel in the radar balloon. Engine room, make ready for the surface speed of twenty-five knots. Clear the bridge." As soon as the hatches were closed, Boyington turned on the ship's intercom.

"This is the Captain. Apparently, we are at war. Our sister ship, the USS San Antonio apparently launched nuclear strikes against either China or Eastern Russia. At this time, I don't know which. The San Antonio went down under attack by three Chinese submarines, two of which the San Antonio managed to sink before she went under. I know some of you had friends on the San Antonio. Say a prayer for them. It is obvious we are at war with at least China. Now it is our turn. That is all."

CHAPTER VII

IN AN ALTERNATIVE NATIONAL control center outside Vologda.

"What choices do we have Comrade Proboff? Only by the grace of God are we personally saved. Being in your dacha away from Moscow saved us. Many areas of our major cities in western Russia are burned to a crisp. We cannot feed the people any more. People are fleeing the destroyed cities with whatever they can carry in the middle of winter. While many parts of the cities remain undisturbed, everyone is afraid of radiation sickness. No one will deliver grain or foodstuffs to the devastated areas. Our troops are reluctant to enter the areas to provide support. They remember Chernobyl all too well. Our winters are so severe the people will not survive without shelter. Those who remain on the outskirts of the blast area will surely suffer radiation poisoning. They cannot stay in radioactive areas. The countryside cannot support very many of them even if the country people open their homes to them, which I doubt. People are freezing to death on their death march. It is like Leningrad in World War II all over again except people can escape this time if they have the resources to survive-which they don't. All vehicle engines are magnetized. People are evacuating on foot."

"We will move our timetable forward a month, perhaps two, weather dependent replied Comrad Proboff. At the latest, we will move into Europe on the first of May with whatever forces we have left. Those positioned along the Baltics are relatively unscathed. We, our forces, will have to live off what is available in Europe. The Europeans have not experienced the devastation of infrastructure that Mother Russia has. We will colonize Europe as a new extension of Russia. We have always dreamed of Europe as an extension of the Motherland. We will bleed Poland, Belarus, and Ukraine as it becomes necessary for their grain and meat.

I fear we must revise the size of our country. Russia will now be European Russia. Far Eastern Russia is another matter. Between the Far East and European Russia, the vast expanse of our interior will have to be neglected for some time. All the territory east from the curve of the river Ob at Khanty-Mansiysk south to Petropavlovsk on the Kazakhstan border, to the river Lena, will have to be on its own. They have been in a different world ever since Genghis Khan anyway. They will have to muddle through on their own. We might not be able to even control much of the land to the west of that line.

No doubt Ukraine will continue to resist Mother Russia. Ethnic Russians in Ukraine will have to fend for themselves against Ukrainian nationalists. Let us hope we left enough small arms there for our Russian citizens. The eastern seaboard of Russia is devastated. Due to the enormity of China in area and population, they will survive. We will quite likely disintegrate. Between European Russia and Far Eastern Russia lies an enormous land mass we can no longer control. Our former provinces of the USSR are now independent nations that have managed to avoid nuclear destruction. Should they choose, they can exert undue influence, even advancing authority over vast regions of what was our interior. God only knows what has happened to China and how they will react. So Potyr, what do you think our plan of action should be?"

CHAPTER VIII

"GENTLEMEN, WE NEED A GOOD ANTENNA for the shortwave stoled Gypsy. The flag pole will have to suffice. We'll move it from the front to the rear of the house. That is the shortest route for the wire. There are two sacks of ready-mix concrete to stabilize it in the big garage. Ethan, if you or one of the boys will dig a hole about two feet deep and a foot in diameter, we'll set it by the sunroom. We can drill a hole for the antenna wire through the wall and connect it to the transceiver. The boys should know Morse code by the time the concrete hardens. I'll make an array for the top of the flagpole so we can receive multiple wavelengths."

Gypsy went to work on building a satellite receiver. She wired and soldered with a hand-held propane torch using scraps she raided from the neighboring houses. All of the commercial civilian satellite receivers from the various satellite companies were burned out. Her biggest handicap was not knowing what wavelengths the European satellites utilized. She perceived all of the American satellites were down, but the European satellites probably remained as possibly those of Russia and China. That way they were not limited to short wave radio broadcasts from ham operators. She was right in that all of the American communications and spy satellites were simultaneously attacked within one or two minutes of the EMP burst. Russian satellites were maneuvered close to American satellites and were destroyed either by a cannon-sized blast of #00 buck shotgun pellets or a high energy pulse that burned them out.

May 1, 2025

Russian armored forces surged out of the Baltic States south into northern Europe. The non-Muslim populations of Europe had been reduced by perhaps as much as 50% by the Muslims who declared jihad on non-Muslims. The general order to Russian troops was to kill on sight anyone who appeared to be a Muslim or simply on the mere suspicion of it. The order included women and children since they were often used as suicide bombers. Muslim women quickly shed their burkhas. Muslim men were very quick to shave. Native European citizens came out to cheer the Russian forces as liberators, an action they would soon come to regard with apprehension. Local communist committees emerged from the woodwork in France, Spain, Italy, and right wing nationalist parties, skinheads, emerged in Germany. Muslims that could flee across the Mediterranean did so as fast as they could escape the Russians. After a week of rest and consolidation, the Russian brigades pushed into France and the Benelux countries. With much of Russia destroyed and radioactive, the average Russian soldiers tended to view Europe as their new home. Russian soldiers were under strict orders not to provide arms and ammunition to the "liberated" Europeans.

Nevertheless, many French and German citizens acquired AK-47s and ammunition from dead Muslims and many were abandoned by fleeing Muslims. An act that in the future, would serve them well. British aircraft strafed Muslims attempting to flee across the sea. British destroyers and corvettes attacked boatloads of Muslims in the Mediterranean and the English Channel with a bitter vengeance while street fighting was still occurring in Liverpool, Birmingham, and London. No quarter was given by the British citizens or soldiers alike. Too many rapes of young women and girls and castrations of young boys had occurred for any show of mercy. British aircraft strafed Muslims attempting to flee along highways. Muslims and those who even appeared of Middle Eastern descent were shot or attacked and killed by whatever means were at hand. One British farmer began to use a pitchfork to skewer individual Muslims when he could catch them alone.

30 May 2025

Russia launched invasion forces headed for Anchorage, Alaska from the Petropavlovsk-Kamchatskiy complex on the Kamchatka peninsula. After all, Alaska was known as Russian-America until Russia sold it to the United States in 1867. The purchase was brokered by the Secretary of State Seward, and it became known as Seward's folly. Now, gold, timber, uranium, nickel, and other minerals made it easy to plunder.

1 June 2025

Commander Saunders aboard the SSBM USS Fort Worth in the northern Pacific.

"Send up a buoy to monitor civilian radio traffic. Use the frequency jumping mode until we can pick up something in a language we can understand. We need to replenish subsistence and consumables, so we need to find a safe home port."

By June the details of the Chinese grave diggers had cleared sufficient stalled vehicles and the corpses they contained from the highways to move east of Los Angeles. The stench in the June heat was overwhelming. Chinese planners had not considered the enormous effort required for the disposal of the dead. Bulldozers were critical for providing mass graves. The decision was made to forget about the corpses as much as possible. Push on to the east. The Chinese initially thought to use fuel supplies from depots and refineries in the United States. Belatedly, they discovered that all of their pump controls were digital and fried. Fuels had to be removed from storage tanks manually and distributed, which required a great deal of time. Farther north, from San Francisco to Seattle, the odor was not as nauseating but sufficient to slow their progress.

Another factor slowing their progress was the immediate acquisition of a taste for American liquor by the average Chinese soldier. No liquor store contained any, but the Chinese soldiers took to looting houses looking for liquor and beer, ignoring the often rotting corpses. Not many homes had liquor left, but that did not dissuade their attempts to find any. Inebriation became something of a discipline problem. The accident rate increased as drunken soldiers attempted to perform their assigned work. Chinese officers pushed even harder to get out of the metropolitan areas.

In Seattle and other more northerly port cities, the survivors in the Korean populations became a Chinese problem. The Koreans had a different mindset than the average American. They came from a land with a history of brutality and martial preparedness. Even the second and third generation Koreans, filled with stories of the brutality and destruction wrought on their native land by Japanese, were prepared to fight to the death. Other Americans would not. After the destructive riots of the last two decades, many, if not most Korean Americans, had acquired firearms which they had hidden.

As fast as Chinese ships could transit the Pacific and unload, mechanized forces proceeded eastward along the highways in front of an ever increasing number of Chinese civilians who were determined to initiate spring planting in what they were told fertile valleys of the American West. In areas just east of the coast, Chinese wanna-be farmers often burned the corpses they removed from farm and ranch houses.

Farming implements were slow in coming from China; their distribution was even worse. Replacement parts for the burned out electronics on American farm implements were routinely mismatched by brands and models. Many Chinese would be farmers entered the fall and winter seasons without getting any crop planted at all. They could not utilize the fertile river valleys and lands of the states of Washington and Oregon. The more industrious ones turned small garden plots by hand with whatever shovels and hoes were found on the premises they occupied. Then the lack of seeds for garden vegetables became a problem. The would-be Chinese farmers pedaled their bicycles into the small towns where Chinese administrators had set up distribution centers for seeds, mechanized implements, and food stores that were not forthcoming.

Reports of Chinese farmers being shot were initially very few and far between. As the summer progressed, they became more frequent. Somehow word of mouth reports of the Chinese invasion had spread to some of the rural survivors farther east. Some of these survivors moved their remaining foodstuffs to hidden locations as the weather warmed, so there was not a threat of their loss to spoilage.

Due to the dust in the atmosphere and massively increased cloud cover, the spring was not anywhere as warm as normal. The nuclear attacks on Russian and Chinese cities had resulted in something of a mild nuclear winter. Growing the usual gardens would be difficult. Where normal spring daytime highs in late March in the midwest were in the eighties, they were now in the sixties. Plants more attuned to northern climates should have been selected for planting. A nuclear summer was not considered in the planning.

Much of America's rural population was smart enough to prevent loss of their canned foods through the use of root cellars, especially in the south and Midwest, or moving it sufficiently close to their wood stoves to prevent freezing.

As sniping of the Chinese farmers increased in Oregon and Washington, they demanded protection from their local administrators. California's anti-firearms laws prevented California's surviving citizens from protecting themselves. The Chinese army initially refused to detail soldiers to protect the individual farmers at their occupied locations. The snipers, moving at night from ranch and farm to ranch and farm began to take a psychological toll on the Chinese in the outlying areas, ten or more miles from the Chinese administration centers began to move into these centers for food and protection. The administration centers were slowly being overwhelmed.

The Chinese government decided to bypass all but the smallest towns and villages as the army moved east. Leave the dead to rot in place. Move into the productive farmland. By late June, the decision was made for a massive push into the midlands where late crops might still be planted. Guarding the Rocky Mountain passes became a priority for surviving Americans.

Surviving ham operators who protected their equipment from the EMP with Faraday cages were broadcasting first the eastward progress of the Chinese army, than their civilian farmers. Chinese officials did not initially realize the threat that ham radio operators posed. When they finally recognized the threat, they began to systemically identify and execute those they could catch.

Sam had been routinely monitoring ham radio traffic all along. Ethan required both boys to learn Morse code. They could both send and receive at better than ten words per minute. Both had novice class licenses, but never really developed much interest. Ethan, however, recognizing the threat of identification and elimination, reinforced his order that no broadcasting is to be permitted under any circumstance. Sam began to pick up reports in Morse code on a single sideband that Chinese and European hams were broadcasting about the EMP attacks on the United States. There were unconfirmed reports of retaliatory strikes by the United States on China and perhaps on Russia. Some of them described the massive flooding of the Yellow River as a result of the destruction of the Five Gorges dams. Hundreds of thousands if not millions of Chinese were said to have been drowned or are unaccounted for. Confirmed reports detailed riots in many Chinese cities. Reasons were not specified, but Ethan deduced they were over food when Sam described the reports. The Chinese are starving. The desertification of Sinkiang continues unabated. The desert is marching eastward, destroying what little food the area can produce. Clouds and lower temperatures than normal as a result of nuclear strikes reduce the growing season. Unconfirmed reports from Vietnam and Cambodia describe an invasion by Chinese soldiers. Refugees from the nuclear strikes in northern China begin to pour into Russia.

"That is why China is invading us. They need our food production. They are starving, realized Ethan. Boys, we need to become bigger and better gardeners. I'm glad you put in a large garden last summer. It is even more important than ever."

10 June 2025

The USS Fort Worth in the middle of the northern Pacific had surfaced each night at 0015:00 hours for one hour at a time for four months. It had never received any messages. Now their stores of food were almost depleted. Frustrated, Commander Saunders decided to exercise his initiative. He proceeded northwesterly at a snail's pace remaining in the thermocline to avoid detection as much as possible. After surveying the area at periscope depth, he surfaced five miles off the island of Adak. He observed no lights at midnight. The summer sunlight might be sufficient he thought, to preclude the use of artificial illumination on the base. He returned to the thermocline. At 06:00 after a fitful sleep, Captain Saunders ordered a signal buoy to be released. It picked up a lot of ship traffic noise but no radio signal from Adak.

"Skipper, I am picking up a lot of sonar traffic. Lots of ships, large ones, headed east around fifteen knots. It sounds like a large convoy stretched out, or maybe two convoys several miles apart. They are south of us by about thirty miles."

"Any indications of a sub around?"

After listening intently, the sonar man replied, "Sir, it sounds like there might be one screening on the southern flank of the convoy."

After an hour of listening, he ordered the radioman to have the buoy sweep the electromagnetic spectrum for other signal traffic.

"Sir, I'm getting all kinds of signals and am honing in on them now. It is voice traffic in a language I don't understand."

Commander Saunders picked up the headset. He studied Russian at the US Naval Academy and was reasonably fluent in the language. He recognized that it was radio traffic sent in the clear between the Russian ships of the convoy. It could mean only one thing. They did not feel threatened in any way. The only way that could occur was if the prospect of detection, let alone of retaliation, had been eliminated. They did not feel any need for communications security. He ordered the buoy reeled in.

Commander Saunders immediately ordered "All quiet" throughout the ship. The Fort Worth remained at neutral buoyancy in the thermocline and just passively listened. After six hours, the Captain questioned the sonar man on duty about what he heard.

"Sir, the ships have passed south of our position. The sub stayed on the flank of the convoy. They are well past us. On a course of that seems to be changing. They are now headed northeast, on a course of about 40 degrees north."

"The only place they could be headed for is Anchorage. It is an invasion of Alaska. A convoy that size is carrying troops," suddenly dawned on Commander Saunders.

"What in God's name do I do now?" The only way that invasion force would act that way is if the United States has been destroyed, or at least incapable of retaliating. "

Saunders spoke into the intercom, "All officers, Chief of the Boat and chiefs to the officers' ward," ordered Saunders.

"We have received no instructions from any higher headquarters; not from COMSUBPAC, CNO, Joint Chiefs of Staff, or anyone else. I am opening our sealed orders as directed in the presence of all officers and Chief of the Boat. Our marine guards are standing outside the door. We have all wondered exactly what might be going on. I received these orders personally and have been more or less under Marine guard since receiving them and for this entire cruise. Now I think we all know why and we will find out our real mission." The Exec handed Commander Saunders his key to go along with Saunder's key. He opened the attache' case he had retrieved from his safe.

His orders read that "In case of any extended communications failure of more than two months duration, of any evidence of attack upon US Forces in the Pacific, or on the continental United States, or on Alaska, you are to attack the Russian military complex at Petropavlovsk-Kamatchatskiy on the Kamchatka peninsula. (There are two Petropavlovsks, one just inside the Kazakhstan border, the other on the Kamchatka peninsula). You are not confined to any time frame after twelve weeks. Use your own discretion. It is your duty to see that the entire complex is completely destroyed by any and all means available. If it is unnecessary to use all of your missiles for complete destruction, you are to expend them on strategic targets of opportunity within missile range given your situation. Your first two missiles are pre-programmed for that attack. The remainder is to be used at your discretion and will require programming." Signed, George Reagan, Admiral, Chief of Naval Operations. No one said a word. All realized that in all probability, the continental United States had suffered a nuclear attack.

"Mr. Snider set a course for Kamchatka. We will fire one hundred miles off the coast. We will launch one missile with ten multiple independent warheads to spread the damage across the complex, perhaps then lay low for twelve hours.

Afterward, we will sail in close to assess the damage and see if a second strike is necessary. Exec, accompany me to my cabin now. That is all."

At midnight, the USS Fort Worth surfaced. Her first missile streaked out; its flaming tail visible for all to see within twenty-five miles. It arched high, the warheads released, to hit five kilometers apart. The flight, release, and detonation took two minutes. After a delay of ten minutes, Commander Saunders ordered the second missile with an identical spread of warheads to make sure that no military capability was left on the peninsula. He ordered to dive and maneuvered south at 180 degrees. When he reached the thermocline, he ordered the word to be passed for all officers and the Chief of the Boat to meet in the Officers' wardrobe.

"Gentlemen, you all know what we have just done. God have mercy on our souls if I have initiated World War III. Having said that, I am confident that we have struck in retaliation. We are almost out of subsistence, we have no place to retreat, the Russian convoy is heading for Anchorage, and we have eight strategic missiles left. What I propose is to destroy Russian cities when I reach within range of them in the Sea of Okhotsk. Depending on what decisions I make and if we receive any information to the contrary, we might have a missile or two left for China. I will save the last missile for the Russian convoy headed for Alaska.

Chris, as our primary communications officer, when you feel it is appropriate to monitor worldwide radio traffic, inform me. We will surface to two hundred meters and quietly listen to chatter through the buoy. In the meantime, I will select more Russian cities as targets. Please inform your people by word of mouth. Mike, as our missile officer and programmer, please remain. For the rest of you, that is all for now."

After the rest of the officers left the wardrobe, Commander Saunders sighed and poured the two of them a cup of coffee.

"God, I wish I had some good Canadian whiskey to sweeten this coffee, Mike."

Mike grinned, "Command is a hell of a burden, Roger. I'm sure you are one hundred percent correct. If it is of any consolation, I would have made exactly the same choice. No doubt that Russian convoy is aimed at invading Alaska. Wait here. After a few minutes, Saunders returned with a bottle of Canadian Club whiskey. Roger laughed.

"Wish I had thought of smuggling something aboard Sir!" He laughed as he poured each of them a stiff drink in their coffee cups.

"The next two problems are where to go for food, especially fresh fruit and vegetables, and what do we do with our remaining nukes. Let's break out some charts and see what is important. Maybe radio chatter off some satellite will give us some clues since we have heard nothing at all from the good old USA, not even commercial radio broadcasts."

"I really don't want to get trapped within the Sea of Okhotsk, having to sail between the Kuriles. I would rather find some place out in open waters to launch if we can find suitable targets in range. Ideally, I would like to level Vladivostok, but that could be even worse, boxed in the Sea of Japan. My only question is what to do about the Russian invasion fleet. What do you think?"

"Frankly, I think we are toast no matter what we do. No place to go, the massive air-independent killer-hunter submarine fleets the Russians and Chinese have built, no choices about what to do or where we go. So, what the hell, let us burn the bastards to the greatest degree. I reckon those Alaskan pioneer types can ultimately handle the Russian invasion fleet with a little help from us. The Russians are probably counting on support and resupply from the mother country. If it isn't coming, they will have a hard time. They will die on the interior of Alaska without support. I think we should expend our remaining missiles on more important targets, ones to do the most damage."

I'm not so sure. I think we can reprogram to put one fifty kiloton MIRV, (multiple independent re-entry vehicles) out of the ten on one missile on that Russian fleet headed to Alaska. Those Russian troops are bound to be well trained in Arctic warfare. Those Alaskans could sure use some help."

"Damn, Mike. I knew there was some reason I really liked you. Let's plot some courses and targets starting with Vladivostok then we'll go after that convoy with our last missile."

The Russian convoy carried a division of arctic troops, well trained for the harsh climate of the arctic. Their initial objective was Anchorage, with its harbor. The 50-kiloton warhead exploded in the middle of the convoy. Several ships immediately capsized. Most had their communications and controls fried. Several suffered massive war page from the heat, becoming twisted wrecks of metal, their crews, and troops aboard dead from the heat. The heat of the blast penetrated some bulkheads on several ships' peripheral to the convoy, not enough to warp the ship but enough to kill some exposed crew members close to the bulkhead and to the flash. In some ships, their ammunition exploded. Their ships were not prepared for nuclear decontamination. Their officers decided not to inform the troops on the surviving troop carriers of the degree of their radiation exposure. The surviving ships sailed on.

American forces in Alaska planned a stall and retreat strategy, putting up firefights and then quickly retreating starting at the harbor. Many booby traps were placed in homes, stores, buildings, and other facilities. They denied all they could to the Russians by early evacuation of civilians and military families to the interior and destruction of what they could not move. A few days after landing the surviving Russian troops began to succumb to infections as a result of radiation exposure. Meningitis, diarrhea due to several pathogens as well as to what would otherwise be innocuous agents, exhaustion, and lethargy began to take their toll.

CHAPTER IX

ETHAN WISHED TO GOD he had a couple of hundred pounds of the plastic high explosive C4 to seal off the Wind River Canyon to the south and the Shell Canyon to the east. Other routes into the Big Horn Basin, through Yellowstone National Park along US 16/20 and US 287/20 would have to be closed by the local militias to the west. Winter snows would be a formidable blockade through the Park in season. The real route into the Basin would be from the north, down from Billings. They might traverse south down Interstate 90 along the east slope of the Big Horn mountains from the north and then turn east at Buffalo. Ethan thought that if the Chinese army and civil administrators had any brains at all, they would bypass the Big Horn Basin because of the lack of rainfall. It is a desert country, receiving only six to eight inches of rain a year, suitable only for irrigation farming, which potential they destroyed with their EMP attack. It is barely suitable for grazing, requiring about fifty acres to support one cow/calf unit. Their options are to cross the high mountain passes only once to reach the Great Plains. Their best chances to do that are along the four- lane interstate highways, such as Interstate-80 to the south and Interstate-90 to the north.

By the light of a single Coleman lantern on the kitchen table, Ethan made Sam and Josh read Army Field Manuals on guerilla warfare. They saved the electricity from the bicycle generator. Sam found several civilian and military publications in his grandfather's library on homemade explosives, improvised weapons, guerilla warfare, tactics, weapons, and explosives. One such publication was a fifty-year-old paperback book called The Anarchists Cookbook.

Gypsy and Ethan also sat at the table. Gypsy would read novels while Ethan tried to devise ways to blunt the Chinese thrust. In the case of homemade explosives, Ethan deferred to Gypsy. Even though she was a physicist, she also had several courses in both inorganic and organic chemistry. She knew what would work, how well it would work, and what would not. The only viable plan he could devise was to leave the Basin with a small force of only a few men. They would require horses or bicycles for mobility. They would have to operate in the foothills. Actions would be limited to small raids. If we can kill enough Chinese wanna-be farmers along with Chinese soldiers, we can instill fear in them. If they want to eat until they can grow food here, they will have to ship it from China. We can drive them back on themselves. The civilians will be a burden on their army, which would have to feed and protect them. We must stop them at or before the Rockies.

Ethan sat there thinking, *"God, what of Sam and Josh and Gypsy? I don't want to risk them, but how can I restrain them. This is their country. Is it worth the risk of their lives? Would it be better not to risk them so that they can survive to rebuild the country? What unique skills can they offer in rebuilding? With 100% objectivity, they are or should be fighters. Which, or both, should remain to protect Gypsy and grow the garden, hunt, and slaughter the occasional stray cow."*

Ethan decided to go alone. The boys should protect the garden, Gypsy, the hearth, and be the hope of the future. He considered several options. He could take a bicycle and pedal north into Montana. Once out of the Basin past the northern end of the Big Horns, he could turn east to interdict the Chinese if they headed south along Interstate-90. Chinese traffic along Interstate 94 in Montana would have to be covered by others. His other option for going east would be to cross the Big Horn Mountains along US Highway 26 over to Buffalo and interdict them along Interstate-90. No! That would be too late. How could he travel alone over the Big Horn mountains with deep snow on the passes? He must be in position prior to the arrival of Chinese forces. They must be stopped on the west slope. Country snows would block both of the eastern options until sometime in June. He would have to go west. He would travel south through the Wind River Canyon, over to the South Pass and onto the western slope. He would have to pack jerky and hope to pilfer what he could and hunt along the way. Most certainly all foods would already have been consumed by locals he would pass en route. He would take a Government Model 1911 with 100 rounds of ammunition, and a bolt action scope sighted .30-06 with 100 rounds. He figured he would encounter people who might be of assistance or even join him. He thought he might encounter people in Thermopolis if any people at all. He would have to risk being shot by some excitable citizen who would view him as a threat. He decided to travel mostly at night where there was less a possibility of a chance encounter.

In the morning at breakfast, Ethan informed his family. If they break through the Rockies, you boys will be on the front line. I believe they will pass north and south of the Big Horn Basin, over the Central Pass in the south and along Interstate 90 to the north. They might send an exploratory mechanized infantry company or battalion to look over the Big Horn Basin. If so, I doubt they will find anything of much interest. The wells are all shut down due to the EMP. It could be a battalion they send but more likely just a reinforced mechanized rifle company in armored personnel carriers. I have decided to continue the fight, but not from here. Sam and Josh, your missions are to protect your mother, grow the garden, defend it, and stay alive. I am the least valuable, most knowledgeable, and experienced soldier in the region. My job is to find a few erstwhile survivors and form a guerilla force. I don't know if we will ever see each other again. It is doubtful. I'll leave right after breakfast. Know this. I love each of you more than life itself.

Boys, from now on, when you swim or bathe in the river, keep your guns handy, right on the bank. Keep the brush cleared along the bank and away from it so no one can sneak up on you. Better still, one stand guard while the other swims, then trade places. You might want to lay a stone stair steps to keep your feet from getting muddy when you climb out, or maybe even build a small dock down there to stay clean. Up to you. Give you a chance to have a bath every day and help Gypsy keep your clothes cleaner."

One change of clothes, a down sleeping bag and closed cell sleeping pad, Boy Scout mess kit, and knife, fork and spoon set, a small bottle of bleach for water disinfectant, guns and ammunition, and jerky would be what he could pack in the bicycle saddle bags and his backpack.

Ethan determined, "If the Chinese have half a brain, they will recognize several axis of advance. One will be the southern route, the old California trail in reverse. From Los Angeles through the southwest; the central route over the South Pass in Wyoming, and the northern route used by the Burlington Northern Santa Fe railroad across the top of the U.S."

Ethan's only logical choice was the South Pass through the central Rockies in the southwest corner of Wyoming. Every Wyoming state map had the routes delineated. His route would be south through the Wind River Canyon, west to Lander, up to the mountain to South Pass City and on across the continental divide. Somewhere in the western foothills, he would make his stand. He considered he might meet the Chinese coming east as soon as the snow melted at the pass. He would take the chance. He had no way of knowing of the nuclear retaliation against the Chinese mainland. Much of the Chinese mainland political apparatus had been vaporized. The surviving mainland Chinese government refused to acknowledge the destruction of the homeland to preclude demoralizing their forces in North America. Neither the Chinese nor Russian Central Committees were aware of the rogue Chief of Naval Operations ordering the boomers to strike without the knowledge of the acting U.S. President, the National Security Council or anybody else.

The retaliation was completely unexpected, and consequently, no preparations were made. While severely wounded, China, with its large population and huge land mass, and expansion into Southeast Asia, could survive. Russia, on the other hand, with a far smaller population, with most of its large land mass in a much more northerly climate, was mortally wounded. It would die a slower, agonizing death. Ethan had no way of knowing what was occurring in the Baltics, the nuclear strikes on Russia or the difficulties of the invading Chinese.

A week after leaving Wasatch County, he arrived at the deserted gold mines at South Pass City. Stopping overnight there, he shot a mule deer at sundown. He boned out the meat and cut the longissimus dorsi muscles, called the back straps in lay terms, into long, thins strips for jerky. He cut several large steaks from a hindquarter and roasted them spitted over the fire for his supper. He built the fire up to have a large bed of coals for the morning.

In the morning, he cut more muscle into thin strips and hung them over a stick suspended two feet over the bed of coals between two forked sticks stuck in the ground to dry the meat while he inspected the mine. Ethan found a steel spud bar, a six-foot-long pry bar, and used it to pry the hasp off the door of a suspicious looking tool shed away from all other structures. As he hoped, the shed contained dynamite, fuses and blasting caps. He spent most of the day making jerky and scouting for ambush sites if he had to retrace his steps.

The next day he packed the jerky, two dozen sticks of dynamite in one saddle bag, fuse and blasting caps and fuse in another. He refilled his canteen from the steam fed by melting snow, added six drops of bleach to disinfect it, shook it, turned it upside down and let a few drops dribble out to disinfect the threads. He slung his rifle over his back and peddled off. From there, it was more downhill than up.

Iran seized Iraq after Sunnis of the Islamic State of Iraq and the Levant, sometimes referred to as ISIS or ISIL, slaughtered the Shiites of southern Iraq. Taking a lesson from the history of the Spanish Civil War, Shiite forces posing as civilians invaded southern Iraq, acting as the classic "fifth column on the inside," identifying and slaughtering local Sunni leaders and their families at night. Then "Volunteer" Iranian forces invaded Iraq from the east to defeat the regular Iraqi Army units and reversed the overall slaughter. Russia controls Shiite Syria through its puppet president. The two warring factions eye one another across the Syrian-Iraqi border. Iran is fomenting unrest in the Central Asian Republics, turning Shiites against Sunnis. Shiites believe the Twelfth Imam will return to rule the world as a caliphate when the world is bathed in blood. China watches with interest as Russia and Turkey become increasingly agitated with the Islamic internecine warfare in the states between the Black and Caspian Seas. Turkey, a Sunni state, concentrates the majority of its forces along its borders with Iraq and Syria. Foreign forces have pulled out of Afghanistan. Afghanistan has reverted to a twelfth-century amalgam ruled by a half dozen warlords who have divided what was the country between themselves.

The House of Saud fell to the riots of its youthful population. The state of Saudi Arabia no longer exists. Local sheiks, heads of clans from other than the House Saud, set up local territories as their own fiefdoms, especially around water sources. Shiites were murdered by Wahhabi Sunnis whenever they could be caught. Saudi Arabia is primed for invasion. The only questions are who will invade and when. House to house fighting continues in Lebanon.

Sam, Josh, and Gypsy pedaled their bikes into town; rifles slung across their backs. The streets were empty; perhaps one person visible every four blocks. They turned off on a side street, a block short of the main drag through the center of town. Josh recognized a high school girl sitting in the April sunshine on the front steps of a house. She was a senior in Sam's class. They stopped, and she lifted her head off her arms folded over her knees as Sam and Josh approached. Sam had asked her for a date once, but she refused. Her very gaunt face revealed sunken eyes. She watched as the boys approached her. She couldn't believe it. They looked healthy and had not lost any weight.

"Hello, Donna. How is your family," asked Sam.

"Starving. Why aren't you?" asked Donna.

"We live outside of town and stored some long term dried foods, vitamin pills, and canned goods. It is not all that palatable and not a lot of variety, but we are not starving."

Sam looked at Gypsy and Josh. Josh made no movement. Gypsy shrugged and said, "Your call. You're the only one who knows her. Is she a good girl, will she be a good woman, will she be a good, faithful wife?"

Donna looked at Gypsy with a mix of alarm and puzzlement.

Gypsy approached her. "Look, young lady, I have two healthy sons. There are very few if any, healthy young women for them to have as a wife. It will be decades before any degree of normalcy is restored, before any population can be built. Most of those who are left will die, most likely of starvation or disease. Not one person in a thousand, maybe not one in ten thousand, will be alive in five years. We have no idea what is transpiring outside this county, state, or country. It is even possible we are being invaded. It is not to pick and choose the time. It is up to Sam if he will take you for a wife and if you will accept it. You better think hard on it. If he says yes, will you be a good and faithful lifetime mate? We can accept only you. No other family member of yours and you will have to decide with a few hours. The only exception is if you have a sister that will take Josh as a husband and he says yes to your sister as a wife."

Donna started crying. Gypsy laid her bike down and approached her. Gypsy sat beside her and put her arm around her. "Young lady, we are offering you your life if you and Sam can agree on the marriage."

"What must I do?"

"Gather what you can put in a child's wagon or a grocery cart and backpack if you have one. If you have any firearms and ammunition of your own for them, you must bring them as well. We will be back.

Sam held out a Granola Bar. She stared at it, then grabbed it, tore off the wrapper, almost swallowing the first two bites without chewing.

"If you have a bicycle or can get one, do so."

"Remember, we'll be back in an hour or two. Be ready."

Donna turned and almost tripped going up the steps. The trio moved over to the main street and through the center of town. They moved their rifles to hand in front of their chests. Every storefront had been smashed and broken into. Display windows had only shards of glass, and all stores had been looted. At the end of the street, the largest food store in town stood with its doors wide open. Sam took a grocery cart from inside, put it behind his bicycle and went back in to find some string, wire or rope to tie it behind his bicycle. He found some electrical wire attached to one of the coolers. He ripped it free and stripped off the outer insulation with his pocket knife. He took the three copper wires it contained and wired the grocery cart behind his bicycle with one. Gypsy stayed outside with the Mini-14 across her back while Josh wandered through the store. He found nothing of value until he entered the butchers' area behind the meat display case. In the dark, he could barely discern a roll of butcher's paper which he immediately picked up and carried outside.

"Sam, are you going to use all three strands of that copper wire?"

"Nope. You want to wire a cart behind your bike?" eyeing the roll of butcher's paper.

"It might come in handy. Donna will have some extra stuff, and more than likely can fill more than one cart. Besides, we might find something else we want to haul."

Sam handed Josh the green-clad grounding wire. Josh made short work of wiring the cart behind his bike. Off they went. Donna was waiting with as many clothes as she could put on the steps. Donna had no bike. She didn't know where to get one. They loaded the two carts with her clothes. Sam put her on his bike.

"Can you pedal while pulling the wagon?" Gypsy asked as she looked at the emaciated girl.

"Donna, you take my bike. I'll pedal Sam's. He and I can alternate walking and pedaling." Donna's family came out and hugged and kissed her. No father was in evidence. Donna's mom hugged Sam and Gypsy and said "God Bless You" through the tears. Josh led off, with Donna wobbly pedaling behind. Sam followed at a brisk pace. After Four hundred yards, they had to stop to let Donna rest and Sam to catch up. No one bothered them, especially if they noticed Sam's rifle slung across his back. And so, it went, for the seven miles out of town.

When they reached the house, Donna staggered, too exhausted to stand. Sam easily scooped her up and carried her inside while Josh held the door. Sam laid her on the sofa where she burst into tears. Gypsy made her a glass of Tang. Sam and Josh unloaded the carts into the bedroom, put the bikes and carts in the garage. Donna was asleep, and Gypsy was starting supper. Josh fed the stove while Sam carried in more wood. Josh set the table for four. When supper of rice, pinto beans, homemade bread and reconstituted butter from butter powder and canned ground venison was ready, Sam woke his new wife and sat her at the table. Gypsy took Donna by the hand and looked into her eyes.

"Donna, please understand that we are going to slowly feed you increasing amounts of food for a good medical reason. People who have been starved and then suddenly have plenty to eat, usually die. It is due to a massive overgrowth of certain kinds of bacteria in your intestine. Thousands of concentration camp prisoners died from it after being liberated from the concentration camps in World War II. In humans, it is called a pig gut. In veterinary medicine, it is called overeating disease. Cattle and sheep feedlots often vaccinate to prevent it. God knows why the names are not reversed between human and veterinary medicine. Nevertheless, over the next week, we will gradually increase your food intake, so you don't get necrosis of your intestine from Clostridial species bacterial overgrowth. Eat slowly drink lots of water, get rest, and sleep. You'll get three modest meals every day for a week, and then we'll increase your food intake. You will sleep alone in the bedroom until you are healthy and ready to be a wife. The boys will continue to sleep by the stove. No one will touch you without your consent. Now we will say grace and eat."

Gypsy put two tablespoons each of rice and beans and one of meat on Donna's plate. Gypsy buttered one piece of bread and set it on Donna's plate. Donna cried again. They all ate in silence. Sam poured Donna a cup of hot tea without sugar.

"We will sweeten your tea a little at a time in the future. We don't want a sugar load for bacteria to feed on and cause bloat and bacterial overgrowth. Eat slowly, chew every bite."

Sam smiled at his new wife and sat down beside her. She looked him in the eye, picked up a fork, and began to eat and cry again. In two weeks, she was devouring one plate full, no seconds. At one month, she was allowed to eat her fill. At two months, she was a healthy five foot six inch one hundred and twenty-pound young woman. She and Sam were slowly falling in love. Idyllic, thought Josh although he was a little jealous, he kept it to himself.

In June Donna began helping in the garden. She tired easily, but she never quit. After a few minutes of rest, she would resume pulling weeds, hoeing, working side by side with Sam. Sam bucketed water from the river and watered the garden. Sam did all the watering.

"Okay Sam, your girl is healthy enough to learn some new tricks. It is time she developed some handgun skills," staled Gypsy.

"Ok, Mom, I'll start her out with the Ruger Single Six .22 for the basics. She can learn all the basics in the house until she's ready for live fire. Grip, stance, sight picture, trigger squeeze, I'll make sure she masters them all. She can dry fire away. After she has learned on the revolver, I'll put the .22 conversion kit on a .45 Government model frame. Her hands are big enough to handle one. Then, outdoors we go. When she is good with that, we'll transition to a full house — .45 ACP load. I'll get her started with the AR-15 as well. With a scope on it, she should be able to handle that by next week. I'll get her set up with a couple of holsters and a belt. She can take her pick. We have plenty. I suspect a cross draw will be best, but I'll leave the choice to her. Whatever she is comfortable with."

Sam took her down the hill to use the base of the hill as a backstop. "Always bring the gun to eye level unless they are ten feet or less away from you. If they are within ten feet, then shoot from the belly button level. LOOK AT THE FRONT SIGHT! DON'T LOOK AT THE TARGET. LET THE FRONT SIGHT BE CLEAR AND CRISP IN YOUR VISION AND THE TARGET BLURRY! Don't ever let anyone get close enough to you to grab the pistol. Kill them if they attempt to advance within twenty feet of you, given they are not already that close to you. If they have a weapon of any kind, shoot them regardless. Don't stop to think or give them a chance. Don't let them start talking. If you want to live, they must die. That is how you will survive. We are in very severe times. I want us both to live. Don't take any chances. No one else's life is worth any risk to yours. When you have mastered the basics, we'll start firing with the .22 conversion kit. It won't be long before you graduate to full power .45 loads. It will be easier than you think."

Donna selected the cross draw on a pants belt because it fit best in the curve between her hips and waist. She mastered the draw, sight presentation, sight picture, cocking the hammer on the draw, and dry firing. Sam made her keep both eyes open, stressing the need for situational awareness. When she felt she had mastered the single action, Sam put the .22 long rifle conversion kit on one of the Government Model 1911 .45 ACP semi-automatics. It was a new learning curve.

Sam instructed to her "Keep the hammer cocked with the safety on. Learn to swipe the safety off as you draw. Grasp the pistol with both hands. Lock your off hand that is the left hand, over the right, interlocking the fingers just under the trigger guard."

Donna went through 500 rounds of .22 long rifle ammunition with the conversion kit developing her skills. She was cat quick. When Sam switched out the conversion kit for a .45 ACP slide and barrel and spring, she was ready. After a week, she could outshoot Sam with what became her own .45 Government Model 1911A1. Gypsy smiled at the two of them. "All right, Donna. From now on, you wear your .45 all of the time. It is the first thing you put on after you pull on your pants. You only remove it from your holster when you are ready to remove your pants. From now on, keep a round in the chamber, safety on at all times. It is called Condition One, locked and cocked. Just be sure you don't shoot one of us!"

One warm fall day while Donna was working in the garden, Sam just stepped up to Donna, put an arm around her waist, and gently kissed her on the mouth. He smiled, said nothing, and went on hauling water for the garden. Now an old eighteen, Donna intuitively knew she would truly be a wife sometime soon.

The boys would skinny dip in the river after a day of hard work when they were covered in sweat and dirt after Donna and Gypsy went up to the hill.

"We girls each get a hot bath once a week in the tub unless we are unusually dirty and sweaty" said Gypsy. "We get ten gallons of hot water, and we do it on a different day from the boys. We get the tub on Friday nights, and they get the tub on Saturdays. We don't have to work as hard on Saturdays. Sunday is kind of a day off for us. We believe in the Lord and take Sundays as a day of rest. If we really get dirty, we get an extra bath. Otherwise, we take a sponge bath each night and wear pajamas to save the sheets."

The Chinese armored scout company had stopped along Interstate 1-80. The tank commander was standing in the open hatch of the cupola, observing the hole in the pavement. The bullet caught him in the temple and arched his body over the side of the cupola. The tank crews did not immediately recognize what happened to their platoon leader. The noise of the engine masked the report of the rifle fired from 300 meters away. The Chinese sergeant in the armored personnel carrier (APC) behind the tank saw what happened and immediately ducked inside, pulling the hatch closed over himself. He excitedly reported over the radio net to the rest of the column of sniper activity. Periscopes on armored vehicles swiveled around looking for any movement or sign from where the shot originated.

Ethan ducked down behind a rock and was smart enough not to reveal himself. Two truckloads of infantry from farther down the column fanned out seeking Ethan. Ethan slow crawled along his pre-planned escape route. He planted a false trip wire half visible along the path. On both sides of the trail were real booby traps with improvised detonation. After he crawled several hundred yards, he stood to a crouched position and began to run in the timber. A loud boom told him at least one Chinese infantry man lost a leg. With any luck, several others were wounded by the loose pile of gravel placed over the dynamite to act as shrapnel. A second boom made him smile.

The Chinese infantry advanced much more slowly. After 15 minutes, the infantry company commander blew a whistle recalling his men. In the interim, he sent two men forward to inspect the blown hole in the pavement. The two found no evidence of a mine or booby trap and reported back. The Captain in charge of the company ordered the column to proceed, bypassing the ruptured pavement.

Bradley noted that the Chinese infantry fighting vehicle (IFV) had copied the mine-resistant design from American IFV used in the Middle East. They were also resistant to attack by Molotov cocktails. Ethan pondered on how to defeat them. All he could think of was anti-tank weapons, tube-launched optically guided missiles called TOWs most certainly, but maybe not by light anti-tank weapons, or LAWS "Thank God they don't have anything like the man-portable Switch Blade tactical drone because if they did, I would be dead meat, "thought Ethan. He pulled the camouflage poncho over himself for the next five minutes. Ethan abandoned his bicycle and packed everything in the backpack. He hid the bicycle under a brush pile and put a blaze on each side of the nearest tree with his hatchet.

Four men with long hair and beards saw smoke from the chimney from the highway. They looked at each other and nodded. No one spoke. They approached the house which had all the doors and windows open because of the heat from the wood burning cook stove. Any breeze that would blow through the house to help reduce the heat was welcome. The leader motioned at two of the men. One man went around each side of the house. Two went to the front door and opened it. Gypsy and Donna were in the kitchen about to set the table. Sam and Josh were down the hill, skinny dipping in the river to wash the dirt and sweat off from hoeing in the garden. Chess was in the water splashing around with them. They were not visible from the house. Before they knew it, two men were standing in the kitchen behind Gypsy and Donna. The other two which had circled the house came in together in the back door. Surprised, Gypsy and Donna stood there for a minute.

"Get out. You are not welcome here." Gypsy stood in front of Donna and turned so that her right side was not visible. She screened Donna who also grasped the butt of her .45.

"Now look Lady, we're hungry. We want food and some feminine company. You and your daughter there look mighty inviting for both." The man who spoke cradled a shotgun. The man behind him rested a rifle on his shoulder. The man in the rear just grinned and turned to look at the two men who just entered the back door and addressed them. "Looks like we scored! We get food and fucked!"

With that, Gypsy drew her .45 Government Model and shot the man closest to her in the face. The man who just spoke looked at Gypsy with a surprised look, but could not bring the rifle off his shoulder before Gypsy also shot him in the face.

Donna was momentarily stunned, then her training took over. She drew her .45 and started shooting at the two men who came in the back door. She hit one in the chest, and the other bolted for the back door as quickly as he could retreat.

Hearing the shots, the boys swimming in the river simply slipped on their boots, grabbed their pants with their holstered sidearms, picked up their rifles and ran up the steps as fast as they could. They arrived butt naked at the back door except for their boots. Sam noticed the one man fleeing. Josh stuck his head in the door.

Gypsy shouted, "We're all right, but we have three men shot in here. They are not threats anymore."

Josh looked down at his nakedness, but Sam ran around the front of the house. The man was almost 200 yards away running down the street when Sam shot him in the back with his .308. The man lurched forward and fell face down on the pavement. The boys stopped, looked down at their naked bodies with considerable embarrassment. Josh looked at the three men on the floor, two not moving and one groaning. He stepped back, pulled off his boots, and put on his pants. Sam returned from the front of the house when he saw Josh dressing. He laid down his rifle, picked up his pants where he had dropped them and did the same thing.

Donna was hyperventilating, a surprised look on her face, then she started to giggle, then cry, then giggled some more. Gypsy kept the three men on the floor covered with her .45 the whole time, just in case the two were only unconscious. As soon as they had their pants on, Sam and Josh searched the three men. Two were dead, the third gravely wounded, none had anything of value on them.

"Let's get them out of here," said Sam. "Josh, will you please get the polyethylene sled from the garage while I strip these guys down to their shorts. No, I'd better do it outside as I see these two dead guys have bladder and bowel release. Let's get them out of here so Mom and Donna can clean the floor while we haul these guys to the river."

They loaded the bodies into the sled one at a time and dragged them out on the grass. There they stripped them down to their underwear. Their pants stunk of urine and feces and body odor from being unwashed for weeks.

"I figure we'll keep what we can of their clothes, boil them good, patch them and use what we can't wear as rags," said Sam.

"Good idea, Big Brother. I'll strip this one if you bring out the other one. Let's see what Mom has to say about the wounded one."

Josh proceeded to strip the two bodies while Sam and Gypsy loaded the wounded one in the sled and hauled him outside. His wound was a sucking chest wound. He looked Sam and Josh, and then Gypsy. You could see him begging with his eyes. Josh bent over him and looked him in the eye.

"You have a sucking chest wound. There is no medical aid or treatment available anywhere around here for it. You're going to die, and no one can do anything to help you, except maybe put you out of your misery. You wanted to rob and rape, and you'll get no sympathy here." Josh looked at Gypsy and Donna, and said: "Why don't you girls see what needs to be done about blood on the kitchen floor?"

His crassness surprised Gypsy, Donna, and even Sam. He spoke with authority in his voice. As soon as the women were in the house, Josh drew his sheath knife from his belt and plunged it into the man's heart. The body shuddered for a few second, then lay still. Sam watched but said nothing. Josh looked at his brother, not caring whether Sam approved or not. He stripped the body and rolled it into the sled. He then hauled the body to the river and dumped it into the water. He pulled the sled back up the hill and loaded another body in it.

"I'll take this one, Josh, and you take a breather." Josh nodded and sat down to catch his breath. "Hell, of a thing before supper" was all he said. Call it the survival instinct or the killer instinct. Whatever it was, Josh had plenty of it.

Together they walked down the street to inspect the fourth body. They stripped it where it lay and left it lying crossways in the middle of the road as a sign to others to not come on their street.

Ethan was hungry. He had lost thirty pounds of body weight. He was out of rifle ammunition. He figured he had killed at least fifty Chinese out of the 100 rifle rounds. Several times he approached isolated ranch houses, only to be shot at or near to drive him away. He had not been able to get within pistol range of the now half-wild cattle. He figured he was somewhere around the Wyoming-Utah border. He was careful not to stray too far from a water source.

CHAPTER X

KASHMIR FLARED, THEN EXPLODED and burned. Ethnic Pakistani Muslims attacked scores of ethnic Pakistani Hindu villages. Mumbai had enough. The Indian government decided not to escalate the war incrementally. Rather, the initial response was nuclear and complete. Indian fighter bombers flying under Pakistani radar delivered nuclear bombs up to 20 kilotons in size; initial targets were Pakistani air assets and air defense networks. The second wave strikes concentrated on Pakistani army forces. Third wave attacks concentrated on ports, critical infrastructure, and political targets. Peshawar, Islamabad, Rawalpindi, Gujrat, Lahore, Faisalabad, Sialkot, and Sukkur all received devastating blows. The naval base at Karachi ceased to exist along with much of the city. In order to achieve complete strategic surprise, Indian army units did not receive mobilization orders until the third wave strikes were completed. Damage Assessment determined that the potential for Pakistani retaliation was minimal and most likely non-existent.

Five days after the mobilization order was issued, three divisions of first-line Indian mountain troops moved into Kashmir. Surviving Muslims were given the option of leaving with whatever they could carry into what was left of Pakistan. Those Muslims who failed to comply immediately were shot where they stood. A few females and small children were spared.

The retreating Muslims had little knowledge of the nuclear devastation and the accompanying danger of residual radiation.

China went on full alert and mobilization. All Chinese reserve units were ordered to report status in twenty-four hours of receipt of the mobilization order. The Chinese Central Committee called an emergency meeting. The Chinese Premier addressed the Assembly:

"Why should we waste the opportunity? Our forces are in place for deployment, manned, fully equipped; morale is high; it has cost us hundreds of millions of yuan in lost production. We should use this unanticipated gift to recoup some of the expense by removing an internal threat and secure our borders. Comrade, no one is foolish enough to invade the interior of China. That lame excuse would never be accepted on the world scene, although admittedly, with the rest of the world in turmoil, who would notice, let alone care? Perhaps it is as you say, to secure our borders. Let us, however, not think so limited. How far into the Middle East has Iran advanced? Let us consider the internal security problem as perhaps the next phase of consolidation of our empire. Our New Silk Road has suffered enough guerilla attacks from these Muslims based in their wastelands on or adjacent to our borders. The governments of the Islamic Republics that comprise the Central Asian Republics are quite probably encouraging these attacks by failure to hunt them down. Certainly, some of their bases are in these countries. Our intelligence indicates that many of these guerilla bands are actually Iranian soldiers.

They are taking lessons from the American experiences of railroad sabotage during the great western expansion of the United States. Certainly, they have studied T.E. Lawrence, the Lawrence of Arabia fame. They are pulling the spikes holding the rails in place in canyons and narrow defiles. These are preferred locations because of the difficulty in unloading and removing the cargos from the railroad cars that tumbled off the tracks prior to recovery of the cars. Locations, where tracks are adjacent to rivers and other bodies of water, were also places preferred for sabotage. I have ordered the army to institute flying observational drones along the entire line. Bases of the sabotaging crews are now known. Soon armed drones will begin to accompany the observation drones. Our satellite reconnaissance has revealed some of their training bases in Iran. Even though our railroad can provide them an inexpensive, easy to ship their oil, the Central Asian Republics obviously regard it as a threat to their pipeline enterprises.

Let us discuss what our options are and appropriate plans. Due to the nuclear devastation from the EMP blast of the United States, our building of an alternative to the Suez Canal through Nicaragua has been put on hold. With the Muslim turmoil in Europe, the "cancellation" if you will, of the North American market, it might not be a profitable financial venture to continue. Besides, the earthquake potential is increasing according to our geologists. We can utilize the existing canal for an eastern approach with our smaller ships. Our fleet of larger tankers will, of course, be fully utilized per our strategic plan.

General Wu, how far should we allow the Iranians to extend their lines of communication? What is the opinion of the General Staff? What does PLAN recommend? Can we afford extended operations by opening a western front? Your liaison with our Russian friends seems to be proceeding well behind the scenes. Our North American effort must have first priority. What of fallout? Can the Iranians armies turn against us with any measure of success? The Central Committee is very concerned with this development of Iranian intransigence. What of the Muslim Central Asian Republics? Our intelligence net informs us that these Muslims Republics are very sympathetic to the Muslim cause even though they are almost all Sunnis. They fear the rise of Christianity in Russia less than they fear Shiite Iran and their loss of revenue from oil flowing through their pipelines on their soil to Europe. Of course, it is all of Muslim making."

"Comrade Premier, the Iranians are advancing quite rapidly. The Shiites in southern Iraq where they are a majority have been armed and have essentially driven out or killed the Sunnis. Under Shiite Iranian protection, they are setting up their own country which will, in essence, be an extension of Iran. This will give Iran control of the entire northern and eastern littorals of the Persian Gulf. It threatens the United Arab Emirates, Bahrain, and Qatar. I anticipate in the not too definite future, and they will "petition" for annexation by Iran. Sunni Saudi Arabia will probably cease to exist. Our temporary ally Russia has harmed itself and us by selling the Iranian mullahs state of the art fighter and fighter-bomber aircraft. Their large sales of Uranium 238 ore and plutonium to the Iranians have encouraged their nuclear weapons program. Still, they could not have manufactured more than ten or fifteen bombs no larger than twenty-five kilo tons. Sunni Egypt is marshaling to invade across the Sinai into Jordan, with tacit Israeli approval to cross their southern border. Turkey is in a quagmire, on which borders to defend; its eastern border with Iran or its southern border with Iraq and Syria. We are uncertain of Russia's intentions in the Caucasus region. Certainly, they would resist Iranian expansion into Azerbaijan. Chechnyian guerillas would most certainly harass Russia's supply lines in the region. It is mountainous terrain, ideal for guerilla warfare. Then there are always the Kurds and the Armenians, small, but very angry populations.

The area is essentially Muslim. Who can predict how the majority of them will act? Can we allow the Iranians to control the Persian Gulf oil, the Iraqi oilfields, and the Saudi Arabian oil fields? Then the only major sources of oil are Africa and us. I submit that the real goal of Iran is the conversion of everyone to the Shia brand of Islam. Can we destroy their center or centers and leave their forces hanging out on a limb in the field to be destroyed piecemeal? Can we destroy the controlling mullahs and allow the Iranian population to return to their former status as in the 1970s?"

September 15, 2025

Ethan was tired, hungry, dirty, and above all, disappointed for general lack of resistance he saw by American civilians. Maybe they just weren't threatened yet by the invading Chinese. Perhaps they had not been threatened enough, or are too involved in their own survival. Ethan had been shot at twice as he approached isolated ranch houses in the last two days. One bullet clipped his backpack. He presumed the other was a warning shot. He figured he appeared to be the occasional straggler or possible miscreant who was perceived as a threat by the survivors. Every attempt he made to establish contact with other Americans resulted in failure. He had not had a bath in weeks. He smelled bad; he knew it, he tried washing in ice-cold streams pouring off the mountains without soap. It helped to some degree. Always hungry, he had killed the occasional deer or cow and made jerky when he could. He was in need of fresh fruits and vegetables in his diet, and he knew it. He had lost over fifty pounds of body weight. He was tired. He had expended all of his rifle ammo. The Chinese army had made it to Salt Lake City, but not much farther. They had not calculated on the resistance mounted by the Mormon Church and armed patriots who had refused to surrender their firearms to the federal government.

Ethan had pedaled hundreds of miles, over the South Pass on Highway 28 and into the desert beyond. He avoided towns and major highways wherever possible. Only when the need for resupply forced him did he venture into a village. He observed and finally entered Kemmerer, WY at the next set of foothills, hoping to find food, ammunition, and rest. No such luck. Then traveling on Highway 189, mostly by night, he crossed the Salt River Range and beyond into Utah.

It was in the foothills of the Wasatch Range where he encountered the first significant Chinese forces. Other encounters had been with small probing units exploring avenues of approach. This is where Ethan had expended the majority of his rifle ammunition. Killing a single Chinese soldier each time, trying to pick off an officer or a Non-Commissioned Officer, and beat a hasty retreat. Several times cannon and machine-gun fire searching for him came very, very close.

Ethan watched a Chinese brigade camped below from a mountainside. Chinese patrols regularly combed the foothills seeking any potential snipers such as Ethan. *"Why in the hell am I doing this?"* he thought. "Am I the only one fighting a guerilla war? What is left of our regular army? Where are the reserve units, where are the patriotic citizens? I'm tired and growing old. Why don't I just go home?"

At midnight Ethan packed his sleeping bag and cautiously proceeded east towards home and Wyoming.

Ethan traveled mostly at night, choosing to stay off the roads when convenient. He headed in a general northeasterly direction. Water and food were his greatest concerns. Now in mid-September, he could see snow on the higher elevations of the mountains to the east. There was more of a chill as the night temperatures dropped into the upper twenties, but he was still warm in his sleeping bag. He figured he better cross the mountains soon or he would be snowed out on the west side of the Central Pass. Somewhere out of Cokeville, Wyoming, he camped on a forested hill. He built a small fire and boiled the last of his jerky for his supper. Tired, he unintentionally overslept. He woke at dawn to discover he was overlooking a ranch house.

As he packed his sleeping bag and pack frame, he looked at the ranch house he saw a Chinese vehicle pull up. Four Chinese soldiers climbed out and started for the house. One walked around the back of the house towards the barn when a man emerged from it. The Chinese soldier shot the man on sight. The other three Chinese entered the house when he heard another gunshot.

Ethan left his pack and moved down the hill, staying out of sight as much as possible. As he approached the front door which the Chinese had entered, he dropped his rifle and drew his .45. He could hear a woman crying and begging. He peered in around the door frame, then very quietly opened the screen door. The front door was standing open. In the living room, a middle-aged woman lay dead with a bullet wound through her chest and a shotgun next to her body. He quietly stepped towards the sounds of a woman crying.

In the bedroom were four naked Chinese men holding down a girl across the bed. One held her arms over her head, one held each of her legs apart by the ankles, while the fourth was raping her. The first to notice Ethan was the one holding a leg on the far side of the bed. Ethan shot him in the middle of the forehead. He next shot the one closest to him, who was holding her other leg. The man holding her arms had a look of surprise as Ethan shot him in the face. The rapist rolled off the girl to the side of the bed on the floor opposite Ethan. Ethan walked around the bed where the soldier was crouched on the floor. As he attempted to rise, Ethan shot him in the top of his head.

The young girl was crying hysterically and pulled a blanket over herself. Ethan drew his Cold Steel Recon Scout knife and plunged its seven-inch blade upwards from underneath the xiphoid cartilage through the diaphragm into the thoracic aorta of each soldier in turn. He wiped the blade of his knife on the shirt of one of the soldiers and returned it to its sheath on his pistol belt. He removed the magazine from his pistol and replaced it with a loaded one before holstering it.

"Young lady, listen to me. Your parents are dead. You cannot stay here. The next Chinese patrol that comes along will take you as a sex slave to be raped or tortured to death. You better get up and get dressed. Do you hear me?" Ethan started shaking the girl. He pulled her over to see her face. "Now, get up and wash yourself and get dressed. I say again; you can't stay here.

Are there any guns in the house? Food? Get up and pack your clothes, winter clothes have first priority. Then spring and fall and summer clothes. I'm going to check out the Chinese vehicle. Get things packed and put them on the front porch."

Ethan picked up the Chinese rifles and webbed gear. One webbed belt had a pistol on it. One of their uniform shirts had some yellow stripes on it, so Ethan figured he was the sergeant in charge of the detail. Ethan carried their gear out to their vehicle. He checked each rifle to see a round was chambered and the safety on as he loaded them.

He climbed into the driver's seat and started the vehicle. No key was required. He noted fuel tanks behind the house off to the side of the barn. He drove to them. He pulled the rancher's body into the barn so his daughter wouldn't see it. He took a handkerchief from the body and stuffed it part way into the gas tank of the vehicle. He wanted to determine if it was gasoline or a diesel engine. He withdrew the handkerchief and smelled it. Diesel. He went over to the fuel tanks and lifted the hose off the larger one and let a little dribble out. Diesel fuel. He pulled the vehicle up to it and filled the tank. Then he looked around the barn, then moved to another outbuilding which was a garage and tool shed. There he found two five-gallon jerry gas cans. He took them to the fuel tank and filled them, then put them in the back of the vehicle with the rifles. He drove around to the front of the house and added his backpack and rifle to the back seat.

Inside, he found the girl had not moved, still crying on the bed. "Now look, young lady, things are desperate here. If you want to live, you better do as I say and start moving right now. Get up and get dressed. Another Chinese patrol could come along at any time."

With that, Ethan pulled the blanket away from her and off the bed. He folded it and walked into the kitchen where he started going through the cabinets. He found a box of salt, pepper, a jar of jam, some fresh eggs, a slab of bacon, and two loaves of homemade bread. In the firebox over the wood burning cook stove, he found a pie. He put most of the eggs in a sauce pan with water and set them on the stove to boil. Thank goodness the lady of the house had started a fire. Ethan added more wood to get the water boiling as quickly as possible. He quickly sliced as much bacon as he could put in the frying pan. He returned to the girl. She was almost dressed. Ethan shook the pillows out of the pillow sacks and handed them to the girl.

"Stuff your clothes in them and put them in their vehicle out in front."

Ethan picked up the shotgun beside the deceased woman. He dragged her body out of the living room into an adjacent bedroom to remove it from the girl's sight. Ethan took a quick tour of the rest of the house.

When the girl emerged, she was carrying the two pillow sacks stuffed with her clothes.

Ethan asked, "Are there any more guns here? If so, get them, we'll take them with us. By the way, my name is Ethan. I am, or was, a Marine General Officer, now a lone guerilla fighter. You do not have anything to fear from me. Let's eat quickly and leave. I haven't had a hot meal, or any good meal, in weeks. I'm very hungry. You should eat if you can."

Ethan turned the bacon, got out two plates, set the bacon equally divided on them. Then he broke four eggs into the skillet, with popping hot bacon grease. He sliced four pieces off one of the loaves of bread and put two on each plate. As soon as the eggs were done, Ethan put two on each plate on the bread. He sliced two more pieces of bread and put them in the skillet to soak up the grease. He set the plates on the table, sat down, and ate. The girl watched him out of scared eyes.

"Look, young lady, you better eat. We need to get moving now. Sit and eat. I'll load what I can in the vehicle, and we are out of here in the next few minutes." Ethan quickly finished eating as the girl just started to eat.

Ethan went to the first bedroom and removed blankets and one pillow which he carried out and put in the back seat of the Chinese vehicle. Ethan went back for more blankets when he glanced in the master bedroom dresser mirror. He couldn't believe that the reflection he saw was his own. His face was haggard, dark circles under his eyes, an unruly growth of hair on the back of his neck, and worst of all, a very scraggly beard.

Ethan went through the drawers of the bathroom sink. He found a straight razor, shaving brush, a mug of shaving soap, a fine whetstone and a strop. He never shaved with a straight razor before. He went to the water pump in the front yard and pumped a two-quart saucepan of water. He put it on the stove, put wood in the stove and returned to the bathroom to strop the razor. He took the hot water from the stove, found a wash cloth and tried to soften his beard with the hot water. Then he started to scrape his face. When he emerged, he was more or less clean-shaven, but bled from about a dozen small cuts. He rolled the razor, brush, strop, shaving mug and whetstone in a towel, one to each roll of the towel. He quickly went through the medicine cabinet and removed everything there, then the toiletries in the linen closet, putting them in another pillowcase.

The girl ate her food as she watched Ethan move around. Ethan poured the boiling water off the boiled eggs and with a spoon lifted them into a pitcher. He put the rest of the food in a turkey roasting pan and carried it to the truck. He started the engine and came back into the kitchen.

"Get whatever guns you have and ammunition for them. I already have your shotgun, but didn't find any ammunition for it. I'm sure your Dad had at least one rifle, probably two or three and maybe a handgun. .30-06 and .45 ACP ammunition are a priority if you have them. Those are the firearms I am carrying. Get your guns, ammunition, and coat, and let's go now!" The girl came out of the house carrying two rifles.

"There are ammunition and a revolver, but I can't carry everything at once."

Ethan climbed out of the truck and said, "Show me."

They walked into the house where the girl had piled several boxes of ammunition and a double action .357 magnum revolver on the desk of what appeared to be an office. Ethan grabbed it all, and they returned to the truck where Ethan threw it in the back seat... Ethan looked up at the flagpole in the front yard. An American flag was at the top. Ethan pulled down the flag, drove to the barn where he found a shovel. He tied the flag to the shovel handle and wedged the blade of the spade between the fender and the bumper.

"Which way to the highway? We're headed for Washakie County, Wyoming, to the northeast. I'm sure you know where it is." Ethan wanted to get the girl talking. The girl pointed to the right, and Ethan pulled out of the yard and onto the road.

"I hope we have enough fuel to make it all the way home. We'll do what we can to find more fuel as necessary en route. By the way, my name is Ethan, Ethan Bradley. I have a wife and two teenage sons at home. That's where we are headed. Our older son is Sam. Hopefully; he has found a young lady this spring. Our younger son is Josh, short for Joshua. My wife is a brilliant scientist. She is, or was, a Ph.D. candidate in astrophysics. I think you will get along famously with the family. What is your name, young lady?"

"My name is Carol, Carol Youngston. Did you find my father?"

"Yes. I found him. He was in the barn. Let's not talk of him anymore. Of more concern right now, is your health, both physical and mental. You are severely traumatized, and I expect it will take you some time to recover. I will be blunt. I don't know how many of those bastards had their way with you. I am sure you don't want to be pregnant. So where are you in your menstrual cycle? I mean your period?"

The girl looked at Ethan and wondered, "What kind of asshole is this guy?" I'm due in a couple of days. I didn't think to grab any sanitary napkins."

"Well, maybe we can raid a pharmacy or grocery store or something along the way for you."

"Why did you tie the flag to the shovel and put it on the truck?"

"I wanted other guerillas, if there are any out there, to know that this is now an American truck, not a Chinese one. I don't want to encounter any friendly fire. We don't need that!"

"Are you really a Marine General?"

"Yes, I am, or I was. I commanded a Marine Division on the east coast when my wife had something bad happen. I came home on leave when we were nuked. There is no way in hell I could have returned to my command. Besides, my family needed me more. My Assistant Division Commander was capable. He will do OK, as best as can be done, given the circumstances. That means I don't know what in hell the national picture looks like."

"I know we lost all our power, and the vehicles won't start, but I never understood why."

"Our country was attacked with nuclear weapons tailored to deliver more of an electromagnetic pulse form of radiation as opposed to ionizing radiation, heat, and blast. Of course, those elements are still present in any nuclear detonation, but the great percentage of energy went into the formation of the electromagnetic pulse. That fried all electronics, circuits, digital equipment and so on. They must have spread several bombs at low altitude, probably twenty to forty miles high, to blanket the entire country. I expect four powerful nukes at around forty miles high would blanket the entire country. It will take us decades to recover. It is obvious that the Chinese, perhaps in conjunction with the Russians, want our country for, as Adolph Hitler used to say, 'lebensraum' or room to live and our agricultural production. China can't support its own population with the agricultural production inside its borders. They ruined too much of their agricultural land through various forms of pollution. I'm guessing that they might have also expanded into Southeast Asia. The Chinese are desperate for food. The South China Sea area and into the Indian Ocean is one of the world's last, greatest fisheries. The Chinese are starved for protein. That means fish to them. Western China has been experiencing massive riots for years. That is a major reason China expanded into the South China Sea with their artificial islands and air bases, to control the fisheries. China has been attacking fishing boats of other Southeast Asian nations for years, sinking them with gunboats and then disappearing. The American people are never really informed. Looney liberal socialist control of the media never really reports how bad things are in the rest of the world. That might require a balanced budget and greater defense spending instead of social welfare programs to keep them in power. "

"How long before things can return to normal?"

"Things will never return to normal in my lifetime; perhaps not in yours. Casualty estimates that means how many dead, will probably be 250 million Americans, maybe more, out of 325 million or so. Most will die of starvation or be killed by their fellow citizens in the quest for food and potable water. Our cities no doubt have quickly evolved into jungles; survival of the fittest. I suspect cannibalism is how many are staying alive. Only people in rural areas, farmers and ranchers, such as your family, stand a chance of survival. Now it appears that the Chinese will kill off all of those they can catch. I doubt there is any semblance of government left anywhere, national, state, or local. It is going to take a long time for us to recover. Our only hope is outlying farmers and ranchers and very small towns that are self-supporting. We must hold off the Chinese. That is our next primary threat."

They drove on, not speaking for several hours. Around noon, Ethan stopped at a small bridge crossing a free-flowing stream. He filled his canteen and added a few drops of bleach as his usual disinfection method. *"I wish I had grabbed a funnel, he thought."* Looking around, they saw a plastic half gallon soda bottle. He cut the bottom off and stuck the neck in the fuel tank. With some difficulty, he poured diesel fuel into the fuel tank of the truck until it overflowed.

"Where are we going?"

"Frankly, I am returning to my home. Remember I said Washakie County. I made a critical mistake. I put my duty to my country over my family. I have been waging a one-man guerilla war against the Chinese invaders since spring. I left my family, my wife, and two teenage sons at home to manage without me. I have been more or less like many family men in the great stock market crash of 1929, only for a different reason. Men left their families and homes to fend for themselves while they prowled the country in search of employment, in search of food, or some cases plunder and rape. I left out of a sense of duty to my country. In retrospect, my country, our country, deserted us by the failure of preparation. I do not intend to carry on a winter campaign against the Chinese alone. I do not know the Chinese strategy. I don't know if they will continue to push eastward over the winter. That is where we are going to my home.

To be perfectly honest about it, I am more or less kidnapping you. My sons will need wives. You are elected unless you want out now. I don't really see you have many choices. We can feed you and care for you, but that is up to you. We have a small place in the Big Horn Basin with a large garden that we water by hand. We occasionally kill a stray cow or deer. My sons and wife are wonderful people. The biggest problem I see is that there are only one of you and two of my sons. I hope that we can find a second young lady for them. I don't want my sons fighting over a young woman. If you agree, welcome to the family. Hopefully, you will fall in love with one of them and that one in love with you. Nobody has many choices these days. If not interested right now, you have two choices. Tell me where you want me to let you out, or you can wait to meet them. No doubt, you will be welcome. I don't know what has transpired these few months that I have been gone. Again, it is entirely up to you. Out here or go home with me and see what your options really are. You certainly could not have waited around for the next Chinese patrol. By the way, how old are you?"

"I'm about to turn eighteen."

"My sons are, or were, a high school senior and a sophomore. If things were normal Sam would be a graduate and into college and Josh a junior. You'll fit right in between them. More likely, the older one, Sam, will be the one, by mutual consent, that you will pick. I just hope to God my family is still alive and well."

Ethan turned off US 189 onto what appeared to be a forest service road onto the Seedskadee National Wildlife Refuge about thirty minutes before dark. He looked for a place to park out of sight but still had wood and water. Ethan hid the car in the brush alongside the lake. He started a small fire and retrieved the roasting pan with food. Carol sat, just watching, not quite knowing what to do as Ethan prepared their supper. After eating, Ethan washed the dishes with sand along the riverbank. Then he sat by the fire and lit a cigar, one of those he took from the desk at Carol's house.

"General, why did they attack us?"

"Well, it boils down to geopolitics and the world's resources. Russia wanted the Middle East for Oil. That gives them control of the great majority of the world's oil supply. They now control the world's oil market. They can dictate any price they want for it, either in currencies or commodities. I'm sure they reached some accord with China on how to divvy up the world's energy resources. China wanted Africa for oil and the natural resources to keep their economy afloat for internal consumption. They will bleed off their excess population by colonizing Africa I am sure and displacing native Africans, by force or starvation. Russia gets Europe with its captive population that it can keep quiescent by controlling energy and by force and starvation if necessary. They also get the latest technology in manufacturing and research of Europe along with the captive population. Any brains, I mean intelligent people, who want to eat and stay warm in the winter, will have to cooperate with the Russians.

China needs food. So, the USA is the garden spot of the planet for food production. Russia gets the Middle East and Europe. China gets North America and Africa. Everybody is happy except for the rest of the world. China has a sense of superiority to the rest of the world. They claim 5000 years of civilization that makes them superior to every other people and nation. We made very feeble attempts to block China's expansion into Southeast Asia and the South China Sea. They resented our efforts regardless of their ineffectiveness. We did not respond with massive force to their expansionist overtures. Both Russia and China will deal harshly with Muslim attempts and world domination. The Central Asian Republics, if they have any sense at all, will recognize that any attempts at furthering a world caliphate will be dealt with most harshly by both Russia and China. Both will have some initial problems with Muslim countries on their borders, but they won't last long. Neither will put up with any rebellious movements. I suspect they will go in and crush Afghanistan, sparing no one. Russia has never forgiven us for supplying the guerilla forces that defeated them in Afghanistan. Now, if they crush Afghanistan as I suspect, they will have the march to a year-round warm water port right through Pakistan. That will probably come in a year or two. If Pakistan resists, they will be toast as well."

"Did we bomb them or do anything in retaliation? We didn't start this, did we?"

"No, Carol, we did not start it. It came as a complete surprise. I only wonder how, or if, part of the assassination of the President-Elect and military takeover of Washington, DC was part of the plan. If it was, we have some traitors to deal with. I have no idea about retaliation. If there is any, the only hope is the US Navy's ballistic missile submarine force. It is outdated and equipped with outdated missiles. The bastards in government thought it was more important to maintain their offices by buying votes with welfare programs than keeping the nation safe."

"I'm scared, General. What if I don't like your sons?"

"We can't feed you if you don't fit in. Ultimately, you will have to share in the work. You can leave at any time. I'll pack you a lunch, and you can hit the road."

CHAPTER XI

"WELL ALEXI, WHAT DO YOU THINK NOW? Has the population of New York City been sufficiently reduced that we can continue with our original plan?" Alexi smiled once Again. Based on our experiences in the siege of Leningrad in World War II, the only survivors there are the cannibals. They have few if any, weapons. We should thank the mayor and politicians of New York for disarming themselves. The survivors can be hunted own easily enough if they cause any difficulties. Our canine cohorts, the military dogs, can sniff them out and we can eliminate them on contact. I suggest that if they do not bother us, we not bother them."

"Perhaps we should emulate the Chinese and invade the American east coast, Alexi. After all, we lost a significant portion of our urban population in their retaliatory strikes. We, along with our families, were fortunate to survive by evacuating our families to the safety of the countryside prior to the unpleasantness and our persons to the hardened shelters beneath our buildings. We had not originally countenanced the invasion of America; that was not part of the deal with China, but then no one calculated on the US Navy submarine force showing any initiative and moving out on its own without any orders or higher authority knowing it and striking back. Probably less than half a dozen SSBNs were involved.

The Chinese claim to have sunk all those in the Pacific. I am not so sure, but where could the surviving ships go? They no longer have a home port. After all, much of our rural population survived, and they are agrarian. They would readily take to the eastern half of the USA with its rich farmland. That could block Chinese expansion east of the Mississippi River and provide us with a much better climate and food production. We will have to draw on our European segment of the population, that of western Russia. We cannot have our eastern provinces with their Asian populations accompanying us to North America. Of more immediate concern, I fear rumblings in the Muslim —stan nations. They did not suffer the nuclear strikes as our Mother Russia did. Do you think they would take the opportunity to invade us if they think we are sufficiently crippled to resist their invasion?"

"That is something to ponder, Comrade. Let's see what our satellites tell us about Chinese advances in North America and any military buildup in our so-called Muslim neighbors. After all, China is seizing Africa. But first, let us see what our satellites say about New York City. Another major concern is our lack of ports. Our major eastern ports no longer exist. We will have to use European ports, which means we must take at least part of Europe."

The few remaining, surviving citizens of New York City looked like walking skeletons. Sixty days without food left many unable to resist common cold agents. A cold winter that stretched into a cold, wet spring contributed to the demise of many. They easily succumbed to pneumonia and or diarrheal diseases. Those few in the suburbs with wood burning stoves ran out of furniture to burn in thirty days. Chain saws with a digital ignition system had succumbed to the EMP, but not the Bradleys'. The Faraday cages where they were stored when the EMP attack occurred allowed continual use of their chain saws. Josh and Sam insured plenty of gas by siphoning gas from the tanks of the neighbors' vehicles and adding fuel stabilizer. This gas they held for longer-term use.

"It's a good thing Dad had us put up a dozen one-gallon jugs of bar and chain oil, and about a gallon of two-cycle gas engine treatment. If he hadn't, we would surely burn a lot of calories using saws and axes," remarked Josh. Josh and Sam continued to drop trees on the neighbors' lands, so they could dry and be ready to burn next year.

"Then, Alexi, we shall inform General Azimov to proceed. He should be able to grasp the gold near the airport first, then proceed to the main stash at the Federal Reserve Bank of New York. At one time the Americans allegedly had over twenty tonnes (1000 kilograms) of gold to support the dollar. Now they claim they are down to eight thousand tons. It was supposed to be in Fort Knox, Kentucky and West Point, New York, but in reality, a part is stored in the vault of the Federal Reserve Bank of New York on Liberty Street in New York City, for trading. The gold held there really doesn't belong to the United States. Rather, it belongs to many nations and is held there for trading purposes. They just move the gold around from one section to another, from one foreign account to another marked off on the floor. Another three thousand tons is held near the JF Kennedy airport for shipment as required when other nations demand their gold being held by the United States. Finally, the Hong Kong Shanghai Bank of China maintains an estimated five thousand tons in its vault at 39th Street and 5th Avenue. President Richard Nixon, in his infinite stupidity in the 1970s, removed the dollar from the gold standard under the concept of a floating currency, making the dollar relative to the other currencies of the world. That was partially in response to the French under Charles DeGaulle, who continually redeemed dollars for gold, depleting the American gold reserves. That allowed the Federal Reserve Bank to initiate inflation to the accumulation of immense wealth by the elitists of their capitalist society. They made about four percent per year, which compounded into enormous wealth. It was really the average stupid American who did not understand what was happening, that suffered inflation. The elitists blackmailed then President Woodrow Wilson into establishing the Federal Reserve Bank."

"How did they do that, Vladimir?"

"Wilson was having an extramarital affair with the wife of one of his subordinate professors at Princeton University. They held that over his head as the stick. For the carrot, they promised him the Presidency."

"Who were they, Vladimir."

"They were the moneyed capitalists of the time. The Morgans, the Rothschilds, the Rockefellers, and the other capitalist barons. Recall that Wilson promised to keep American out of World War I. After he became President, they pressured him to do an about face to get the United States into the war. They made billions on the war industries. Never let it be said that war is not profitable for some, as long as you can make someone else bleed for it."

General Azimov ordered his task force to board two troop carriers from the Black Sea fleet in Sevastapol. Accompanied by two destroyers, the small flotilla passed through the Dardanelles, the Mediterranean and into the Atlantic. There the flotilla rendezvoused with two Russian submarines and a missile cruiser from the Northern Fleet that survived the nuclear response by being at sea at the time. The task force was in New York harbor two weeks later.

With detailed street maps, Azimov ordered his infantry brigade to set up a security perimeter around the Federal Reserve Bank of New York.

On board his flagship, Azimov was pondering his next move when a knock on his door broke his concentration.

"General, I'm having difficulty in radio communications. I don't know if our satellites are not working or something happened, but I cannot contact Moscow. I don't know if the EMP damaged our own satellites or what. None were supposed to be over the United States at the time of demolition. I can't seem to pick up other radio chatter either except for a few American amateur radio operators."

"Keep trying Admiral and keep me informed the minute you can make contact. Perhaps you can pick something up from our Chinese friends on the west coast or one of our fleets."

"That is disturbing. Why can't we pick up something off our satellites?" thought General Azimov. He decided to observe personally how robbing the Federal Reserve Bank was progressing. He had his driver take him there immediately.

"Colonel Patronin, how are things going? Can you give me any kind of time frame, Colonel?"

Colonel Patronin commanded the engineering brigade who turned to Lieutenant Colonel Simonov, who commanded one of his engineering battalions. Simonov was a civil engineer and explosives expert. Another engineering battalion commander was busy maintaining generator driven electrical and water and all other support services for the task force.

"Right now, I can only give you an educated guess on a time frame General. Based on the information we have, there are two potential pathways into the vault. Our informant employee of the bank was very detailed in diagrams and descriptions. One is through the door, and the other is through a tunnel that leads to the wall of the vault. As soon as I can finish digging a tunnel to the foundation of the Bank and blow a hole, I can give you a better answer. I have studied the photographs of the door of the vault, but have no information on the walls of the vault. That is what I need. According to our plan, we are operating on both approaches."

Colonel Patronin turned to General Azimov. *"I expect we will be here one to several weeks General."* I have planned for two engineering companies from Lieutenant Colonel's Simonov's battalion so that we can work around the clock, so a platoon from each company is always working on each approach; one company to attack through each avenue. We'll make a contest of it. Whoever succeeds in penetrating the vault first will have a forty-eight-hour pass in the city to do whatever they wish. The loser battalion will get only a twenty-four-hour pass. We will probably use a modest amount of explosives in the tunneling operation. What we know of the door will probably require several diamonds tipped drilling bits if we try to blow the door bolts. Oxyacetylene torches can possibly remove the hinges, but the retaining bars or bolts might be something else. No doubt the EMP fried the digital lock. We might have to place explosives around the hinges, then perhaps we will know. We can finish the job with oxyacetylene torches. We might have to blow away the wall that suspends the door. We might be able to bring in a small bulldozer to drag the door out of the way as it weighs several tonnes if we can get one into the basement. I have my doubts about that."

The support companies of each battalion set up field kitchens and temporary barracks. The fall weather was turning much cooler than normal. Off duty, soldiers searched the immediate surrounding area for souvenirs and warm clothing. Outdoor sporting clothes, such as down jackets and insulated boots, camping supplies and tools from hardware and sporting goods stores in the area were favored targets. Several neighborhood liquor stores were discovered, and their contents looted. It created a problem with drunkenness on duty. Quality scotch, American bourbon, and Canadian blended whiskeys quickly became the favorites.

A graves and disposal company began the odious task or removing bodies from around the building and in the floors going down to the basement. The bodies were hauled a dozen blocks away and dumped on the street.

The responsible engineering battalion restored electrical power to the elevators to move men and equipment from the main floor to the basement. Lieutenant Colonel Simonov's engineering battalion then began the penetration of the bank. First, they tunneled down an incline from the street side, then laterally towards the basement of the building. In the bottom of the bank was the twelve foot in diameter hardened steel door that guarded the vault. The engineers brought in diesel driven generators to produce electricity for lights and the drill in the basement. They strung lights throughout the basement, not just around the vault. A ventilation system was installed to remove the diesel fumes and dust. The engineers set up reinforced scaffolding on which they mounted an electrical drill that automatically fed drill bits forward. Water sprayed on the bit tip kept the tip from overheating against the hardened steel based on the pressure of the bit on the vault door."

Two days later, General Azimov returned to the Bank for a second time. "How does it go, Colonel Patronin?

"We are making progress General, although a bit slower than I hoped. The tunnel tends to collapse because of the rainy weather and the steel on the door is extremely hard. We have worn out two diamond bits trying to drill through the lock."

"Have you tried the demolitions?"

"I am about to try plastic explosives and or thermite grenades on the hinges of the door to see if I can drop it out of its seat. To do so, we will have to evacuate the basement and might damage the elevators, the lights and pumps we have put in place and inadvertently hinder our progress. Since the tunnel is in close proximity, it could also be damaged. The oxyacetylene torches seem to be the best effort so far. We have managed to cut through two hinge sections that way, but it is slow going. The steel is a high chromium vanadium molybdenum alloy steel which produces a slag that rehardens as soon as heat is removed.

"Can you increase the tempo, Colonel?"

"I will order the increased use of oxyacetylene torches, but in subterranean conditions that increases the hazard. Perhaps I should try something different in the tunnel operation."

"Please immediately do so, Colonel. I want the tempo of this operation increased. I want to get out of here as quickly as possible. If you have not noticed, the weather is unusually cool and cloudier than was forecast. There is more rain than predicted. I suppose it is no reason for concern, but still, I wonder. I am anxious to examine the contents of the vault. It will be most interesting to see if the eight thousand tons of gold the U.S. government claimed to have stored here really exists, or if they sold it off under the Clinton, Bush and Obama administrations to support the dollar. We still have no contact with Moscow."

Roving security patrols by squads were established. The command was given to shoot any observed survivors on sight. That order was disregarded in the case of any young woman or girl. Any observed woman that was young resulted in an effort to capture her. Very few women were caught. A few managed to escape in a labyrinth of buildings. Older ones were immediately shot. The captured younger women swiftly became the property of her captors in that patrol. They kept them sequestered in locations known only to the members of that patrol who would more or less rape them at their off duty leisure. The girls were semi-feral from starvation and cold. At least some of the more civilized Russians soldiers shared their food with their captives. Hunger is a powerful weapon, and most were willing to allow themselves to be used in exchange for a meal and a warm place to sleep.

With the last explosives detonated in the drill holes in the basement walls, the concrete crumbled, leaving mostly a mesh of steel reinforcing bars. The bars quickly yielded to oxyacetylene torches. An eight-foot wide hole was created.

Electric lights were strung by powerful flashlights as an electric generator was hand carried into the vault. Once lit, the lights revealed dozens of pallets of gold bars. A human chain was formed to pass the gold bars from one to another while the entrance was enlarged with pneumatic drills to allow a small forklift to operate. They were loaded on trucks which immediately proceeded to the dock as soon as they were full, where the crew of a support ship carried them aboard.

"Colonel Patronin, you have done well. No doubt you and your people will be adequately and justly rewarded for your performance. This gold will help repair the damage done to our cities by the Americans retaliatory strikes."

"Yes, General, it will. I thank you for your indulgence and recognition. I estimate that we have indeed, rescued at least five thousand tons of gold from the vault." As he spoke, Col Patronin wondered to himself where, or with whom, would Russia now barter the gold? Or store it? Will it once again become the world's standard of money as it has historically been? Personally, he would have liked to open the safe deposit boxes of the banks' officers and the rich of New York City. He thought that gold weighed too much and required too much storage room for large amounts. Perhaps the rich elitists had large home storage safes? They would want their gold in one-ounce coins or smaller since they are untraceable or for barter and perhaps bribes. Perhaps they left it in personal accounts in the vault of the Federal Reserve Bank? Or perhaps many had traded their gold for diamonds or other precious stones that lack the bulk of gold.

Perhaps Comrade, we should have had a separate force to explore the vault in West Point, NY. After all, West Point is really just a short distance north of New York City, on the Hudson River. Fabled Fort Knox will have to wait. We will see what transpires with the Chinese and what forces we have left to invade so far into the United States."

The Russian task force sailed for home. Only when the gold was unloaded in Russia, did they discover the real nature of the gold painted bars. Approximately ninety percent of the bars were in fact tungsten, painted gold. They surmised that the only real gold bars were the ones on the top of each pallet. All those beneath were tungsten. Apparently, the Federal Reserve Bank had secretly sold off America's gold supply in an effort to support the U.S. dollar. Now, China held more gold than the rest of the world. Russia had the second largest cache and India the third. The Chinese had demanded the U.S. Treasury redeem the ten-year Treasury bonds which they had accumulated for over thirty years, believing in the soundness of the dollar. When President Biden would not redeem them in 2022, they dumped three trillion U.S. dollars of U.S. Treasury bonds on the market, which caused a massive crash in the U.S. Dollar. In an attempt to support the dollar, the Federal Reserve Bank secretly sold off the U.S. gold supply.

CHAPTER XII

"ADMIRAL, WE HAVE NEARLY DRAINED the fuel tanks on the tank farms adjacent to the harbor for our ships. Our engineers have begun to operate the refineries to restore the supply, but are having difficulty without a trained labor force to operate them. It goes very slowly. It might require us to bring several supertankers with diesel fuel to replenish our ships for the return voyage in order not to break the cycle. Perhaps the wise Admiral might request more engineers capable of operating the refineries in the next shipload of personnel from our homeland. Our land forces are burning through more fuel than we planned. Their tanker trucks are making continuous circles to provide fuel to the forward elements. It is in our best interest to restore the refining capacity here as quickly as possible. Our fuel consumption estimates were too low."

"I will look into it, Colonel. I'll send an immediate dispatch to Peking to see how many American trained refinery engineers can be sent in the next personnel shipment. I'll also request the immediate dispatch of two more tankers with diesel fuel. I realize the difficulties we face if we do not breach the Sierra Madre Mountains before snow falls. We need to link up with forces advancing from the south over South Pass.

Iranian forces advanced across southern Iraq, where the majority of the Iraqis are believers in the Shiite branch of Islam. A1 Basrah offered no resistance. They seized the southern oil fields. One Iranian army proceeded up the Euphrates River, the other up the Tigris River. The Iranians continued northwest seizing city after city as the Sunni populations fled. Only when the northern army reached, Bagdad was any significant resistance encountered. A1 Hillah, Karbala, Ramadi fell in turn. At Ramadi, the southern army rested and refitted while the northern Army reduced Damascus. They surrounded the city in a double envelopment, pounded strongpoints with artillery, killed any civilians they sighted, and ceased operations for a week. They rested, refitted, evacuated their wounded back to Iran, and sacked those parts of the city that was deserted. The southern army turned north to link with the northern army at Samarra. The civilian population of Samarra fled north in the face of the invasion. They moved towards Kirkuk, the center of the Kurdish world. There, they were turned back. Those that tried to force their way into the Kurdish defenses were killed without mercy. Slaughtered, and hated for their belief, the Kurds had suffered massive atrocities at the hand of Sunni Iraqis, Sunni Turks, and Shiite Iranians. Never having a land of their own, they were fighting for their very existence, their very survival. Now, in view of a nuclear exchange, they had little hope except to kill as many of their traditional enemies as possible before they were totally annihilated.

"Georgi asked Vladimir What do you think of these damned Iranian mullahs? If we initiate a conventional invasion, they will launch their Intermediate Range Ballistic Missiles with their ten and twenty kiloton warheads against our cities, the cities that were spared in the American Submarine Launched Ballistic Missile attacks. Recall these mullahs consider us the second Great Satan, second only to the United States. Now they wish to take advantage of our wounds and our deployment in Europe. They greatly resent the rise of the Russian Orthodox Church in our homeland. They are marshaling armies around Tabriz and Khvoy.

Our intelligence reports indicate at least fifty divisions. Their infantry divisions consist of 14,000 personnel. Do they mean to march through the Caucasus, destroying Christian Armenia en route? Then they will have access to both the Black Sea and the Caspian Sea. They will have Sunni Turkey's entire northern border on the Black Sea. Then the Bosporus and the Dardanelles are open to them. So, what suggestions might we be pondering? The nuclear response, nerve gas, which is really a tactical weapon, or strategically deployed biological weapons? What should we do with this menace that threatens our Republics between the Black and Caspian Seas? I do not see the use of conventional forces. Ours are mostly tied down now in Europe."

"Georgi, I think that assessment might be wrong. Instead, they will more likely attack Sunni Turkey. They will avoid the mountainous Caucasus. First, they will take all of Iraq and Syria. That will give them the southern flank of Turkey, access to the eastern Mediterranean littoral, isolate Israel's northern flank, and threaten Turkey on both its eastern and southern flanks. I think that since they are not vaccinated against many biological agents, we should select one that our population is protected against by vaccination, perhaps a virulent strain of influenza, or smallpox, or a pneumonic form of bubonic plague that allows person to person transmission. They would have difficulty in proving a deliberate attack if it is carried out in a proper manner. After all, their ultimate goal is a caliphate ruled from Jerusalem. That is their ultimate strategic objective, the city of Jerusalem. Tehran is a long, long way from Jerusalem. Certainly, a biological attack will not risk any infrastructure."

"And Georgi, what if the genie escapes from the bottle?"

"If the genie escapes, where could it go before it could be contained? Afghanistan, some of our former provinces, Turkmenistan, Uzbekistan, Kazakhstan, Pakistan, Iraq, or even Saudi Arabia which is now in the throes of civil war? All of them are Muslim. I think our biologists could come up with a satisfactory vaccine if we don't already have one. Of course, if we select an agent for which we are well prepared, that problem hardly exists. When we had a national vaccination campaign for hepatitis B, we could have included an immunogenic component for another agent. Perhaps we should have had a national booster campaign and include an antigen for a biological weapon of choice. In fact, we have done just that. Less than one hundred people know of it, and most of them are dead."

CHAPTER XIII

"MR. PREMIER, COLONEL GENERAL LAZIMOV is here. He says it is urgent."

Good morning, Mr. Premier."

"And a very good morning to you, General. Have you had breakfast? Would you care to join me, for a full breakfast or even tea or coffee?"

"Thank you, Mr. Premier. I had breakfast a little while ago. I just wanted to inform you of recent developments."

"And they are, General?"

"Our satellite photographs reveal that China has launched twenty divisions of mounted infantry into the western parts of Sinkiang Province this morning at 04:00 on multiple axes. They have been attacking every village, town, and city of the Uighers for the last four hours. We were initially not certain if it was to be a limited attack or a strategic one. Their follow-on supporting forces are quite large and moving westward from a variety of marshaling sites. It now appears that they are attempting genocide against this fundamentalist Muslim population, quite possibly through the entire province of Sinkiang. No doubt they are driving toward their nuclear facilities in the western desert to prevent their possible seizure. We interpret that as an intermediate objective. Their strategic objective appears to be the elimination of the Muslim population."

"Well, General. I am sure that China has the reserve militia to carry that out. The Uighers are only lightly armed if at all. They seem to be eliminating a Muslim menace on their western frontier. Keep me casually informed of their progress, General. No need to be greatly concerned unless something of unusual consequence happens. Thank you for the report. I'll see you in an hour."

"That could have waited for another hour until our usual meeting at 09:00. I wonder if there is something else that Lazimov is not telling me or didn't want the rest of the staff to know," thought Proboff.

The Russian Northern Fleet, or what was left of it after the nuclear attack, sailed out of Murmansk through the Iceland-United Kingdom gap to stand in the North Sea while negotiations took place. Hidden from the world was the loss of manpower of their crew members to radiation poisoning and burns. Those ashore suffered the worst. Most ships had skeletal crews at best. The city of Murmansk was mostly destroyed, along with most of the harbor facilities and support installations. More than a dozen Russian warships stood at anchor off the coast of Scotland.

The Russian ambassador received orders to negotiate new home ports for the surviving ships with the British government. The old American nuclear submarine facilities on the body of water known as Holy Loch across from Greenock in Scotland were first on the list for negotiations. Was the British Navy ready to challenge the remains of the Russian Northern Fleet for a home port? Russian supersonic jet bombers known as the Tupolov 160 "Blackjack" initiated conducting daily low-level flights over the base as an intimidation factor. The British government agreed to "lease" the base for five years for a modest sum.

Although it was their second summer of living in Wyoming, Gypsy, Donna and the boys all noticed the cooler than normal weather. The cloud formation was unusually heavy, worse than last summer, with a lot of rain, most unusual for summer in the Big Horn Basin. Gypsy began to be concerned about the vegetable garden. It was slow in growing, in maturing. Why she wondered.

"Oh, Crap!" She thought. She dug the Geiger Mueller counter out of the basement and took it into the garden. The readings were far higher than they should have been. Gypsy realized that radioactive fallout had occurred with the unusual rains and cloudy weather. These conditions should not have occurred with a nationwide EMP attack. She realized that multiple nuclear explosions must have occurred in other parts of the world. Radiation fallout was being spread by weather patterns. She said nothing to Donna or the boys and quietly returned the Geiger counter to the basement. She made certain everyone took their iodine tablets at supper every night thereafter. The cabbage, brussel sprouts, carrots, beets, potatoes, and kale were doing acceptably well; the corn, not so well. It appeared stunted. The strawberries hardly bloomed at all. The spring was simply unusually cold. The blueberry bushes, however, we're doing quite well. Thank God we planted crops high in vitamin C to see us through the winter. The cabbage can be made into sauerkraut for long term storage.

Gypsy dug out the books on gardening. She discovered cabbage should be grown away from other Brassica species. *"Next year we will have two gardens, so there won't be any problems with the Brassica species,"* she thought.

It was nearly dark when Ethan pulled into the driveway. He honked the horn, turned off the engine, and climbed out of the vehicle to stand in front of it, armed folded, smiling. Carol joined him, a scared look on her face.

Inside, the boys each grabbed a firearm; Sam went out the back door and around the house with a shotgun; Josh out the front door with his .45 with Gypsy standing by in the doorframe, shotgun in hand as a backup.

"Dad," cried Josh. Gypsy laid the shotgun down and ran and literally jumped on Ethan, burying her head between his shoulder and neck. Sam came around the side of the house and ran up to his dad. He hugged Ethan and Gypsy together. Josh was jumping up and down and made it a foursome love-in. Donna came out smiling. Ethan looked at Donna, then at Carol.

"This is Carol. She just might be joining the family.

Who is this young lady?" nodding at Donna.

"I'm Donna, and I think it is preordained that I am soon to be Sam's legal wife if we can ever find a preacher. Not that I am already; as I am not!"

Ethan had tears starting down his face. He wiped them away as he turned to Carol.

I found Carol over by Cokeville. Her parents were killed by Chinese soldiers. I figured I couldn't leave her in that situation. I told her she could stay or go as she chooses, as long as she pulls her own weight. I figured she might be a mate for Sam, but I see he has resolved that! Congratulations, Sam and Donna!" He smiled at Sam and gave his son a bear hug.

Donna went to Carol and took her by the arm. "Come on in Carol. You will find some supper ready, and then we'll talk at your leisure."

Gypsy couldn't take her arm from around Ethan. Ethan gave her another hug, his tears wetting her face.

Carol wolfed down the venison stew and biscuits. Sam ate more slowly. Josh couldn't keep his eyes off Carol, who noticed his stare about halfway through her large bowl of stew. She just continued to eat, glancing at him about every third spoon full.

Donna said, "Josh, quit staring?! You're disturbing the young lady!"

Josh blushed in embarrassment while the rest of them just smiled, except Sam who chuckled.

Gypsy said, "Sam and Donna can have the spare bedroom. They might as well start playing house. I don't think they have shared a bed, but it is only a matter of time. Might as well be now; that is if you two concur. Josh, you can go on a cot in the basement. We'll have to make a pallet or cot for Carol in the sunroom, by the safe. I'll heat some water for you, Carol, so you can have a bath before you retire. I'll lay out some blankets, a sheet and a pillow for you."

"Gypsy, said Ethan, I need a haircut and bath. I feel like a sheepdog and a dirty one at that. After Carol can get a bath, I want to soak for a few minutes to get the grime and grease off me before we crash."

"I'll get the manual hair clipper and give you a haircut while Carol gets a bath. I presume she hasn't had the opportunity to bathe since being attacked."

"No, she hasn't. We had a quick meal, packed out of her house and hit the road; that was two days ago."

After Carol bathed and retired, Donna and Sam closed their bedroom door. Gypsy heated water for Sam so he had a hot bath and shaved. She scrubbed his back from top to bottom, concerned over how much weight he had lost. Ethan and Gypsy crashed in each other's arms.

Gypsy was up before everyone else. She decided a big breakfast was in order. She filled the wood stove with wood, sliced bread for the four corner stove top toaster, dug into the powdered eggs, cut the leftover venison roast into small pieces, poured oil into the largest skillet, and served a massive bowl of scrambled eggs and meat on the table, putting more bread on the toaster as soon as the first four slices were done. Ethan emerged in clean clothes and put his arms around Gypsy's waist and buried his head on her shoulder. She just stood there, smiling. Sam and Donna emerged and made a dash for the latrine outside. Josh came up from the basement, waited until Sam and Donna returned, then visited the latrine. The commotion woke Carol, who emerged.

"The latrine is out back", said Gypsy, motioning with a wood spoon.

"Breakfast in five minutes or less everybody." Carol made a dash for the latrine behind the house.

They sat down to eat, and without further word, Gypsy said grace. Gypsy poured hot tea for everybody and passed the sugar bowl around. No one asked Carol anything about herself. They were certain she would talk when she was ready.

"What's on the day's agenda, Guys?" asked Ethan.

Gypsy spoke up. "We're working in the garden. It has been a pretty poor year for the corn, but the cool weather crops have done OK. The corn could have done better, but the squash and beans of the three sisters have done well. So have the apples. We will be making some applesauce later this week. Sam will be the potato digger while Donna brushes off as much dirt as practical and stacks them in boxes for storage in the basement. We butchered a stray cow a couple of weeks ago and canned it, so we are OK for meat for a couple of months. Josh, why don't you take Carol fishing down at the river? Adding some canned or smoked trout to the larder would be pretty good for this winter. You can get some worms from Sam digging potatoes, and perhaps Carol can catch some grasshoppers or other bugs for bait."

Josh took a shovel from the tool shed to dig worms; he didn't have enough. He picked out two rigged rod and reels, put on a fishing vest with lures, a stringer and pliers in the pocket as Carol watched. She noticed that Josh was wearing his .45 but said nothing.

"Have you done much fishing, Carol?"

"Not much at all. I went a few times with Dad when I was younger, but nothing since."

"Would you rather spin cast outfit or fish with worms and a bobber that you can watch?"

"I'll take the worms and cork."

"I have a can of worms that I have saved, so we'll take them with us."

Josh slung a mini-14 over his back and led Carol to the river where he baited a worm on a hook a foot below a small sinker, attached a cork and cast it upstream to watch it slowly float down steam. He did the same for a second rod and sat next to Carol.

"I suppose I am to be your girl or wife or whatever." Said Carol.

"Well, that is pretty much up to you. You have to earn your keep if you stay. I don't think you will find another boyfriend around here. If you do, and you select him over me, you will have to go with him. We can't take him in. We can't feed another person.'"

"I'm no virgin."

"Carol, I really don't care. I don't know your history and don't want to know it unless you choose to share it. All I know is that you are the only girl in sight that isn't spoken for. I don't know if you will ever love me or if I will love you, but I find that you are an attractive girl. I hope you are as intelligent as you are physically attractive to me."

"I might be pregnant."

"I don't know about that; I don't want to know unless you want to tell me, now or any time later. If we fall in love and you have a baby by somebody else, I will have no choice but to love it and be a father for it."

Carol was silent, but tears formed in her eyes. Josh didn't say any more. He noticed the tears running down her face. By noon they had caught three fish and so climbed the hill for lunch.

After the kids left, Ethan asked, "Have you heard anything on the national picture? Josh pick up anything on the short wave? How about on your satellite receiver?"

"I'm not getting much there at all. The short wave gives us the best picture of what is going on."

"Josh hasn't mentioned much. It seems the Chinese are advancing in the north, into Idaho, maybe into the eastern mountains there. It seems they are having a hard time of it though. Militia groups are harassing them. Have you heard or seen anything?"

"The Chinese are coming from the southwest in a major thrust towards Texas, and some are also allegedly swinging northwards to attempt the Central Pass. I guess they are stopped in the center by the Sierra Madres. I found Carol outside of Cokeville. Chinese soldiers killed her parents; four of them were raping her when I intervened. I'm sure she is pretty shaken over it all. That was a good idea to send her and Josh fishing. I don't have any idea about her thoughts, how long it will take to get over the trauma, whether or not she will suffer PTSD. Wouldn't surprise me a bit if she has or develops it. I told her if she didn't fit in here, we would pack her a lunch and say adios. If she is as bright as I hope she will stay; she really has no other choice. I also hope that she and Josh will be compatible and love each other. I just hope Josh doesn't rush things. I can imagine how he felt with Sam having a mate and him no girl at all. I sure am glad Sam found a mate. I couldn't be more pleased. They seem pretty happy together.

Chinese motorized convoys are probing eastward. I don't think they will cross the mountains in any strength before winter. That gives us a little time. I saw absolutely no evidence of armed resistance. I was it. What about here?"

"We had to fend off a few looters. Both boys have killed now. They handled it well. I think there has been a nuclear exchange somewhere in the world, probably a number of nukes went off. I haven't said anything to the boys. It accounts for the cool summer. The Geiger-Mueller counter registered a lot higher than I like. Alpha radiation, more than I like to see, by particles attaching to dust and debris sucked up into the atmosphere. It washed out with the rains and cooler weather. Strontium 90 and Iodine 131 is another story. We have to protect our thyroid glands. We needed the potassium iodine tablets and thanked God I bought half a dozen bottles. It might be a couple of years until all the fallout is settled. We must have retaliated in some way. How I don't know. There is a lot more radiation than just a few nuclear bombs going off. Something must have happened in other parts of the world. I can't imagine anything in the southern hemisphere though.

The Mormon neighbors pulled out shortly after the EMP strike. The town is essentially deserted, last time we were in. I have no idea as to its current status, population wise, probably very few, if any around. Did you see many populations in your travels?"

"Only on a few isolated farms and ranches. Most of them shot around me to prevent me from coming too close. Can't say I blame them. I saw no evidence of organized resistance. That is what really concerns me.

What I did see was Chinese killing any Americans they saw. What is our food supply? Will make it through the winter without serious hunger?"

"We can. We have enough, although I would like to have had more produce from the garden to can. Vitamin A and vitamin C are major concerns. We need them every day. Hopefully, we can supplement our diets with more meat and fish. The summer was a lot cooler than it should have been. The boys and Donna worked hard all summer long in the garden. They realized it meant work or starve.

While we now have an extra mouth to feed, I can't tell you how happy I am to see a girl for Josh. I am really glad you found her. The boys have also worked hard to keep us in firewood as well. While we have plenty of gas from abandoned vehicles, its quality concerns me. Even adding fuel stabilizer, it will with time, turn to varnish. Then the chain saws will be essentially useless. It will be crosscut saws only. The boys have stacked about a dozen cords behind the garage. Making firewood and carrying it up the steps has been a big expenditure of calories, but it has really made the boys tough and strong. They are lean and mean. They are grown men now."

At supper, Ethan said, "I saw no evidence of any kind of organized resistance. I am guessing that the Chinese apparently have advanced perhaps to the west slope of the Rockies. I saw only advance scouts, probing actions really, so I can't say for sure. I don't think they will force a winter crossing. I don't know what will happen in the spring. I don't know what is happening in up the North, Idaho, and Montana. Hopefully, they will pass north and south of the Basin, but that is anyone's guess. I wouldn't count on it. Have you boys picked up anything of strategic importance on the shortwave?"

"I'm getting, or was, getting some reports out of Europe and a few from South America," replied Josh. "It seems the Russians have invaded Europe and have really kicked Muslim ass, all the way back across the Mediterranean and eastward into the desert sands. I did get one funny broadcast, couldn't make much of it; I think it bounced off a satellite or something and became garbled. It seems some kind of war going on in Central Asia that didn't make a lot of sense. Then I heard a broadcast from Europe in English, but with a Russian accent, in voice, not code, that China is doing something big time in Asia. I pick up a few broadcasts occasionally from around the USA here, but nothing really significant. Only that things are hard everywhere. I'm not picking up nearly as many broadcasts as I did three months ago.

A couple of days ago, I got one from up north. It sounded like the Russians were trying to take Alaska, but somehow or another maybe caught an atomic bomb. It sounded like there was more than one big flash across the northern Arctic. I think the report came from some Canadian or Japanese fishing boats talking back and forth. I don't know if Alaska was the target, but I understood the flash came from the west, from Siberia. That suggested to me that someplace in Asia got burned. What do you think that could have been, Dad?"

"It sounds to me like one of our boomers hit the major Russian naval base at Petropavlovsk on the Kamchatka peninsula. I sure as hell hope so. If that is accurate, it means we hit them elsewhere as well. Maybe more than one nuclear sub retaliated. Maybe somebody got Moscow and Peking and elsewhere. Russia won't survive then, if it took multiple hits, not without taking Europe. China can absorb multiple nuclear strikes and survive, but not Russia. If the Europeans can kick the Russians to death, they can survive. The trouble is, NATO became so hollow I don't think they could fight their way out of a paper bag. They just relied on us too much to save their bacon. Their citizens weren't allowed any privately-owned firearms to repel any invaders, Muslim or Russian. Josh, did you and Carol catch any fish today?"

"Donna, you have obviously mastered your handgun. What about your rifle? Have you picked out one that you want as your go-to rifle?"

"No, haven't. I rather like the Winchester 94 .30-30, but the recoil is just a bit much. I don't like shooting more than two or three rounds through it, but I like its lightweight, easy carrying, and quick firing."

"I'll put a recoil pad on it for you. I have a couple of spares. How is it for length? Is the stock too short or too long?"

"No Dad, the stock is just right."

"Then I'll saw the same amount of wood off and fit the recoil pad for you. I have a Kick-Eze recoil pad that will tame that thing."

Ethan spent the next week shortening the stock and gluing and screwing a recoil pad on the .30-30 for Donna. It took an awful lot of wood rasping and sandpapering to get a good fit, then refinish the stock, but it was worth it. Donna took it out into the backyard and fired three rounds through it.

"That's your dedicated rifle from now on, Young Lady."

Donna was very pleased.

CHAPTER XIV

THE THREE DRUNKEN RUSSIAN SAILORS tumbled out of the pub at Greenock. "Wait, Sergei, I have to pee!" They laughed and staggered into the alley behind the bar. When they were inside the pub, they harassed a young colleen, groping hands on her breasts and up her skirt. One held her arms while the others fondled her. The bartender informed them that they had best leave before trouble started. One young man followed them outside, observed them turn into the alley, then went back in the pub.

"They went into the alley, probably to piss." Three men left the booth when the bartender nodded at them, then without a word, handed them each a nightstick. Two other men went out the front door. The drunken Russians took turns to see who could urinate the highest on the side of the building. One of the two men who went out the front door coughed, drawing their attention to them. The three who went out the back door came up behind them. With one swift blow, the nightstick came down on the head of the rearmost sailor. He slumped to the ground. The next sailor turned around to catch a cross-handed blow of the nightstick across his face. The third sailor, when he turned to face the three with the nightsticks received a well-aimed blow to his left kidney. He opened his mouth but could not scream because of the pain. Another followed. A fist to the base of his skull just below the ear rendered him unconscious. The five men stood around, taking turns kicking and stomping on the unconscious Russians. One man deliberately crushed their larynxes with a well-placed heel.

"What do we do with them?" If we leave them here, the Russians will retaliate by closing the pub at the least, maybe hanging or shooting some citizens or raping some women. If we simply throw them into the water, their bodies will ultimately be recovered. The Russkies will know they were beaten to death. They need to disappear forever. If they go in the water, they should be out to sea with weights. If inland, they need to be buried where they won't be found. Our ancestors used to bury their sacrificial dead and criminals in the bogs. Jock, what about you, Mike and I taking them out of town and dropping them in the peat bogs? It's a bit of a drive, but it will dispose of them where they won't be found any time soon, if at all."

"I'll get my lorry and bring it around into the alley. It will be an all-night effort, but worth it." They loaded the bodies, then stacked some vegetable boxes in the back to hide them and drove north, to the bogs.

The sailors were listed as AWOL, absent without leave. Russian authorities questioned a number of people on the streets and in the pubs, but no one saw or knew anything.

"I see Sam shaves every day now and that Josh is starting to. What are they using for razor blades?" asked Ethan.

"Sam was shaving before you left. He has his own three blade safety razor. Josh started shaving a month or two ago, using one of your old safety razors. I bought them each a new razor and about a dozen blades at Walmart earlier. I see you have several small cuts on your face. I don't know what the boys, or you, will use when the razor blades are gone. The boys seem to be stretching them as much as they can. Did you try shaving with a hunting knife or something?"

"I used Carol's father's straight razor. I brought his shaving gear with me. I'll no doubt cut myself a few more times before I'm good with it. I did not get a close shave at all with it the first time. What are the boys using for shaving soap?"

"We had enough bath soap stored that we all use. Still, have several dozen bars. In spite of that, I saved tallow from the deer and steer and made soap with some of it. I have also saved some of it in quart Mason jars after rendering it to use as a cooking oil in the future. Hog lard would be better, but we can't be choosey. I made the boys save the ashes from the stove to drip lye. We built a trough from some 2"x6"x12' boards and put the ashes in it. Then I pour boiling water over the ashes and catch the runoff in baking pans at the end of the trough. We made some very crude soap, but at least it is soap. It will get us clean and let you guys shave with it. After it hardened, I cut it into bars and have it stored in the garage. It will improve with age. Sooner or later we will have to use lard or find some other kind of oil to make candles by dipping. The Coleman fuel can't last forever."

In the privacy of their bedroom, Ethan and Gypsy discussed the girls getting pregnant, especially Donna now that she and Sam were having sex as man and wife.

"It looks like we now have at least one daughter-in-law, perhaps two. I observed that when you put Donna and Sam in the bedroom together that was your seal of approval and that it is OK to be sleeping together. What are they/we, doing about birth control? The kids are too young to be parents. We certainly are not ready to be grandparents!"

Gypsy replied, "I have discussed the rhythm method of birth control with the kids. I hope to God they practice it. The period around the time of ovulation is the time of greatest desire in the woman. That is hard to resist. Withdrawal doesn't work worth a damn. Very few men have that kind of control. I know that from experience with you, Darling. I don't want to be delivering any babies. I don't have any skills in that department. The two of them were really lonely and just formed a union. It was bound to happen. Finding Carol was a Godsend. Now Josh won't be jealous, I know he was, even though he tried not to show it. All of the kids have been fantastic. They have really worked, knowing our survival depended on it. We have all really missed you."

"I see the boys have moderately short hair."

"I have been cutting their hair with the electric clippers whenever they ask for it. One of them rides the bicycle generator to run the clippers while I cut the other one's hair. Then they trade places. Short hair is a lot easier to keep clean, and they realize that."

"Do you think the Chinese will push through in the spring?" asked Gypsy.

"I would bet on it unless we can find some way to stop them. As far as I know, I was a lone wolf out there. I killed as many as I could without getting captured or killed myself. I didn't see any other signs of resistance. I don't know how it will play out, but it won't be good."

"For whatever it is worth, we have had an unusually wet summer, cloudy and cool. It dawned on me; I got out of the Geiger-Mueller counter. We're hot, Ethan, there has been a pretty good nuclear exchange. We didn't get hit here in the Basin, but there must have been multiple bombs in other parts of the world to drop the alpha radiation on us the way we have it here. Everything is mildly contaminated. I put us all on Iodine-131 tablets to protect thyroid glands."

"Enough talk. Come over here. I have missed you more than I can say."

CHAPTER XV

"GYPSY, ETHAN, DO YOU THINK it would be all right if some of us went into town on our bicycles to check on my parents?" asked Donna. "It is now the middle of October, and I expect that they have not survived. I would like to bury them in the backyard if I can. What do you think?"

Sam, Ethan, and Gypsy looked at each other. "Ethan nodded. It is OK with me if Gypsy thinks it is safe enough. What do you think, Dear?"

"I understand her concerns. I think three of us with a couple of shovels could manage it. Why don't Sam, Donna and I pedal in and check things out? You and Carol can rest, and Josh can hump a load or two of firewood up to the hill and perhaps catch some fish for us. One of us is usually in the gazebo now with a rifle covering whoever works down the hill. Seemed like a prudent thing to do after what has happened."

"And what was that," asked Ethan.

"Well, a couple of guys thought they were going to take over this place. Donna and I took out two of them here in the house; Sam and Josh did the other two outside. Threat eliminated. Enough on that."

Sam, Donna and Gypsy pedaled into town, rifles on their backs and shovels tied across the handlebars of Sam and Donna's bicycles. They pulled the shopping carts behind their bikes. They saw no one.

When they reached Donna's house, Donna cried out, "Hello," with no answer. She opened the door, "Mom, Dad, anyone here?" No answer. Donna walked into the kitchen, where she found a note on the table held in place by a salt shaker.

"Dear Donna, we hope you are alive and well and can read this someday. Everyone around here is starving, so we decided to try and go where we might find some food. The Hendersons, Franklins, Thompsons and us decided that we should all try and walk to Casper together. We hope there are some Civil Defense food supplies stored there. We thought we might be able to shoot something for some food if we could find a cow or a deer or an antelope or something along the way. Cattle around here within walking distance have already been butchered. No use in sitting here in the house just to starve. People really turned nasty and violent here; I guess driven that way by hunger. We love you and hope you have a long and happy life. Love, Mom, and Dad."

Donna started crying. Then she went through the house to pack some more clothes in pillowcases. She took as many of her father's clothes as she did of her own for herself and Carol. They bundled the stuffed pillowcases on their bicycles and pedaled home.

"What we gals miss most is decent napkins," complained Gypsy. "We have tried rags in conjunction with a thin belt. It works, but not very well. Talk about primitive. I guess the old biblical tale of the Red Tent is true. Primitive people sent their women to isolated huts during their menstruation. No luck with that one!"

Ethan just chuckled. He knew that he and now the boys, no, now men, could not do without their women. Even though Carol just arrived, he knew Josh would court her in earnest, taking whatever time would be required; at least he hoped so. He wanted them to genuinely fall in love, not rush things, or have a relationship based solely on the necessity of survival. He rolled over and embraced Gypsy.

CHAPTER XVI

"**SAM, I AM VERY CURIOUS ABOUT** the rest of the world, as well as Chinese progression inland from California" stated Ethan. "Can you spend more time on the radio? Josh, have you learned how to operate the radio? Do you know Morse code as well as Sam?"

"Not as well as Sam, Dad, but I can read about ten to fifteen words per minute. Do you want me to step up?"

"I sure do. In fact, that would be a good thing for Carol to learn. She can become our primary radio operator. Do you mind learning Morse code and how to operate our radio station, Carol?"

"No, I have no problem with learning that. I want to know what else is going on in the rest of the world. It would free up Sam for more time for wood cutting and whatever other chores he has. Glad to do it."

"Great! Josh, get her up to snuff as soon as possible on the whole shooting match; operating the radio, learning the code. I am beginning to wonder if we should now identify ourselves. Maybe we should let somebody else know of our existence. There is always the chance though, of Chinese signal interception and paying us a visit once, or if, they cross the mountains."

"I'll get Carol up with the key and a lesson plan. She'll know the code before the week is out. By two weeks, I'll bet she is reading twenty words a minute."

"Josh, when you two need a break from being radio operators, get her up to snuff with a .22 handgun. Then move her on to a revolver or .45 ACP, whatever she prefers. Get her started with a good holster as soon as she moves past the .22. She knows how to handle a .22 long rifle; brought her own, but I want her to learn a high powered rifle as well. So, one of your duties is to get Carol capable with firearms as quickly as safety and time permits."

"What is today's program, Dear?"

"Sam and Donna and I can work in the garden. We're digging potatoes and putting them in the basement. We have picked the apples off the neighbors' trees and will make apple sauce in the next couple of days. We picked the corn but still have to shell it. I decided to let it dry out and then shell it so we can grind it into corn meal. It is a lot easier to store than corn on the cob and more versatile."

"Dad, I picked up a broadcast this morning in English; I think from Moscow. They called it an evening report. I wrote down the frequencies. I think it was aimed at England. They said they had liberated Hungary, Poland, Romania, Austria, and Czechoslovakia from the Islamic threat. I think they mean that they purged Muslims from Eastern Europe. I haven't heard any response from England. I also heard from a ham in Canada, Vancouver, I think. He said that some Russian fleet got knocked off, nuked, around the Aleutians. What does that mean?"

"I think, I hope, it means that a Russian invasion force headed for Alaska took a nuclear strike from one of our boomers, that is, one of our nuclear ballistic missile launching subs. God knows how they survived."

"He also said that Russia is recovering very fast from the vicious sneak attacks by America on Russia. I guess that means we hit them too?"

The Chinese militia army proceeded west through Sinkiang. They stopped at Urumqi. After resting, they were recalled and moved southeast. The Uighers ceased to exist except perhaps in very small, isolated groups of no more than a few individuals.

With Iranian forces seizing Iraq and threatening what was left of Syria, Sunni Turkey observes the turmoil in the Islamic states between the Caspian and Black seas very closely. Shiite Iranians increase guerilla warfare in Chechnya, Azerbaijan, and Nagorno-Karabakh.

Shiite Islam believes the world must be bathed in blood to allow the return of the Twelfth Imam. When that occurs, he will rule an Islamic world seated on his throne in Jerusalem.

With Iranian forces beginning to form a horseshoe around Turkey's eastern end, Turkey's President Erdogan orders the first step of a general military alert. Iranian forces cross the Persian Gulf and seize Qatar and Bahrain. The royal princes, princesses and other members of the royal family of the House of Saud flee to Cairo aboard a dozen Boeing 737s. The remnants of the Saudi Air Force flying F-15s purchased from the United States escort the royal family where they surrender their aircraft to the Egyptian government. Oil production in Saudi Arabia completely ceases.

Captain Sherman, making his routine figure eight patrols in the northeastern Pacific aboard the USS Robert Howard, watches with growing dismay at the Chinese convoys circulating in the Pacific, from China to the U.S. west coast. When he observes the third convoy exceeding thirty ships in five days, all flying the flag of the Peoples Republic of China, he realizes this is not just normal trade. His attempts to contact COMSUBPAC are never answered. After one broadcast, a pair of Chinese frigates instituted a search for him. Slipping quietly into the thermocline, he lay quiet and motionless for three days. He chose a circuitous route to reach 200 miles off the west coast opposite Seattle. Raising a radio buoy, his electronics suite of personnel could detect no civilian radio broadcasts on any frequency. He pondered the meaning for three days as he steered a southerly course avoiding more Chinese convoys where he encountered other Chinese merchant ship convoys headed east, he presumed for southern California.

"God, the USA must have just disappeared. What the hell do I do now? I have two SLBMS each with six missiles, each containing 145 kilo ton warheads. If I launch a nuclear attack on China, do I start World War III, or am I just catching on to the tail end of it."

His radioman had informed him that he was picking up ship to ship transmissions in what he presumed was Chinese. His automatic language translator informed him that it was often gregarious comments about how the USA will soon be China America. Sherman reached the conclusion that the United States no longer existed. His sonar man had informed him earlier of several significant seismic events. It now dawned on Captain Sherman that they were the result of nuclear explosions. He reached the unalterable conclusion that the United States had suffered a nuclear attack and quite likely no longer existed and or the United States had responded accordingly.

"To the crew of the USS Robert Howard: This is Captain Sherman. Some of you have probably guessed from the numerous Chinese convoys we have observed headed east and our failure to raise any contact with either Hawaii, Alaska, or the continental United States, that we, at least the continental United States, have been successfully attacked. The probability that the United States no longer exists as we knew it is almost a certainty. Therefore, given the numerous Chinese convoys traveling and broadcasting in the open, I must assume that China, and perhaps in consonance with Russia, has attacked the United States with at least limited nuclear weapons. Our multi-language translator has revealed several comments about the new China America being broadcast ship to ship among the convoys. Unless I receive or can confirm that all is well in our nation, I must assume that we are at war with China. I am acting accordingly. We have tremendous firepower aboard this craft, and I intend to use it to inflict maximum damage upon the Peoples Republic of China. If anyone has heartburn over this presumption, please express it to me. That is all."

"Lieutenant Picore, plot us a course for southeast China. All officers and Chief of the Boat report to the stateroom."

"Gentlemen, I have no desire to waste our nuclear firepower on targets that our boomers might possibly have already hit. Neither do I wish to reveal our presence by sinking any Chinese ships until we have expanded our nuclear capability. After that, it is open season on anything Chinese. I don't know what those Chinese convoys are carrying, but I surmise they are Chinese pilgrims. So, what would be the best use of our torpedoes; Chinese naval vessels or those full of Chinese settlers. Let's give it some thought. I wish we knew what, if anything, our boomers have accomplished. From now on, I want our multi-lingual translator tuned to everything Chinese. Perhaps we can garner a few leads."

"Gypsy, Thank God I started my period, but I don't have any sanitary napkins. What do I do?"

"We girls have been using rags in kind of a sanitary belt mode. Come on, and I'll show you how we do it."

Gypsy gave Carol a thin belt and showed how they used a rolled rag secured by a thin belt.

Carol started crying. Gypsy tightly held the girl and told her, "Anytime you want to talk about it, let me know. I'm the mother figure around here. We girls have to stick together." Carol nodded but didn't say anything.

Later that evening Gypsy said, "Ethan, I'm sure you have noticed that the last two weeks have had a noticeable weather change. The days are cooler, but the nights are simply getting colder. It is nearly freezing now in the early morning. We need to harvest all of the vegetables before it freezes. There has been hoar frost several mornings in the last ten days."

"I'll help by digging potatoes tomorrow, carrots too."

"The girls and I will start canning the cabbage and carrots. We'll start washing the jars along with the reusable canning lids and bands. Carol can help with the canning. I'm hopeful she has done it before. Those 50-pound bags of table salt I bought from the Co-Op last summer are a lifesaver."

On the first day of October, the temperature plunged to an overnight low 20 degrees Fahrenheit. Snow started falling. By midday, the temperature rose to 35F, and the snow began to melt. The sky remained overcast.

"If it is not too muddy, we will continue to dig the potatoes. After we finish digging the potatoes which won't take very long, it might be a good idea boys, to start carrying more wood up the hill and stacking it behind the barn. This looks like the harbinger of a hard winter. Those steps can get pretty treacherous when they are ice covered. You better resort to your routine of one carrying wood and one overwatching from the gazebo than trading places. Don't want a repeat of last spring."

The boys nodded as Gypsy dished them each a plate heaped with biscuits and gravy and fried sliced venison on top. She gave the girls a slightly smaller helping on their plates as well as on her own. Ethan's, she stacked high to get his weight back to normal. Carol looked from Gypsy to the boys but said nothing.

That evening Donna and Sam were sitting in the gazebo in down jackets, holding hands. Not too far away, some animal howled.

"God, did you hear that Sam?"

"Yeah, I did, and I don't like it. I never heard a coyote or a wolf before, but I'll bet that was a wolf. If so, I don't like it. That means they are moving out from around Yellowstone Park into this area. They will be a threat to the deer and now wild cattle. We better be sure and tell everybody we heard it. The wolves the Game and Fish people imported in the 1990s aren't the wolves that previously occupied Wyoming. They brought in the Alaskan subspecies of wolf. They are much larger. They preyed on reindeer, elk, even bison and moose. Some wolves weighed over 200 pounds. I saw a picture of one shot over in Idaho that weighed 250 pounds. They can bring down a cow. We better carry a handgun at all times and keep a long gun handy."

In the distance, a howl was heard again. It was answered by another from a different direction.

CHAPTER XVII

THE UNDERWATER DEMOLITION TEAM (UDT) in northwest Scotland supposedly at a classified base moved south by truck with their inflatable zodiacs. A convoy of seven trucks is difficult to conceal. Using night vision goggles and infrared filters on the headlights they traveled only after 22:00 hours. One contingency plan mapped their route where they could conceal themselves in barns and buildings by day. Explosives and detonators were divided between the trucks. Somehow, the Russians failed to plan for a Spetsnaz team to destroy the UDT team at their base. Now the teams disbursed along several miles of their route of march. The team commander, LT Michaels, and the Petty Officer First Class Summers hitchhiked from Inverarry to Dunoon. A local farmer stopped to give them a ride.

"Aye, you lads be Americans, I'm a 'thinkin'," said the farmer, judgin' from the way ye speak."

"Yes, we are, but please ask us no questions. We're just a couple of civilian sailors who got stranded when the war broke out. We've been living on Scottish hospitality for months. If anyone should ask, you have not seen us, let alone spoke with us."

"Ye boys know the Russians have taken over your old base at Holy Loch, don't ye?"

Michaels and Summers looked at each other, wondering if they should reveal what they knew.

"No friend, we've not heard that. The last news we heard was that Russian troops moved down through the Baltics into Germany, and France and even closing in on Italy, at least somewhere around there. We've not had much communication, and don't know the world situation, can you help us?"

"Well Lads, the Russians caught some nuclear bombs on their homeland. Apparently, western Russia is rather devastated. It seems surviving Russians are moving west into Europe however they can. Word is a lot of them are dying of radiation poisonin' along the way. That's the rumor anyway. Russian sailors are throwing their weight around in Dunoon and Greenock. Them Russian ships, two cruisers, a couple of transport ships, and a destroyer are scattered 'round. Womenfolk isn't safe, I'm told. The Russian sailors are pretty arrogant and rugged, or so they think they be. I don't know if they are aware that much of Russia has been devastated. They'll find out soon enough, I suppose. Wonder what they'll be thinkin' then. I hope they ain't thinkin' these Isles are the new Russia."

Michaels and Summers looked at each other, but neither spoke.

"Summer here's been a lot cooler than normal. Crops aren't doing well at all. Don't know if the Russkies will pay me for what this load of last year's potatoes is worth. If they won't, it'll be the last load they get from me.

Turnips are doin' OK, but not much else. So, what you are Yankee sailors going to do in Greenock?"

"Oh, if you don't mind, we'll walk the last mile into town. We just want to look around, really carefully like. Is there a pub you can recommend for Nessie Water?"

"Aye, the Grey Seal '11 give you a cold Guinness or two. Well, this is about a mile or two out if you Yanks don't want my company."

"We'd appreciate it very much if you didn't tell anyone; and I mean anyone, about us. We're much obliged for the ride. We hope you get a good price for your potatoes."

Michaels and Summers slowly walked around Greenock. The Russian ships were anchored in the Firth, rather than in the port of Glasgow. They waited until nearly closing then entered a pub close to the harbor. They each ordered bar food and a pint of Guinness dark ale, locally known as Nessy Water. As they were served, Michaels asked the barmaid about the Russia ships and troops. She said most of the troops spend their nights aboard the transports. The Russians are working on finding homes to billet them without pay, of course. Sooner or later, they'll all be in town, all over town., thousands of them. They've only been here four days now. Already there have been several nasty gang rapes by those bloody bastards. Soon no girl will be safe at all. It's a shame you Yanks pulled out of Europe. Nobody appreciated you until you left. Now we all wish to God you were back, but I understand there's no chance at that. You've your own survivors to worry about now."

Michaels sighed, didn't say anything, and laid a twenty-pound note on the table. He and Summers walked the shore again to note the position of each Russian ship on the water. Which has the easiest approach? Which is the most valuable target? How to approach? Concentrate on one or several. They hot-wired a car and drove back to their central location. They called the team together. LT Michael decided the two transport ships with the sleeping Russian soldiers would be the most profitable. The soldiers could do the most damage on land. The cruiser would be the third target if they can strike again.

"5000 Russian dead seems like a good idea to me, Sir."

"Thank you, Jamison. We want the ships to go down fast to drown as many troops as possible. We will plant four mines on each side of the two transports to simultaneously detonate. Ignore all else, all threats, get the mines in place. We'll set the fuses before we even hit the water. We'll go in from the shore at 01:00 hours tomorrow. Each man will plant one mine. Chief, you and your seven men, will take the transport closer to the east bank. I'll take the rest of the team for the larger ship closer to the west bank. All fuses will be timed for 02:30. Let's hope they have no swimmers of their own aboard, and that they don't have an active sonar going that can detect us. We'll leave the shore from two different points. Chief and your team leave from Dumbarton. I'll take off from Greenock. Steal a small boat if you can; if not use a zodiac or swim. It's your call on your side, Chief. We won't have a lot of time to make it back to shore. Leave civilian clothes in the trucks for a fast change. We'll meet back here around dawn if all goes well. If necessary, try and eliminate any road guards that try to stop you as quietly as possible. Shoot only if you have to. Good luck, God help us all."

"Question, Sir. LT, what about the USA"?

"The USA, as we knew it is gone. Our families are deceased or have little or no chance of surviving. There is no way we can get to them. The best we can do is kill as many Russians as possible in revenge. Europe is the only sanctuary for us as individuals. Europeans must expel the Russians, succumb to them, or assimilate them. Only time and decades will tell. I doubt that the National Command Authority made it to any suitable shelter. If nukes were launched from the International Space Station, we're talking one or two minutes to detonation. If SLBM launched from around our seacoasts, from five to ten minutes, from China or Russian territory, thirty minutes. The last would give those SOBs in Congress time to reach shelter within a mile or two of the Capitol or White House. They are the ones responsible for this.

Now, there might be a secret place in the immediate vicinity of the capitol of which I am not aware, a place where the rats can scurry into in a few minutes. It might be in some subterranean chamber below some government or even a private building to where they could retreat. A government-owned building disguised as a private building, within a block or two of the capitol building. They could stash their mistresses in it, come to think of it, as cover. It could be a place for their secretaries and staff who wouldn't know anything about its real nature. That would be very convenient. Hell, some of those bastards might even have an apartment there in their own names. That would be a legitimate cover. Just call their mistress to come on in! We will have to depend on Europe to defeat Russia first; then and only then can they help us rebuild our country. Of course, they will take care of their own needs first, then the rest of us. It will be the recolonizing of North America, Twenty-First-century style. I expect it will be thirty years, maybe more, before we see any hope of that. Now let's sink some ships and kill some rats."

Explosions ripped through the night. The two transports both sank within ten minutes, taking most of the sleeping Russian soldiers with them. The ships shuddered as gaping holes in their hulls just below the waterline allowed rushing water into them, sealing off the decks below. Those sleeping on decks below the ruptured hulls could not escape as fights for access to the stairs broke out among panicked soldiers. Of the thousands of sleeping Russians, only a few hundred managed to escape from their ships. Some of them drowned while trying to swim in the cold waters of the Loch. The cruiser had its propellers blown off, leaving it a crippled ship.

"What do the kids think, Gypsy, or do they?"

"I think the boys know enough to realize how bad things really are. I doubt the girls really have much of an inkling; perhaps only a vague idea. I don't think any of them want to think about it. In the meantime, we have to ensure our own survival, especially the kids. I don't know what in hell we will do when the girls get pregnant, as they inevitably will. I'm open to suggestions."

CHAPTER XVIII

"MR. PRIME MINISTER, THE AMERICAN people and us have been deceived. We wanted to verify the gold bars brought back from the Federal Reserve Bank by General Azimov. When we drilled into one, then many, we found they are not gold. Rather, they are tungsten-painted gold. We then instituted checking each bar. The tungsten bars are slightly lighter in weight but volumetrically the same as gold bars. Without very close inspection, they can pass as gold bars. Each has to be verified by weight and volume. To date, less than five percent are found to be gold."

Proboff thought for a moment. "General Roussof, the Chinese, and the Indians must not discover how fraudulent the Americans were and how we have been deceived. It appears that you have tested every brick. See that this is classified at the highest level. Send those who are knowledgeable of it to a duty station where they cannot reveal it. Keep the fraudulent gold separate, but ensure that it is listed in our inventory with a code that will identify it."

On 1 November, twelve inches of snow fell. The temperature plunged to ten degrees Fahrenheit above zero. The boys alternated carrying wood into the house. Donna went outside to help Sam carry in an armload of wood.

"Boy, I'm sure glad Mom made us carry all this wood up the hill earlier. It would have been dangerous to carry fifty pounds of firewood up snow-covered steps now. Now, we only have to carry it from behind the bar to the stove!"

"Sam, as of tonight, we're married. I love you. We've been informally married, I want to make it formal. I want you. And besides, it is too damned cold to sleep alone. If we close the door, we'll have privacy but not heat, so let's have privacy and each other. So, you are my husband, and I am your wife. Tonight, after supper, let's make the announcement. I want a wedding ring though, sometime, somehow."

"After we make the announcement, we'll find a way to get you a ring, sooner or later." Donna threw her arms around Sam's neck and kissed him on the lips. Sam picked her up in his arms and spun her around in a circle.

"Do you know how hard it has been just waiting to hear you say that! I love you and I will be your husband forever and ever."

At the dinner table, Donna couldn't quit giggling. Sam couldn't stop chuckling. Ethan and Gypsy looked at each other and silently laughed. Josh and Carol didn't quite figure it out.

"We know there won't be a chance of a ceremony, but Donna and I now consider us married." announced Sam. "She would like a wedding ring sooner or later. I want to give her one."

"The town is completely deserted. We won't find a minister around here for the next 40 years, but perhaps we can find a wedding ring for you, Donna, one way or another.

Congratulations, kids!" Josh and Carol jumped up, and the four all hugged each other. Gypsy and Ethan joined in.

Ethan opened the safe. He found his father's wedding ring in a cigar box. He gave it to Sam, saying "It was your grandfathers. Donna, we'll find a wedding ring for you."

Josh came up and shook Sam's hand again, then father and son hugged each other, smiling and laughing. Donna and Gypsy hugged Carol. Ethan, with tears in his eyes, hugged his older son and said, "Welcome to the family, daughter-in-law" to Donna. Josh looked at Carol, who looked away. Josh decided she wasn't ready for a proposal of marriage. Heck, she had only been there a month.

On 16 November, Paris had six inches of snow.

London had an overnight low of 15 degrees Fahrenheit. Moscow, or what was left of it, had fifteen degrees below zero. The Russian supply of natural gas to Europe failed. The food supply in Europe was dangerously low due to a poor harvest. The grain crops in Ukraine were down by thirty-five percent. The Russian people were ordered to leave their homes and report to the nearest school building, which would be heated. They were ordered to bring all the food they had and their bedding. There, communal living would offer consolidated meals, a warm environment, and security by police forces. South America shuddered at the thought of fallout as the seasons rotated south of the equator.

Throughout Central Asia, especially in Afghanistan, warlords seized power through the rule of the gun. The warlords didn't initially appreciate it, but they lost their financial power with the loss of markets for heroin and hashish in Europe and North America. The cities in Southeast Asia and South Asia fell into anarchy as governments fell into dictatorships. Shiite Islam celebrated the destruction of the Great Satan of the USA and considered this the first major triumph in the establishment of a worldwide caliphate, ruled by their Imam from Jerusalem. The Shiia concept is that the world must be bathed in blood before the Twelfth Imam would return to rule a universal caliphate from

Jerusalem. The Iranian Guards developed their plan to march through Saudi Arabia and Syria, killing Sunnis en route to destroying Israel before seizing Jerusalem. They anticipated Sunni Turkey would fall before their display of power.

"Dad, Donna really has her heart set on a wedding ring. Do you think we could find one in town?"

"I've had the same thought, Sam. There is no jewelry store in town. It is very bizarre, but what we will have to do is rob the deceased. I doubt if anyone is left alive in the town. We will have to go house to house, to see if we can find a dead lady that will contribute her ring. While I don't like the idea, it is the only practical way to find one. With a little bit of luck, we will find a matching pair for you and Donna. Don't tell her about how they are acquired. Sooner or later, Josh and Carol will want the same. As soon as the crops are harvested and canned and we get a cow or another deer or two, we will go ring hunting."

Ethan asked "Honey, how are we fixed for food; not just for the winter but through the next spring and summer as well?

"What we have now will have to last until we harvest the garden a year from now," answered Gypsy.

"I keep wondering if we will have enough to satisfy our needs for vitamins. Humans must have vitamin C, and ascorbic acid, every day. Vitamins A, D, and E are essential too. I remember Dad giving vitamin ADE shots to cattle when he was in practice. We need to get out the field guides and see what wild plants are edible. What did the Native Americans eat for vitamins before the arrival of the white man? Does anybody know of any beekeepers where we might salvage some honey?"

Gypsy broke the nerve to Ethan "We're on our last tank of propane Ethan. I have husbanded it as much as I could. That's one thing we should look for, although I doubt, we will find any. I hate the thought of having to can in the kitchen on the wood burning stove. If that is what we have to do, though, that is what we will do. We have cabbage and kale to can or preserve. That will help with vitamin C. I'm concerned though, about our apple trees. We have a modest crop. We can make perhaps six quarts of apple sauce and maybe a half or more bushels of apples we can wrap in newspaper and store in the basement. Apples have some vitamin C but not like citrus fruits. We have carrots and beets that did OK as well. We still have half of the cow we canned. Getting another cow or a couple of deer would satisfy our protein needs. It is the necessity for vitamins that concerns me. I am afraid we will be eating a lot of stew, breakfast, lunch, and dinner, as just about everything we have is, or will be canned. It is the fresh fruits and vegetables that we will really miss. We didn't get enough blueberries or raspberries to can, so we ate them fresh as they ripened. It is the possibility of the apple trees freezing if we have a really cold winter that worries me the most. I sure wish we did better at tanning deer hides. Do you think we might find some more 50-pound bags of salt at the Co-op? We could sure use some iodinated salt to can meat and fish. We could use it to make jerky as well."

"Carol, how are you doing on the radio operator bit?"

"Great Sir, I'm learning fast."

"Don't call me, Sir. I'm your father-in-law or probably will be. Call me Dad or Ethan. You've been here what, how many months now and you are family, like it or not. So, what's with the radio business?"

"Sam and Josh alternate on the bicycle driven generator for power. I'm getting so I can read much of the Morse code, but I'm still a lot slower than Josh. Sometimes we can pick up a voice from Europe. The news there is not good. It seems the Russians are giving the Germans and French problems. The Muslims aren't mentioned anymore so I guess they have been eliminated. I get more from England in English, but I rely on code from the continent. My high school German is not that good. I wish I had a German-English English-German dictionary. That would help a lot."

"Maybe we can find one at the high school next time we go into town."

"That's a great idea, Dad!"

Ethan smiled. "That is the first time you called me Dad."

Lying in bed, Ethan put his arm under Gypsy's neck and snuggled against her. "Wife, after we can all the vegetables and meat that is possible, I think we should consider a scavenging party in town. I was initially thinking of it, but perhaps it would be better if we all went. You know, security in numbers and all of us well armed. I doubt we will find any survivors in town, but if there are, we might be considered a tempting target. No bunching up. We'll need to pull wagons and shopping carts behind our bikes. I think we should look for good blankets and down comforters. I think we will have a cold winter. We need to take a few tools, screwdrivers, a socket set, and a couple of adjustable wrenches. We'll leave the dogs inside to guard the house."

Ethan didn't mention it, but he thought a heavy-duty pair of pruning shears might be necessary to remove fingers from the dead to acquire wedding rings.

"God, what a morbid thought" he wondered to himself as it occurred to him. He would not want the kids to witness it, but he determined he would go through with it. The kids need as much of a normal life as possible.

"It's true the girls could use some winter clothes asnwered. They need to try them on. I don't think they want any contact with the dead, but maybe we could ransack some closets and dressers and let the girls try them on in the living room or somewhere they won't come in contact with the deceased. You guys could stand guard around the house. We'll need to visit a number of houses. We could all stock up on clothes. Socks, underwear, jeans, sweaters, even headgear. We might need it for the next forty years. You never know."

Gypsy smiled. She didn't say anything, and she just rolled over on top of Ethan.

15 November 2025

That night, tremors shook the house. Gypsy and Ethan awoke, but the remainder slept through it. The morning revealed a large plume of smoke emanating from the area of Yellowstone National Park, 150 miles away. All of them stepped out of the house to observe what appeared to be the first eruption of Old Faithful as a volcano in over 640,000 years.

"What do you mean Honey"? asked Ethan.

"Well, with all the nuclear explosions, I anticipated the major fault lines along the crust of the earth to make some adjustments. No doubt some have, just how violent and where I can't say. I strongly suspect the so-called Ring of Fire around the Pacific is experiencing some possibly harrowing times. Let's hope and pray that Yellowstone doesn't have a major eruption. If it does, we could be in real trouble. While lava might not flow this far, the ash, the clouds, the potential fires from expelled lava could be very, very dangerous. California, Washington, Oregon just might be sliding into the ocean as we speak. If we are fortunate, the pressure will be relieved in a number of smaller eruptions and the numerous vents in the Park. That is just smoke and steam from the caldera. It is probably boiling away Yellowstone Lake. If the deeper chambers of the volcano blow, it will be a massive blow to the environment. I suspect we are on the verge of a nuclear winter. Much will depend upon what has happened or will happen around the rest of the globe. Only God knows how long it will all continue."

The kids all looked at each other and then at Gypsy and Ethan.

Gypsy was right. San Francisco and Los Angeles and all up and down the Pacific coast experienced major tremors. The docks of San Francisco, Oakland, and Los Angeles slid into the sea, taking much of the Chinese efforts with it. Seattle did not escape. A tremendous tsunami swept in from the Pacific Ocean, a one-hundred-foot-high wall of water traveling more than a mile inland as a result of the land west of the San Andreas Fault falling into the sea. Chinese ships at sea capsized. Those close to the former shoreline who were not killed by falling buildings and debris in the cities, drowned.

Unknown but surmised by the Bradleys, other nuclear exchanges occurred in other parts of the world. Those delivered by India were much more devastating than those delivered by Pakistan. Pakistan essentially ceased to exist as a nation. India's rockets were much more accurate. Pakistan was forced to revert to essentially a patchwork of tribal-controlled areas. Earthquakes shook the entire region, from the Zagros Mountains east through Mongolia. Whole mountains fractured and slid away along fault lines. Afghanistan and Pakistan, or what was left of them, both suffered major earthquakes. Ownership of Kashmir was no longer a question. The Kashmiri Muslims that hid and refused to flee earlier did not survive their exposure and were quickly killed by the dominant Hindus.

"OK kids," announced Gypsy, "enough of the canning. We'll take tomorrow off and go on a treasure hunt. Let's break out the bicycles and head into town tomorrow morning right after breakfast. We need to gather a few things. We're looking for more winter clothing for everybody, more rope, more nails, more of just about everything. We'll raid some houses if we have to. I don't think any stores have anything left on their shelves. We'll work in pairs or a team of fours. Not that I expect to encounter anyone, but you never know. We won't enter any residence without first announcing ourselves. We'll select the larger houses of the richer citizens first. Nothing like robbing the dead. In fact,

I think you kids ought to be one team of four; Dad and I will do our thing."

The parental thing was to find matching wedding rings for young couples. Ethan slipped a pair of heavy-duty pruning shears into his pocket when no one was looking. A good tool to remove fingers that would not yield wedding rings.

They all jumped on their bikes and pedaled into town, Sam, Ethan, and Josh towing wagons behind their bicycles. At the edge of town, Ethan said, "OK kids, set your watches for 09:00. We will meet here at noon and head for home. Good hunting in the meantime."

"Gypsy, do you know of any relatively young couples or rich older ones, and where they lived in this town? That might save us a lot of time hunting around."

"No, I never did establish much social contact here. We'll just have to hunt until we find what we want. We won't find what we are looking for in the heart of town. We need to go to the west end where there are some nice houses. We should find something there."

For some reason, most of the houses they explored were deserted. When they found nice, usable clothes, they loaded them into the wagon behind Ethan's bike. In the tenth house, they found a dead couple, lying in bed. There were bullet holes in their skulls and a revolver in their hand of the man. Sam slipped off their wedding rings and put them in his pocket. She had a very nice diamond ring, and he had a matching band. He took the revolver and put it under his belt. In another home, they found a deceased couple with a nice pair of matching bands, but no diamonds. Sam collected them. They all met at noon, with wagons loaded with clothes, tools, and anything they thought useful, pedaled home. They saw no one; no one alive.

CHAPTER XIX

PREMIER PROBOFF ADDRESSED THE DUMA in a special session in a theater in Moscow.

"Comrades, the question has become how far do we allow the Iranians to advance? They have crossed the Persian Gulf and seized the Emirates, Qatar, and Bahrain. Their land forces have taken Kuwait. They are advancing north from there. They crossed the Zagros Mountains and took Baghdad and Ramadi. Three divisions of Quds Guards have taken Irbil. That puts Kirkuk in a pincer movement, north from Baghdad and south from Kirkuk. The House of Saud is doomed if any of it is left. It seems that one virulent branch of Islam, the imams of Shiia, is about to annihilate the other virulent branch of Islam, that of Sunni Islam, the Wahhabis. To their destruction, I say good riddance. Hopefully, they will bleed each other to death, although the odds greatly favor the victory of the Iranian mullahs. The critical questions are what will Sunni Turkey do, what is Iran's next move and what should we do?

Our options are limited. It is not logistically feasible to turn our northern forces away from Western Europe. We have already advanced through the Baltic States, established bases in the United Kingdom, and are on the borders of the Benelux countries and Germany. Western Europe could, as it should be, our new western settlement.

Will Sunni Turkey allow virulent Shiites to exist all along their southeast border? After Syria falls, the Iranians will have access to one-third of Turkey's southern border. They will have access to the Mediterranean Sea. From there they could also threaten Sunni Egypt and the Suez Canal. If they do, it would likely be fatal, and I am convinced the Egyptians know it. They might reach a temporary truce, but the Iranians would only use it to rest and rearm. Turkey realizes this, I am sure. Iran's eastern flank is protected by the worst and highest mountain regions of the world. The former Soviet Republics are mostly Muslim. I doubt that China could force its way through Kazakhstan in order to turn south through the Caucasus region to attack Iran from the north. Alternatively, the Muslim Central Asian Republics, Kazakhstan, Uzbekistan, and Turkmenistan might allow the Chinese forces to cross their territory. I doubt this. High-level discussion with all parties will be necessary. If Iran breaches Turkey, Europe is then open to Iran. I recommend we discuss with our Chinese neighbors the possibility of a combined nuclear strike against Iran. We will not have to occupy the territory, but rather we would leave the overstretched Iranian forces without logistical support. They would be isolated and forced to live wherever they are.

Is it possible for the Chinese to continue on their South Asian conquest and still mount an offensive against Iran? Any threat of interference by Pakistan and India has been essentially eliminated by the nuclear exchange between those two nations. The nuclear genie is out of the bottle. Why not continue to release it? If nuclear strikes are limited to modest-sized nuclear weapons against military targets only, with no boots deployed on the ground is proposed, will the Chinese think it necessary to advance any farther than Sinkiang to address their Uigher problem? What is the probability of an uprising of ordinary Iranian citizens against the mullahs? Surely the average intelligent

Iranian would realize that it is the fanatical mullahs that brought death and destruction from two directions. Should we approach Turkey for a temporary alliance to halt the Iranian advance? Ladies and gentlemen, let the great discussion begin. We will meet again in forty-eight hours."

Politburo Briefing.

"In the last 96 hours, three divisions of the Iranian Army have moved against Armenia where they are slaughtering everyone. Their goal appears to be to eliminate Christian Armenia. No one is exempt. All who are found are killed. Armenians are fleeing northward by any means they can. The Iranians have occupied the eastern half of Iraq, on a northwest-southeast axis with Ramadi as its center. This puts the Iranians on the southeast and eastern flanks of Turkey. They are resting and resupplying. It is likely they will push westward across the Iraqi desert as the Americans did in the Gulf War. If they move through the rest of Iraq and into Syria, the land borders of Sunni Turkey are essentially occupied. The remainder of Turkey is surrounded by water. We are uncertain, but their most likely strategic objective is Israel. Will Israel respond with tactical nuclear weapons? Probably. The question is, where have they drawn the line and will Iran mount a pre-emptive nuclear strike. It is doubtful that Iran will use tactical nuclear weapons in a pre-emptive strike, but it cannot be ruled out. Saudi Arabia is essentially no more.

China is advancing in the South China Sea. Their objective is to control the Straits of Malacca. That means they must control Malaysia. We seriously doubt they are willing to take on Indonesia. They can watch each other across the Straits. We cannot expect any help from China. If anything, they would have to advance across the southern Central Asian Republics to even strike at Iran's eastern flanks. To avoid Pakistan and India, they would have to utilize a northeast axis of approach, through Kyrgyzstan, Uzbekistan, and Turkmenistan. With their thrust into Southeast Asia, it is highly unlikely they will do so. We have no indications of such a strategy.

As for us, Mother Russia, we have certainly been degraded, but not destroyed. Most of our naval assets have been eliminated. Most of our western cities have experienced nuclear attacks. Still, we persevere. The greatest threats now are starvation and adverse weather and militant Iran. Our conquest of Western Europe has provided some new homelands. Now, the only real threat to stopping Iran is Turkey. Ukraine and Belarus are already ours. The Baltic States are ours. I suggest our new national borders are the Ural Mountains in the east, and a line running from the Baltic States south across the border with Poland, Slovakia, Romania, and Moldavia. We must now address the threats of starvation and nuclear winter. Our other major threat is Iran and the Shiite belief of bathing the world in blood. After all, we are a Christian nation and the second Great Satan."

CHAPTER XX

THE DECISION WAS MADE. A secret vote was cast in the Duma. The only way to stop the advance of Iran would be through the use of biological weapons. Turkey was not informed of any such decision. Nuclear weapons had already inflicted such ecological and physical damage as to limit their deployment to a last minute stand to prevent total annihilation. Russia learned its lesson when the Soviet Union broke apart. The public health system had broken down. As a result, they experienced tens of thousands of cases of diphtheria alone, with thousands of deaths. Thereafter public health received considerably more support and appreciation. The powers that be decided that they would never allow an epidemic to occur again, either natural or manmade. Consequently, their secret stores of biological weapons were brought into play at the beginning of the twenty-first century. All of their citizens were vaccinated against what the epidemiologists considered to be the most likely agents deployed in bio-warfare. The former Soviet Union had 125 different strains of smallpox in their virus laboratory. Their researchers used recombinant DNA techniques to perfect a vaccine that would protect against all known strains. School children were required to be vaccinated before being allowed entry into school. The public was not informed of precisely which diseases it was being vaccinated against as it was incorporated into a multiple agent vaccine. Thus, the majority of the population received influenza, bubonic plague, diphtheria, typhus, typhoid, and smallpox vaccinations as well as measles (rubeola), chickenpox (Herpes zoster/varicella), Hepatitis B and C. These are the classical disease of major plagues. The Central Asian Republics did not receive any such vaccines. In what was left of Pakistan, Central Asia, and Korea, tuberculosis was beginning to make itself felt in populations compromised by inadequate diets, and exposure to harsh environments. Body lice became a growing threat, and with it, the threat of epidemic typhus.

Smallpox has historically been considered a close contact aerosolized transmission virus. Genetically "improved" strains engineered by Russian virologists allowed for far more efficient aerosol transmission. The Soviet smallpox library contained 125 strains, providing an enormous number of potential recombinations of the virus. Close person to person contact was no longer required. A sneeze laden with the virus would fill a room with infectious particles called virions. Modified long-range aircraft were painted with Iranian air force markings and equipped with aerial spraying equipment that flew low, flying under Iranian radar. They took off from airfields around the north end of Lake Baku on the western shore of the Caspian Sea.

One squadron sprayed a wide path that covered Tabriz, Zanjan, Tehran, Esfahan, Shiraz and Bandar Abbas. It landed in Dubai. Another squadron flew more westerly, down the western side of the Zagros Mountains. It distributed its lethal cargo over Arbil, Kirkuk, Ramadi, Karbala, Al Hillah, An Najaf, Basra, Abadan, Al Kuwait, and Bahrain.

Only a modest amount of spray was required over each city. The small droplets of the spray could not be observed or felt. The open country was spared to conserve the spray. The local transmission would handle its spread. This squadron also landed in Dubai. Now, all Russia had to do was wait. Without support, an army soon grinds to a halt. Soon, tens of millions of people in the Middle East would experience an epidemic the likes of which had not occurred since the bubonic plagues of the Middle Ages. Cold weather increased the death toll. The advancing Iranian forces were cut off from their logistical supply lines, without food and fuel, forced to live however they could, wherever they were. Soon, they too began to suffer death by the thousands.

CHAPTER XXI

1 DECEMBER 2025.

THE CENTRAL ASIAN REPUBLICS grew more fearful of their northern neighbor. Like a seriously wounded beast becomes more dangerous, so they viewed Russia. While they escaped much of the radiological fallout, they did not escape the climatic changes that Russian malevolence had induced. Being essentially tyrannical Muslim states, they had no love for what they perceived as Eastern Orthodox Christian Russia. Their primary source of wealth was oil. Now their markets were critically disrupted. Leaders feared a popular uprising with good reason as the standard of living dramatically declined. Smallpox erupted in Turkmenistan.

The geology of East Asia is extremely complicated. Multiple fault lines and tectonic plates mash against one another. Over two dozen fault lines exist in mainland China. Earthquakes begin in the Hindu Kush, Zeravshan Range in Tajikistan, the Tianshan Range, Kunlun Shan, and the Ladakh Ranges. The Sagaing Fault splits Myanmar from north to south. The two halves of Myanmar slide into the sea. The Ring of Fire of seismic activity in the Pacific engulfs Japan. Coastal cities are drowned. Earthquakes never seem to end. The Tarim Plate boundary goes north through Myanmar, through China into Mongolia where it intersects with another plate south of Lake Baikal. The Somalia plate pushes eastward against the India plate. The Indian plate pushes straight north colliding with the Eurasian plate to be subducted by the Himalayas and the Tibetan plateau. The subduction zone lying beneath Bangladesh, Myanmar and eastern India release a 10. 0 earthquake on the Richter scale. Tectonic plates meet below where the Ganges and Brahmaputra rivers meet to form the world's largest delta that drains into the Bay of Bengal. What was left of Pakistan becomes completely obliterated under a series of massive earthquakes. Very few survive. Pakistan simply ceases to exist.

The north edge of the Persian Gulf experiences massive earthquakes. The city of Shiraz, Iran, is destroyed. Then diseases began to take their toll. Food and waterborne diseases quickly spread among the few survivors. Cholera, a food, and waterborne disease rages through the survivors. Characterized by the massive shedding of cholera bacteria in uncontrolled dysentery, contamination of surface waters becomes widespread. Death is by dehydration through massive water loss through the digestive system. Victims pass liters of watery diarrhea. China's ten nuclear power plants on the East and South China Seas are disrupted, releasing massive amounts of radioactive water into the ocean in a repeat of the Fukushima disaster of Japan.

"Boys and girls, I think we better double our efforts in getting firewood up to the hill. Things do not bode well for the world in general and us in particular. We better go hunting. We had best to find more canning jars and lids and can more meat and vegetables. We might be in for a long dark winter. On our next trip to town, we will raid the library for books, all kinds of books. Our winter nights are going to be very long and cold. You boys and your wives," and Gypsy hesitated, realizing what she just said meant for Carol and Josh, "will alternate days carrying wood up the hill and going hunting. It would be ideal if we can kill another cow. This time we'll skin it as well as bone it. We have to do better in the hide tanning department." Carol looked down and then looked at Josh to see him watching her.

"Look, we're not man and wife until you are ready if you ever are. I won't push it." Josh turned and walked away, leaving Carol to console herself on her future.

The British people had enough. Surviving Russian sailors began to fall to snipers' bullets in Scotland. Small arms taken from Muslims began to be used with good effect against Russian patrols in France, Belgium, Netherlands, Spain and especially Germany. Russian patrols in the Thuringer Wald were often annihilated to a man. Prostitutes used themselves as bait to lure Russian soldiers into alleys where they were beaten to death or had their throats slashed. Russians began to retaliate against the civilian populations. After all, what they wanted was the land, not the native people. Guerrilla warfare, both urban and rural, began in earnest. The Germans remembered how they suffered from the Russians in retaliation for World War II. 100,000 German women in Berlin alone gave birth to babies in 1946 from being raped by soldiers from the Asian divisions Stalin employed in taking Berlin. Weapons taken from Muslims came out of closets. No individual Russian was safe. Russian patrols expanded from ten to twenty men. Russian forces began a slow retreat, from Finland through the Baltics to western Ukraine. Fuel was in short supply for Russian forces. Many vehicles were abandoned. Russians retreated on foot, using trucks for the wounded. Occasional guerilla forces sniped at the retreating Russians, harassing them day and night.

Sam and Donna were more than a mile down the stream from the house. They were moving as quietly as they could, hoping to surprise a deer. Donna heard a noise, turned around and then gasped. Not more than thirty feet behind them was a pack of wolves. Sam turned around; he recognized the danger.

Donna worked the lever of her Winchester as fast as she could. Sam got two rounds off with his bolt action .308. Four wolves went down, but one of them got up and limped away. Sam snapped another round off after it as it disappeared in the brush. Donna was shaking so violently that she dropped every other cartridge as she tried stuffing them through the loading gate of her rifle. Sam looked back at her. He was visibly shaking as well. He picked up her dropped cartridges and wiped them clean with his handkerchief. He took her rifle and stuffed them into the magazine of her .30-30. Then he topped off the magazine of his own rifle.

"Let's get out of here. Those wolves were tracking us. We better circle around and get home pronto. It is too far to carry a deer even if we saw one now. I don't want any smell of blood in the air."

They circled around, walking up the ridge rather than backtracking to climb the bluff. They arrived home shortly after dark.

"Well, where have you two been?" asked Gypsy. "See anything?"

"Yeah, a pack of wolves stalking us. We killed three and wounded a fourth about a mile down the river."

The parents stared at them, "Donna and that .30-30 saved our skins. She cut loose with that thing so fast the wolves didn't know what hit them. I got two quick rounds off to her six. Those she hit didn't take more than a few steps. Seems like she hit them dead on in the chest. Dad, those wolves are huge!"

Both were still shaking when they sat down at the table. Gypsy went to the cabinet and brought out four glasses and a bottle of Canadian Club whiskey. She poured a gill into each glass and handed one each to Sam, Donna, and Ethan and kept one for herself.

"Tomorrow we will go skin them. Think you can find them?"

"Yes, I think so, Dad. It was around the bend where the shore narrows between the river and the bluff."

After breakfast, Ethan said, "Sam, Donna and I will go skinning; Josh, Carol, Gypsy, stay close to the house. No telling if the rest of the pack trailed you here. From now on, nobody goes out without a large centerfire rifle or shotgun. No more .223s. Sam, you take the 870 Remington Magnum loaded with buckshot, put a dozen rounds in your pocket. Donna, your .30-30 and I'll take an Ml-A. Honey, will you pack some sandwiches for us? No telling how long we will be out there. Sam and I will take a canteen each in case we stray from the river."

"I baked some honey oat bars yesterday. I'll pack some of those in the newspaper as well."

"Wow, would you look at the size of these beasts!" exclaimed Ethan. "Grab the front legs of that one, Sam, let's see if we can guess its weight."

They couldn't lift the dead wolf high enough to get it's back more than a few inches off the ground. In fact, they could barely lift it, even though its head was still on the ground.

"This wolf has to weigh over 200 pounds, maybe even 250," exclaimed Ethan.

"Sam, you skin that one, I'll skin this one. Donna, you stand guard with that .30-30!"

It was mid-afternoon and already growing dark when they finished skinning. Ethan rolled the hides and tied them to his pack frame. "OK, kids. Let's head for home. Let's make it before it gets dark and cold."

CHAPTER XXII

MUCH OF HARBIN, THE PARIS OF THE EAST, disappeared under the massive mushroom cloud. It was a 100 kiloton burst, more than five times the size of the blast over Hiroshima, set at 500 meters altitude. The fires spread over a gigantic area. Unlike Russian weapons tailored for electromagnetic pulse, this one was tailored for heat and blast. Millions died in the initial heat and blast, and millions more died in the fires. Structures were leveled for several miles radius to the center of the blast. Survivors on the periphery of the blast area gathered what they could carry and moved out onto the steppes. They ate whatever they could find after they devoured whatever they could carry.

On the steppes lived a marmot, scientifically known as Marmota Siberia, the Mongolian marmot. It is a very closely related species to the groundhog of the eastern United States, Marmota monax and the marmot of the western United States, commonly called the rockchuck, which is properly known as Marmota flaviventris. People began to shoot and capture and trap by any means these little mammals to eat. In the early part of the twentieth century, the Mongolian marmot was trapped by the thousands or tens of thousands on the steppes, for their fur. Barrels and barrels of hides were shipped out of Mongolia. In 1910 something happened. An outbreak of plague occurred in these rodents. Spread by fleas, Mongolian trappers were soon infested with plague-infected fleas. Only in 1910, it was different. Instead of developing the more common form of plague, the bubonic form, it developed into the pneumonic form. Bubonic plague is primarily an infection of the lymphatic system, while the pneumonic form is an infection of the respiratory system. This allowed direct respiratory spread from person to person. Every time a victim coughed, he spewed plague bacillus into the air to share with more people. An estimated 46,000 to 60,000 people died of a pneumonic plague before the disease ran out of victims in 1910-1911. Now, the disease once again raised its head-in-the pneumonic form. The steppe was soon littered with the dead and dying. Most of those who escaped the nightmare of nuclear war in Harbin died on the steppe of an ancient disease.

The fiercely independent Finns looked upon the Russian invasion as an opportunity for revenge. They were well aware of the dire straits of the Russians. The Finns produced some of the finest rifles in the world, if not the finest. Anyone who owned a Sako brand rifle can testify to that. The Finns on their skis took to the snow as they did in the Russo-Finnish war of 1940. Ultimately, the smaller nation had to sue for peace in that war, but not before they taught the Russians some mighty hard lessons on winter warfare. The Russians moved the international border thirty miles west in that conflict, now the Finns wanted their territory back. The Finnish army passed out rifles and ammunition to civilians who requested them. So did the Swedes and Danes.

Christmas, December 2025

Citizens of the Baltic nations who were not of Russian ethnicity began to turn on their neighbors who were. Many of the Russian ethnicity initially supported the Russian invasion. Some of those of Russian ethnicity fled south, into Poland. Their welcome there was a whole lot less than favorable. Poland lived in fear of the Russian bear for much of the latter half of the twentieth century. For fifty years they lived under the heel of the Soviets. Into the twenty-first century, they were threatened by Putin's renewal of militancy. Many Russian refugees were beaten and robbed, some were killed. With nowhere to go, many turned back north to face the wrath of their fellow countrymen.

An extraordinary thing began to occur in the United Kingdom. Some Russian soldiers were deserting the Russian forces, asking for asylum and British citizenship. They gladly turned their weapons over to British citizens who would conduct guerilla warfare. A few of them spoke broken English, which made it less difficult. Some volunteered to lead patrols or at least accompany them to ambush their former Russian colleagues. The Scottish people no longer supplied the few remaining Russian ships with food. The Russian army officers sent out foraging patrols, many of which were ambushed. Most came back empty handed as no one would sell to them and they could not raid far into the countryside out of fear of being cut off and ambushed. The decision was made to withdraw from British waters. The decision was not difficult. Murmansk was the only choice.

An early winter gripped Europe. Arctic storms swept down in late November. The temperature plunged below zero. Refugees, especially Russians, began to freeze by the hundreds, then thousands. Germans and Poles killed them whenever they could.

Sam and Ethan built a hide scraping platform based on an illustration from a book on trapping. They scraped and scraped on the wolf hides, removing all tissue down to the basal layer of the skin. Ethan found a book on tanning hides the Native American way and so they scraped and rubbed and stretched and sawed the hides back and forth on a smooth pole with one end stuck in the ground and five feet above it. They called it their softening pole. They rubbed fat into the hides. Native Americans used the brains of the animals as a source of the fat. After quite a bit of work, they decided the skins were soft enough that they could make garments out of the wolf hides.

CHAPTER XXIII

FINLAND REMEMBERS. Finland remembers the 1940 Finnish-Russian war. Russia demanded to move the border thirty miles west so they would have more freedom of action for World War II. Finland waged a superb winter war against the Russians. Ultimately, Finland had to sue for peace and so surrendered some of their homelands. In retrospect, the Russians learned much about the winter war from their experience with the Finns. Now Finland wanted their land back. Finland didn't ask for it back. They attacked. Russian border guard stations disappeared under withering fire. Finns on skis had not forgotten how to ski or how to fight. Their marksmanship has always been spectacular. Guerilla groups attacked the Kola Peninsula. Russians were not safe on the streets. Russia is now being squeezed from both east and west. Sensing blood, Kazakhstan marshaled their modest forces along the western border, north of the Caspian Sea and the Naryn Qom Depression. Waiting.

"Come on everybody, let's get seated. Everybody washed?" cried Gypsy as she removed a pan from the oven. Ethan strolled into the room grinning like a Cheshire cat, holding his hand behind his back as the family gathered to sit at the table. He set a bottle of wine on the table and pulled a corkscrew out of his hip pocket.

Donna jumped up from the table and said "I'll get some wine glasses." She moved quickly to the kitchen cabinet and in two trips set six glasses in front of Ethan. Ethan opened the wine and filled each glass which drained the bottle. Gypsy sat a huge venison sirloin roast on the table in front of Ethan's place. Ethan sliced the entire roast into thin slabs. "We are ready, Mom." he stated as he sat down. Gypsy took her place at the foot of the table.

With bowed head Ethan began, "Lord, grant us continued security and safety. Keep our family intact through the coming decades. Please restore the goodness and rights that we once had in this country as when you first blessed this nation. Guide us in all our endeavors and in all things. We pray for those who have not been so fortunate as us. We pray that righteousness and goodness will be restored to the world and that evil will be punished and eliminated. In Your name, we pray, AMEN.

Milton Keynes UK
Ingram Content Group UK Ltd.
UKHW041351041024
2011UKWH00002B/8